C000260463

SHOW ME

NICK PIROG

© Nick Pirog 2017

This is a work of fiction. Names, characters, businesses, places, events and incidents are either the products of the author's imagination or used in a fictitious manner. Any resemblance to actual persons, living or dead, or actual events is purely coincidental.

Origin of how Missouri became the
Show-Me State:

"I come from a state that raises corn and cotton, cockleburs and
Democrats, and frothy eloquence neither convinces nor satisfies
me. I'm from Missouri. You have got to *show me*."

—Congressman Willard Duncan Vandiver in 1899

PROLOGUE

Tuesday, October 9, 2012
Tarrin, Missouri

She rarely got sick. The last time was four years earlier. She remembered because it was during the first week of the Summer Olympics when they were held in Beijing. Peggy loved watching the diving. She'd been a diver in high school herself, though far from a standout. Her best dive was a Reverse 1 ½. It wasn't the hardest of dives, but one she routinely received her highest scores on. So, yeah, she obsessed over the diving coverage during the Olympics. Only she'd gotten a horrible cold and her head had been spinning for days, and she missed it.

Peggy hoped this cold wouldn't be quite as bad, though it had swept its way through her office building like a swarm of angry locusts. Still, most people were back to work two or three days later.

It hit her about halfway through her second game. It was bowling night. She and Roger joined the league last year. She'd been terrible when she first started. She hadn't bowled in more than fifteen years, not since she and Roger's first date. But now that their oldest was thirteen, they felt comfortable leaving the boys alone for a couple of hours on a Tuesday night.

Peggy rolled a 178 her first game. Roger was so excited he'd given her a little pat on the butt. She blushed, then looked around to make sure nobody saw. No one had. They were too busy bowling themselves or eating wings or drinking beer or watching the Cardinals' playoff game that was on the big screen.

The third frame of her second game, she knocked down six pins with her first ball. The four pins remaining were all on the right side. It should have been easy for her to pick up the spare. She picked up the ball, a purple eleven-pounder Roger bought her at the end of last year after she complained about putting her fingers "where a thousand people's fingers had already been." She was all set to roll when she sneezed twice—her sneezes had always come in pairs—then twice more. It was hard to cover her face with the ball in her hand, and Roger and the couple on the lane next to them all started laughing.

Not knowing what to do, she wiped her nose on her shoulder and rolled the ball down the lane knocking all four pins down. The spare symbol flashed on the screen, and Roger stood up to give her a high five.

"I think I'm getting sick," she told him.

And she was.

By the sixth frame, she started to feel feverish. She was so careful. She had little tubes of hand sanitizer stashed everywhere. She even had one on her keychain. But then, so many people had gotten sick the last two weeks, Peggy supposed it was inevitable. And now she had it.

She didn't want to roll the last couple frames, but Roger begged her to finish out. He had a great game going; he would end up getting a 237. And if she didn't finish, it would hurt their seeding come the tournament in two weeks.

Once the game was over, she told Roger she was heading out to pick up some medicine. They'd come in separate cars, Peggy having to stay late at work to finish writing a report.

It was closing in on 8:30 p.m., and Peggy hoped the grocery store—Save-More—was still open. Technically, it closed at 8:00, but Odell, the owner, usually stayed open an extra half hour.

As she neared the store, Peggy could see there were still a few cars parked outside. When she was growing up, the store was called McBride's and had been little more than a six-aisle grocery store. Over the past thirty years, Odell had expanded the store, changing the name with each remodel. Ten years ago, it became McBride's Market, then five years ago, Save-More.

Peggy parked, jumped out, and rushed inside. She grew light-headed and stopped to take a couple long breaths.

Odell McBride, an exceedingly pleasant man in his early sixties, made eye contact with her. He was checking out the last of the customers. Tarrin being a small town of just two thousand, Peggy knew both men in line and waved hello. "Hi Jack, Hi Dr. Lanningham," she said, then turned to Odell and asked, "Can I grab something really quick?"

"Sure, but make it snappy," he replied with a soft wink.

"I will," she promised, then started toward the medicine aisle.

She passed a woman standing near one of the two other checkout lanes. The woman was wearing a cowboy hat and had her face buried in a gossip magazine. Though Peggy recognized her from town, she couldn't recall her name.

In the medicine aisle, Peggy grabbed a box of Theraflu and some throat lozenges, then made her way back up front. Odell had finished with Jack and was checking out Dr. Lanningham, Peggy's longtime veterinarian. Behind Dr. Lanningham was a young man in his mid-twenties, whom Peggy recognized from the lumberyard. He asked, "You got it too?"

She glanced down into his basket and saw a similar assortment of medicines.

"Yeah," she said. "Hit me hard about thirty minutes ago."

The front doors opened and a man walked in.

Neil Felding.

Peggy and he had gone to high school together. He'd been valedictorian if she remembered correctly. She heard he'd recently moved back, though this was the first time she'd seen him.

Right behind Neil was a second man.

The hairs on Peggy's arms pricked.

It wasn't the gun in the man's hand, though that was frightening enough. It was the look on his face.

Rage.

He smashed the butt of the gun into Neil's back, sending him flailing into a bin filled with an assortment of Halloween merchandise.

"Lowry!" yelled Odell. "What the hell are you doing?"

Lowry Barnes, Peggy realized.

He was in his late twenties. Thinning brown hair. Freckles. Vacant brown eyes. The last time Peggy had seen him was three weeks earlier when he'd still been working at Save-More and had bagged her groceries.

Peggy wasn't sure why he'd been fired, but she assumed it was either drugs or alcohol. At least that's what landed Lowry in jail. Or so went the gossip.

"Over here!" Lowry screamed, waving the gun. "Everybody over here!"

Odell.

Dr. Lanningham.

The woman in the cowboy hat.

The young man from the lumberyard.

Neil.

And Peggy.

Everybody.

"You don't have to do this, Lowry," Dr. Lanningham said calmly. He was in his late fifties, with a head of salt-and-pepper hair. It was the same voice that had told Peggy it was time to put her golden retriever, Betty, to sleep.

"Yes I do!" Lowry screamed.

He pointed the gun at Odell and said, "You never should have fired me. You should have just given me a warning or something."

"I did give you—"

"No! You just threw me out on the street."

Odell didn't answer.

"Now move! Everyone to the back of the store!"

Peggy waited for someone to dart toward the door or make a run into one of the aisles.

No one did.

Everyone obeyed.

Everyone but Peggy.

Her legs seemed incapable of moving.

Lowry pointed the gun at her chest and shouted, "I said move!"

The young man from the lumberyard gave her a reassuring nod, then took her arm and guided her toward the rest of the group.

Lowry ushered the six of them to the back of the store and into the freezer bay. It was the size of a small bedroom, half filled with frozen items.

Lowry told them to sit on the floor, and Peggy fell to the cold concrete. The young man was to her left, Dr. Lanningham to her right.

Lowry stood in front of them. "I didn't deserve it," he said.

He pointed the gun at Odell and pulled the trigger. Odell's head flopped backward, and he fell to his side.

Peggy screamed.

Lowry pulled the trigger again, the bullet hitting the young man next to her in the throat.

Peggy closed her eyes and said a quick prayer.

It would be her last.

Chapter 1

Friday, May 27th, 2016
Seattle, Washington

I got fat.

Capital F.

Capital A.

Capital T.

FAT.

There were a lot of variables. Lack of exercise. Netflix. That new Dairy Queen Blizzard with all the fudge in the center. But those all came after the fact. *After* Gina moved back to Bolivia.

I met Gina Brady under dire circumstances the previous summer in South Africa. She was a doctor with the World Health Organization and had been living in a small village in Bolivia for the couple of years before we met. After we started dating, she moved to Washington and took a job at a clinic. Everything was going great, we were even talking about moving in together, when there was an outbreak of tuberculosis in her old village. That's when she dropped the bomb.

The B-bomb.

She was moving back to Bolivia.

And she wanted me to come with her.

Let's see, stay in a beautiful house overlooking Puget Sound or live in a hut in the freaking Amazon.

So I went with her.

Just kidding.

I declined her offer and watched a *Naked and Afraid* marathon on television. And I ate an entire pizza.

That was the beginning.

Of the fatness.

In the past, I would have been able to dig myself out of the funk that I found myself in. I would have gone for a couple of long runs, maybe phoned up an ex-girlfriend, maybe shot down to Tahiti for a couple of weeks.

But I couldn't.

Get my legs to work.

I loved Gina. And to be honest, I considered moving with her to Bolivia. It would only have been for six months, just until the WHO could get a couple more doctors down there who spoke the language. But I couldn't leave Harold. He could die at any second. I mean, when you looked at him, you would think he already had.

So I stayed.

On the rare occasion that my legs did cooperate, I let them carry me to the Willow Springs Nursing Home, also known as *Fake Key West for People Who Are Like Seriously on Death's Doorstep.*

There isn't a whole lot to do at a nursing home, and if Harold and I weren't watching horse racing or playing chess—which Harold would unabashedly cheat at, constantly swapping his dead queen for pawns and thinking I wouldn't notice—we were eating at the cafeteria.

Salisbury steak.

Macaroni and cheese.

Beef Wellington.

Pizza.

Tacos.

Salisbury steak.

Apple pie.

Cherry pie.

Peach pie.

Salisbury steak pie.

And then there were the cakes. Someone was always celebrating something. Mable is one hundred and ten, get her a cake. Wally's third hip isn't making that weird creaking sound anymore, get him a cake. Blanche's niece just had a recital, get her a fucking cake.

By February, I'd put on ten pounds, which might not seem like all that much weight. But for someone who'd been running five miles nearly every day for twenty years, this was a colossal amount.

But I didn't stop there. I put on another eight pounds in March. Then another twelve in April. And as of three days ago, I was two hundred and fifteen pounds, which was forty more than I usually carry on my six-foot frame.

That was the day Harold died.

~

You would think it would have been cancer or emphysema that got him in the end. I mean, he did smoke two packs of cigarettes every day for fifty years. At least that's what he said. But not everything Harold Humphries said was true, and you had to take some of his admissions, stories, and anecdotes with a grain of salt. For instance, when he confided in me that he was voted "Most Handsome" his senior year in high school. Granted, I only saw what he looked like seventy years later, but it was hard to believe the wrinkled, spotted, Gollum-ish looking specimen had once been anything in the vicinity of attractive.

I asked him countless times to provide evidence to this fact—a photo, a drawing, a bronze bust—but he never complied.

Now I'm not saying the old guy was a liar. I'm just saying he was prone to the occasional hyperbole. Winning $10,000 at the racetrack in 1967 might have only been $5,000. Or the twelve corndogs he ate at the town fair. I mean, maybe it was only ten.

All that being said, the most important story—the story of how he met his first wife and how he gave their baby daughter up for adoption when his wife died during childbirth—this was true.

I had Harold's and my DNA tested against each another. Harold was my maternal grandfather. The little girl he gave up for adoption was my mother.

Anyhow, like I said, it wasn't the cigarettes that got him. It was, of all things, his beloved ducks.

Each day at lunch, Harold would get two pieces of bread from the cafeteria, and he would make his way out to the little pond in the courtyard of the nursing home. He had one of those steel walkers with the tennis balls on the bottom, and you could watch *Braveheart* in the time it took him to walk out there. He would sit on the wooden bench near the pond and toss bits of bread to the ducks. He would always try to throw the bread between two of them and hope for a bit of a wrestling match. That would always get him going.

Three days ago, Harold was feeding the ducks when apparently one of the ducks hopped up on the bench next to him and stole an entire piece of bread. I didn't have to be there to know this would have thrilled Harold beyond words. And he would have laughed and laughed and laughed, and then he would have died.

He was ninety-two years old.

I was numb when the phone call came. I always expected I would have time to say goodbye, that he would catch pneumonia or something and I would get a week to prepare. That I would be able to tell him how much the last couple years meant to me. Though, in hindsight, it was better he went out the way he did. No suffering. Just sunshine, ducks, and laughter. We should all be so lucky.

Still, it hurt.

Still, three days later, I was raw.

~

There was a knock at the door and I craned my neck up off the sofa. I wasn't expecting visitors, nor had I had a visitor in many months.

I pushed myself up with a grunt and plodded in my bear claw slippers to the front door. I was also wearing gray sweatpants and a Seattle Seahawks sweatshirt, size XXL. There was a grape jelly stain on the front of the sweatshirt that looked remarkably like Texas.

So yeah, I looked good.

I pulled the door open.

"Mr. Prescott?" inquired a gentleman in a tan overcoat. He was holding a blue umbrella, which shielded him from the unremitting Seattle drizzle.

I didn't acknowledge I was or was not this Prescott fellow.

"I'm Mark Jones with Hershey and Associates," the man said. Mark was fortyish and trim.

"You look a little old to be selling candy bars," I told him.

"Hershey and Associates the *law firm*."

"So, no Mr. Goodbars?"

He ignored me.

Sometimes this is best.

He did say, "Our firm represents the estate of Harold D. Humphries."

My throat constricted at the sound of Harold's name, a python tightening around my Adam's apple like a vice.

"May I come in?" he asked.

I sidestepped and he entered. Still dazed, I led him to the kitchen. I cleared my throat and asked, "Do you want something to drink?"

He declined.

"I would offer you some waffles, but I'm down to my last six boxes."

He seemed slightly thrown by this statement and shook his head. He set a briefcase on the kitchen island and snapped it open. He said, "Your name came up in the will."

My eyebrows jumped. "Really?"

My first thought was that it had something to do with my mother, maybe her birth certificate or some baby pictures or some other memorabilia.

Mark the Lawyer handed me a piece of paper. After quickly skimming it, I gazed up.

"You had no idea?" he asked.

"No...I mean, *no*." I shook my head. "Why didn't he give this to his kids? Why me?"

Mark shrugged. "I couldn't tell you. But, if you don't want it, I'm sure they will. Those two have been calling nonstop for the last forty-eight hours trying to get their hands on the will."

Harold had a son and a daughter. The daughter was somewhere out east and the son down in Portland. In all the times I visited Harold, easily more than a hundred, I never encountered either of them. I once asked Harold if it would be okay if I got in touch with them, as they were technically my aunt and uncle.

"You don't want none of that," was all he said.

As far as inheritances went, Harold had worked for Boeing for nearly forty years. He never discussed his finances with me, but I assumed he had some money stashed away.

Looking down at the paper a second time, I said, "I can't believe this is still in the family. He never mentioned it."

"Well, it's yours now," Mark said with a grin.

It was the farm Harold grew up on in Missouri.

It belonged to him.

And now, it belonged to me.

~

I knew a bit about the probate process from when my parents died, but Mark the Lawyer explained things to me like I was a seven-year-old with a learning disability.

I listened politely, but my thoughts kept wandering to the farm. Harold had told dozens of stories about growing up on the farm in Missouri, each story more Rockwellian than the last. Waking up at the break of dawn to milk the cow. Cleaning out the chicken coop. Feeding the pigs. Skipping school during the fall harvest.

For my thirty-fifth birthday a few months earlier, my sister sent me a couple of coloring books. When I first opened the package, I thought it was a gag gift, another of my sister's hilarious pranks. Turned out, she was serious. Evidently, adult coloring books were all the rage.

The coloring books sat unopened for many weeks, but then one day I started flipping through one. Then I started coloring. It's hard to admit, but for the next week all I did was color.

My favorite of all the pictures was a farm scene. Barn, tractor, fence with a rooster, a cow, a horse, a couple chickens. I was so proud of it that I hung it on the refrigerator.

I found myself glancing in the direction of the picture as Mark continued to prattle on. I think he could sense my preoccupation and attempted to wrap it up. "Anyhow, it will take a few months until the property is legally yours."

I nodded, then asked, "Do you think his kids will contest the will?"

"Possibly, but the will is ironclad. They won't have a leg to stand on."

"How much did they each get?"

"The nursing home bills and the property taxes on the farm cut into his nest egg some, but after everything is squared away, they'll each get a nice chunk."

"And the farm?" I asked.

He smirked as if to say, *there it is.*

I was tempted to tell Mark that my parents had left my sister and me a sizable inheritance, enough money to go see *Hamilton* every day for the rest of our lives.

I didn't.

"One point four million," he said. "And that's low. In the late eighties, early nineties, Harold probably could have gotten two million for it."

"When did Harold inherit it?"

"His father passed away in 1985. His mother and both his sisters were already dead. Neither sister had any offspring."

I nodded.

It appeared our interaction was over and Mark made his way toward the door. He took down my cell phone number and promised to keep me updated on any developments.

As he was grabbing his umbrella, I asked, "Do you know if anyone is living on the farm right now?"

"No one legally. Harold rented the land out from 1985 until the early 2000s, but no one has been there for over a decade." He gazed at me, then asked, "Why do you ask?"

"Oh, no reason," I lied.

~

I'd never been to the Midwest.

I was born in Seattle and spent the better part of twenty-six years there. When my parents died, Lacy, my kid sister, was a junior in high school. The next year, she got a full athletic scholarship to Temple—she was a star swimmer—and the two of us moved to Philadelphia.

Job-wise, the move couldn't have come at a better time. As a second-year detective with the Seattle Police Department, I beat a suspect to within an inch of his life—don't worry, he deserved every last kick, punch, and purple nurple—which resulted in the city being sued for $7 million. To complicate matters, I slammed my partner's face into his locker when he defended the scumbag.

Sorry, Ethan.

R.I.P.

I thought these two events should have resulted in me getting a promotion, possibly even my own TV show, but instead, I was sent packing.

While in Philadelphia, I began consulting with the FBI's Violent Crime Unit helping them track down several serial killers and even cracking a few cold cases. Everything was going great until one day when Lacy got dizzy at swim practice. Two weeks later, the verdict was in: multiple sclerosis.

The day my parents died was hard. That day was harder.

A year later, Lacy and I ended up in Maine. Lacy revitalized her spirit and I, well, I chased a serial killer, got shot twice, fell off a cliff, drowned, then died. But like Jon Snow, I came back from the dead. The case in Maine put me on the map. I couldn't go ten feet without someone telling me I looked like that douchebag detective on the cover of *Time* magazine. That's because I was the douchebag detective on the cover of *Time* magazine.

Two years ago, Lacy moved to France, and I moved back home to Seattle.

Wolves.

Just saying.

So, I'd done a good job of straddling the United States. West Coast, East Coast, then West Coast. But I'd never been to the Midwest.

According to Google, the drive was two thousand miles and would take me thirty-one hours.

Years later, someone would ask me why I drove there that day. And I would tell them the truth. I was all out of coloring books.

Chapter 2

About the time a small ceremony for Harold was being held at a church opposite the nursing home, I was stopping at a gas station in eastern Washington to fill up my dad's fifteen-year-old Range Rover. I bought a blue Powerade, a couple bags of Cheetos, some beef jerky, and two Mr. Goodbars, the latter of which I was craving since thinking Mark the Lawyer had been there to sell me candy bars.

I went through a half dozen radio stations as I drove east on I-90 through Idaho and into Montana. I slept in my car at a truck stop in South Dakota for a few hours then continued south on I-29 through Iowa and into the flat lands, prairies, and plains of Nebraska. The landscape changed little over the course of the next ten hours: wispy yellow grass, cows, and miles and miles of open road.

Once into Missouri, I left the interstate on the outskirts of Kansas City and headed east on Highway 36. The flat lands slowly gave way to lush, green hills and copses of leafy, green trees. White clouds stretched thin and sat low on the horizon, further evidence of the increasingly moist and humid air.

It was another three and a half hours until I reached the fertile soil of Audrain County, located in north central Missouri—forty miles north of the Missouri river, ninety miles west of the Mississippi—and home to the small town where Harold grew up.

Tarrin, MO.

Population: 2,153.

I'd seen my fair share of small towns, mostly when I was living in Maine. But Maine was peculiar. It was a tourist destination and many of those small towns were overrun with New Yorkers, Bostonians,

Europeans, and others during the summer months. During the off-season, the populations of those towns dwindled, sometimes down into the hundreds.

Small-town Middle America would be starkly different. There wouldn't be a tourist in sight.

I exited the highway toward Tarrin, drove for a handful of miles, then followed a sign to Main Street. It was a late Sunday afternoon and there wasn't much activity.

Main Street was wide with diagonal parking on both sides. The street glistened from a quick rain that had passed through some time earlier. Tan, red, and gray two-story buildings ran the length of an entire block. Second stories were peppered with thin rectangular windows gazing down on shingled overhangs.

A few cars, but mostly trucks, filled the diagonal parking in front of a potpourri of shops: a real estate office, a live bait shop, a True Value, a law firm, a barbershop, a tailor, an art gallery, an ice cream shop, an accounting firm, a repair shop, a bookstore, a vet clinic, an insurance office. Many of the businesses had flags hanging in their windows, some the American flag, some a green and yellow flag with a tiger on it, some the St. Louis Cardinals' flag.

It was, in a word, charming.

I continued through a traffic light.

I passed a community center, a post office, a fire station, and a police department. There were two squad cars parked outside the Tarrin Police Department, and I wondered how many officers it took to police a town of two thousand. I guessed four full-time officers, five tops. This was a far cry from the nearly fifteen hundred it took to police Seattle. Then again, if Tarrin was anything like the small towns I experienced in Maine, they were mostly dealing with petty crime, drugs, DUIs, and maybe the occasional domestic dispute, not the ghastly murders and gang activity that plagued the big cities.

To the right was a high school with a football field in the far distance. There was a sign out front that read "Go Tigers," which would explain the flags I saw earlier.

Just past the high school were two churches. The first, Lutheran. The second, Baptist. They were both set on sprawling manicured lawns, but still more or less across the street from each other. I imagined the two groups standing on their respective lawns, dressed in their Sunday best, judging each other from across the way. I mean, I don't think it was like the Yankees and Red Sox, but there had to be a touch of rivalry there.

We have the best choir.

No, we have the best choir.

Past the churches, there was another block of businesses: a feed store, a bike shop, a Sonic Drive-In, a bank, a gas station, a liquor store, a fitness center, a motel, a grocery store, a bowling alley, a dry cleaner, a dance studio, a small hospital.

After the next traffic light, small houses began popping up. I took a left on a side street and drove slowly. The houses were small and sturdy. There were no fences, the yards running together in a melting pot of leafy trees, well-tended lawns, and children's toys. The vehicle of choice was a truck, with an overwhelming amount of Fords. There were a few sedans, even one Prius, so it wasn't against city ordinance to own a foreign car.

I found my way back to Main Street then continued on. The Humphries Farm was eight miles from town. I followed the directions I'd printed off the internet, taking a turn onto County Road 34, then another on County Road 52.

One farm led into another, tractors moving through corduroyed fields of budding corn, soybeans, or the like. Opposite one of the farms was a small lake. Behind the lake was a giant house. Immediately, I recognized both from Harold's stories.

I pulled the Range Rover over on the side of the road and rolled down the window.

The King family lived in the mansion in the 1940s. The Kings owned nearly all the land in the area, and Harold's father leased his land from them. The lake was the one Harold jumped in to save a girl from drowning. That was how he first met Elizabeth, the young woman he would later marry, and who would give birth to my mother.

I'm not sure if it were thoughts of my mother, or Harold's death, or guilt for having missed Harold's funeral, or lack of sleep, or the eight Mr. Goodbars I'd eaten in the last thirty-six hours, but I felt my eyes begin to well with tears.

I wiped the tears with the back of my hand, then glanced at my reflection in the rearview mirror. The extra weight had given my face a certain roundness, my angular jaw hidden beneath a thick sweater of fat and stubble. My eyes, a grayish-blue, were bloodshot from thirty hours of driving, and my finger-length brown hair was matted and oily. Someone had once described me as looking like Matthew McConaughey after a bad car accident. Whatever that means. Anyhow, it took me a long minute to compose myself, then pull the car back onto the road. I passed several more farms before coming to a dirt road leading through a broken gate. A family of crows were perched on the ramshackle fencing. Tall, unkempt grass and weeds led to a faint farmhouse in the distance.

"This must be it," I muttered.

I drove through a large puddle then continued toward the house. Unlike the other farms, whose plots were neatly sectioned off, the Humphries Farm was wild and roaming. It was an adolescent with no guardian and no curfew. Tall grasses freckled with little yellow flowers extended a half mile in every direction.

Halfway to the house, I stopped the car and squinted into the lowering sun. There was a tractor out in the field, but unlike the others, this one wasn't moving. It was long deceased, engulfed by the very field it once plowed.

Mark the Lawyer said the farm had been uninhabited for the past ten years, but it looked like no one had lived there for thirty.

A road snaked between a series of large trees then gave way to a small farmhouse. The farmhouse was two stories, white clapboard. The paint was peeling, leaving the dull gray of the beaten timber beneath exposed. The roof was a checkerboard of black squares where a quarter of the rain-battered shingles had fallen off.

To the house's left was a giant oak. Having gone untrimmed for several decades, like a monster uncurling its fingers, the branches reached precariously over the house. Behind the tree was a tall, cylindrical, gray brick structure, which was either a silo or a guard tower. To the right of the house, maybe fifty feet away, was what I presumed to be a chicken coop. Farther right, a football field away, was a barn. Both the coop and the barn were the same white clapboard, the same peeling paint, the same underlying grayness.

Unlike my picture on the fridge, there was a lack of color. Everything was muted. Everything acid-washed. Everything the color of an approaching thunderstorm.

I should have taken that as a sign.

A sign of things to come.

Chapter 3

I opened the door of the car and stepped out, sinking shin-deep into the tall overgrowth. My black T-shirt stuck to my back, and I didn't know if it was from the long drive, the fatness, or the dense Missouri air.

I trudged through the tall grass to the front porch where two rocking chairs sat in disrepair. I wondered if they dated as far back as Harold, wondered if Harold sat in one of those chairs, rocked back and forth, drank lemonade, and whittled something while he listened to his beloved St. Louis Cardinals on the radio.

Bugs of all makes and sizes skittered up and down the wooden porch and railings.

"Don't mess with me and I won't mess with you," I told the bugs, hoping they would share our understanding with the rest of their tribes.

A screen door was held open three inches by an invisible force. I pushed it back and tried the door. Locked. I knocked a couple times. Part of me expected someone to open the door. Someone with half their teeth, a shotgun, and a bottle of moonshine. But since it wasn't 1890, this didn't happen.

I pressed my shoulder against the door and gave it a nudge. It held firm. I pondered kicking it down but decided I should first explore my alternatives.

I made my way around the tall oak and to the back of the house. The back door was also locked. I continued around, peeking through several of the windows. Most were opaque, fogged by decades of dust and grime, and in the few that had areas of visibility, the view was blocked by curtains. I tried to open several windows, but none budged.

Back at the front door, I took a couple deep breaths then kicked it with my foot.

The door didn't waver.

Farmhouse: 1. Thomas: 0.

I shook my leg out then went the shoulder route.

Blamo.

Same result.

Farmhouse: 2. Thomas: 0.

I walked to the Range Rover, popped the hatch, pulled out a tire iron, and said, "You have messed with the wrong guy."

I should mention I was slightly delirious.

I needed food.

And sleep.

On my way back to the house, I noticed one of the second-story windows was open a few inches. I also noticed it wasn't all that far from where the tall oak fed into the roof.

I dropped the tire iron and began climbing the tree. It was harder than I expected. On account of the fatness.

After a long couple of minutes, I crawled out onto one of the branches. My face was beaded in sweat and I was wheezing. The branch was softball-size in diameter, which would have held Fit Thomas just fine but creaked under the weight of Fat Thomas.

"Please hold," I wheezed.

I'd survived too much in my life to die climbing a fucking tree.

I set my feet and prepared to leap to the roof.

Crack.

The limb snapped clean off.

I braced for impact and landed on my side with a loud thud.

"Oh, God."

I lay groaning for a long minute, then did a damage assessment. I fell on my left side with my shoulder, ribs, and thigh absorbing most of the impact. I doubted anything was broken, but I wouldn't be starting Pilates the next morning like I intended.

I pushed myself up with a grunt, holding my tender ribs with my arm.

Farmhouse: 3. Thomas: 0.

I picked up the tire iron and shouted, "You dirty rat! You killed my brother!"

Did I mention I was delirious?

And now concussed.

I smashed the tire iron against the front door. Once, twice, three million times. The door died a horrible death. I pushed open what remained of the door, a light breeze sending ten years of dust into the air. I sneezed.

The sneeze sent a bolt of lightning through my bruised ribs, and I fled back to the porch.

The dust would need a few minutes to settle, and after the pain in my side lessened to mildly excruciating, I decided to do some exploring. First stop, the chicken coop. The roof was slightly angled, and there was a thin door. The door was ajar, and I stuck my head in. Inside were thirty little cubbies. No chickens.

I walked around to the back and saw the small opening where the chickens could go in and out. Hypothetically, of course. Like I said, there were no chickens. The ramp leading to the opening was gone, most likely scavenged by someone many years earlier.

I continued plowing through the waist-high grass until I came to a barn with a steeply sloped roof. The entrance to the barn was two large sliding panels, but they were held together by a thick lock and chain. I put my ear to the crack between the two panels and listened. I could hear a bit of rustling, but that was probably my subconscious wanting a family of barn owls to be living there.

I was headed back toward the farmhouse when a rectangle of fencing hidden in the tall grass caught my eye. It took me a long minute to reach the crumbling enclosure: a 1000-square-foot area of dirt with the occasional outcropping of weeds.

It was a pigpen.

Harold had told several stories about the pigs on the farm, about how smart they were, and how they each had a different personality. He said it always broke his heart when they had to slaughter one.

They were just pigs, I remembered thinking. *Delicious pigs.*

A few minutes later, I returned to the farmhouse. The dust had settled and I stepped inside. Mark the Lawyer had said that Harold rented the land out from the mid-eighties up until the early 2000s so I half expected the inside of the house to be nicer than the outside.

And it was.

Marginally.

The interior walls were covered in wallpaper—beige with maroon flowers. At the corners, the wallpaper was peeling away, and a few sections had fallen and were lying prostrate on the brown tiled floor.

From the entry, there was a dining room to the right and a living area to the left. The dining room was filled with a scarred wooden table and three chairs. A chandelier hung above the table at a thirty-degree angle. The many light bulbs were colored nearly black by time. Cobwebs clung to the chandelier, stretching to the brass rods and thick beige curtains that held the sunlight at bay.

I slowly peeled the curtains back—sending years of dust sprinkling into the air—then unlocked the window and pushed it upward with a loud creak. I did the same with a second window, then made my way to the living area.

The living area was occupied by a gray upholstered couch, a wooden rocking chair, and a tan La-Z-Boy, which easily could have been the first one off the assembly line. A rectangular rug, striped brown and white, centered the room. An oval coffee table sat atop the rug. Everything faced an oak entertainment center where a monstrosity of a TV stood.

I sat down in the rocking chair and rocked a couple times, the chair's stiff joints groaning under my weight. I pushed myself up and out of the chair and drew a smiley face in the layer of dust caking the sixty-inch, half-ton Zenith.

There was a light switch against the wall, and I flipped it up. The lights didn't turn on, which didn't mean a whole lot since few light bulbs lived to see their teenage years. Still, I made a mental note to find out the names of the utility companies.

Next, I made my way to the kitchen. There was a large steel oven with huge handles which made me think about the oven Hansel and Gretel shoved the mean old witch into. Above the oven hung a series of cast iron pots and pans. I gave a skillet a light push, sending it rocking back and forth.

Next to the stove was a small sink, and I turned the faucet. Nothing came out. No water. No air. No noise.

Lastly, I checked the fridge. It was light blue and looked fit to survive a nuclear holocaust. I pulled the door open. It was empty.

On the counter next to the fridge was the solitary anachronism. An espresso machine. It must have been left over by whoever last rented the place or was brought over later by some extravagant squatters.

I chuckled lightly then headed for the staircase opposite the kitchen. The wooden stairs creaked loudly, and I was reminded of that one time when I climbed out onto a tree branch and it started to creak. And then I fell twelve feet.

I involuntarily shuddered.

Delirious.

Concussed.

And now I had PTSD.

Awesome.

Keeping with the color scheme, the top floor was maroon carpet. A narrow hallway connected three bedrooms: one master, then two identical smaller ones.

I checked the master bedroom first. There was a queen-size bed with a floral bedspread, but other than that, the room was void of any character, its trinkets and possessions long boxed up or given away. Next, I checked the two smaller bedrooms. Both had a single bed, stripped to the mattress and two naked pillows. The sun shone through the lone window of the bedroom facing west, a box of gold on the maroon carpet. I sat down on the mattress—sending a plume of dust jettisoning into the air—and knew the room once belonged to Harold. It sounds odd, but I could feel him in the room, could sense his spirit. Almost as if the millions of dust molecules dancing in the sunlight were his ashes.

"Sorry I didn't get to say goodbye," I said softly.

I waited for Harold to answer. For a quick gust of wind. For the rattling of the window. For the ashes to spell out "Goodbye, Thomas" on the floor.

But Harold had better things to do.

Two minutes later, I was asleep.

Chapter 4

The diner was called Dina's Corner Dine-In.

It was half full at 7:00 a.m. on a Monday, and I guessed it was slammed come the weekends. The patrons were mostly men, a healthy mix of white collar and blue collar. Slacks sat next to blue jeans. Wingtips conversed with work boots.

I could feel the stares as I walked in and took a stool at the counter. Maybe it was because I was limping. Maybe it was because I was grimacing with each step. Maybe it was because I was the first new face they'd seen in weeks. Either way, the looks were brief, the conversations halted for a single breath before resuming.

The counter was black Formica, clean and polished. Half the stools were occupied, and I took the one on the far left. The man to my right had a thick mustache and was clad in a flannel shirt and a tan Carhartt jacket. Warm for what promised to be a day in the mid-eighties, both in temperature and humidity. The hand cinched around his coffee cup was worn and callused, a farmer's hand.

I glanced at my hands. I had a blister on my thumb from playing Tetris, but otherwise, my hands screamed of a life of money and privilege.

A fiftyish woman politely but efficiently took my order for two Belgian waffles, a double order of bacon, an apple juice, and seven Percocet.

I'd slept from sundown to sunup and I felt rested, but my body was in shambles. There was a deep bruise on my left buttock that ran down the length of my thigh. My left shoulder was swollen and stiff, and I could barely lift my arm six inches. But both of these injuries paled in comparison to my ribs. Each time I exhaled it felt like someone was spreading my ribs with a crowbar.

There was a stack of *Tarrin Weekly* near the entrance and I'd grabbed one on my way in. I flipped through the small paper, reading about the many church revivals the coming weekend, a couple of teachers who were retiring after the school year ended the following week, the results of the Little Miss Tarrin pageant, and Mayor Paula Van Dixon's reelection bid for her tenth straight term.

A different waitress appeared behind the counter and said, "I hear you're looking for some Percocet."

She was cute, early twenties. Her stomach was just starting to round out, and I guessed she was halfway into her pregnancy.

"Or a morphine drip," I quipped.

She laughed, then handed me four blue capsules.

I squinted at the pills. "Um, I think these are Advil."

"Best I could do." She smiled. "But, I mean, at least they're gelcaps."

"Hallelujah," I muttered, then added, "Don't think I won't Yelp about this."

She snickered, then asked, "What's the other guy look like?"

"Green and about thirty feet tall."

Her eyebrows furrowed.

"I fell out of a tree," I explained.

I told her the story.

A few minutes after she left to greet a table, my food came. I ate two bites of waffle, then two pieces of bacon, then washed the four Advil down with apple juice.

The cute waitress returned after checking on her tables and asked, "The Humphries Farm? Did you buy it?"

"It was handed down to me in a will."

"Are you a Humphries?"

"Not technically. It's a long story."

Her gaze told me that someday she would like to hear all the details, and I started to have serious doubts that the father of little Billy-Bob-To-Be was still in the picture.

Who knows, maybe she was a chubby chaser.

"No one has been out there for a long time," she said.

"Yeah, it's in pretty bad shape."

While I had her there, I asked her the names of the electric, gas, and water supply companies. She let me borrow one of her pens, and I wrote the names down on a napkin. Then I asked if they had a Yellow Pages.

"A *Yellow Pages?*" she asked in disbelief. "Why?"

"So I can find out the phone numbers of these places and call them."

"Why don't you use your phone?"

I pulled my phone out of my front pocket and showed her.

"A flip phone? I didn't even know they still made those."

A group of five men walked through the door, and the waitress told them she'd be right with them. She pulled an iPhone out of her apron and slid it over to me. "Here, you can borrow mine. Just, um, don't scroll through the pictures."

I finished off my breakfast, then spent the next ten minutes looking up the utility companies on the waitress's phone and setting up accounts with each. I could expect both the electricity and gas to be turned on at some point later in the day. The water supply company said they would send someone within the hour.

I was still wearing the same thing as yesterday: jeans, a black T-shirt, and blue Asics, and I was in desperate need of a shower and shave.

Speaking of getting clean, I searched "Tarrin cleaning services" and got one hit. A company called Tarrin Cleaning Services.

Creative.

I called the number, but no one answered, and I left a message.

The waitress stopped by a minute later, and I gave back her phone. I told her all the nude pics I saw were extremely tasteful.

She enjoyed this.

I attempted to give her twenty bucks for her troubles, but she wouldn't accept it.

Back outside, the traffic on Main Street had doubled. A number of kids with backpacks were walking on the sidewalks, headed to their respective schools. One kid had a cowboy hat on, but for the most part, the kids were dressed just like the city kids. Lots of skateboards. Big headphones. Bright colors.

I drove to the middle of town and parked in front of a home goods store called, quite fittingly, Kim's Home Goods.

Why was it that every store had to be someone's?

Dina's Corner Dine-In.

Joe's Automotive.

Nancy's Music and Jewelry.

Morris's Loans.

Bob's Accounting Services.

Maybe I should open a shop.

Thomas's Buttons.

A bell rang as I entered the shop, and two women chatting near a register smiled. They were both in their late forties and looked similar enough to be siblings.

"Well, hi there," they both shouted too enthusiastically.

I waved a quick hello.

"What brings you in here today?" asked the one striding toward me. She was clad in a beige sweater, blue jeans, and red designer glasses. *Did these people not know how hot it was here?*

"I just moved here and I need a bunch of stuff."

"He just moved here and he needs a bunch of stuff," she yelled to the other woman.

Turning back to me, she asked, "Where'd you move in?"

"The Old Humphries Farm." I hadn't anticipated adding the "Old," but after seeing the place and sleeping a night there, it seemed necessary.

"He just moved into the Humphries place," she echoed.

The other woman started clapping.

I pondered running to my car and driving back to Seattle.

As if sensing this, the woman grabbed my arm. "Now, what all do you need?"

I told her I needed a lot of the necessities, towels, bedsheets, and "all that jazz."

Annie, that was her name, gave my arm a tug and said, "Well, all right then."

~

An hour later, I walked out with two sets of bedsheets, three pillows, a quilt, four towels of different dimensions, a blender, a toaster, and an invitation to attend both women's church revivals the coming weekend.

My next stop was the hardware store. The two men working were busy with other customers, and I got out of there quickly with a deluxe toolbox and some bolt cutters.

As I was putting the tools in my car, my phone rang. It was the cleaning service. I scheduled to meet two cleaners at the farmhouse in an hour. The woman on the phone didn't ask for an address. The Humphries Farm seemed to suffice.

After the call, my phone rang a second time. It was the electric company confirming the power had been turned on, which meant I could buy some groceries.

I decided to walk to the grocery store rather than drive, hoping the short stroll would help loosen up the stiffness in my leg.

I remembered seeing the grocery store a block and a half past the traffic light and headed in that direction. After a block, I reached a small park, which I hadn't noticed the previous day. The park was located on the corner of the busiest intersection on Main Street. It would have been a prime location for commerce, possibly even the most sought after lot in all of Tarrin. The park was as out of place as the espresso machine in the farmhouse kitchen.

There was a stone bench, a couple small trees, two rectangular flower beds, and a large rock. Leaning against the rock was a handful of yellow flowers.

The rock was twenty yards from the sidewalk. The sun reflected off its shiny surface. It took me a moment to realize it wasn't the rock reflecting the sun, it was a bronze plaque.

I stepped onto the grass and approached the rock. It was four feet wide and came up to my waist. It was granite, a kaleidoscope of gray, white, and black. The face of the rock sloped down gently where the plaque was secured.

Inscribed on the plaque was:

In Loving Memory:

Peggy Bertina
Will Dennel
Neil Felding
Tom Lanningham
Odell McBride

October 9, 2012

You will never be forgotten

I leaned down and looked more closely at the flowers propped against the rock.

Tulips.

Five of them.

The park was a *memorial*.

My brain started whirring. The first theory that popped into my head was that the park seemed so out of place because there had previously been a commercial business there. Then something happened.

A fire.

There must have been a fire and five people died.

I gave the memorial a departing nod, then found my way back to the sidewalk. A half block later, I came to the town grocery store, Harvest Food & Market. Though it was half the size of the Whole Foods where I shopped in Seattle, it had a decent selection. I pondered buying health food, but I was in no shape to exercise, and I decided to postpone Operation Fitness at least a few more days.

The checkout clerk was an acne-faced kid with dark hair.

"You guys don't have any chocolate chip waffles," I informed him.

"Oh," he said, his eyebrows jumping. "I don't think we have those."

"Yeah, you don't. Who do I talk to about ordering them?"

"Travis, but he's not here right now."

"Well, if you can get Travis to start carrying chocolate chip waffles, I'll give you fifty bucks."

He smiled and said he'd see what he could do.

While he was bagging my groceries, I asked, "What's the deal with the memorial down the street? Did a business burn down?"

"You aren't from around here?"

"No, I'm not."

He took a deep breath and said, "It wasn't a fire. There used to be a grocery store there, but then some guy came in and shot up the place."

"And five people died?"

He nodded, then sighed. I could tell he knew at least a couple of them. Heck, in such a small town, he probably knew all five.

I asked, "What was the name of the place?"

"Save-More."

Chapter 5

The next day was May 31st.

The two women who cleaned the house were there for close to six hours the previous day. With the layers of dust gone, the cobwebs cleared, the tile floor scrubbed, the carpets vacuumed, the windows cleaned, and the electricity, gas, and water working, the house was a stark contrast from when I first entered just a day and a half earlier. The house had been hit with a defibrillator. Brought back from the dead.

Just like me.

I'd put the clean sheets on the bed but I slept fitfully. Finally, at around 3:00 in the morning, I gave up.

Part of the reason I couldn't sleep was my aching ribs. The other part was that I couldn't turn my brain off. My brain was a dog with a bone, the bone being the five people murdered four years earlier.

What happened? Who did it? Did they catch them? Had they already made it into a *Dateline Saturday Night Mystery*?

For the first time, maybe ever, I wished I had a fancy iPhone. I could have learned every detail about the murders. I did the next best thing, which was to call my sister. France was seven hours ahead, and I caught Lacy on a break from painting.

"Hey, Fat-ass," she answered.

I laughed. I'd kept Lacy well apprised of my weight gain.

"What are you up to?" she asked.

"Just hanging out at my farm."

"*Your* farm?"

I spent the next twenty minutes bringing her up to speed. She couldn't believe it and asked, "That farm was still in the family?"

"Apparently."

Lacy had only met Harold a handful of times. She came back to the

States for two weeks the past October, and we went to visit him several times at the nursing home. Like me, she fell in love with him and even considered moving back home with Caleb so she could spend more time with him. He was the only living relative we had left. She was crushed when she found out he died, and she nearly jumped on the first flight out. I had to convince her flying back wouldn't do him any good. And it wouldn't do me any good. She'd relented.

"So I fell out of a tree yesterday," I told her.

When my sister thinks something is funny, she goes into a giggle fit, and the idea of me falling out of a tree to my near death sent her reeling. Once composed, she excitedly told me she sold one of her paintings for twenty grand and that she and Caleb were trying for a baby. "So when those days come around," she said, "Caleb and I screw like bunnies."

I begged her to stop telling me about her sex life, and in turn, she began describing it in graphic detail.

I said, "I'm two seconds away from climbing that tree and doing a swan dive."

She laughed, and I told her why I really called. I asked her if she could look something up on the computer for me.

She huffed, but agreed.

"Search 'Save-More murders.'"

"Holy shit," she quipped a moment later. "This happened there? I didn't think that kind of stuff happened in small towns."

"Me neither."

She found an article from the *St. Louis Post-Dispatch* and read it to me.

The short of it was:

October 9th, 2012, a disgruntled ex-employee went to the Save-More right before closing. The manager, who had fired the guy two weeks earlier, was checking out the last of the customers. The killer forced his six victims to the back of the store at gunpoint, all of which was caught on the surveillance cameras. He then ushered them into the back freezer bay where, unfortunately, there were no cameras. But it wasn't hard to figure out what happened. The enraged ex-employee shot all six of them, killing five. The manhunt for the killer didn't last long. He was found in his car on the side of the road with a hole in his temple. He'd committed suicide.

I asked Lacy if she could tell me a bit more about the killer, but she said she had a meeting she needed to get to.

I finally fell asleep an hour later.

~

The first time I tried to cut through the chain with the bolt cutters, the flexing of my arms sent a shockwave through my ribs so violent that I nearly vomited. I wouldn't have tried a second time, but my first attempt cut a nice groove into both sides of the chain and it wouldn't take much to finish the job.

I planted my feet, situated the bolt cutters in the grooves, and clasped the handles together. The chain split, then rattled against the door.

Holding my ribs with one arm, I gingerly pried the barn doors open.

A wave of musk washed over me before diffusing into the warm sunshine. I waited a few seconds, then stepped inside.

The afternoon sun shone through foggy windows high in the steepled ceiling, illuminating the dirt floor and many brittle stacks of baled hay.

"Hedwig!" I shouted. "Where are you?"

I listened for the rustle I heard the previous day but was rewarded with silence.

There was a ladder lying on the ground and I hefted it up and leaned it against the ledge of the wooden loft. If there were any owls, the loft would be where they built their nest.

I started up the ladder, climbing until my stomach was level with the hay-covered loft floor. A moment later, the rustling I heard the previous day returned. There was something moving through the hay. And whatever it was, rat, mouse, possum, or tiger, it was headed right toward me.

My body tensed.

A breath later, it wiggled its way out of the hay two inches from my chest.

I screamed.

Even worse, I leaned backward.

I could feel the ladder pull off the ledge and begin moving backward with me. I let go of the ladder and jumped. I over rotated and hit the ground. On my left side. Again.

"Oh, God."

My eyes welled with tears.

I lay there for a long minute praying for death to take me into its warm embrace. The pain was so fierce it took my brain a couple minutes to reload the video of the creature that surprised me.

A little piglet.

~

"How did you even get up there?" I muttered, leaning down to pick up the ladder with a groan.

I replaced the ladder and started climbing.

Each step was a battle.

Pain vs. Piglet.

Once I reached the loft, I called out, "Come here, little piglet."

I pulled myself up and onto the loft, which was one of the most painful experiences of my life. And remember, I was attacked by a pack of wolves. And shot. And drowned. And fell out of a fucking tree.

I stood up, the angled roof hovering just overhead, and started searching the hay for my attacker. At the far back of the barn, I noticed a large lump. I eased forward. It was a pig. A full-grown pig, pinkish white with black markings. I only saw the piglet for a moment, but it had the same coloring.

I gave the pig a slight shake.

She was dead.

After a decade of solving murders, tracking serial killers, and reinvestigating cold cases, my brain was wired to seek answers. You see a dead body and you backtrack. How did it get there? And why?

The pig must have wandered over from one of the neighboring farms. Maybe she left on purpose, maybe by accident. She was pregnant, her motherly instinct told her to seek shelter. She found entrance to the barn through some opening. Somehow, she made it up to the loft. Then she gave birth to a piglet. I only saw the piglet for a moment, but it didn't appear to have just been born. It was a baby, but not an infant. It was about the size of my sister's pug Baxter when he was six months old. So five, maybe six pounds.

As for the mother pig, I tried to narrow down her time of death. She wasn't bloated, which meant the putrefaction process was yet to start. That's when the bacteria and enzymes still alive in a body began to break it down. The bacteria were what caused the awful smelling gas people attributed to death. That usually started around the end of the second day, ergo, Miss Piggy had been dead less than forty-eight hours. How much less, I couldn't be certain, though the little piglet was a good indication. A baby piglet couldn't survive too long without food. Certainly not much longer than a day.

The case solved, I turned on my heel.

"Hey, little piglet," I called out. "I know you're hungry."

I got down on all fours, moving my hands through the hay.

"I know you haven't eaten in a while. And I bet you're thirsty."

I crawled another couple steps.

There was a rustling.

A head popped up.

"There you are," I said, grinning. Then my face fell. The piglet that surprised me was pink with black markings. This piglet was *tan* with black markings.

"There are two of you!"

As if on cue, five feet away, the other piglet popped its head out.

It took me five minutes of crawling through the hay before I caught both of them.

"Okay, are there any more of you? Because I'm running out of hands."

If there were more, I was going to have to come back for them.

~

I made it to town in ten minutes.

Pink, who was anatomically a little girl, sat on my lap, while Tan, who anatomically had a tiny little piglet pecker, thrashed about in the backseat.

I drove past the vet clinic the previous day, and I screeched into one of the parking spots out front. I grabbed the two piglets and pushed through the door. There was an empty reception desk with a vase of flowers and a small bell. My hands full with the piglets, I hit the bell three times with my elbow.

"Just a second!" a woman shouted.

A moment later, she emerged. She was petite with blond hair. She was wearing a blue shirt, jeans, and a white lab coat. I put her in her late twenties, early thirties. She was straight out of central casting: Attractive Country Veterinarian. For a moment, I nearly forgot I was holding two little pigs.

"Look at you guys," she said, her eyes lighting up.

"I found them in the loft of my barn."

She ignored me and felt both piglets' noses, then looked into their eyes. Only then did she appear to realize there was a fourth mammal in the room.

"The loft?" she asked, glancing up. Her eyes were the color of honey. "How did they get up into the loft?"

"Their mother was up there. I think she must have given birth to them up there?"

"How did she get up there?"

"I have no idea."

"Where is the sow now?"

"Sow?"

She sighed. "The mom."

"Oh. She's dead."

"No wonder they're so dehydrated."

She took Tan from my arms and said, "Follow me."

I followed her through a hall and into an examination room. She set Tan on a small metal table, grabbed a stethoscope, and gave him a quick examination. Then she stuck a thermometer up his rump, which he didn't like one bit—*SQUEAL!*—and I was reminded I was due for my first prostate exam.

She went through the same rigmarole with Pink, who was remarkably unfazed by the piece of glass in her rear.

"They're different colors," I said.

The vet raised her eyebrows and said, "You picked up on that, did you?"

Her sarcasm took me by surprise.

"I did."

She fought down a smile.

I said, "The girl is the same color as the mom, but the boy is totally different."

She glanced at me for a long second. "Sorry, sometimes I forget not everyone is from here."

"I forgive you."

She rolled her eyes, then explained that a pig's litter can have piglets with all sorts of different colorings and markings. The sow (female pig) and boar (male pig) are usually different breeds, and the piglets may look like one or both parents. "Odds are the boar was an Oxford Sandy and Black."

"A what?"

"Oxford Sandy and Black. A breed of pig."

"Like a German shepherd?"

"If that helps you," she said, a dimple surfacing for a breath before disappearing back to the depths.

Gina who?

"Okay," she said. "Let's get these kiddos some food."

She disappeared into the back and left me with the piglets. Both sat on the table staring at me with their large brown eyes.

"What?"

They didn't answer.

The vet returned with two bottles. She handed one to me.

"I never got your name," I said.

"Sarah."

She nodded at the bottle and said, "Just gently—"

Without prompting, Pink sucked the nipple into her mouth and begin suckling.

Sarah said, "You're a natural."

"I nursed until I was nine."

She cut her eyes at me, then finally cracked a smile.

A second dimple surfaced.

Here we go again.

"Good girl," I coaxed, turning my attention back to Pink. She suckled away, her little jaw moving up and down.

"That's a good boy," Sarah cooed to Tan.

The two piglets sucked the bottles dry, and I asked, "Can they have another one?"

"Not right now. They could have gone a day or more without food, so we don't want to overwhelm their systems. You can feed them again in a few hours."

"Me?" I scoffed. "What do you mean?" I had assumed I would leave the piglets with her.

"When you take them home."

"But they're not my pigs."

"Then go find out whose pigs they are and give them back. Any farmer out here will be happy to take them."

My brow furrowed. "And what will they do with them?"

"Depends. Breed 'em, eat 'em, or sell 'em. There isn't much else."

"But—"

She looked at me.

"Okay, I guess I can take them."

She told me she could give me enough formula for the next two days, but I would have to go to the feed and supply store to pick up more. Then she told me about some website I should visit so I could read all about how to care for them.

"I don't have the internet."

"Even on your phone?"

I shook my head.

She sighed, her third by my count, and said, "Okay, I'll print some stuff out for you. Meet me up front."

Five minutes later, she met me at the reception desk with a ream of printed pages. She put them in a bag with the formula, then rang me up for the visit. All of $40.

I said, "It's got to be more than that."

"First-timer's discount."

I set the piglets down and reached for my wallet.

I groaned.

In all the piglet hullabaloo, I nearly forgot I was lucky I wasn't paralyzed.

"What's wrong with you?" Sarah asked.

"I fell out of a tree."

"Oh."

"And then I fell off a ladder."

She fought back a smile. "Really?"

"Sadly, yes."

"Want me to take a look?"

"Uh, I'm a human."

She narrowed her eyes at me.

I can be annoying.

"Do you want me to take a look or not?"

"Yes, please."

She came around the counter and asked, "Where does it hurt?"

"My whole left side, butt, ribs, and shoulder."

She ushered me out of the lobby and a few feet into the hall. Then she said, "Okay, pull down your pants."

I raised my eyebrows and said, "Isn't that second visit sort of stuff?"

She gazed at me. I knew the look. It was the *I wish I had access to a time machine so I could go back and never have met this guy* look.

"Sorry." I unbuttoned my pants and pushed my jeans down halfway. On my right quadriceps, a half inch below where my boxer briefs ended, there was a nickel-sized area of dimpled skin. There was a similar scar on my left shoulder.

Bullets will do that.

Sarah cast her eyes to the scar, but said nothing. She checked the bruise on my butt and thigh, then said, "Now, lift your shirt."

Err.

"What now?" she said, throwing up her hands.

"It's just, I'm kind of chunky right now."

She forced down a smile.

I think I was growing on her.

That happens sometimes.

"Just lift your shirt."

I did.

She prodded my ribs.

"Yowee!"

"Are you always like this?"

"I think I might have PTSD."

"I think you have brain damage."

I laughed, which hurt, but appeared to make Sarah happy.

After another minute of pressing, prodding, and overall pain infliction, she said, "Well, first off, for falling out of a tree and falling off a ladder, you are incredibly lucky. It's probably a good thing you're, as you say, 'a little chunky.'"

"I'm joining Weight Watchers."

"Good for you," she said, then rolled her eyes.

Three sighs, two eye rolls.

"Anyhow, like I was saying, you might have a couple hairline fractures in your ribs, but there isn't much you can do for that except grin and bear it for six weeks."

"Six weeks?"

She walked around the counter and pushed through the door. She returned thirty seconds later with a Ziploc bag containing a handful of white pills.

"This is Hydrocodone. It should help alleviate some of the pain and help you get some sleep."

It wasn't quite as powerful as Percocet, but it would do the trick.

I thanked her and asked, "What do I owe you for it?"

"Nothing. It's from my personal supply. But if you crash your car in a ditch, you didn't get them from me."

"Deal."

She told me to get my pigs and go.

~

Back in the car with the piglets, who were now both sitting on my lap, I realized a couple things.

First, the pills Sarah gave me were not Hydrocodone. They were Tylenol. And second, the flowers on the counter. They were yellow.

Yellow tulips.

~

I left Pink and Tan in the car when I returned to the farm. Then I spent ten minutes making sure there weren't any more piglets in the hay loft.

Hey, little piggies.

Come here, little piggies.

Are there any more little piggies hiding in the hay?

Satisfied that I'd saved all the little piggies I could for the day, I made my way back to the car and opened the front door. Both piglets were sitting on the driver's seat. Pink was sitting down, gazing up at me with her big brown eyes. Her nose was pink with a black ink spot, and she wiggled it from side to side. Tan was lying on his back, glaring up at me with as much disinterest as he could muster.

"What am I going to do with you guys?"

The logical answer was to put them in the pigpen, but the small fence would first need to be repaired.

"I suppose I could put you guys in the chicken coop?" I said, thinking out loud. "That might work."

The final option was to lock them in the barn, but there was an opening somewhere I would first need to block. Also, I didn't want them in there with their dead mother. Speaking of whom, I would need to find a way to get down from the loft at some point.

I let out a long exhale and said, "Well, I suppose you can come into the house with me for tonight."

I had to feed them every few hours anyhow.

I grabbed a piglet in each arm and carried them into the house. I set them down, then went back outside to the car to grab the bag of goodies Sarah had given me. For a brief moment, I thought about the yellow tulips.

This was far from an assurance that Sarah was the one who left the flowers at the Save-More memorial, but it did give probable cause.

But who's to say there wasn't a sale on yellow tulips somewhere and half the town had vases filled with the same exact flowers this very moment?

I would have to look into it further.

Back inside, the piglets were roaming around, sniffing this and sniffing that. I put out a water bowl, and they both took a few cautious laps.

They both gazed up at me as if to say, "This isn't as good as that other stuff."

I checked the time on my cell phone.

"Another hour and you guys can eat again."

I made myself some food, a peanut butter and jelly sandwich, then swallowed down three of the Tylenol.

I grabbed a couple pillows from upstairs, pushed the oval coffee table off the rug in the living room, and lay down. Pink immediately ran over and sniffed me and licked my hand. She rolled over on her side and I tickled her tummy.

A short time later, Tan came over. He was a bit more hesitant, but after a while, he too gave me a couple licks.

For the next hour, I skimmed the printouts on how to care for the piglets. I looked at Tan and said, "Did you know you guys don't sweat?"

That's why the mud in a pigpen was so important, it's what the pigs used to regulate their temperature.

"Sorry, this place doesn't have any A/C," I told them.

At 5:00 p.m., I fed the piglets.

Tan let me hold him like a baby and suckled away.

We were bonding.

Then I took them outside where, to my utter amazement, both of them went potty.

Back in the living room, I lay back down on the ground. My body was devastated, and I was drained from the day's events.

Ten minutes later, I was asleep.

~

When I woke up, both piglets were snuggled into my side.

I checked the time on my cellphone.

11:51 p.m.

I'd slept for almost seven hours. I grabbed two more bottles of formula and fed the hungry pigs.

How does that taste?

Oh, you guys were hungry.

Come on, Pink, just a little more.

Dang it, Tan, that's your sister's.

I shook my head, realizing I couldn't call them Pink and Tan forever. I picked Tan up and gave him a good once-over. He was bald except for a whisper of hair on his forehead. Plus, he was kind of cranky. Just like *him*.

"I christen you Harold."

I set him down and picked up Pink.

"Now you, my dear."

She was so delicate.

And sweet.

I racked my brain for a name.

"Trisket?"

"Latifah?"

"Spammy?"

"Little Heidi Klum?"

"Jennifer?"

"Mable?"

"Piglet?"

"Beyoncé?"

"Ruth?"

"Molly?"

"Polly?"

"Dolly?"

"Tina?"

"Winnie?"

"Sara?"

"Sara Lee?"

"Pound Cake?"

"Mindy?"

"Cindy?"

"Destiny?"

"Hermione?"

Nothing fit.

I looked at the phone.

It was 11:59 p.m.

Just one minute left in the month of May.

I smiled.

That was it.

I held up Pink and said, "You will be Miss May."

Chapter 6

The first day of June was a Wednesday.

After eating breakfast and feeding the piglets, I drove into town. There were a couple of errands that needed doing. I needed to stop by the feed and supply store to buy more formula for Harold and May. I needed to get some lumber from the hardware store so I could repair the pigpen fence. I needed to buy some more Tylenol from the supermarket to numb my aching body. But first, I needed to get on the internet.

The Tarrin Public Library was across the street from the high school. It was an aging red brick building, two stories tall. There was a small parking lot, which at 11:00 a.m., was half-full.

I parked and walked inside.

There were a few people sitting at tables reading and another few on laptops. Like all libraries, the lighting was low and there was a pervasive smell of carpet deodorizer. There were a few computer terminals against the back wall, and I settled in behind one.

I tried to log onto the internet, but I was unsuccessful. A young man next to me informed me that I needed to first have a library card and then I could create a login.

Ten minutes later, I was the proud owner of a Tarrin Public Library card.

I logged onto the internet and searched "Save-More murders," then skimmed the same article Lacy read to me over the phone the previous day. I found the list of the victims—Peggy Bertina, Will Dennel, Neil Felding, Tom Lanningham, Odell McBride, Victoria Page—and looked at their pictures and read their bios.

Nothing jumped out at me until the fourth one.

Tom Lanningham.

He looked to be in his fifties, with receding gray hair and thick glasses. His bio read: *Tom Lanningham was fifty-eight years old. He was a veterinarian for almost twenty years, all of them in his hometown of Tarrin. He is survived by his daughter, Sarah.*

Was *Sarah*, Sarah Lanningham?

It would make sense, the age seemed right, and maybe she'd followed in her father's footsteps.

This was more circumstantial evidence Sarah was the one who left the flowers at the memorial. Of course, in this technological age, it would be easy enough to verify the daughter Sarah was also the veterinarian Sarah.

I'd been in such a rush with the piglets that I hadn't noticed the name of the vet clinic.

I searched "Dr. Sarah Lanningham."

A moment later, I clicked on the link for the Big and Small Vet Hospital. The website had a picture of Sarah. I found myself grinning at the sight of her. In the picture she was wearing the same white jacket and holding a kitten.

The mystery of the yellow tulips solved, I returned to the article from the *St. Louis Post-Dispatch.* At the bottom of the article, there was a blurb about the killer.

His name was Lowry Barnes. He was twenty-nine years old, married, a father of two. He was a convicted felon for burglary, with minor offenses for DUI and drug possession. He did a couple small stints at the county jail then a two-year prison sentence for the burglary. He was paroled in early 2012 and worked at the Save-More for six months. Then he got himself fired. Two weeks later, he would exact his revenge.

Three agencies had been involved in the investigation: the Tarrin Police Department, the Audrain County Sheriff's Department, and the Missouri Bureau of Investigation.

That being said, there didn't appear to be much of an investigation. There was no question who did it or why he did it.

According to the article, surveillance footage clearly showed Lowry Barnes entering the store with a gun raised, then rounding up his victims and marching them to the back of the store and into the freezer bay. Lowry Barnes was found an hour after the murders, parked on the side of the road. Overcome with guilt, he'd taken his own life.

I pondered searching the internet for the surveillance video or perhaps photos of the crime scene, but it didn't seem necessary. The case was what we refer to in the business as "open and shut."

~

"I need some baby formula for some piglets," I told the guy stacking large bags outside the feed and supply store. "Do you guys sell that sort of thing here?"

The man dropped the bag he was holding, put both hands on his back, and said, "Sure do."

He was wearing a green John Deere hat that I suspected had resided on his shaggy gray hair for the better part of a decade. He waved me to follow him inside the large store and said, "Baby piglets, huh? Where's the sow?"

"She is currently decomposing in my barn."

His eyes widened, and I gave him a clipped version.

"Miracle those little guys survived," he said. "Can't go more than a day without eating."

I nodded.

"You thought about finding a surrogate?" he asked, making his way through the store to a refrigerated section.

"A what?"

"Another sow. They're pretty good about letting other piglets join their litter. Course, every once in a while, they don't take to it, and it can get ugly."

I ran a simulation of a big mama pig going crazy when Harold and May tried to suckle on her teats. "I think I'll stick with the formula for now."

"Suit yourself, but make sure you're givin' those little piglets all the love in the world." He grabbed me by the shoulder, his thick, calloused fingers heavy and strong. "You're their mama now."

"Don't worry," I said with a laugh. "If anything, they're getting too much attention."

The three of us had slept on the floor together. I woke up with May tucked into my side and Harold between my legs.

Once at the refrigerator, the man showed me my two options for piglet formula—sorry, *Proprietary Sow's Milk Replacer*. I chose the more expensive one. Only the best for my piglets.

Walking back up front, the man asked, "You the guy who bought the Humphries place?"

"Yeah, though I didn't exactly buy it. It was willed to me."

"By Harold?"

I smiled. "You knew him?"

"Not really, but I met him at his dad's funeral way back when."

He told a quick anecdote about Harold's father. How Harold's father was the best farmer he'd ever known. How, when he was little, Harold's father would hire him to help with the harvest. "That there is some of the best land in all of Audrain County."

I raised an eyebrow. "It's a glorified landfill."

"I'll admit it doesn't look too good these days, but it's all about the soil, and that's the best soil I've come across in fifty years."

I paid him for the formula, and he asked, "You thinking about planting anything this year?"

"I hadn't given it much thought."

"Well, you should." He grabbed a pen and scribbled on the back of my receipt. "Call this number if you're thinking about getting that farm back in shape. Guy I try to throw some work."

I stuffed the receipt in my pocket and told him I would think about it.

~

Sitting at the last stoplight headed out of town, I rolled up the windows and cranked the A/C.

In the three days I'd been in Tarrin, the air had grown incrementally warmer and stickier each day. If it kept at this rate, by the end of the summer it would be like walking through molasses.

The light turned green, and I gently eased down the gas pedal. There was a hundred dollars' worth of lumber tied down to the top of the Range Rover—which a guy from the hardware store loaded for me as my ribs and shoulder were still too sore to do any heavy lifting—and it made a soft hum against the headwind.

Main Street turned into County Road 34, and the speed limit changed from thirty-five to fifty. There wasn't another car on the road, and I sped up to sixty. The humming quickly escalated into a violent rattle, and I slowed back down. But it was too late.

I was so preoccupied with the lumber, I failed to notice the cop car parked on the side of the road.

In my rearview mirror, I watched as the Tarrin Police Department cruiser spit up a cloud of dust, fell in behind me, then flipped its siren. I let out a long exhale and pulled to the side of the road. I rolled the window down, the Missouri afternoon at equilibrium with the cool synthetic atmosphere for half a second before pressing in entirely.

In the side mirror, I watched the door of the cruiser open and a man step out. The officer was small, a head shorter than me, with blond hair curling from beneath a Tarrin PD ball cap.

"Howdy," he said as he came even with the window. He had two days of stubble and a defined butt chin.

"Howdy," I returned.

"You know why I pulled you over?"

"Because I'm not driving a Chevy?"

He laughed, revealing flawless teeth, and said, "Naw, we don't do that here. Unless you're driving one of those little Minis, then it's mandatory."

He seemed like a nice enough guy, and I gave a chuckle.

"You were going a little fast back there."

"I was trying to get the wood on top of the car to fly off and go all over the road."

He didn't laugh. He did say, "I clocked you going fifty-seven. Speed limit is fifty."

"Right."

"Where are you headed?" he asked.

It's the way he said it that tipped me off. A little too matter-of-fact. It's a slippery slope, asking questions you already know the answer to. Pulling me over wasn't a coincidence. He was waiting for me.

"I'm headed to the Humphries Farm."

"Oh, yeah," he said, keeping up the charade. "What business you got there?"

"It's my farm." My tone was a touch less friendly.

"Yours? You buy it?"

"Don't worry about it."

His eyes narrowed. "What did you say?"

"It's not much of your business."

He glared at me for a long second, then said, "License and registration."

I handed them over.

He looked at my license, then he looked at my registration. He handed my registration back and said, "This is an old Blockbuster receipt."

"Oh, sorry. This is my dad's old car. I thought that was the registration."

Hahahahaha.

I stuck my hand in the glove compartment and rooted around. "Is this it?"

He glanced at it. "No, that's another Blockbuster receipt."

"Sorry, they look the same."

They do not.

I thought about handing him another of my father's many old Blockbuster receipts filling the glove compartment, but Officer Tiny's hand had moved dangerously close to the gun on his hip.

I found the registration and handed it over, and he walked back to his cruiser.

I gazed forward and pondered why Officer Tiny was waiting for me. Was it because I was the new kid on the block? Was this some sort of small town initiation? Did this happen to everyone or had he made special considerations for yours truly?

Officer Tiny returned and handed me back my license and registration.

If he did a comprehensive background check on me, he didn't say. Though I had a feeling he already knew a thing or two about Thomas Dergen Prescott before he pulled me over.

"I'm gonna let you slide on the speeding today," he said, forcing a smile. "You being new and all."

"That's awful kind of you, sir." Sir came out *suh*.

He leaned down, his chin-ass where the window would have been, and said, "Can I give you a piece of advice, Thomas?"

I jutted out my chin, the international signal for *let's hear it*.

"Leave it alone," he said.

Then he smacked the top of the Range Rover and walked back to his cruiser.

~

"This little piggy went to the bathtub," I said, setting May in the two inches of warm water. She sat down on her rump and gave the water a couple licks. "And this little piggy went to the bathtub." I picked up Harold and set him next to his sister. He looked down at the water, then back up at me, as if to say, "I don't like this one bit. Not one bit."

I squeezed some Johnson's baby shampoo in my hand and began scrubbing the two of them. Drying them off, I set them on the bed and gave each of them a little piglet backrub. Then I fed them for the last time and took them outside to go to the bathroom.

Lying down in bed, the two little piglets smelling like heaven and snoring, I reminisced on the advice Officer Tiny had given.

Leave it alone.

There was only one thing he could be talking about.

The Save-More murders.

And the only way he could have known I'd taken an interest is if he was tipped-off about my internet search at the library. They must have a program that alerted them when someone searched specific keywords. And then traced it to my login.

"Leave it alone," he'd said.

And I would have.

If only he hadn't told me to.

Chapter 7

The barn smelled horrific.

"What do you think?" I asked Randall.

Randall Jones didn't look like he belonged on a farm. He looked like he belonged on a football field. He was wearing a floppy straw hat and had a spongy black beard an inch thick that was three shades darker than his skin. He wore a near-constant grin that revealed a small gap between his two front teeth.

"I think," he said, his voice as gruff as his beard, "that you have a dead pig in your loft."

I stared down at Miss Piggy, whose carcass was now bloated and covered in maggots, and said "Yep."

I initially called Randall—his phone number had been scribbled on the back of my feed store receipt—to help me repair the pigpen. My body was still in too much pain to lug around lumber and wield a hammer.

When he arrived in a beat-up Ford Bronco, I decided that Harold and May's deceased mother was higher on the priority list than the busted pigpen. The piglets would just have to sleep in bed with me for another day.

Darn.

"We could just roll her off," I said. "Let her fall to the ground."

Randall shook his head. "Nope, she'll explode, then you're never gonna get rid of that smell."

"What if we move a bunch of the hay bales underneath us then roll her onto those?"

He mulled this over. "Probably be soft enough to keep her from exploding."

We spent the next ten minutes moving hay bales to the drop site.

Back up top, Randall asked, "You ready?"

We both took two deep breaths then began pushing the huge pig toward the edge. Three hundred and fifty pounds of dead weight feels like twice that, but luckily Randall was even stronger than his frame indicated.

Miss Piggy fell over the precipice, and I yelled, "Timber!"

We both watched as Miss Piggy dropped into the hay, then, like hitting a trampoline, bounced off the hay bales and fell to the earth.

Where she promptly exploded.

Randall cut his eyes at me, then tilted his head back and let out a riotous laugh. Soon we were both in hysterics.

A minute later, wiping his eyes, Randall said, "I guess that didn't work after all."

~

Randall handed me a pair of purple kitchen gloves and said, "Put these on, you don't want to get that stink on you."

Randall had backed his Ford Bronco up to the barn door. A trailer was attached, the bed of the trailer covered in a blue tarp. We spent the next twenty minutes heaving what remained of Miss Piggy into the trailer. My ribs screamed out at me, but, if possible, the stench of the exploded sow took sensory precedence.

Most of what exploded, the entrails and some of her guts, was contained by the bedding of hay on the ground, and we were able to pile this into the trailer as well.

Just as we finished, a plume of dust swirled at the edge of the hill; a truck was driving up the road. The truck bounced over the many ruts, splashed through the ever-present puddle, then parked a few feet from Randall's Bronco.

There was a glare off the windshield, and I couldn't make out who was behind the wheel. The door opened, and a woman stepped out.

"Hiya, Wheeler," Randall said. "I thought that was you."

Sarah Lanningham was wearing jean shorts, a gray tank top, and a red St. Louis Cardinals hat. For the first time, I realized she was hiding some spectacular curves under her doctor's coat.

Hubba hubba.

"Hiya, Randall," she said, walking over to give him a quick hug. "What are you doing here?"

He glanced in the direction of the trailer hitched to his Bronco and said, "Helping get rid of this here sow."

Sarah leaned over the edge of the trailer, showcasing she'd put in her time on the elliptical, and peered down. "What the hell did you guys do to her?"

I pointed at Randall and said, "He did it."

Randall opened his mouth and threw up his hands. He didn't cop to it, and I explained, "We tried to roll her off the loft and onto some hay bales, but it didn't go as planned."

Sarah said, "She looks like she got hit by an IED."

Randall let loose a laugh, and I could tell he was running the clip back over in his head. Just the look on his face started me laughing, and soon we were both giggling like children.

My eyes were watering, but I could see Sarah wasn't amused. She shook her head and said, "I came to check on the piglets." She looked around. "Where are they?"

I cocked my head toward the house. "Inside." Then nodding at Randall, I said, "Randall here was going to help me fix up the pigpen."

Sarah said, "Oh, well, I can come back some other time."

"No, no," Randall interjected. "You two go on. I'll take care of the pigpen myself."

"You sure?" I asked.

"Yeah, you'll just get in the way."

He was probably right.

The lumber I bought the previous day was still strapped to the top of the Range Rover, and I asked, "You need any help getting the wood down?"

He shook his head and waved for the two of us to leave him be.

I thanked him and started toward the farmhouse.

"Good to see you, Randall," Sarah said, joining me. "Make sure you get Roscoe in for a checkup here pretty soon."

Randall promised to do just that.

She turned to me—her honey-colored eyes had taken on a slight amber hue under the red ball cap—and said, "Roscoe is his black lab."

"That's a great name," I said, then added, "Speaking of names, why did he call you Wheeler?"

We were a couple steps from the porch, and she stopped. "Most people around here still call me that. It's my middle name."

"You don't seem to like it."

"I don't."

"Then why go by it?"

"It wasn't by choice. In first grade, my class was fifteen kids, eight girls, and three of us were named Sarah. Sarah Graves, Sara Whitfield, and me. My teacher just started calling me by my middle name the first week, and everyone has called me Wheeler ever since."

"Where did Wheeler come from?"

She sighed. "It's my mom's maiden name. It comes from the old English days when your last name was what you did for work."

"Like Blacksmith?"

She nodded.

"So what did a Wheeler do?"

"Um," she said, giving me a sideways glance. "They made *wheels*."

I forced a laugh. "Right."

First chunky.

Now dumb.

I was tempted to tell her I once got a B- on an algebra test in high school, but I didn't want to add bragger to that list.

I said, "My middle name is Dergen."

"Dergen?" She stifled a laugh.

"What?"

"You don't know?"

I shook my head.

"That's what we call cow shit out here." She laughed and said, "That cow just took a big old dergen."

"Oh, man."

"Yeah, I'd keep that to yourself if I were you."

We moved up the porch and toward the front door. It was still technically on its hinges, but it was hanging by a thread.

Wheeler asked, "Was the front door like this when you got here?"

I told her about how after I fell out of the tree I grabbed the tire iron from my car and went *The Shining* on the door.

She found this amusing.

"How's your body feeling these days?" she asked.

"A little better. Thanks again for those Hydrocodone, those really helped."

She shrugged.

"Except they were Tylenol."

"Like I'm gonna give some strange guy off the street prescription drugs."

"Yeah, that was probably smart of you."

We entered the house, and I called out, "Harold! May! We have a visitor."

There was a pitter-pattering, and the two little piglets came barreling around the corner. Both Wheeler and I crouched down and let the piglets attack us.

"Oh, thank you for the kisses," Wheeler said, picking up May. She sniffed, looked at me suspiciously, then asked, "Why do they smell so good?"

I shrugged.

"You gave them baths, didn't you?"

"I plead the Fifth."

She picked up Harold and said, "You must be Harold."

Harold wiggled his little tail and oinked.

We headed into the dining room, and she gave each of the piglets a quick exam. When she finished, she said, "Well, I half expected to come here and find two little dead piglets, but it appears you have done a pretty good job so far."

"Is that a backhanded compliment?"

She shrugged, then asked, "What time did they last eat?"

"It's been a few hours."

We made our way to the fridge, and I filled two bottles with formula. I fed May and she fed Harold.

As May suckled away on the bottle, I couldn't help stealing glances at Wheeler. The care with which she held Harold. The look in her eyes as he sucked on the bottle. There was so much love there. I wondered if she had the same love for every animal she treated. How big was her reserve? And what happened when she couldn't fix one of them?

It must take its toll.

I thought back to my days as a homicide detective. One of the first rules is: don't get attached. To the victim, to the victim's family, or to the investigation itself. You let yourself get attached, and it will slowly chip away at you. You won't make it three years.

I only made it two.

That's because I couldn't draw a line in the sand. I couldn't see the body of a seventeen-year-old girl and not imagine it was my kid sister lying there.

When you're a homicide detective, you're on rotation, and when your number is called, there's no "Thanks, but this one isn't for me. I'll grab the next one."

After I cracked, after I was let go from the Seattle Police Department, I started taking on cases with the FBI. But with the Feds, it was different, I could pick and choose the cases I investigated. And that's why I loved the cold cases. It was easier to hold on to your emotions when you were dealing with a crime that happened five, ten, twenty years earlier.

At least, most of the time.

"The yellow tulips," I said, glancing up. "Are you the one who put them at the memorial?"

Wheeler raised her eyes, but didn't answer.

"I know your dad was one of the people killed."

She set Harold down, rinsed the bottle in the sink, then turned back to me. "Yes," she said flatly.

I set May down and she scampered out of the kitchen to wherever her brother had absconded to. Then I opened the fridge and grabbed two beers. I twisted off the tops, then handed one to Wheeler. She took a sip in silence, then followed me out front. I pondered chancing the two rocking chairs, but they both had a bad case of osteoporosis, and I feared they would collapse under our weight.

I nodded at the chairs and said, "I ordered those from the Old Dilapidated Farmhouse store. They are strictly decorative."

I could tell she was still thinking about her dad, and she didn't laugh.

We plopped down on the front steps, a foot apart. A huge beetle, easily an inch long, rumbled past, stopping for a quick moment to glance up at Wheeler.

Even the bugs were impressed.

The big beetle made a U-turn, probably headed back to tell all his buddies about the hot chick on the porch steps, when he banged into my foot. Then he started climbing up it. I shook out my foot, but he held on tight. I leapt from the porch and swatted him off with my hand.

I may have screamed.

Wheeler laughed

I said, "He was attacking me."

"I could see that."

Once I composed myself, I said, "I heard the bugs were big in the Midwest, but it's still a shock."

"You haven't seen anything yet," she said with a light shake of her head. "Wait till the middle of July."

"What happens in July?"

"You ever see Jurassic Park?"

"Sure."

"You know the scene with the pterodactyls."

I laughed. "That bad?"

She took a swig and nodded.

I matched her swig, then asked, "So did you ever leave this place?"

"I went to undergrad at the University of Missouri, then vet school out east."

"Where out east?"

"Cornell."

"Ah, Delaware."

"Upstate New York, actually."

"Right."

"How 'bout you?"

"I went to the University of Washington for a few years."

"Didn't finish?"

"It wasn't for me."

"So what did you do?"

"I went to the police academy."

She sat forward a couple inches. "You were a cop?"

"I was a beat cop for a few years, then a homicide detective in some capacity or another for almost a decade."

She cocked her head down at my leg and said, "Is that how you got shot?"

"That happened up in Maine, when I was working a case later on."

"Maine? How did you end up there?"

"I was a second-year homicide detective in Seattle when my parents died. My kid sister was just finishing high school and got a scholarship to Temple so I moved to Philly with her."

"Geez, I'm sorry." She paused, then asked, "What happened to your parents?"

I recounted how my parents were flying back from a Rolling Stones concert in my father's company jet when the plane crashed into the Sierra Nevadas.

"Where is your sister now?"

"France. She got married last year. Now they're trying to start a family."

"Uncle Thomas."

I hadn't given this much thought, and the idea made me smile. "Yep."

"Anyhow, she's a badass painter." I bragged about Lacy for a few minutes, then segued into Lacy's MS diagnosis and how we ultimately ended up in Maine. I touched briefly on the case that led to my being shot, but it wasn't one of my favorite topics to dwell on and I shifted things in her direction. I asked, "How old were you when your dad was killed?"

She deflated slightly at the mention of her father. "Twenty-eight."

"And that was four years ago?"

She nodded.

"So you're thirty-two?"

"Yes, math wizard, I'm thirty-two."

I grinned then asked, "What about your mom?"

"My parents got divorced when I was twelve. My mom moved to North Dakota and got remarried. I have two stepbrothers up there."

"You ever go visit?"

"Every couple years. The town they live in is even smaller than here."

The soft pounding of a hammer caused me to glance up. Randall's wicker hat bobbed above the tall grass in the distance.

I turned back to Wheeler and said, "When I first got here, I was surprised at the size of Tarrin."

"Smaller than you thought?"

"Bigger."

"Really?"

"I mean, you guys have a Sonic."

"Yeah, that was a big day," she said smiling. She glanced down between her feet, and I could see the memory loading. Her head lifted, one of her dimples winking. "Half the town camped out in their cars the night before it opened. They actually ran out of hamburgers, and people had to wait an hour for someone from the Sonic two towns over to bring more meat."

"So you got your burger?"

"You kidding me?" she scoffed. "Chili dog all the way. Three of them."

I smiled.

My kind of girl.

She tilted her beer, which was empty, and said, "You want another one?"

"Sure."

I made to push myself up, but she said, "I got it."

She sprang up and was back twenty seconds later with two cold ones.

I twisted the top off the beer then pointed the mouth of the bottle at her red ball cap. "You a big Cardinals fan?"

"You have to be around here."

"You go to any games?"

"Usually a couple. Haven't gotten out there yet, but it's early in the season."

"How they doing?"

"Couple games back of the Cubs," she said. "You follow baseball?"

"Not really, but my grandpa loved the Cardinals." I pointed to the rocking chairs on the porch and said, "He would tell stories about his entire family huddled around a little transistor radio listening to their games."

For a moment, I felt myself travel back to the 1940s. The paint on the farmhouse a brilliant white. The rocking chairs pristine. Harold in one of the chairs with one of his little sisters on his lap. The sound of the announcer's voice crackling over the radio.

"Thomas?"

I broke from my reverie "What?"

Wheeler said, "I asked if you and your grandpa were close."

"We were, but I only knew him for a couple years."

"How did you only know him a couple years?"

I'd only told a few people the story. I'm not sure if it was the 1.2 beers I drank, Wheeler's beckoning glance, or the flashback I just had, but the story came spilling out of me.

"Two Thanksgivings ago, I moved back to Seattle. I hadn't been back in eight years, but my parents still owned a house on the cliffs overlooking Puget Sound. One day, the phone rang and it was this old man. He asked for someone by name—I think he asked for someone named Bobby—and I told him he had the wrong number. I don't know what would have happened if I hung up the phone that day, but thankfully, I didn't. I ended up talking to him for twenty minutes, mostly just listening to him ramble on about the nursing home he was living in. Then he asked me to bring him some stuff."

"What did he ask for?"

"*Maxim*, Sour Patch Kids, Red Bull, chocolate chip cookie dough, lotto tickets. Your run of the mill nursing home contraband."

"*Sour Patch Kids*?"

"Yeah." I laughed, then continued, "Anyhow, I didn't have a whole lot going on in my life at that point, and I would go visit him a couple times a week. We ended up becoming friends."

"What would you guys do?"

"Watch horse racing, play chess—well, Harold's version of chess—eat at the cafeteria, play bingo. I took him for Slurpees at 7-11 once. Whenever it was nice out, he liked to go sit on this bench and toss bread to the ducks in the fake pond."

"That's adorable."

"Yeah, he was pretty great." I found myself smiling. "But the best part of each visit was listening to him tell the story about how he met his wife and how she gave birth to my mother. Only I didn't know he was my grandpa at the time. I thought he was just telling a story."

"He didn't tell you he was your grandpa the first day you came?"

"No. Not for a few months."

"And you kept going to see him even though he was just this random old man who accidentally called you?"

"I told you I didn't have a whole lot going on at the time. Well, aside from investigating the murder of the governor of Washington."

Her eyebrows arched.

"But that's another story altogether."

"Let's circle back to that," she said nodding.

I laughed. "Sure thing."

"So how did you find out this guy was your grandpa?"

"Each time I would visit, he would tell me a bit of this story, little snippets at a time. Started when he was eighteen, living right here on this farm. He wanted to join the army—I think it was the second or third year of World War II—but his dad wouldn't let him, said he needed him to help with the farm. But Harold had his mind set on fighting in the war and stole his dad's—or as Harold called him, 'his Pa's'—truck and was headed to the train station when he saw a young girl playing on a lake."

"Which lake?"

"You know that big house with the lake out front?"

She nodded. "The Crowly house."

"Back then, a family named the Kings lived there."

"That sounds familiar. Rich family, owned half the land in Tarrin, then just up and skipped town one day."

"Yeah, they left because of my grandpa."

Wheeler slid a couple inches closer to me and we were only separated by two beetles. Her knee grazed mine as she said, "What did he do?"

"I'm getting to that." I took a swig of beer, then said, "Harold was driving to the train station when he saw a young girl out on the lake. Turns out she wasn't playing. Her dog had fallen through the ice and she was running out to try to save it."

"I don't like where this is headed. Tell me right now, did the dog die?"

I nodded.

She hung her head down for a moment, sighed, then glanced back up. "Okay, keep going."

"Well, the girl came to where the dog had fallen in, and the ice broke around her, and she fell in. Harold watched this all unfold from the road. There happened to be a long span of rope in the back of the truck. He grabbed it, tied it to a fence post, then tied it to his waist, then went after the girl."

Wheeler was grinning from ear to ear. Both of her dimples were showing. She reminded me of myself when Harold told the same story.

I said, "So he runs out on the lake, jumps in the water, and saves this girl."

"Who turns out to be your grandma?"

"Well, not for a while. She was like fourteen years old at the time."

"Right. Continue."

"Harold pulled her out, wrapped her in a blanket that was in the car, and carried her up to the house. Instead of thanking him for saving his daughter's life, the father threw rocks at Harold and told him to get off his property."

"You're kidding?"

"I wish."

"What did Harold do?"

"He left, got in his truck, and joined the army the next day."

"What about the girl?" Wheeler exclaimed. "If this doesn't have a happy ending, I'm never talking to you again."

"Remind me never to watch *The Notebook* with you."

She said, "It doesn't have a happy ending, does it?"

"Just listen to the story."

"Dergen!"

I laughed and said, "Just listen."

"Fine." She took a drink of beer.

"He joined the army. Then when he'd been in for about two years—I think he was stationed in Poland or somewhere—he gets this huge stack of mail. Turns out, the young girl, Elizabeth, had been writing him a letter every day for over a year."

"Holy shit," Wheeler shrieked.

"Harold wrote her back, and they fell in love. When his enlistment was over a year later, he came back to Tarrin. Elizabeth said she would be waiting at the train station for him, but she wasn't there. Turns out her dad found out she'd been writing to Harold, and that's when they just up and left."

"What an asshole."

"The only good news was that after the Kings left town, they stopped paying property taxes, and after a few years all their land was turned over to the county. Harold's father was able to buy the acres he'd been leasing for well below market value. If the Kings hadn't up and left, I wouldn't be here right now."

"No one cares about you," she said with a forced sneer. "Get back to the story, Dergen."

"Right. Well, the Kings moved to Seattle. Harold found that out and he moved there as well. He took a job with Boeing and spent years looking for her. Then, one day, he finally found her. He spotted her leaving the movie theater with a big group of girls. He followed them in his car back to an all-girls university."

"This is getting good."

"Just wait. It gets better. Sometimes the girls went weeks without leaving the campus, but Harold needed a way to get a message to Elizabeth. So he quit his job at Boeing and he joined the gardening crew that tended the grounds. Took him about a month, but they finally came up with a plan. They let a bunch of mice into one of the classrooms, and all the girls came running out. That's when he slipped her a note."

"What did the note say?"

"To meet him behind the school later that night."

"Did she come?"

"She did."

"Yay," she said grinning. "And they lived happily ever after."

I sighed.

"What?" she asked. "What now?"

"The dean of the school found out about their romance."

"So what?"

"The dean of the school was her father."

"The asshole who threw rocks at him?"

"Yeah."

"What did he do?"

"He forbade Elizabeth from seeing Harold. Said that if she ever saw him again, she would no longer be part of their family."

"What did she do?"

"She chose Harold."

Wheeler grabbed my wrist.

I let out another sigh.

"Oh, no," she said.

"They got married, and Elizabeth got pregnant. But then she died during childbirth."

"Oh my God." Wheeler's eyes began to glass over under her hat. It wasn't just animals.

I said, "Harold didn't know what to do so he put the little girl, my mom, up for adoption. He got remarried, had two more kids, but he never told them about Elizabeth. In fact, I was the only person he ever told."

Wheeler wiped the tears from her eyes and asked, "What about your mom?"

"He kept tabs on Lily, that's my mom, over the years."

"When did he finally tell you he was your grandpa?"

"We were actually on a ferry ride when he pulled an old tattered piece of newspaper from his sock and showed it to me. It was a news article about when my parents died."

She rocked back lightly, then said, "That's crazy. And then after he died, he gave you this farm?"

I nodded.

She took a long swig of beer, then said, "Now let's hear about this governor of Washington murder."

"Maybe some other time. I want to hear more about you."

"Okay."

I asked, "What did you do after vet school?"

"I stayed out east."

"Why did you come back here? Didn't like city life?"

"I was three months into my first job when my dad was murdered. I came back for the funeral and decided to take over his practice."

"Is it just you that works there?"

"Mostly it's just me. My dad's old receptionist comes in for a few hours a week to tidy up and to help file. If I need help with a surgery I usually call one of the other vets to assist."

I nodded, then said, "That was actually my first time in a vet clinic."

"Really? You've never had any pets?"

"I had a hamster for two weeks when I was little, but he ate his leg off and then died. And then I won a fish at the fair once, but I think he was dead by the time I got him home."

"That's too bad."

"My sister though, she has a little pug named Baxter. He has narcolepsy." I began laughing. "He once fell asleep with his head in a gopher hole."

"That's not funny," she said, giving me a light slap on the shoulder.

"I beg to differ." I asked, "You have any pets?"

"I have a little shih tzu named Margo. She's twelve. She was asleep on the ground behind the front desk when you came in." Her eyes fell to the ground. "She was my father's."

I decided now was as good a time as any and asked, "You mind if I ask you a couple questions about the murders?"

She bit the inside of her cheek, took a breath, and nodded.

"Did you know this Lowry guy who did it?"

"Yeah, I knew him. He was a few years younger than me in school."

"When you heard it was him, were you surprised?"

"Yeah. Lowry was pretty quiet, but nice enough. I was gone so I didn't know about all the trouble he got himself into over the years."

"The drinking?"

"Yeah, and I think he broke into a couple of homes."

"But that's a giant leap to shooting six people."

She nodded silently and I asked, "When did you start putting the flowers at the memorial?"

"A couple years ago, I bought some flowers to put on my dad's grave, and I was walking past the memorial and I just decided to leave five of them there. Then it became a habit. I try to do it every few weeks."

"Did you ever question what happened at the store? That it went down the way everybody said it did?"

"There was nothing to question. Most of it was captured on video, and what's not, Victoria was able to tell."

"Victoria?"

"Victoria Page. The only survivor."

"Where is she now?"

"Still here. She's the town comptroller."

"Comptroller?"

"Like a treasurer. But she only does that part-time now. Mostly, she breeds horses. I was actually out at her place just last week."

She took the last drink of beer, set the bottle down, then asked, "Why do you care about the murders so much? You miss the old job?"

Because I was forever the skeptic. Because something about the murders seemed off. Because some douchebag told me to leave it alone.

"Just curious," I said.

We were both silent a moment, then I said, "I got pulled over yesterday."

"Really?"

"Yeah, right on County Road 34. For speeding."

"Really? I've never heard of anyone getting a speeding ticket around there."

That's because he was waiting for me.

"I was wondering if you knew the police officer. Little guy, butt chin." I squished my chin together with my fingers.

She looked at the ground, exhaled, then glanced up. "Matt Miller."

"You know him?"

She puffed out her cheeks and nodded. "I was engaged to him."

~

"You were engaged to him?" I asked, my disdain for the guy increasing ten-fold. "What happened?"

"We were high school sweethearts. Actually, we were middle school sweethearts. I started dating him when I was thirteen."

"Thirteen?"

"Seventh grade. I asked him to the Sadie Hawkins."

"Remind me what that is again."

"It's the school dance where the girls ask out the guys."

"Right."

"So I asked him, and we were together until I was twenty-one."

"Weren't you in college by then?"

"Yeah, we both went to the University of Missouri. He wrestled for them. We got engaged after our junior year, then I called it off."

"Why?"

"He was the only guy I'd ever been with. I wanted to see what else was out there."

"Understandable."

"Anyhow, after I broke up with him, he messed up his knee and lost his scholarship. He moved back home."

For just a split second, I felt a twinge of empathy for the guy. He makes it out of his small town, then he loses his girl, then his knee, then he has to head back to Tarrin with his tail between his legs. And he was just *so* small.

"What happens when you guys see each other now?"

Her face flushed slightly.

"I should have said that I was engaged to him *twice.*"

"No!"

She lowered her head. "I know."

"So, what? When you moved back home four years ago, you guys got back together?"

"Yeah, we dated for another couple years, then he proposed again. We moved in together. Even had a date set."

"And then you backed out?"

She let out the longest sigh I'd ever heard. "Yep."

"You are a terrible person."

"I know."

"A monster."

"Stop." She covered her face in her hands.

I laughed and said, "I can't believe you stuck around."

"Trust me, I thought about moving to Alaska, but keeping my dad's practice going…" Her breath caught and her soft hazel eyes began to water. "Working there just makes me feel like he's still around."

"I get it."

She wiped her eyes then looked at her watch. "I should get going."

I walked her to her truck and shut the door.

I grinned and said, "Thanks for stopping by, *Wheeler*."

"My pleasure, *Dergen*."

Chapter 8

The next day was Friday.

I parked the Range Rover in the Tarrin Police Department parking lot, then headed inside.

"Is the Chief in?" I asked the woman behind a small reception desk. Behind her there were three small desks. Two empty, one filled by a female officer in uniform.

When you get thrown in jail, they say the first thing you should do is find the biggest, scariest guy on the block, and knock him out.

That's what I was doing.

The woman furrowed her brow and asked, "What is this regarding?"

"The Save-More murders."

Her breath caught. Evidently, the words "Save-More" were the equivalent of "Voldemort" in this town.

The woman picked up the phone, turned her back, then spoke softly. A moment later, she turned back around. "He wants to know your name."

"Thomas the Magnificent."

She relayed this.

If for no other reason, I was certain he would see me just to put a face to the name.

The woman put the phone down and said, "I'm gonna need to see some ID before I can let you back."

I pulled out my wallet and handed her my license. "Don't look at the weight. I'm a little pudgy right now."

She forced a smile and said, "I'm just gonna make a quick photocopy of this," then disappeared from view.

I didn't wait for her to return but headed toward the back of the room and to a door that read "Chief Leonard Eccleston."

The door was ajar, and I pushed through.

Chief Eccleston sat behind a black desk. He was in his late fifties, but had the jowls of a man twenty years older. His face was badly sunburned, his forehead and nose peeling in chunks.

"Chief," I said with a nod.

He pushed back from the desk and surveyed me, soaking up my now only thirty-seven-pounds-overweight frame and rugged good looks.

"What can I do for you?" the Chief asked, his loose jowls shaking with each word.

He reminded me of that cartoon dog.

Droopy.

Well, if Droopy had fallen asleep in the sun for thirty hours.

Anyhow, I wasn't sure if Droopy was responsible for the threat Officer Tiny—aka Officer Matt Miller, aka Officer Dumped Twice by the Same Girl—had delivered, but there was only one way to find out.

"I'm interested in the Save-More murders, and I was hoping I could have a look at your case files."

My request fell somewhere between downright absurd and utterly ridiculous. Closer to the latter.

The Chief's forehead creased, sending a flurry of dried skin into the air.

"Who exactly are you?" he asked flatly.

I smirked.

Late last night, I received a text message from an old acquaintance in Seattle, Erica Frost. She was an ex-girlfriend, and we parted on semi-decent terms. Semi-decent because I broke up with her by text which, according to my sister, should be on my permanent record. Anyhow, she was a homicide detective at the Seattle Police Department. Her text simply said: **Heard your name today. Some police chief in Missouri asking about you. Just a heads-up.**

"Cut the shit. You know who I am."

His facade broke. "You're right, I do."

"Which begs the question: why exactly are you doing background checks on me?"

"Just doing my due diligence on the newest member of our community."

"Bullshit."

He glared at me, then said, "As for your request, that's not gonna happen."

I held his gaze.

"And just out of curiosity," he asked, "what is your interest in the Save-More murders?"

"Just doing *my* due diligence on my new community."

He didn't respond to this, and I said, "You know, there's probably a video on YouTube that will show you how to apply sunblock properly."

If he found this amusing, he didn't show it.

He said, "You think that just because you were some hotshot homicide detective, that because you were on the cover of *Time*, that because you come from the *city*, you think you can just waltz in here and demand to see our files. You got some nerve."

"First, I was on the cover of *Time* and *People*. Second, I have no idea how to waltz. And third, I didn't demand anything, I *asked* to see your files."

He stared at me for a long second, then said, "Your old boss said you were a prick."

"That might be the case. But if you did your proper homework on me, then you would know I've put a shitload of bad guys away, that I helped track down four serial killers when I was working with the Feds, and that I broke open several cold cases that were considered not cold, but frozen in ice."

He put his hand up to speak, but I wasn't finished.

"I've seen more murders, more depraved shit, more death, and closed more cases than everyone in your little podunk police department combined. You should feel blessed that the gods have looked down upon you that I might offer my services and take a look at your case files."

He stood. He was taller than I would have thought, at least six-three. He said, "Forgive me if I don't bow down and wash your feet. And for the record, I was a homicide detective for nine years in St. Louis before I came here, so I can assure you, I have seen just as much depraved shit, and I can guarantee I solved more cases than you. And if Sherlock Holmes himself walked through those doors, I would tell him the same exact thing I'm gonna tell you: it will be a cold day in hell when I let anyone outside of this department look at a sensitive case file."

If I were a dog, my tail would be between my legs hiding my genitalia. If this were a rap battle, I would have just been booed off stage. If this were *Hell's Kitchen*, Gordon Ramsay would have just told me to "get out of his fucking kitchen."

After a few recovery breaths, not to mention a couple Stuart Smalley self-affirmations that I wasn't a complete loser, I asked, "St. Louis?"

St. Louis was routinely ranked as one of the most dangerous cities in the United States.

He nodded, his jowls hiccupping up and down.

"I guess I had you all wrong," I said. "But just so you know, Sherlock Holmes is a fictional character. I think you might be confused about that."

"I know, I was just making a point."

"It's just you made it sound like he was a real person who could come walking through the door, but he can't."

"I kno—"

"He's not real."

It would seem I'd officially worn out my welcome, and he pointed to the door. "I think it's time for you to go."

When I was halfway through the doorway, I turned and said, "They sell it at most grocery stores. Heck, they probably even sold it at the Save-More. You know, before the murders."

"What?"

"Sunblock."

I winked at him, then made my way back to the entrance. I hit the reception desk, and the woman called out, "Mr. Prescott. Your ID." She held up my license.

I took it.

I could feel the piece of paper taped to the back of my license the moment I took it from her, but I didn't dare look at it until I'd driven from the parking lot and down a few blocks. Peeling the small white piece of paper off the back of my license, I unfolded it and read the message:

Talk to Mike Zernan.

Then there was an address.

And so it began.

Chapter 9

There were seven churches within the town limits, and I was invited to three of their summer revivals.

Two Lutheran.

And one Baptist.

Walk into a bar.

Just kidding.

Apparently, the festivities lasted all day Saturday and most of Sunday. I didn't want to hurt anyone's feelings and I decided to make a pit stop at all three. My plan was to hit a couple today, then one tomorrow.

I contemplated dressing May and Harold up and taking them with me, but I wasn't sure what the rules were with pigs and churches. Deities? Dinner? It was a slippery slope.

Anyhow, I put them in the pigpen. When I walked away, they both started oinking up a storm.

"It's okay, guys," I kept saying. "I'll be back in a few hours."

I could still hear their whining as I drove from the farm. I did a U-turn, came back, and let them into the house.

I was not the alpha.

I started my revival marathon at Randall's church. I was starving, and he promised delicious barbeque.

Holy Trinity Lutheran was on the south side of town, and I pulled into the parking lot. All of the one hundred black people who lived in Tarrin, plus another twenty white people, were dressed in their Sunday best and hovered under four large white tents set up on the church's front lawn.

The men were wearing suits, and the women were clad in dresses of every color imaginable.

According to Randall, over the course of two days it would be many hours of preaching, followed by long stretches of eating, plus games and activities for both the kids and adults.

I parked the Range Rover and stepped out.

I was dressed to the sevens, which was about as high as I could go with the clothes I packed—at least the ones that still fit. I was wearing tan slacks and a blue button-down, which, due to my increased girth, was testing the limits of the cotton gin. I nearly added a tie, but after three failed attempts at tying it, I gave up.

Randall was huddled with two men and two little girls. He spotted me as I strolled across the grass and headed in my direction. He looked dapper in a black suit with a red tie and his beard was a half inch shorter than it was a couple days prior. It was the first time I'd seen him without his trademark straw hat, and his bald head reflected the noon sun.

"Dergen!" he shouted, pulling me into a hug.

"She told you?"

"I took Roscoe in for his checkup yesterday, and she told me." He clapped me on the shoulder. "Could be worse. Your first name could be Holy!"

He laughed at his own joke, then ushered me back toward the group and introduced me to his two brothers-in-law and his two daughters. The girls were twins named Keesha and Kaylin. They were seven. Keesha had on a bright yellow dress, and Kaylin's was lavender. Their skin was a caramel brown, and I guessed their mother was white.

Next, Randall ushered me to a table stacked high with barbeque. There was a beautiful woman behind the table. She was curvy with brown hair and sharp green eyes—Randall's wife, Alexa.

She came around the table and gave me a long hug, thanked me for giving Randall some work, then loaded my plate high with ribs and pork shoulder.

"She seems great," I told Randall, sidling up next to him at a picnic table.

"She's the best. She teaches English at the high school."

"How long have you guys been married?"

"Nine years."

I didn't know how to phrase the question so I just came out with it. "I know this isn't exactly the South, but how does that go over in a small town?"

"Interracial marriage?"

I nodded.

"It's gotten a lot better here over the past couple of decades. A lot of the hate died off with the last generation. Sure, it's still there. Hell, Alexa's dad didn't take to me for about three years."

"And now?"

"We're like this." He crossed his fingers.

He wrestled down half a rib, then changed the subject. "So, your farm?"

I knew where he was headed and I said, "I'm in."

He raised his eyebrows. "It's not gonna be easy."

"Why live on a farm if you're not gonna fucking farm?"

He laughed, nearly choking on the meat in his mouth.

I patted his shoulder. "Careful, I can't have my head foreman dying on day one."

He slapped his chest with his hand, coughed, then said, "How 'bout I stop by on Monday and we can go over what needs to be done?"

"Sounds good."

There was a loud whistle, and Randall said, "Eat up. The service is about to start."

~

A sixty-something black preacher gave an impassioned sermon about resisting sin during these next three months of summer. He pleaded with the youth to stay away from the "devil's brew" and to chasten themselves against the "temptations of the flesh" on those hot, humid nights.

The sermon lasted two hours. Make that, *I* lasted two hours. The sermon could have lasted six for all I knew. I slipped out under the guise of using the bathroom, then darted to the Range Rover, and found my way back to Main Street.

Tarrin Baptist was on the south side of Main Street. Lutheran United was across the street on the north side. More than two hundred people permeated the front lawns of both churches, and many tents were sprawled on the street, separating the two. If there were any resentments between the two factions, they'd set aside their differences for the day.

Or so it seemed.

It took me a few moments to locate Annie from the home goods store, who, to my great pleasure, was standing behind one of the tables in the buffet line. In front of her were two metal dishes stacked high with glistening fried chicken.

I guess I would start my diet tomorrow.

Annie forced me to take four pieces—two breasts and two thighs, which she thought was hilarious—and I happily obliged her.

I was headed back to snag a drumstick when a woman grabbed me by the arm.

"We need you," she said.

I traded glances between the metal pan of glistening chicken and the enchanting blond woman tugging on my arm.

"Can I just grab—"

"No!" she yelled. "There's no time."

"What's going on? Is everything okay?"

"The tug-of-war," she said, pulling me across the street toward Lutheran United at a jog.

I couldn't help but notice the uppermost of her pink dress bouncing up and down as she ran.

We made it around to the back of Lutheran United where there was a large grass courtyard and a sand volleyball pit. The volleyball net was gone and lying across the length of the sand was a rope.

"We've lost five years in a row," the blond said, coming to a stop.

For the first time, I got a good look at her. She had light blue eyes and high cheekbones. Her lipstick was the exact shade of her dress, a light pink. She was barefoot, yet she was only an inch shorter than me.

She was a tall blond goddess.

She dragged me to the pit where two pastors stood across from each other on opposite sides of a thick rope. Both men's faces were stern, and both were doing stretches.

This *was* Yankees vs. Red Sox.

"Pastor John, look what I got," the blond said.

Pastor John appraised me to the point I thought he was going to ask to see my teeth, then said "Nice work, Caroline."

Caroline.

"I hear you've lost five years in a row to Lutheran United," I said, unable to think of anything else.

Pastor John shook his head. "We *are* Lutheran United."

I turned and looked at Caroline. She'd poached me from the Tarrin Baptist front lawn.

On this note, a woman ran over and said, "Oh, no! He's with us."

It was Annie.

"Not a chance, Annie," Caroline barked. "He's with us."

"Thomas?" Annie asked.

"Thomas?" Caroline echoed.

I froze.

Brain: Thomas, you know the right thing to do.

Dick: Yeah you do, buddy.

Brain: Must I remind you that you were at Tarrin Baptist to see Annie? You were eating her fried chicken. Four pieces.

Dick: Dude, must I remind you that you haven't been laid since Gina left? Which was, oh, I don't know, SEVEN MONTHS AGO!

Brain: Did you hear the preacher, Thomas? "Chasten yourself against the temptations of the flesh."

Dick: Did you see her running, Thomas? That was like some Baywatch style bouncing, my man.

"I'm sorry," I said, taking a step closer to Caroline.

Annie's face fell.

Brain: I'm so disappointed.

Dick: Yahooooooo!

There were ten spots on each side. Pastor John walked me down the line, and like a baseball manager staring at his lineup card, he switched a couple people around, then put me in the eighth spot.

I wrapped my hands around the rope.

Someone yelled, "One minute!"

The crowd around the volleyball court quickly doubled.

Let's go, Lutheran!

Let's go, Baptist!

Lutheran!

Baptist!

Lutheran!

Baptist!

Someone counted down from ten, then a gunshot erupted. And not some fake starter pistol. A rifle shot.

Everyone started pulling.

I heaved, a blinding pain shooting through my ribs.

Brain: Karma.

The pain in my side was nearly as bad as when I first fell off the ladder, but Caroline screaming my name—Come on, Thomas! Pull, Thomas! Harder, Thomas!—kept me going.

Dick: Pull!!!

A minute later, it was over.

Baptist won for a sixth straight year.

Caroline made her way over to me and asked, "Are you okay?"

I might have been lying on the sand holding my ribs.

"Uh, yeah," I groaned.

I told her how I fell out of a tree and then fell off a ladder.

"Oh, honey, why didn't you say so?"

~

I filled up the Range Rover at the small gas station and while I was there, I asked for directions to the address the Tarrin Police Department receptionist had taped to my license.

It took me five minutes to find the place, a small house on the outskirts of town. There was a dirt road leading to a house set back on a couple of acres. A blue Toyota Tacoma was parked in the dirt out front.

I knocked on the front door, but no one answered. I walked around to the back of the house and saw a man working on a hot rod.

"Hey," I announced.

He glanced up from the engine and squinted in my direction. He had a thick Selleck mustache, and his hands were covered in grease. There was a shotgun leaned against the front tire of the car, and he picked it up and ambled toward me.

He stopped five feet short and asked, "Whatcha need, partner?"

"Was thinking maybe we could chat."

"What, exactly, would we be chatting about?"

"The Save-More murders."

He glared at me, then looked down at his gun, then back at me.

"Or we could just talk about the Cardinals," I said.

"Now we're talking." He stuck his hand out. "Mike Zernan."

"Thomas Prescott." If my name meant anything to him, he didn't show it.

"You know anything about cars, Thomas?" he asked, waving me toward the hot rod.

The last time I attempted any car maintenance myself, I put window washer fluid in the radiator.

"Can't say I do."

He seemed to second-guess putting his gun away, took a breath, then tilted his head toward the hot rod. "This here is a 1930 Ford Model A Pickup."

The hot rod frame was black with an exposed chrome engine. Two exhaust pipes stuck up from the engine like the pipes of a church organ. The wheels were thin, black rubber with concentric circles of white and red. The frame of the truck hovered six inches above a small patch of gravel. It looked in excellent condition, save for the front headlights which were both cracked.

He said, "I've been restoring her for going on a year and a half now."

"Looks like you're almost done."

"Yeah, just a few more little projects."

"What are you working on today?"

"Waiting on a couple headlights to be delivered. Supposed to be here an hour ago, if Pete would get off his lazy ass."

I laughed. "Who's Pete?"

"UPS guy. Probably down at the bowling alley drinking a beer."

I didn't pry further.

Mike cracked his neck, then said, "Just been fiddling with the engine most of the morning. Trying to squeak out a few more horses." He leaned over the engine, then said, "Come here."

I joined him.

He fiddled away for a good ten minutes, detailing his every move, then said, "Jump in and give it a whirl, would ya?"

I opened the driver side door and slid in. The key was in the ignition, and I turned it. The engine rumbled to life.

"Gas it!" Mike yelled over the thrum of the engine.

I did.

The engine rumbled two octaves louder, the entire car vibrating. It made my father's Range Rover seem like a Big Wheel.

"Okay, kill it!" he yelled.

He waved me out, wiped his hands on his jeans, and asked, "What did you think?"

"Instant Viagra."

He smiled. "You want a beer?"

"Sounds good."

He disappeared inside, then returned with two longnecks. He motioned toward the hot rod and said, "Let's get away from these bugs for a while."

We both got into the truck.

He flipped the radio to an old fifties station, then turned to me and said, "So the *Cardinals*? What's your interest in them?"

"Someone told me to ask you about them."

His lips pursed under his mustache.

I said, "I was looking into one of their games from a couple years back and I was having trouble getting any stats."

"You're not very good at this," he said.

I laughed.

He said, "So you're looking into the Save-More murders?"

I nodded.

"Why?"

"Curiosity at first. Stumbled on the memorial, and old habits die hard." I gave him a quick summation of my life in law enforcement.

"I heard about that case up in Maine," he said. "What was the nickname they had for that guy?"

The case had been three years earlier. It garnered a lot of attention because a woman named Alex Tooms—who would later go on to shatter my heart into a million little pieces—wrote a true-crime novel detailing the murders. It had been on the bestseller list for nearly three months. Only, the murders hadn't been solved. The killer, Tristan Grayer, had still been out there, biding his time before going on another killing spree. This time, targeting women close to me.

"The Maine-iac," I replied.

"That's it," he said. "Didn't you get shot and fall off a cliff?"

I took a deep breath. Involuntarily, I could feel my knuckles go white around the beer bottle in my hand.

"Yeah. I got lucky."

Before he could ask any follow-up questions, I asked, "So why would the receptionist at the Tarrin Police Department tell me to talk to you?"

"I was with the TPD for fourteen years."

"Did you head up the Save-More investigation?"

"I did," he said solemnly, leaning his head back against the seat.

I knew he was back there, back at the crime scene, back standing over five dead bodies. Just like I'd been back on that cliff a moment earlier.

"What happened?" I asked.

"With the murders? Or the investigation?"

"More the investigation. And more why you no longer work as a police officer."

Something told me that if it weren't for the Save-More murders, Officer Mike Zernan would still be gainfully employed.

"Well, as you would expect, it was a real shit show. Everybody—the TPD, County, and Missouri Bureau—all jostling for jurisdiction. Eventually, the TPD won out, mostly because it wasn't a whodunit. It wasn't a hate crime or terrorism—it was a revenge killing. Then the shooter killed himself. It was pretty cut and dry."

"So it seems."

He raised his eyebrows.

"What did you find?" I asked.

He glanced outside, then turned back. "Just some inconsistencies."

"Yeah, like what?"

"Still kind of *buggy* in here." He sat on the word buggy.

I nodded.

"Where are you staying?" he asked.

"The Humphries Farm."

We talked farming for a couple minutes, then we talked actual baseball. When our beers were gone, we exited the car.

On my departure, Mike shook my hand, leaned in, and whispered, "Give me three days."

Chapter 10

Saturday's Revival marathon tuckered me out. I met a lifetime quota of hallelujahs and the tug-of-war did a number on my ribs. So I canceled the second leg, staying home and playing with Harold and May.

I added some water to the now working pigpen, and the piglets rolled around in the mud for over an hour. Then I gave them baths. And, of course, backrubs. And yes, they still slept in bed with me.

Monday morning, as planned, Randall came by and we set up a plan to get the farm back into shape. He gave me a quick rundown on everything we needed to do: buy or rent a tractor, get rid of the overgrown brush, till the soil, fix the irrigation, decide what crops to plant, buy seed, and so forth.

I handed him my credit card and gave him carte blanche, though I knew he would exhaust himself finding the best deals on everything.

He said he had a good chicken guy, whatever that meant.

It was now a little after 2:00 p.m. and I was driving to Page Ranch. As in Victoria Page, the sole survivor of the Save-More murders.

I called my sister, aka my Google, and Lacy did a quick internet search on Victoria, then found her present address easily enough.

I continued over rolling green hills for fifteen minutes, took a few turns, then pulled onto a dirt road leading under a giant sign that read "Page Ranch."

I expected to see a bunch of cows, but instead I saw horses. The horses were the color of chocolate: milk, dark, white, and even one that looked like that Hershey's Cookies and Cream. Most were standing still. A few romped around.

I drove up the dirt road for a quarter mile and parked in front of a large house. There were several trucks and horse trailers. To the left of the house was a giant, red wooden stable.

A moment later, I knocked on the door of the house. No one answered, and I started toward the stable. Even from a hundred feet away, I could hear horses neighing and stomping.

I opened and closed a high steel gate, then walked through the wide entrance. A woman and two men were standing with their backs to me. I looked past them into an open stall and saw two horses. The male horse was huge. He was the Dwayne Johnson of horses. He reared up on his hind legs and thrusted what looked to be an old Soviet missile, but was actually his dick, into the girl horse.

I feared for the female horse's life, but as quickly as it started, it was over.

The woman shook the hands of the two men. She noticed me in her peripheral and turned. She was medium height with a cowboy hat atop unnaturally red hair. She was what people would refer to as a handsome woman. I guessed her to be in her early sixties.

"Can I help you?" she asked.

"I'm looking for Victoria Page," I said, though I was nearly certain this was she.

Her brown eyes directed me to the entrance, and she said, "Give me a minute."

I nodded and exited.

A minute later, the two men led Dwayne Johnson from the stable with a post-coital twinkle in his large amber eyes. His now flaccid dong hung like the world's largest piece of strawberry taffy. He glared at me and snorted.

I'd never felt so emasculated.

The two men gave a quick howdy, then led Dwayne to one of the horse trailers. They drove away, and Victoria Page walked from the stable. She had a noticeable limp, dragging her left foot slightly.

"First time you see two horses going at it?" she asked.

"What makes you think that?"

"Just the look on your face back in there, like you saw a ghost."

"I expected a bit more foreplay."

She laughed.

I said, "That guy horse was enormous."

"That's Diamond. He won the Futurity two years ago."

"Futurity?"

"The All-American Futurity. Race down in New Mexico."

"He's a racehorse?"

"One of the best."

"He run in the Kentucky Derby?"

She shook her head. "Those are thoroughbreds." She looked toward the horses across the way. "These are quarter horses. Different breed. They run shorter distances."

"Got it."

I thought back to Dwayne/Diamond. "Does that big guy still race?"

"He's retired. Now he just does what you saw."

"Goes around screwing."

"Pretty much."

"So he's a gigolo?"

"Basically."

"How much do his services cost?"

"You wouldn't believe it if I told you."

"Try me."

"What you just saw cost a hundred grand."

"That's some expensive semen."

"Yes."

"How long have you been doing this?"

"My dad passed away about fifteen years ago and left me some money. That's when I bought my first horse. Been doing it ever since."

She took a long inhale, then said, "But I'm guessing you aren't here to buy one of my horses."

I shook my head.

"Then why are you here?"

I told her.

~

Victoria Page handed me a glass of water and then took a seat on a chair opposite the couch I was sitting on.

I declined her offer for something stronger, but this didn't stop her from pouring herself a martini with two blue cheese olives shipwrecked at the bottom of the glass.

We were in a sitting room. There were two giant windows, with satin curtains glowing in the afternoon sun. Hanging on the walls were a series of watercolors, beautiful landscape paintings filled with horses.

On the far side of the room was a glass display case filled with a collection of trophies and ribbons.

Victoria took a small sip of her martini, set it down, and said, "I can't believe it's been four years."

"Does it seem longer?"

She'd taken off her hat and she ran her fingers through her shoulder length hair, which on closer examination was dyed a near scarlet.

"It's funny," she said. "It seems like it happened a lifetime ago, but it also feels like it was yesterday."

I nodded. I could relate.

She could sense it in my eyes and asked, "What happened to you?"

"Which time?"

Her eyebrows raised slightly.

I explained, "I'm a magnet for mayhem."

This earned a small smile.

She seemed reluctant to talk, and I decided to regale her with a couple stories, which should give the vodka time to loosen her up.

Truthfully, of all the crazy stuff that had happened to me—being shot, falling off a cliff, drowning, being held hostage by South African pirates, going to third base with Becky "Valtrex" Del Vicio—by far, the most traumatic was being attacked by a pack of wolves.

According to my therapist—my sister Lacy—this wasn't just because I nearly bled to death in the middle of the forest or because I had to get more than a hundred stitches or because I still couldn't throw a frisbee very well, it was because the trauma was planted years earlier when I was a child.

Young Thomas Prescott was nine years old when he went on a field trip to the zoo. He thought the exhibit was full of dogs and he wanted to pet those dogs. So Thomas climbed the fence and squirmed his way up the ravine and he went to pet the dog. Which was a fucking wolf.

The wolf was shot by zoo security, and I escaped with only a few stitches. But I did wet my bed for the next five years.

But back to the present.

"There was this big black one," I told Victoria. "His name was Cartman."

"Cartman?"

"Yeah, like from *South Park*."

"What is that?"

"It's a show. One of the park rangers helping with the wolves' release named him. But it kind of fit. You could just feel him plotting behind his eyes, figuring out a way to eat you."

I ran through the rest of the story. The snowmobile. Only room for Erica. Hearing the wolves howl. Seeing them coming. Running through the open snow to the trees. Trying to climb one but unable to find footing. Then the first wolf leaping. Smashing into me, his jaw clamping on my shoulder. Fighting for my life.

I leaned back on the couch and took a few long, deep shuddering breaths. Okay, so maybe I was exaggerating just slightly, but I wanted Victoria to know I could empathize with her trauma. And, to be brutally honest, the memory of the wolves, with their jaws locked into my flesh, did quicken my pulse.

"Here," Victoria said, offering me her drink, "take a sip of this."

I took a sip, then handed back her drink. "Thanks."

"That sounds terrifying," she said. "When I tell my story to most people, I know few can relate."

She popped one of the olives in her mouth and said, "It was the only time in my life I remember having no control over the outcome. I was at the mercy of this man and, I suppose, God's will."

I nodded, but didn't dare speak.

"I was making cookies for my niece's bake sale. I make incredible chocolate chip macadamia nut cookies." Her lips flexed into a smile ever so briefly. "I ran out of butter so I made a run to Save-More. While I was there, I picked up one of those gossip mags." She let out a long sigh. "If I hadn't stopped to flip through that magazine, I would have been out of there before Lowry came in. I would have been on my way home, getting ready to bake another batch of cookies.

"I was next in line to check out when Neil Felding came in. Right behind him was Lowry. Lowry had a gun in his hand and he started waving it at Odell, the manager, screaming that he shouldn't have been fired. Then he forced all of us back to the back freezer."

"Who is *us*?" I asked, though I knew the names already.

"Dr. Lanningham, he was the town veterinarian; Peggy Bertina, who I didn't know personally; Will Dennel, a nice looking kid who worked over at the lumberyard; Neil Felding, who I didn't know all that well, but had just moved back into town; Odell, the store owner; and me."

"Did you ever think about making a run for it?"

"Of course. But then I figured that would get me killed for certain. I still thought there was a good chance Lowry was just gonna give us a scare then let us go."

"Why did you think that?"

"Just that it was Lowry."

"You knew him?"

"He cut my lawn for five or six years when he was younger. He even stayed the night at my house a couple times when he needed to get away from his old man."

"You didn't think he was dangerous?"

"No. I mean, he did some stupid stuff. The things that landed him in jail. Boozing mostly, but that ran in his family, so it wasn't a surprise."

Her eyes glazed over, which was possibly due to the vodka, and she said, "I still remember one time when he was cutting my lawn. He found a dead fawn in the leaves. He was sixteen, maybe seventeen years old, but he was crying like the dickens. He dug a hole and buried her, then planted some flowers on top of her."

"People can change a lot in ten years."

She was silent for a couple moments, and I prodded, "So he took the lot of you to the back freezer?"

"Yes."

"Was he talking?"

"Not much. Just giving orders. He made us sit down on the cold concrete."

"Did you say anything to him, you know, since you sort of knew him?"

"Yeah, I said, 'Lowry this isn't you' or something like that, and he told me to 'shut up.'" She took a breath, then added, "That's when I started to think maybe things—"

I finished for her, "—things were going to end badly?"

She nodded.

"Then what?"

"Then he started shooting. Just going down the line." She shook her head from side to side. "I just remember screaming, then..." She paused, took a breath, "...then pain unlike anything I've ever felt before."

"Where did you get hit?"

"One in the shoulder, one in my left hip."

That would account for the limp.

"What did you do?"

"Nothing. I played dead."

"Then what?"

"Lowry left. I waited another couple minutes, then I got a cell phone out of Peggy's pocket and called the police."

She continued, "It seemed like it took them hours to arrive, but it was only three or four minutes. Once I saw the first police officer crash through the door, everything gets cloudy. I remember them putting me on a stretcher. Then the hospital. I was pretty drugged up for the next few days."

I'd been there. In the clouds. Floating. Little montages fighting their way into your consciousness. A face. Lights. Lucid dreams.

"How long were you in the hospital?"

"Five days. I made them discharge me so I could go to the funeral."

"Did they have a big collective one?"

She nodded. "At the high school."

"Did the entire town show up?"

"And more."

"I'm guessing they had private family burials afterward."

Without answering, I knew she went to all five. I imagined her watching Wheeler give her father's eulogy.

Suddenly, I found myself furious.

That was stage two.

Stage one: Curiosity.

Stage two: Fury.

I checked the time on my cell phone.

I needed to feed the piglets.

I stood and said, "Thank you for reliving that for me. I know I'm a total stranger and you didn't have to."

Her eyes looked heavy. The story and the martini had exhausted her. She gave the slightest of nods.

I saw myself out.

Chapter 11

I pushed the door open.

I waited for Harold and May to attack me with oinks and kisses, but they didn't come.

"Harold! Ma—"

She was sitting in the rocking chair in the living room. She was wearing a low-cut purple dress. Her blond hair was teased and curled onto her shoulders. A glass of white wine shimmered in her left hand.

It took me a long second to remember her name.

Carol?

Karen?

Caroline.

"Hope ya don't mind," she said. "I made myself comfortable."

"I can see that."

"I thought—"

I cut her off. "Where are the piglets?"

"Those beasts?"

Beasts?

"Yes, where are they?"

"Outside, of course."

"You let them out?"

"They were in your house," she exclaimed.

I turned on my heel and ran outside. "Harold! May!"

I could hear Caroline push through the door behind me. I turned back and watched as she navigated the three porch steps in black heels. She didn't spill a drop of the wine still in her hand.

I took off toward the pigpen, praying that's where they were, praying they were rolling around in the mud.

They weren't.

I checked the barn.

Then the chicken coop.

Finally, I returned to the house.

Caroline was standing right out front. She hadn't moved.

"Did you see them?" I asked.

She shook her head.

"How long ago did you let them out?"

She took a sip of wine and pondered the question.

I put up my hands.

Finally she said, "I don't know, maybe an hour ago."

"An hour!?"

They could be anywhere.

"Please help me look for them," I pleaded.

"Oh, okay. Yeah, I can do that."

She looked at me, then walked—no, clomped—a couple feet toward the large oak. She leaned down, the dress pulling taut around her backside, and yelled, "Come here, pigs!"

If her desired effect was to take my mind off my two escaped piglets, she only half accomplished it.

I shook my head and took off into the high brush.

Thirty minutes later, still having not found them, the reality that they might really be gone was starting to hit.

The old tractor wasn't far away, and I pushed my way through the overgrown brush and leaned back against it.

"Harold! May!" I screamed.

Oink, oink.

I flattened myself to the ground, pushed a bunch of grass to the side, and peered under the tractor.

Two little piglets smiled back at me.

"Guys!"

They wiggled their way out from the shade and into my arms. My eyes started watering. I was a thirty-five year-old man, and the closest relationship I had outside of my sister was with two little piglets.

Good grief.

I picked up the fugitives and marched back to the house.

Caroline was standing out front as we approached. I couldn't help but notice there was more wine in her glass than previously.

"You found them," she shrieked. "Oh, thank heavens. I don't think I would have been able to live with myself."

I simply stared at her, then made my way inside. I set the piglets down, then headed to the kitchen to mix their formula. Caroline clomped in behind me.

There were two grocery bags sitting on the counter. From behind me, Caroline said, "I came to make you dinner."

I glared at her.

Should I really be that upset?

I mean, yes, she broke into my house. Yes, she let Harold and May out. And yes, she didn't really put any effort into helping find them.

"Do you want me to leave?" she asked. Her face fell. For just a brief moment, there was a break in whatever facade she'd created over the many years.

"What's on the menu?" I asked.

~

Chicken piccata. Lemon butter. Capers.

It was mouthwatering, and I told her so.

She smiled meekly, then took a sip of wine. There was still a touch of tension in the air, but there's something about good food that makes it hard to hold a grudge and I'd mentally signed a treaty. Plus, to Caroline's credit, she made a concerted effort to be extra nice to Harold and May, even going as far as to give them each a couple staged pats on the back. And of course, there was the small fact she looked like she was smuggling cabbages in her dress.

I was telling her the story about finding Harold and May in the barn loft when there was a knock at the door.

I excused myself and opened the door.

"Hi," Wheeler said.

At the sound of her voice, the piglets materialized and attacked her.

"Hi guys," she said, picking up May, turning her over, and giving her a big kiss on the belly. "Don't think I'm not gonna give you kisses too," she said, reaching for Harold.

He turned and ran playfully. Wheeler pushed past me into the house and grabbed him. That's when she noticed Caroline sitting at the table.

Wheeler turned to me, her face ashen. "I'm so sorry. I didn't know you had company."

"Hi, Wheeler," Caroline said. The words hung in the air, two large dripping icicles.

"Oh, hi, Caroline," Wheeler managed, setting Harold down. "I didn't see your car out front."

"I parked around back."

"Right," Wheeler replied. "Well, I just came to check on these little guys."

"Aren't they just adorable?" Caroline said with a giant smile.

Wait, hadn't she called them *beasts?*

Wheeler looked at me expectantly. I wanted to explain that Caroline had broken into my house uninvited, that she'd sprung dinner on me, and that I didn't have the heart to decline.

I opted for silence.

"There's plenty of food," Caroline said, "if you'd like to join us."

From the look on Wheeler's face, it looked as though she'd rather get a pap smear from a crocodile.

"Oh, no, I don't want to be a third wheel."

Caroline smiled in response.

The two women were having their own little conversation, one even a seasoned detective such as myself could only grasp the barest of details. More was conveyed in those few quick exchanges than the Gettysburg Address.

Against my better judgment, I took a moment to contrast the two women. Both women were attractive, albeit in their own way. Wheeler in a short, petite, Scarlett Johansson sense. Caroline in a tall, voluptuous, Jessica Rabbit variety. Wheeler was comfortable in a pair of jeans, a ball cap, and maybe a dusting of makeup. Caroline appeared to feel more at home in a dress, heels, and lipstick. Wheeler preferred beer. Caroline, a white wine spritzer.

Wheeler moved past me and out the front door. I followed her down the porch steps. I asked, "Do you two have history?"

She let out a small laugh. Whatever history they had, she was keeping to herself. She did say, "Enjoy the apple pie. Many have."

Then she got in her truck and drove away.

I headed back to the house and returned to the table. "Sorry about that."

"Oh, heavens. Don't be sorry."

"How do you two know each other?" I asked.

"Oh, Thomas, the first thing you need to learn about a small town. Everybody knows everybody. And everybody knows *everything*."

"And what is the second lesson?"

"The second lesson is that I make the best apple pie on the planet."

Wheeler's departing words came rushing back. Was this Caroline's MO? Break into a guy's house and cook him dinner and feed him apple pie? How many men had fallen into her trap?

I made a mental note of this, then changed the subject to something more benign. "Where did you learn to cook?"

She smiled. "My grandma."

"Did she live in Tarrin?"

"She still does."

"Your grandma is still alive?"

"Ninety-one and still kicking."

"Wow."

"I'm guessing all your grandparents have passed."

I wanted to answer her, but the words were caught in my throat.

"I didn't mean to upset you," she said, concerned she may have ruined whatever progress we'd made in the last twenty minutes.

"You're fine," I assured her. "It's just that my grandpa died a little over a week ago."

"Oh, honey." She stood up and came behind me. She cradled my head and said, "I'm so sorry."

Her touch was soft, and she smelled like honeysuckle.

"This is his house," I told her. "He gave it to me in his will."

She ran her fingers through my hair. It was the first time a woman had touched me in nearly seven months. She stood behind me, caressing my scalp with her fingernails.

Ahhhhh.

"What was his name?" she asked.

I was two-thirds to an orgasm, but somehow managed, "H-H-Harold H-H-H-Humphries."

"He was your grandpa?"

She retook her seat, and I gave her a clipped version of the story. When I was finished, she said, "That's amazing he found you."

I nodded.

"And he was the last relative you had?"

"Yep, now it's just me and my sister."

She was silent a moment, then she dropped her fork. "I don't know why it didn't dawn on me earlier."

"What?"

"Jerry."

"Who?"

"Jerry *Humphries*!" she shouted. "I think you have a cousin here."

~

"Bye, Harold. Bye, May."

The piglets oinked their goodbyes.

I helped Caroline down the porch steps and asked, "You sure you're okay to drive?"

"Oh yeah. I'm fine."

She'd drank half the bottle of wine herself, but she appeared to have all her wits about her.

"I'm sorry again for letting your piglets out," she said.

"It's okay. I didn't even know how attached I'd become until they were gone."

"Well, they are cute, and far less beastly than I thought."

"I'll pass that on to them."

We walked around to the back of the farmhouse where she'd parked in the dirt. Even at 10:00 p.m. the air was still heavy. Still hot. There was something about the sticky air that made it hard to focus. Made it easy to have a lapse in judgment. I bet teen pregnancy was higher in places with high humidity.

At her car, Caroline turned. "Let me know how it goes with Jerry. Like I said, he should be at the bank most days."

"I will. And thanks for dinner. It was delicious. And you were right, you do make the best apple pie on the planet."

She beamed and her fingers brushed against my forearm.

I never wanted to kiss and *not* kiss someone so badly in my life.

She took the decision out of my hands. She leaned forward and pushed her lips to mine. She raked her fingernails across my neck, then she slowly moved her mouth across my cheek.

"The things," she whispered in my ear. "The things I will do."

Chapter 12

"Is Jerry Humphries in?" I asked.

The bank was First Missouri National. Red brick. Two businesses down from the hardware store.

The prospect of having a relative living in Tarrin had been itching at me since Caroline mentioned it the previous night. It was a big fat mosquito bite in the middle of my kneecap.

The clerk, the first Asian person I was yet to encounter in Tarrin, shook his head and said, "He's out for lunch."

"Do you, by chance, know where he went?" I was planning on stopping to get a bite after the bank anyhow.

My mind was still in city mode—cynical, jaded, suspicious—and I was surprised when he answered candidly, "They usually hit the deli, but I heard he and Jim, that's the manager, talking about going to Mexico. There is a great Thai place there."

I still had a hard time not thinking of Mexico, as in south of the border, instead of the town of fifteen thousand, twenty minutes west on Highway 36.

I asked, "If I leave my number, could you have him give me a call?"

"Sure."

I wrote my number and name on the back of a deposit slip, and he promised to deliver it to Jerry when he returned.

I left and walked down to Dina's Dine-In. I looked for the pregnant waitress who let me use her phone, but she must have had the day off. Ten minutes later, I walked out with two club sandwiches and a bag of fries.

I had planned on eating both sandwiches, but I didn't feel like eating alone—and technically it had been three days. So I decided to check in on Mike Zernan.

I made a couple wrong turns trying to find the place from memory, but when I did find it, his truck was parked out front.

It was closing in on 11:30 a.m. There was cloud cover, and it was ten degrees cooler than the previous day. Somehow the air felt stickier; perhaps the moisture was trapped by the clouds above. Still, it was pleasant enough, and I wasn't surprised when he didn't answer the door. He was probably out back, working on his hot rod.

I walked around the house.

The hot rod was sitting in the grass. The busted headlights had been swapped out for pristine halogens and they reflected a couple errant rays of sun shining through a break in the clouds.

Mike was nowhere to be seen.

I made my way to his back door and knocked.

Nothing.

I set the bag of food on a beach chair and moved to one of the windows. I screened my eyes and peered inside.

"Shit!"

Mike was on the floor in the kitchen. He must have passed out or had a heart attack.

I tried the back door, but it was locked. I threw my shoulder into the door, my adrenaline giving me the extra muscle to knock the door from its hinges.

"Mike!" I shouted, falling to my knees. He was on his right side, his left arm draped over his body.

I checked for a pulse more out of ingrained automation than checking for life. He was dead. And he didn't die from a heart attack.

There were deep purple ligature marks on his neck.

He had been strangled.

~

"Did you touch anything?" Miller asked.

It was hard for me to look at him and not see the poor schmuck whom Wheeler had given her engagement ring back to not once but twice.

He was the first officer to respond, though I predicted the entire police force and half the town was en route.

Due to Officer Miller's poor genetic makeup, the brim of his Tarrin

Police Department issue baseball cap was hovering two inches from my chin.

"Do you really have to be so close?" I asked.

He reluctantly took a small step backward and repeated the question. "Did you touch anything?"

"I touched a lot of stuff."

I don't think he was expecting this. "What?"

"After I found him, I decided to whip up some risotto."

His lips began to curl. He clenched and unclenched his fists. "Run me through what happened."

"I brought lunch."

"You brought lunch?"

He acted like he'd never heard of lunch before.

"Yeah, I brought lunch."

"What did you bring?"

"Club sandwiches from Dina's."

"Where are they?"

"Sitting on that chair." We were a couple steps off the back porch, and I pointed to the bag in the chair, which only held one club sandwich now. I ate mine. My blood sugar was getting low, and I knew the next two hours of my life were going to be spent answering questions, though if Miller kept repeating himself, I might not get another meal for three days.

"What time did you leave Dina's?" he asked.

"Maybe twenty minutes ago."

"I'm gonna call and verify."

"You would be a shitty cop if you didn't."

He ignored this and said, "Did you knock on the front door?"

"I did."

"And no one answered?"

"No."

It wasn't a terribly stupid question, but I wanted to scream, "No, you nitwit, the occupant was dead!" I didn't.

"Okay, so no one answered the door. Then what?"

"I walked around to the back. That's where he was last time I c′

"The last time you came?" His eyebrows rose under his ⊦ "When was this?"

"Saturday."

"This past Saturday?"

"Yes, the only Saturday that I've been here."

"Okay."

I could see all the questions rolling around in his head: How did you know Mike? What did you and Mike do last Saturday? What did you talk about? Why did you come here? Was it about the Save-More murders?

He would have plenty of time to ask me these questions later. In a room. Maybe even a locked room.

"You go around back," he said. "Then what?"

"I expected him to be working on his car, but he wasn't. I knocked on the back door. *No one answered,* if you're curious. Then I looked through the window. I saw him on the ground. Then I busted through the door."

"The door was locked?"

"Why would I bust down an unlocked door?"

He didn't answer. He had, without my noticing, crept a step closer to me, and the bill of his hat once again hovered uncomfortably close to my chin.

"Can you, like, get out of my face?"

He took a half step back, and I encouraged him with my eyes to take another one.

He did.

There was a screech of tires on the opposite side of the house. Then two more. Miller had thirty more seconds before he was going to have to start sharing me.

"What did you do when you got inside?" he spat quickly.

"I checked his pulse, more out of habit than anything else, then I didn't do shit. Didn't want to compromise the scene more than I already had."

Three men appeared from around the house. One of them was Chief Eccleston. He walked with purpose, his gut and jowls bouncing in near unison. He came abreast of us and asked Miller, "You been inside yet?"

"Just for a minute." He cocked his head at me and said, "I've been interviewing him."

Eccleston glanced at me.

I waved at him.

Heyyyyy.

He jutted his chin out just slightly. Literally the least he could possibly do to acknowledge my presence.

"Was anything taken?" he asked Miller.

"Not sure yet. The place is ransacked though."

He was right, everything in the house had been overturned. Everything in the kitchen tossed on the floor. Every drawer pulled out and dumped. There was one thing for certain: whoever killed Mike was looking for something.

As a professional conspiracy theorist, my first inclination was that perhaps they were looking for whatever Mike intended to show me. Whatever had taken him three days to obtain.

These ruminations started the moment I saw him through the window. They had only grown in the last twenty minutes. And the look on the Chief's face when he asked if anything was taken, well, that only solidified my theory. Something about the Save-More murder investigation was tainted. And Mike Zernan had proof.

Two more officers came into view.

"Well, I'm gonna get out of your guys' way," I said.

I took two steps in the direction of the back porch.

"Whoa!" shouted Miller. "Where do you think you're going?"

I pointed at the paper bag. "My lunch."

He glanced at the Chief.

Eccleston shook his head. "That's evidence. Leave it."

"My club sandwich is evidence?" I strode toward the chair, grabbed the bag, and walked back to the small group, which now included the two other officers.

I was opening the bag to take out the second sandwich when it was snatched from my hands by Miller.

He smirked and said, "Like the Chief said, it's evidence."

I was tempted to say something about the two engagement rings Wheeler gave back to him, but that was a low blow, even for me. So I said, "Like how the two engagement rings Wheeler gave back to you are evidence that you must really suck in bed."

Miller's face twisted. The Chief and the two other cops gasped in horror.

Point, Prescott.

I turned on my heel and walked away. When I'd gone a dozen steps, a hand wrapped around my arm. This is literally my least favorite thing in the world, and I stopped and stared at the tiny little paw squishing the bat wing of my triceps.

"We need you to come down to the station," Miller barked. "To give a statement."

I wondered if this had anything to do with me emasculating him in front of his friends.

I peeled his hand off my arm and said, "Sure thing, I'll meet you there."

"Why don't I drive you."

"Why don't I meet you there."

He pulled some handcuffs off his belt. "Why don't I drive you."

I ignored him and headed for my car.

He grabbed my arm again, this time three clicks harder than before.

I turned and shoved him in the shoulder.

He took two steps back. Blinked twice. Looked like he probably did when the doctor told him he was in the negative thirtieth percentile for height.

He was a college wrestler, and I wasn't surprised when his hands shot up in front of him, his knees bent, his feet shoulder-width apart. But college wrestler or not, I had him by *seventy* pounds. In a fight, there was no substitute for mass. I was a rhino. He was a squirrel. It was as simple as that.

"You don't want to do this," I said.

The three other officers and Chief Eccleston overheard the exchange and turned. One of the officers took out his phone and began videotaping. Maybe they all secretly detested Miller. Maybe they were looking forward to watching me kick the shit out of him and posting it on the internet.

I would happily oblige.

Miller took two steps forward.

I crouched, ready for him to tackle me to the ground, whereby I would roll on top of him and dangle a loogie over his face until he cried uncle.

Then it happened.

He rose up on his toes, twisted his body around, and pivoted on his front foot. It was lightning quick, and a nanosecond later I was on my ass in the dirt, my ears ringing, and my vision supernova white.

I wouldn't know what happened until I was forwarded the video "Guy Gets Ass Kicked by Cop" by my sister two days later. After it had racked up nearly nine million views.

Miller hit me with a spinning back kick, smashing his foot into my temple at roughly sixty miles per hour.

I'd been punched in the face a handful of times, but I'd never been kicked. Lying on my back in the grass, I ceased to exist for two long seconds.

When my vision cleared, Miller was on top of me. I attempted to wriggle from beneath him, but he had my arms pinned to my chest. I could hear feet clomping in our direction as his fellow officers ran to root him on.

Now I understood why the other officer was recording with his phone.

Miller was some sort of badass.

I bucked up with my hips in an attempt to slip from beneath him, but he dug his knee into my side. "Stop," he said calmly.

"Fuck off," I wheezed. The seven seconds we'd been wrestling exhausted me and I felt like vomiting. It could have been from my poor cardiovascular shape or it could have been from the karate kick to my skull.

I tried to roll over onto my stomach, which I was able to do easily. Too easily. A second later, I knew why. Miller rolled onto my back and slinked his forearm under my chin, the other one behind my neck, creating a vice around my throat.

What we call in the business a "rear naked choke."

I clawed at his arms with my fingers, but he only clamped down harder. I tapped his arm frantically. Finally, after six taps, he released me.

Ten seconds later, I was in handcuffs.

~

"Don't feel too bad," Chief Eccleston said. "He almost made it to the UFC."

I held the can of Coke to the side of my face, which was swollen to near Elephant Man proportions. My lower jaw pulsated, and I was nearly positive one of my back molars was cracked.

"The UFC?"

"Yeah, after he lost his wrestling scholarship, he came back to Tarrin and started getting into Mixed Martial Arts. He won a bunch of amateur fights, then went professional. Did pretty good too, ended up getting on that UFC reality show they do. But he lost, never made it. That's when he came back and went to the academy."

I made a mental note to 1) look Miller up on the internet and 2) ask Wheeler how it slipped her mind to mention her ex was a fucking cage fighter!

I said, "I've thought about it and I don't want to press charges."

Eccleston laughed. "You assaulted him first. You assaulted a police officer."

"He grabbed me."

"He said he gently grabbed your arm."

I rolled up the sleeve of my T-shirt, exposing my triceps. The once rock hard muscle had atrophied by half and hibernated beneath a robust layer of fat. However, in this case, the fat benefited me, as it bruised more easily than muscle. My arm was red and beginning to purple where Miller grabbed me. "Does that look gentle to you?"

"That could have happened during the fight," the Chief countered, "after you assaulted him."

To the Chief's credit, it could have. But it didn't. Miller's hand never touched my arm during the scrum. He was too busy choking the shit out of me.

I was on the other side of the table enough times to know it didn't matter what a police officer did to you. It mattered what you did to them. And I'd pushed—which, sadly, is considered assault—a police officer.

"Fine," I said. "I assaulted him. Charge me, do what you've got to do."

"To be honest, I don't really give a shit about the assault."

I sat up in the chair a half inch.

The Chief took a sip from his can of Mountain Dew and said, "I'm more concerned with why you were meeting with Mike Zernan."

I bet he was.

"And," he continued, "why you killed him."

"Are you out of your mind? I didn't kill him."

"We know you were there on Saturday."

"Yeah, because I told Officer UFC that I was."

Eccleston's jowls flexed.

Maybe he knew a different way.

I hadn't really given much thought to who Mike thought bugged his house. In all honestly, I pretty much wrote it off to paranoia. But if his house really were bugged, then it would make sense it was the Tarrin Police Department listening in, making sure he wasn't talking about the case with anyone.

"Know what I think?" Eccleston asked. "I think you went out there last Saturday to scout Mike's place."

He was baiting me, trying to get me to say, "No, you asshole, I went out there to ask him about the Save-More murders."

"You're right. I wanted to get the lay of the land."

"So you don't deny it?"

"You know I didn't kill him."

"Oh, do I?"

He did. And maybe he even knew who did kill Mike. Or had a good idea. Hell, maybe it was him.

"Pretty convenient," he said, "that you were the one who found him."

"I'm pretty sure I know how to get away with murder."

It was a bold statement, but true.

"Everyone makes mistakes."

"No, amateurs make mistakes. I'm no amateur. And neither are you."

"What are you implying?"

"I don't have any motive to kill Mike Zernan. I don't know if I can say the same for you."

"What did Mike tell you?" he blurted, louder and harsher than he probably wished.

I shrugged.

He composed himself, then opened up a file in front of him. He said, "According to Dina's records, you paid for two club sandwiches and a bag of fries at 11:13 a.m."

"That sounds about right."

"It is right."

"Okay."

"How long did it take for them to make them?"

"I don't know, ten minutes?"

"That's what she said. So would it be safe to say that you left Dina's at around 11:23 a.m.?"

"Sure."

"Then you drove directly to Mike's?"

"I took a wrong turn. Had to double back. But yeah, I drove directly to Mike's."

"What time would you say you got there?"

"I don't know, ten minutes later."

"So 11:33 a.m.?"

"Give or take."

"So let's call it 11:35 a.m."

"Sure."

"According to your statement, you knock on the front door, nobody answers. You go around back, don't see him, then you peek in the window."

"That's correct."

"Do you go peeking into a lot of windows when people don't come to the door?"

"No, but his car was there."

"He could have taken a different car, or been on a walk, or a dozen other things."

"Yeah, but he wasn't."

He snorted, then said, "So you break the door down, then find him lying on the ground?"

 I nodded.

"How long from when you arrive to when you find him?"

I finally saw what he was driving at, where he was going with all this. "I dilly-dallied in his backyard for a while. Checked out the hot rod. He'd put in new halogens."

"That's not in your statement."

"Really? Well, it should have been."

He knew I was lying. He knew I was trying to buy myself a couple minutes. Minutes that were unaccounted for.

"And how long would you say you looked at the hot rod?"

"I don't know, five minutes."

He smirked.

Damn.

I should have said longer.

"Okay, so even with you checking out the hot rod—which we both know you didn't do—you would have broken down the door by, oh, say 11:40 a.m."

I nodded hesitantly.

"So at 11:40 a.m. you break down the door and you find Mike. Do you know what time you called the police to report it?"

I tried to think how long I had poked around Mike's house. At least long enough to eat a club sandwich.

"Probably a couple minutes later," I said, crossing my fingers behind my back.

"12:04 p.m."

Oh, bugger.

"Twenty-four minutes after you found him," the Chief said.

"That doesn't sound right."

"Oh, it's right. The record here and the call record on your phone. 12:04 p.m."

I bit the inside of my cheek.

"Now, I'm curious," he said, smiling for the first time, "what exactly were you doing for the twenty-four minutes between the time you found Mike dead and the time you called 911?"

"I took a shit."

"What?"

"Dead bodies are my prune juice."

He glared at me.

"Seriously, I can't tell you how many crimes scenes I've taken a dump at."

"What were you doing for twenty-four minutes?"

"I was playing Words With Friends." I paused. "On the crapper."

"I think you ate a club sandwich while you were poking around Mike's stuff."

I tried not to react, but my eyebrows betrayed me.

How did they know?

The Chief explained, "We found a piece of bacon on the floor in his garage."

It must have come out when I pushed the door open with the side of my hand.

I said, "That could have come from anyone's club sandwich."

"What were you doing for twenty-four minutes?" he demanded.

I was testing his patience. I mean, I didn't want him to go grab the phone book and start slapping me around.

"You want the truth?" I asked.

He crossed his arms and leaned back a couple inches.

"Mike was dead. He'd been dead awhile. I'm not a pathologist, but I have a pretty good idea of time of death. I'd guess the coroner said he died sometime the previous night. Maybe a three-hour window between 9:00 p.m. and midnight."

The Chief didn't say anything, which meant I was right or at least close.

I continued, "Whoever did it had ample time to make their way to Canada or Mexico if they wanted. So yeah, I waited twenty minutes to call the cops."

"What did you do?"

"What do you think I did?"

He leaned forward, his chair rattling as all four legs found purchase on the concrete floor. "You worked the scene."

I nodded.

It was more reflex than anything else. Once I realized Mike had been murdered, the switch flipped. Not calling the police was a conscious decision. I wanted to give myself five minutes to poke around. I could hardly believe I poked around for twenty minutes. I'd been careful not to leave any fingerprints. On the other hand, I had left a piece of bacon.

I was surprised when the Chief asked, "You notice anything funny?"

I had, but I didn't want to share it with him. Still, I had to give him something.

"I'm guessing the person who did it was left-handed."

His eyes narrowed.

I thought maybe another one of his officer's would have noticed this.

I said, "He fell onto his right side, his left arm draped across his body."

At the scene, I ran the simulation over in my head. Whoever killed him came up from behind him. Mike was a decent-size guy so I'm guessing it was somebody he knew, somebody he possibly invited into his home. Otherwise, it would have been hard to get the jump on him.

I said, "The killer got the cord or belt around Mike's neck, cinched it tight, then waited for Mike to suffocate. When he was sure Mike was dead, he shoved him to the ground. If he shoved Mike with his right hand, Mike would have most likely fallen on his left side. But Mike landed on his right side, ergo, he was pushed to the right, most likely by someone's left hand."

"You might be onto something," the Chief said.

"Yeah, or it could be nothing."

But there was another tidbit that made me think the guy was left-handed.

When I was consulting with the FBI, we were investigating a serial rapist who would strangle his victims with a length of rope. The bruising around the women's throats was always deeper on the left side and it was because the guy was right-handed. After he was caught, he confessed his crimes, even going as far as to show how he wrapped the rope over the victim's head, crossed his arms, and pulled it taut. He naturally pulled slightly harder with his dominant hand, which due to his arms being crossed, increased the bruising on the opposite side of the victim's throat.

In this case, the ligature marks were more pronounced on the right side of Mike Zernan's throat, which led me to believe he was strangled by a left-handed man.

There was another thing. Contrary to what I'd said to Eccleston, I didn't think the murder weapon was a cord or a belt. There was a cut under Mike Zernan's Adam's apple, which I was almost certain was caused by a garrote.

A garrote is a military weapon, a three-foot length of thick wire with handles on the ends, which often cuts into the victim's skin during strangulation.

I didn't tell Chief Eccleston any of this. Sometimes it's better if people don't know how smart you really are.

"Okay, I told you the truth," I said. "Now charge me with something or cut me loose."

~

Another Mountain Dew later and the Chief finally let me go.

On my way out, I bypassed the front desk. The woman who gave me Mike Zernan's name and address was sitting in her chair, a blank expression on her face. We briefly made eye contact, and she whipped her head away like I was the witch from the Narnia books who will turn you to stone.

Guilt can do that.

I put myself in her shoes. She either figured that I killed Mike, which would be her fault because she sent me there, or my going there pissed some people off and they killed Mike. Either way, she thought she was to blame.

Sure, she may have set the ball in motion, but the only person to blame was the asshole who wrapped a garrote around Mike's neck. Or whoever sent him there to do it.

"I'll give you a ride."

I glanced at the door. Miller was holding it open for me.

I nearly forgot that I hadn't driven to the station myself. I must have suffered brain damage from Miller's sleeper hold.

"Don't you have Fight Club to get to?" I asked.

"Fight Club is tomorrow," he said with a smirk.

"The first rule of Fight Club is to not talk about Fight Club."

Idiot.

"Oh, right."

He followed me down the steps and said, "Seriously, let me give you a lift to your car. It's the least I can do." He had the decency not to add, "after kicking the piss out of you."

"I can Uber."

"We don't have Uber."

"I'll get a taxi."

"We only have a couple. Could be an hour or more."

"I'll walk."

"It's four miles."

"I'll run."

He laughed.

"What?"

"You don't seem like the running type."

"I used to run almost every day."

"When?"

I shook my head. I hated being fat.

"Listen, don't worry about me. I'll find my way back to my car just fine."

"Quit being such a pansy and let me give you a lift."

He wasn't going to let up.

"Fine. But I'm not sitting in the back seat again."

"Don't worry. We're not taking a squad car. We'll take my truck."

His truck was an F150. It was on big wheels, and Miller needed the assistance of a step bar to get in. It was obvious the truck was compensating for Miller's small size, and I wanted to comment on this. But I was also still a little dizzy from the fallout from my last ill-advised remark.

I settled in the passenger seat, and we drove in silence for a half mile.

Then I asked, "Why was Mike Zernan let go from the police department?"

Miller glanced at me in his periphery. He seemed to be considering if he should be communicating with a known suspect about the very person he was suspected in killing. After two blocks he said, "He wasn't let go. He was offered early retirement. He was struggling with PTSD."

"From the Save-More murders?"

Miller shook his head. "No, from Iraq."

"He was in the military?" I don't know why this came as such a shock. Many men and women in law enforcement were veterans. Still, from my experience, they usually retained a couple of ingrained idiosyncrasies from their time in the service: cadence, posture, grooming, etc. Mike didn't have any that I'd noticed.

"He did two tours in the Gulf War."

I digested this, then said, "He seemed pretty normal to me."

"On the surface, yeah. But I'd seen him go blank a few times for no reason. Sitting at his desk, eyes glazed over, breathing heavy."

I had those same symptoms. But not from PTSD. From eating an entire pizza and twenty buffalo wings.

Miller continued, "And according to the Chief, he had bouts of paranoid schizophrenia. Thought people were following him. Thought someone bugged his house. It was recommended by the shrink that he should be on meds."

"Well, someone did strangle him. Maybe he had a right to be paranoid."

He didn't respond to this.

I prodded, "You have any idea who it could have been?"

He turned and glared at me.

Maybe he did think I was involved.

He turned back to the road, and I changed the subject to something more friendly. I asked, "So when you ask a girl to marry you a second time, after she's already called off the first engagement, what goes through your head?"

I watched as his hands flexed around the steering wheel. I brought my arms up slightly to protect myself. I didn't think he could kick me in the face while driving a car, but I wasn't taking any chances.

We drove another half mile in silence. He seemed to move past my Wheeler inquiry so I refreshed his memory.

"I mean, she's already broken your heart once. Then you get down on one knee again. Man, that takes guts."

He cut his eyes at me.

I wasn't done. "You must have been so excited. After rejecting you, she wanted you back, then she agreed to marry you. You guys can live happily ever after. Only..."

He slammed on the brakes.

I crashed forward against the seat belt, then smashed my head backward on the seat. My brain, still recovering from his kick, flickered like a bad strobe light.

When I regained my wits, we were parked next to my car.

I opened the door.

I didn't thank him for the ride.

On my exit, he cut his eyes at me and snarled, "Don't leave town."

"I won't," I said.

I had a case to solve.

Chapter 13

My brain has always worked best when my feet were pounding the pavement. I'm not sure if it was the kick of endorphins or that my body went into autopilot, but while running, cold cases had been cracked, text messages from women had been decoded, and the name of the actor in *Apollo 13* who wasn't Kevin Bacon or Tom Hanks had finally come to me.

I did a couple light stretches. Harold and May glanced up at me. They knew I was headed out.

"Sorry, guys. You can't come."

They both whined.

"I have to go running," I told them. "I have to get back into shape. I got my ass kicked yesterday." My jaw was still sore from Miller's kick. But not as sore as my pride.

Harold squealed.

"I know, it was embarrassing."

I picked him up and turned him over. I gave his little pot belly a rub and said, "We really have to start working on your core."

I set him down, then headed out. I started down the long dirt road, down the hill, through the puddle, and to the dusty country road. It was 8:30 a.m. and overcast.

The snapshots from the crime scene came swirling in. Nearly six months of Netflix and *Naked and Afraid* reruns had left my recall as withered as my forearms, and the images were low resolution. Far from the 4K I was used to seeing in my prime. I cascaded through the grainy images: the ransacked living room, Mike's open eyes—the small broken blood vessels spider webbing across his irises, the broken lamp on the floor, the angle of his feet on the carpet.

What was the perp looking for?

My gut told me that whoever killed Mike Zernan was searching for whatever it took Mike three days to get his hands on, whatever he intended on showing me. Proof of something to do with the Save-More murders.

It could have been a simple lump under the skin, suspicious but ultimately benign. Something along the lines of a misstep in the procedure, a lack of due diligence, or a mishandling of evidence. Something that wouldn't have had an effect on the outcome of the investigation.

Or it could have been something malignant. Something metastasizing, spreading from cell to cell, replicating, and with intent. Was it more than simply a revenge killing? Were there more people involved than just Lowry Barnes? What if Lowry had an accessory, someone driving, or someone who helped with the planning? They were as guilty as Lowry. And they were out running free.

Regardless, whatever it was, it was worth killing Mike over.

Then again, maybe I was getting ahead of myself. Maybe Mike's death had nothing to do with the Save-More murders. Maybe whoever killed him was simply looking for Mike's rare coin collection or a signed first edition. Maybe it was a Craigslist murder. A guy came to look at Mike's hot rod and got the sudden impulse to act out one of his dark fantasies. To strangle a man.

Only, Mike wasn't easy prey.

He was in his late fifties, but he was still in relatively good shape. Even shaking his hand, you could feel the underlying brute strength from his time in the military. Which is why I suspected Mike knew his attacker. It would be the only way someone could have snuck up behind him.

But in a small town, where everyone knew literally all two thousand people, this didn't narrow down the suspect pool much.

As far as suspects went, the only suspect on my list thus far was Chief Eccleston. Maybe Mike had something in his case files that proved some level of wrongdoing by the Tarrin Police Department.

I turned around on the country road and headed back. My legs were beginning to itch, a sensation I can only liken to the feeling you get when your feet begin to thaw after skiing. Only this time, it wasn't the cold, it was the cells of my legs reactivating after six months of hibernation.

I pushed the sensation away and found my way back to the case.

Suppose this accessory to the massacre, suppose he was still out there. Did Mike know who this person was? Were they the one who killed him? And what about Mike's mention of bugs?

In the twenty-four minutes I spent poking around his place, I searched high and low for any sign his house was bugged, but was unable to find anything. This wasn't to say the perp hadn't removed the bugs after killing Mike, which would have been the logical thing to do.

And what about what Miller said? That Mike wasn't stable. That he had PTSD and bouts of paranoid schizophrenia.

Was he just a crazy old coot?

My gut said no.

I trusted him.

Speaking of my gut, my stomach began to cramp, and I stopped.

I puked.

I'm not sure if it was a physiological reaction to the exercise or a psychological response to my working theory.

I wiped my mouth, then continued on for another quarter mile. That's when my arm started to tingle. But don't worry, it was my left arm, so yeah, I was having a heart attack.

I considered stopping, but decided I'd rather suffer a heart attack than ever get my ass kicked again. Thankfully, the tingling went away a few minutes later, and I started thinking about my next move in the case.

There wasn't a whole lot I could do. I'd already talked to the only witness. I had no way to see the case files. My only lead related to the Save-More murders had just been murdered himself. Even worse, I was considered a suspect in his death.

If I did anything, I would have to tread lightly.

~

I had three text messages. All are from the same number.

This is Jerry Humphries.

Heard you stopped by to see me at the bank the other day.

What can I do for you?

I texted back.

Hey. Just stopped in to say hello. Just moved here. There's a chance we might be cousins.

I didn't even have time to set the phone down before it chimed. He must have been bored.

Jerry: **What? Seriously?**

Me: **Yeah. Long story. Maybe we can grab lunch?**

Jerry: **What are you doing in an hour?**

Me: **Having lunch with you.**

Jerry: **Damn right.**

Me: **How about Dina's?**

Jerry: **How about we try to squeeze in a quick nine?**

Me: **Nine?**

Jerry: **Holes. Golf.**

Me: **Oh, right. I don't have clubs.**

Jerry: **I have an extra set.**

The last time I swung a golf club was with my dad a decade earlier.

Me: **Okay.**

Jerry: **There's a little course off County Road 34. Three miles north. We can grab some brats there. Let's shoot for noon.**

I told him I would see him there.

He texted back: **Booya.**

I already liked him.

Maybe I should get some shirts made.

Humphries Family Reunion.

Maybe not.

I played with the piglets for half an hour, then headed toward the course.

My stomach was uneasy. I would love to say that I was still recovering from my run, but I couldn't. I was nervous. I felt like I was about to go on a first date with Kate Beckinsale.

Loved you in Underworld.

I still have the outfit.

Check, please.

There were three or four cars in the parking lot. One was a Lexus hatchback. A man in a blue suit was sitting on the back bumper of the car switching out his shoes.

I walked toward the man, trying to mask how sore my legs were from my three-mile run. Paradoxically, they were simultaneously made of Jell-O and stiffer than a puberty boner.

The man pulled on a second shoe and glanced up.

"Thomas?"

I nodded and we shook hands.

Jerry Humphries was slim with thinning brown hair parted to the left. He looked like a politician masquerading as a banker, which I suppose many of them were.

Zing.

"You gonna golf in that suit?" I asked.

"Have to," he said with a chuckle. "I forgot to pack my golf clothes."

He shucked off his jacket and pulled his tie up and over his head. Then he pulled a bag of clubs out of his trunk and heaved them at me. I caught them, my thighs and calves spasming with the impact. "We're gonna get a cart, right?"

He laughed.

I guess not.

"I have to warn you," I said. "The last time I played golf, it was in a bar, and I ended up going in the lava sixteen times." I expanded on this, detailing how my Golden Tee avatar had also fallen into the lava and I was forced to put in six dollars to get him out.

He laughed, which was a good sign, since my sense of humor was "idiotic" according to one man at the Whole Foods, right before he asked me to "please stop putting watermelons in his cart."

"That's alright," Jerry said. "I'll give you some pops."

"Pops?"

"Strokes. I'll give you ten strokes."

I realized then that he wanted to bet. "How 'bout we just play a friendly game?" I hadn't even planned on keeping score.

He shook his head as if the thought of not betting was more absurd than getting a golf cart. Then he grabbed his clubs and walked briskly toward the small clubhouse. To his credit, he paid for both rounds. I thanked him, then asked how long he had before he needed to get back.

"An hour."

"We're gonna play nine holes in an hour?" When my father and I used to play, nine holes would take us two hours, sometimes three. And we had the luxury of a cart. Not to mention the well-endowed cart girl who came around every twenty minutes to drop off more Bud Lights.

"Don't worry, the course isn't very long. Mostly par threes with a couple par fours."

"I can handle that." I looked around and asked, "Where are the hot dogs?"

"Hole five."

I'd never heard of the grill not being at or at least near the clubhouse. "Hole five?"

"Yeah, hole five backs up to the Craisly farm. During the summer, one of their kids is usually out there with a grill."

"Usually?" I was starving. I hadn't eaten anything other than a protein shake.

"You guys are on the tee box," the old man behind the counter said.

Jerry slapped me on the back. "Let's go."

~

We decided to play skins. Five bucks a hole. He gave me a stroke on each hole but he could have given me three. After four holes, he had three pars and a birdie. I had a seven, two eights, and a thirteen.

Not only was I already into him for twenty bucks but I spent so much time looking for my ball in the thick, long underbrush that we didn't even have time to chat. And I had a rash on my legs. And I had a thousand little pricklies in my socks. And I was convinced a snake was stalking me.

Finally on the fifth tee box—the group golfing in front of us was still on the fairway, waiting on the group on the green—we got a minute to converse.

"Usually logjams around hole five," Jerry said. "But that's a good sign. Means the grill is up and running."

Thank God.

My blood sugar was getting low, and I was getting cranky. And I should mention it was the hottest, stickiest, buggiest day yet.

We took a seat on the bench near the tee box, and Jerry said, "So you think we might be cousins?"

My shoes were off, and I was picking the little tan thorns from my socks. "There's a chance," I said, pulling one and tossing it into the wind. "Your last name is Humphries, right?"

"Sure is."

"Harold Humphries was my grandpa."

"No shit?" He smirked. "I guess we are family."

"Did you ever meet him?"

"Once, maybe thirty years ago."

"How are you related to him?"

He was holding his driver between his legs and he tapped it against the grass as he thought. Finally, he said, "I think he was my dad's uncle."

It took me a moment to do the genealogical algebra. "So your grandpa was Harold's dad's brother?"

"That sounds about right."

"Did you know your grandpa?"

"He was around when I was really little, but I don't remember much. He swung his cane at me once when I stole a Werther's Original from the kitchen cupboard."

I laughed.

"What about your grandma?"

"I remember more about her, playing cards and doing crosswords, but they were both pretty old. My dad is fifteen years younger than his two sisters."

"Did the sisters have any kids?" I suppose these would be my cousins as well.

"Yeah, but my dad wasn't very close with either of them. They both moved to the East Coast for college and ended up staying there."

"So you're the only Humphries in Tarrin?"

"Me and my family."

I don't know why this shocked me. Most men in their mid-forties were married with children. Heck, most men in their mid-thirties were married with children. I was the exception. I was an eleven-year-old trapped in the body of a chubby thirty-five-year-old.

Jerry said, "I have two boys. Seven and four."

"Nice. What's your wife do?"

"She stays home with the kiddos."

"How long you been together?"

"About ten years." He paused, then added, "We separated a few years ago, but we worked through things."

I didn't pry, but I did say, "That's good to hear."

He said, "You said it was a long story about us being cousins?"

I gave him the diluted version.

A few minutes later, he said, "That's crazy, man."

"Yeah."

"And then he just up and left the farm to you?"

I grinned.

"You know what it's worth?" he asked.

"I have no idea," I said, not sure exactly why I lied.

He snapped his head to the right and said, "Finally! Let's hit."

I ambled up to the tee box.

"Keep your head down this time," he shouted.

I swung.

I did not keep my head down.

I topped the ball, and it went into the thick overgrowth.

"Nice shot," Jerry said.

I flipped him off and he laughed.

Just cousins being cousins.

Jerry got another par.

I lost three balls in the thick underbrush—which I was now terrified to wade into because of the snake—then spent four strokes in the sand. I ended up getting a whopping sixteen.

Yay.

Fun.

I was at DEFCON 2 crankiness when I saw the little girl manning the grill just on the other side of a low fence.

"Hiya, Gracie," Jerry called out.

"Hi, Mr. Humphries," she said with a big smile. She was probably twelve.

"You got any brats today?"

"Sure do. Just finished casing them a couple days ago."

My eyebrows furrowed, and I whispered to Jerry. "They make their own?"

"Of course."

I could smell the brats on the grill, and my stomach rumbled. I was the hungriest I'd been since being a hostage on a cruise ship.

"Are these pork brats?" I asked Jerry.

"Yeah."

"And pork is pig?"

"Yes, Thomas, pork is pig."

I'd eaten bacon on my BLT just the day before and thought nothing of it, so I wasn't sure why I was hesitating now.

"Do you have any burgers?" I asked.

The little girl shook her head. "Just brats today."

Jerry turned to me and whispered, "Don't tell me you don't eat pork or something. You don't look Jewish."

"I'm not."

"Good." He turned back to Gracie and said, "We'll take two brats."

She pulled two off the grill with tongs and slipped them into two hot dog buns. She handed one to me and said, "Ketchup and mustard are over there, and help yourself to a soda."

Jerry handed her a twenty and told her to keep the change.

We fixed up our brats and grabbed sodas. Barq's Root Beer for me and Pepsi for Jerry. I'd eaten many hot dogs, brats, and polish sausages in my day, but none had ever looked or smelled as divine as the one in my hand this second.

We made our way to the next tee box, and I said, "I gotta take a whiz."

Jerry swallowed down a big bite of brat and motioned toward some trees. "Just go over there."

I walked over to the trees and unzipped my pants. I didn't have to pee. I pulled the brat off the bun and tossed it into the brush. I couldn't eat it. All I could think about was Harold and May.

Little jerks.

I ate the bun, which still tasted pretty good from the brat juice, but it was a tease. I stuffed the last of the bun in my mouth as I returned and said, "Man, that brat was good."

"Told you."

We finished the last four holes. Jerry pared three and bogeyed one, shooting even par for the day. I got double digits on all four holes for a grand total of seven jillion.

I didn't have any cash on me, but I promised to give Jerry forty-five bucks the next time I saw him.

"We'll just run it back next time we play," he said, then drove off. He was in a rush to get back to work.

I was in a rush too. I drove as fast as I could to Dina's and sat down to a big fat burger.

~

When I returned to the farm, there was a package leaning against the front door. It was one of those orange-gold padded mailers. In lieu of my name, it simply read "Humphries Farm" in block lettering. The return address was Phoenix.

I tore the package open and pulled out the contents. It was a small notebook. A Moleskine. My sister had bought me a similar notebook when I started taking on cases with the FBI.

I thought back to what Mike Zernan said.

Give me three days.

Chapter 14

There was a stain on the front cover of the Moleskine, which had saturated the bottom half of the notebook. I lifted the notebook up and sniffed. It smelled faintly of coffee. Mike must have spilled an entire cup. Maybe even an entire pot.

The notebook couldn't have weighed more than ten ounces, but it felt heavy in my hand. Weighted by what was scribbled in the pages, which I was quite confident were all the notes Mike took over the course of his investigation into the Save-More murders.

My heart rate tripled as I flipped it open to the first page.

The page was filled with entries. Neat, block lettering. The first page was dated March 3rd, 2012. The top entry read:

JOSH / PACERS / -3 ½ / $50.

There was a small "L" scribbled next to it that had been highlighted in blue.

If I were looking in a mirror, I would have seen my jaw hanging to the side, looking detached.

The notebook didn't belong to Mike Zernan.

It belonged to a bookie.

I skimmed through the thousands of entries: names, dates, teams, odds, wagers, wins, and losses. Most of the losses were highlighted in blue, which I guessed meant the debt had been paid.

What was Mike telling me? Why had he sent me a bookie's notebook? Was one of the victims a bookie? Who did the notebook belong to? Did Mike think someone other than the manager of the Save-More was the target? Was Mike even the one who had sent the package?

I was brimming with questions. If Mike had sent the package, had gone through all the trouble to send me the notebook, why not add a little sticky note? Why not give me some direction?

Then again, Mike was paranoid about doing anything that might trip someone's alarm. Paranoid about doing anything that might get him killed. But Mike had done something that got him killed.

Was the notebook in my hand the reason he was dead?

If so, then there must be some evidence inside.

I picked up my phone and dialed Randall's number.

He picked up on the third ring. "Hey, boss."

"Hey, buddy."

"I got us a great deal on a used tractor, $13,500. And he said he'd give us $500 for the old one. Whaddaya think?"

"Let's do it."

He updated me on a few more farm purchases, then I said, "Actually, I'm calling about something else."

"What's up?"

"There's a game tonight, and I was hoping to get some action."

He laughed. "I knew I liked you."

"Is there anybody around here who runs a book?"

"There is."

"Can you put me in touch with them?"

"Could take me a couple minutes. I'll text you."

"Sounds good."

"Another weird question, just something I heard. Did one of the guys killed in those murders a few years ago, did one of them run a book?"

"Actually, yeah."

"Which one?"

"Will," he said. "Will Dennel."

I thanked him and hung up.

A couple minutes later, I received a text with a name and a phone number, though to be honest, I wasn't interested in who the current bookie was. At least not yet. I was interested in the former bookie, Will Dennel, who I was nearly positive had been the owner of the Moleskine notebook in my possession.

I flipped to the back of the book. There was a list of names, then amounts. Most had a line through them, which I guessed meant that the debt had been paid. However, there were five people with names and amounts that had not been crossed off.

Josh owed $440.

Ben owed $33.

Nelson owed $125.

Uncle Robbie owed $246.

And one more.

Fuzz.

Fuzz owed $83,000.

In all my years, I'd only heard *Fuzz* referring to one type of person. A cop.

Which meant that someone from the Tarrin Police Department was into Will Dennel deep.

Maybe even deep enough to have him killed.

~

"This is our latest and greatest," the young man at the cellular kiosk inside the Mexico Walmart said. "Samsung Galaxy S7 Edge."

He spent the next couple minutes telling me about all the cool stuff it could do.

"I don't think I need anything quite that fancy."

Although the virtual reality headset sounded pretty cool.

Hello, Kate.

"All I need is to be able to get on the internet." I almost added, "And I don't want the pesky cops three towns over to know what I'm searching."

He pointed to an aisle with a bunch of different phones and purchase cards—TracFone, NET10 Wireless, Virgin Mobile—and said, "Pretty much any of these phones are good for that."

He helped me pick out a phone—a low-end Samsung smartphone—then set it up.

I picked up a bunch of necessities while I was there, plus some fruits and veggies for blending. I also purchased some dumbbells. Then I spent the next twenty minutes at a copy center in the same complex.

Back in the car, the first search I did on my phone was for Thai food.

The second was for Will Dennel.

~

I could see why Jerry and friends periodically drove the twenty-five minutes to Mexico. The Thai was some of the best I'd ever had, albeit a bit spicier than I expected. My eyes watered after each bite, but I couldn't stop shoveling the noodles and chicken into my mouth.

There were over twenty thousand hits for Will Dennel—which wasn't surprising as it was a common name—and I searched "Will Dennel Save-More."

I clicked my way through a dozen results before discovering what I was looking for.

Will Dennel had a sister.

Bree.

There were several Bree Dennels on Facebook, but only one who lived in Missouri. Her profile picture was of a purple-haired girl holding a large cat. Her job was listed as graphic designer, and there was a link to a website. I clicked around her site, scrolling through her portfolio. Her stuff was above average, but not groundbreaking. Still, she appeared to be successful.

Her email and phone number were listed under the Contacts tab, and I punched her number into my phone.

She answered on the second ring.

I didn't beat around the bush. "I need to talk to you," I said, "about your brother."

~

She said she would come to me. She said she had to pick up some things in town anyhow. We agreed to meet at a small coffee shop in the same complex as the Thai restaurant.

While I waited for her to show up, I searched the internet for surveillance footage from the Save-More murders. There was none. Nor was I able to find any crime scene photos or the 911 call that Victoria had allegedly made. There were a few more articles about the murders, but I didn't learn anything that I didn't already know.

The web search for the Save-More murders a bust, I turned my investigation to Officer Matt Miller and his fledgling UFC career. There were several pictures of Miller with his shirt off and the guy was shredded. Not an ounce of fat on him. I watched three of his fights on my phone, cringing when he knocked out a guy with the same spinning back kick that he'd used on me.

Twenty-five minutes later, a young woman walked through the door of the coffee shop. She was clad in yoga pants, a small tank top, and now blue hair cut to her shoulders. I put her in her early twenties. She dropped a laptop bag on the chair opposite me and asked, "You want anything?"

You would never suspect she was meeting with a stranger to talk about her dead brother.

"I'm good," I told her.

She shrugged with one shoulder, then returned a few minutes later with a tall brown drink with extra whip cream. She took a big swipe of the whip cream with her tongue, then raised her eyebrows twice.

I think she was one of those rare breeds who felt so comfortable in their own skin that you couldn't help but admire them.

"So my brother, huh?" she said, plopping down in her seat.

I nodded.

"Out with it," she said. "I mean, you're handsome and all, but there's a guy at the Walmart who I'm dying to go hang out with."

"Is it Carl in electronics? Because I just hung out with him and let me tell you, he's something else."

"No, it's Billy. He's a checker. Works on Tuesdays."

"You're serious?"

She took a long sip of her drink. "Fuck yeah. I've been stalking him for like eight months now. I think he and his girlfriend are on the outs." She glided her hand away from her body and added, "Time for Bree to slide in."

I smiled. She reminded me of Lacy.

"How long was your brother a bookie for?"

"I think he started in high school. Just taking bets from his friends and stuff. Then he went to community college, here in Mexico, actually, and he started getting into it more seriously. He quit after a couple years—school, not bookmaking—then he moved back home and got a job at the lumberyard."

"Did your parents know he was a bookie?"

"My dad was one of his best clients." She laughed to herself, then said, "If my dad lost, he would pay up, but if he won, he wouldn't make Will pay, he'd make him come mow the lawn or do something else."

"To work it off?"

"Yeah."

"He ever have any trouble with other people not paying?"

"I think most people paid. But if they didn't, Will wasn't the type to go breaking kneecaps. He just wouldn't let them bet with him anymore."

I thought about the nickname Fuzz. "What about the police? Did they know he was the town bookie?"

"Yeah, everyone knew."

"They ever do anything about it?"

"Shit, no. Do you know how easy it is for someone to bet online these days? If you're gonna bet, you're gonna bet."

"So he was never arrested?"

"Not that I know of."

"You know if any of the cops bet with him?"

"Not sure. He didn't talk to me much about it."

"Were you guys close?"

She puffed out her cheeks.

"It's okay," I said.

She wiped away a tear and said, "He was just such a nice guy. He didn't deserve to get murdered."

I reached out and grabbed her hand. It wasn't premeditated, it was just what I would have done if Lacy was sitting across from me.

Pulling back my hand, I asked, "Do you think it's possible that your brother was the target of the murders?"

"No. He was just in the wrong place at the wrong time when that wacko Lowry came in."

"Did you know Lowry?"

"I knew of him, but I didn't know him."

"How old was Will?"

"Twenty-six."

"Did he know Lowry?"

"I don't think so."

"So he didn't bet with Will?"

"I think that would have come up."

"Come up?"

"With the cops. You know, during the investigation."

"Right. How many times did they interview you?"

"A few times."

"The Tarrin Police Department or someone else?"

"I only talked to the locals."

"You remember the name of the guy?"

"Uh, yeah."

I already knew.

Matt Miller.

"He's so hot," she said, waving a hand at her face.

"He's like five feet tall."

"I like the dimple in his chin."

"It's called an ass chin."

"Yeah, I like his ass chin."

I rolled my eyes, then asked, "You talk to anybody else?"

"Yeah, there was another guy. But it was like six months later."

"Mike Zernan?"

"Maybe."

I described him.

"Yeah, that was him." She sat up in her chair. "Wait, isn't he the guy who was just murdered?"

I nodded.

"Wait, do you think his death is connected to Will's?'

"I'm not sure."

She took a drink, and I said, "Can you like not tell Billy the checker about this?"

"I don't even know who you are."

I told her.

When I was finished, she said, "I want, no, I *need* to play with your piglets, like ASAP."

"I might be able to make that happen."

She finished her drink, and I told her to follow me to my car.

"We gonna have a quickie?" she asked, giving my butt a little slap.

"What would Billy think?"

"Yeah, you're probably right."

I opened the passenger door and reached into the glove compartment.

"I think you should have this." I handed her the Moleskine.

I'd spent twenty minutes copying every page of it at the OfficeMax. I didn't need it anymore.

She leaned forward and wrapped her arms around me. She sniffed a couple times and said, "Thank you."

~

Graham, no last name, was big and red. He had a cut-off T-shirt revealing muscled biceps, one of which had a barbed wire tattoo encircling it, which he must have had done when such things were still chic. A thick red beard, easily six inches long, engulfed his face and neck.

He was sitting at one of the outdoor tables at the Sonic Drive-In. He wiped his arm across his mouth as I approached.

"Heyya," I said.

Without saying a word, he pulled an envelope from his camo cargo shorts and handed it to me.

I flicked it open with my thumb.

Inside were five twenty-dollar bills.

"Nice bet," he said.

The previous day, I'd bet a hundred dollars on Game 3 of the NBA Finals. I'd bet on the Cleveland Cavaliers to cover the spread, which they'd more than done, winning by thirty points.

"Thanks," I muttered. "LeBron played pretty well." I hadn't seen the game, but I'd checked on my new phone earlier and he'd scored thirty-two points.

"Yep," Graham replied, then asked, "You want any action on the next game?"

"I'm not sure yet," I said, waving the envelope at him. "I might just enjoy my spoils."

He shrugged and tossed back a few fries.

It appeared we were done.

I turned to walk away, then swiveled back.

"Hey," I said, "I got a question for you."

He was unwrapping a burger and gave me a slight nod.

"Any cops ever bet with you?"

His beard cocked slightly. "Cops?"

"Yeah, you know, any *Fuzz*."

He chuckled lightly, then unfolded himself off the bench. He was far more imposing standing up than he'd been sitting down.

A red hulking Hillbilly.

"Why the fuck you so interested in who bets with me?"

He'd already given me the reaction I wanted. If cops didn't bet with him, if Fuzz meant nothing to him, he would have just laughed my inquiry off.

I said, "Small town and all, I was just curious."

"Well," he grinned, "take your curiosity and your fucking bets and shove them up your ass."

He reached out and snatched the envelope back from my hand. Then he calmly sat back down, unwrapped his burger, and began eating.

Chapter 15

"How long do you figure it will take to get rid of all that brush?" I asked.

Randall put both hands on his hips, gazing out at the 250 acres of overgrown farmland. It was 7:30 in the morning and there wasn't a cloud in the sky. According to my new smartphone, the temperature would get into the low nineties.

Since seeing Randall at the church revival, he had stopped by to take care of a couple of odd jobs: installing a new door on the farmhouse, fixing a leaking toilet, and repairing a hole at the back of the barn. But now it was time to farm.

Randall let loose a low whistle, then answered, "With just you and me doing it, probably a week, maybe two."

"That long?"

"We could hire a couple more people," Randall said, "get a couple more tractors going."

"Let's see how today goes."

"Alrighty." He cocked his head at the large tractor and said, "Why don't you drive first?"

"I've never driven a tractor."

"You know how to drive a stick shift?"

"I delivered pizzas in my buddy's Saab in college for a couple of nights."

"How did that go?"

"I ruined his transmission."

He laughed. "Well, good, because this is an automatic."

Attached to the back of the tractor was an eight-foot-wide Brush Hog. It was basically a giant lawn mower capable of cutting down the weed and bush jungle that had overtaken the land.

While I drove, Randall stayed behind, shoveling the cuttings into the back of his truck and trailer. He would then dump them in the wide expanse of dirt in front of the farmhouse where he said we could burn it.

It looked like backbreaking labor, and I decided we were going to need a couple more hands if we wanted to get this done before Thanksgiving.

Keeping my hands on the wheel, cha-chunking my way back and forth across the quarter-square-mile section Randall pointed out, I had plenty of time to think.

I was having a hard time connecting the dots from Mike Zernan's murder to the Save-More murders. It was like trying to get from New York to China but without a plane, boat, or car.

The biggest problem was Lowry Barnes.

He shot six people, killing five. There was no question about that. That was forged in steel. Then he killed himself. Ergo, he could not have killed Mike Zernan. That simple fact would not stop rattling around in my brain.

I said it out loud three times. "Lowry Barnes could not have killed Mike Zernan. Lowry Barnes could not have killed Mike Zernan. Lowry Barnes could not have killed Mike Zernan." Sometimes this leads to an epiphany. Today it did not.

However, I did continue talking to myself.

"Will Dennel was a bookie. Maybe Lowry Barnes bet with him, got in deep, then couldn't pay because he got fired from his job. But even if Will Dennel was the target, why did Lowry commit suicide? And how could this all be connected to Mike Zernan? Unless maybe someone at the Tarrin Police Department was also betting with Will. Maybe whoever *Fuzz* was found out Mike Zernan had taken Will Dennel's notebook and they knew their name would show up."

I nodded to myself.

"Maybe that's what Mike stumbled on. Maybe Mike wasn't even investigating the Save-More murders. Maybe he was trying to find out which cops were betting with Will. Maybe this pissed him off. Shit, maybe Chief Eccleston was the one betting. Maybe that's why Eccleston fired Mike. Told him if he stopped poking around, he would make sure he got his full pension—plus maybe even a little bonus. Then Mike keeps Will Dennel's notebook as collateral just in case Eccleston goes back on his word.

"Then Eccleston gets wind I'm over there talking to Mike. Maybe he's listening in, on one of those bugs Mike thought someone set up. Eccleston thinks Mike is just crazy enough to tell me everything and decides he needs to get that Moleskine. So he goes over there, strangles him, then ransacks the place."

I ran the simulation over in my head.

It was feasible, though far from probable.

I shook my head and noticed in my rambling I forgot to turn around. I'd been chugging along in a straight line for close to half a mile. I looked back over my shoulder and saw Randall off in the distance, hands on his hips, just watching.

I whipped the steering wheel around and cha-chunked my way back in his direction.

"Was Eccleston *Fuzz*?" I asked out loud. "Or it could have been anyone in the Tarrin Police Department. Someone who owed Will Dennel eighty-three thousand dollars. But Bree said Will was pretty lax when it came to collecting, that he didn't threaten people with baseball bats. But still, eighty-three thousand dollars. How had he even let someone get that deep into him? Maybe it was because the guy was a cop. Maybe Fuzz told Will that if he didn't let him keep betting, he would shut down his whole shop."

A minute later, I came abreast of Randall.

He was covered in sweat, leaning on the shovel, belly laughing. "Where were you going, buddy?"

"I got distracted."

"Thinking about Wheeler can do that."

My eyebrows jumped.

"Oh, I saw how you were looking at her." He chuckled. "And I don't blame ya for one second."

We both laughed, then decided we'd earned a break. We walked toward the farmhouse. There was a mountain of grass, weeds, and brush piled three feet high.

"Is it legal to burn that stuff?" I asked.

"No, but everybody does. We'll do it at night. Nobody will even notice."

We entered the house, and Harold and May scampered forward and pawed at both our legs.

Randall asked, "Why did you have me fix the pigpen it you're just gonna let them live in the house?"

"They like it in here."

"*You* like them in here."

I shrugged, then grabbed two beers.

Out on the porch, each of us resting in one of the new rocking chairs I bought the previous day, Randall said, "I just want to thank you for hiring me."

We clinked bottles, then I asked, "So were you born here in Tarrin?"

"I was born in Alabama. My dad moved us up here when I was twelve."

"What part of Alabama?"

"Montgomery."

"How was that?"

He took a long swig. "I was born in 1970, so I was brought up at the tail end of the Civil Rights Movement. My dad was a preacher and he was pretty active."

"What about your mom?"

"She died the year before we moved up here. Brain aneurysm."

I told him I was sorry, and he waved it off. "You said your dad was a preacher?"

"Still is."

It took me a moment to connect the dots. "Your dad? He wasn't—"

"Sure was."

His dad was the preacher at the revival. He had a little bit of white in his hair, but he didn't look nearly old enough to have a forty-six-year-old son.

"How old is he?"

"Sixty-three."

Without prodding, Randall said, "He was seventeen when he had me." He didn't make me ask, going straight into the story. "My mom was two years younger. Only fifteen. When she turned sixteen, they got married."

"You can get married at sixteen?"

"In Alabama you could. Still can, I think, if your parents consent, and both of theirs did. Hell, they demanded it." He paused, then said, "Anyhow, they had two more kids after me. Stayed married for eleven years until she died."

"Wow," I said. "It's rare those marriages work out."

He nodded.

I asked, "Why did your dad move you guys to Missouri?"

"A guy my dad knew from the Movement was opening a church up here and offered my dad the pulpit."

"So he's been preaching at the church—"

"For going on thirty-four years."

"That's pretty cool."

He smiled and took a swig of beer.

"How was it moving from the South to the North?" Before he could answer, I added, "Was Missouri part of the North?"

"The Mason-Dixon line actually goes right through the middle of Missouri, just north of St. Louis. During the Civil War, Missouri was claimed by both the Union and the Confederate, and sent soldiers to both camps."

"So it was both?"

"Geographically, yes. But emotionally, I'd say your average Missourian would say it's part of the South."

"How bad was the racism here, compared to Alabama?"

He scoffed, "That's like asking how the crab cakes are compared to Maryland."

"It was that bad down there?"

He nodded, but said nothing.

There wasn't anything he could say that could make a white boy from Seattle understand.

"What about in Tarrin?" I asked.

"It was a different sort of racism. White kid might call you a nigger, but they weren't gonna throw a rock at you when they said it."

"How many other black kids were there?"

"There were three other black kids who went to my middle school. About ten at my high school."

I punched him lightly on the shoulder and said, "That's enough for a basketball team."

He laughed, then said, "My dad's church was actually one of the biggest reasons more black people started moving to town."

"They all moved here so your father could yell at them?"

He chuckled.

I did my best impression of his father. "On these hot summer nights, keep your dicks in your pants you horny little beasts."

He slapped his knee and nearly spit up the last swig of beer he drank. When he composed himself, he said, "Pretty much." Then he was laughing again.

If Randall recorded his laugh as an MP3, I could listen to it for hours.

"How many black people went to your high school?" he asked.

"Probably a few hundred, but my school was pretty big, a couple thousand kids."

"You get along with the brothers?"

"I played basketball so I was buddies with a lot of them."

"You any good?"

"I had a pretty good jump shot. I walked on at the University of Washington, but I quit after the second practice."

"Why?"

"The coach called me a lazy sack of shit. Then I told him his wife thought I was all hustle."

He laughed again, then said, "So when you say quit, you mean—"

"I was impolitely asked to leave practice by two assistant coaches and a security guard."

"I bet you were a cocky little shit back then."

I grinned. "Thank God that went away."

He smacked me on the shoulder.

I asked, "Did you play any sports?"

"Football."

"Let me guess, offensive tackle."

He grinned, impressed. "Yep, and defensive end."

"You any good?"

"Full ride to Purdue."

"No kidding?"

He nodded.

"How'd you guys do?"

"Not great. Only had one winning season when I was there."

"The pros ever come sniffing?"

"Not really. I was small for a college offensive tackle, I would have been a fruit fly in the pros." He took a breath. "But I got a free education, got a degree in agricultural studies, then moved back home."

"Agricultural studies? You were always into farming?"

"Got into it when I was in high school. One of the assistant coaches had a farm and he'd pay some of us to come work it during the off-season and the summer." He glanced down at his hands and said, "I fell in love with the dirt."

"Is that what you did when you moved back?"

"Started working on my old assistant coach's farm full-time. I would help out with the football team too, as sort of an ad hoc offensive line coach. Did that for a long time, just saving as much as I could. When I was in my early thirties, I took out a loan, and bought a ninety-acre plot."

"Where was that?"

"About six miles east of here. Farmed my ass off for the next five or six years. Made a couple nice returns." His face fell. "Then I lost it."

I wanted to ask him what happened but I didn't want to pry. All I said was, "I'm sorry."

He puffed out his cheeks, took a breath, then said, "But if I hadn't lost the farm, I probably wouldn't have met Alexa."

"God works in mysterious ways," I said. I may have said this in his dad's voice.

He laughed, then said, "You got to stop doing that, man."

"Never."

I asked, "So you met Alexa?"

"Yeah, I went back to coaching the kids at the high school—was the freshman/sophomore head coach—and Alexa was teaching tenth grade. Got married a couple years later, and the twins came a few years after that."

I told him how absolutely beautiful his daughters were, then asked, "What happened with the coaching?"

"About five years ago, they got rid of the freshman/sophomore team. I could have stayed on as an assistant with the varsity team, but I was making more money picking up odd jobs." He downed the last of his beer, then said, "Speaking of that, we ought to get back to work."

~

We spent the next seven hours back in the fields, the two of us splitting time driving the tractor and shoveling the vast amounts of brush into the back of Randall's truck and trailer.

After the sun set, Randall and I returned to the rocking chairs. Along with the chairs, I'd also purchased a bug zapper and a bunch of citronella candles. But even together, the zapper and the candles were overmatched and the mosquitos descended on us. Randall didn't seem the least bit fazed by the swarming insects, immune to them after a lifetime in the Midwest. I swatted, slapped, and inhaled bugs until finally giving in and covering myself in a thick layer of noxious bug repellant.

There was a small cooler of beers between Randall and me, and we sipped brews under the fluorescent blue light of the bug zapper. The first beer, we talked about me. My life, my parents, my sister, a few of my cases. The second beer, we more or less sat in silence, both of us exhausted from a fourteen-hour day in the baking sun.

At one point, Randall took out his lighter and lit the mountain of brush in the dirt in front of the house.

The third beer, we watched it burn.

Chapter 16

The next two days were much the same. Randall showed up on my doorstep at 7:00 a.m. with two steaming cups of coffee. Then we spent the next fourteen hours switching off between driving the tractor and shoveling the brush. Then we drank beers and watched the pile blaze and settle to ash.

On Saturday, we took a half day.

For Mike Zernan's funeral.

The cemetery was on the far eastern edge of Tarrin, adjacent to sprawling mounds of dirt that Randall explained was where the kids went to BMX. As if on cue, a rider emerged over one of the hills, zoomed down a steep decline, then hit a jump, launching himself into the air.

It was a peculiar dichotomy, the cemetery and the BMX park so close to one another. One a final resting place. The other, perhaps the essence of living. And it probably made things super easy when a kid did a backflip and broke his neck.

Just drag him across the street.

The cemetery parking lot was overflowing. I was curious how many people would show up for Mike's funeral. It was a small town, and he had been a public servant for twenty years, but I was surprised at the number of cars.

I parked the Range Rover in the dirt overflow parking, and Randall asked, "Was it really necessary to bring them?"

Harold and May were both sitting on Randall's lap.

"They've been cooped up all day. They needed a little field trip."

"You're gonna end up in the loony bin."

"Says the guy wearing a white suit to a funeral."

"Hey," he said, "I look good. And this is my lightest suit."

To his credit, it was baking hot. To his discredit, he looked like he was about to host *Family Feud*.

A few days earlier, I bought a suit at the only store in town that sold such things. The measurements of the suit were depressing. My waist was once a 34. Now I was a 40.

Sigh.

Randall and I exited the car, both pulling our suit coats from where they were hanging on hooks in the backseat.

I pulled on the navy jacket, my internal temperature jumping ten degrees, then noticed through the window that Randall had left the passenger door open.

I ran around the car. Randall was struggling into his white linen suit coat, and I shouted, "The piglets!"

They were gone.

I whipped my head around and saw them. They were scampering between the grave stones, headed toward the large crowd gathered for Mike Zernan's funeral.

Uh-oh.

I sprinted after them.

The assemblage was close to a hundred people. There were seats for fifty, then another fifty people were standing. Mike's casket split the crowd in half, situated next to a large mound of dirt that would cover his casket after it was lowered into the ground. A small lectern was set under the shade of a birch tree, where a reverend stood speechless. He, like everyone else gathered, watched in stunned silence as two little, funeral-crashing piglets found their way to the large pile of dirt and began rolling around in it.

OMG.

I watched as a couple people attempted to wrangle them, but the two piglets darted away in a game of chase.

By the time I pushed through the crowd, May had her teeth clamped down on a man's pant cuff and was playfully trying to rip them off his body. The man was gently trying to pull her off but Harold was taking great offense to this and squealing at him loudly.

My cheeks rosy with embarrassment—not to mention the hundred-yard sprint—I leaned down and attempted to pry May off the man's pants.

"I'm so sorry," I muttered over and over again.

Finally, after what seemed like two eternities, May released her death grip on the man's pants, and I picked her up.

I turned to look for Harold and saw a woman holding him.

Wheeler.

She was wearing a black skirt and a gray blouse. Her hair was pinned up, and she had a dash more makeup on than usual. Had I not been in the midst of the third most embarrassing moment of my life, I would have told her how beautiful she looked. Shaking her head lightly, she asked, "Did you really bring your piglets to a funeral?"

"They were supposed to stay in the car," I stammered. "Randall let them out."

Speaking of Randall, he was leisurely making his way toward the group, in no apparent hurry to bask in my humiliation.

I turned back to the man whose pants May ruined and told him how sorry I was. It took a moment to register he was the same guy who I sat next to at Dina's Dine-In my first day in town. The farmer with the Carhartt jacket, the thick mustache, and the callused hands.

He waved me off with a smile. "You think that's the first time I've had a piglet chomping at my pants? Hell, happened to me just last week." Everyone within earshot laughed. He gave me a soft pat on the shoulder, then gave May a pet on the head. "You got a strong bite there, princess."

She oinked.

Then he turned to Harold in Wheeler's arms and said, "And you, way to stick up for your sister. I'd go into battle with you any day, buddy." He gave Harold an affectionate rub on the snout.

My cheeks slowly returned to their natural color. The blossoming crowd was still gazing at us, and I noted some familiar faces: Chief Eccleston, Matt Miller, and the other deputies dressed in their blue uniforms; Annie from Kim's Home Goods; and Victoria Page.

Officer Miller sneered in my direction. It was the first time I'd seen him since he kicked the shit out of me. If I'd seen him in any other situation, I would have given him the Ice Man chomp, but the piglets and I already caused enough of a scene, not to mention that ever since he kicked me, my practice chomps were making a weird clicking noise.

"Alrighty, folks," the reverend said from behind the lectern, "let's get things back on track here."

Slowly people turned their attention back to him.

Wheeler and I moved to the outskirts of the group where Randall was just approaching.

"Thanks for your help," I said to Randall.

"Not my pigs," is all he said in reply.

Touché.

Randall gave Wheeler a quick side hug. Wheeler smiled and said, "Nice suit."

He winked at me and said, "See."

I pondered taking the pigs back to the car, but they both seemed exhausted from their prison break and were comfortable being held.

The reverend was speaking, and I tuned in. Most likely, he was a reverend at one of the churches, and he spoke of life and death. I'd been to enough funerals in my short life that I could have paraphrased the various psalms, scriptures, and epithets he relayed.

This made me think about Harold's funeral. I wasn't sure if I felt guilty for missing it or not. Knowing Harold, he would have been tickled pink that I skipped it, driving to the farm instead. Still, missing it nagged at me.

I shook the thought away and tracked my eyes over the crowd. Chief Eccleston was near the lectern facing me. I assumed he would be next to speak. As if sensing my gaze, his eyes moved to mine.

I took one of May's little hooves and waved it at him.

He didn't respond.

Next to him was a woman I'd never seen in person, but whom I recognized from the newspaper and the many campaign signs littered throughout town. Tarrin Mayor, Paula Van Dixon.

She was wearing a black pantsuit. Her face was extreme and angled, as were the gold spectacles riding low on her nose. She reminded me of Meryl Streep, and I put her in the same age bracket.

On the other side of the gathering, clad in a low-cut black dress, was Caroline. I'm not sure what the acceptable amount of cleavage is at a funeral, but whatever it was, Caroline exceeded it by two handfuls.

Unlike Chief Eccleston, Caroline was already glancing in my direction when I looked her way. She gave a soft wave with one of her hands. I gave a light nod in return, then looked away. Though to be perfectly honest, I would have stared a few seconds longer had Wheeler not grimaced in my peripheral.

The reverend wrapped things up, then he introduced Chief Eccleston.

Eccleston waddled behind the podium and cleared his throat. The sun glistened off his blistering scalp. He spent the next few minutes talking about what a senseless crime Mike's murder was, that it was a petty robbery gone wrong, and that they were working tirelessly to find and apprehend the perpetrator. It was more press conference than eulogy.

He then told a couple stories about how great a fisherman Mike was, how he caught the biggest trout the Chief had ever seen. Then he said, "Mike never married, never had any children—the citizens of Tarrin were his children, his family. He felt a need to protect them, from themselves and from others. As most of us are well aware, Mike suffered from mental illness in the last several years. A combination of PTSD—possibly brought on by his military service in the Gulf War— and bouts of paranoid schizophrenia. But we shouldn't let the last few pages of a man's life undo a lifetime of good. He was a great man and he will be greatly missed."

Eccleston stepped down, and the reverend asked if anyone else wanted to speak.

No one did.

The reverend began speaking again, and without thinking, I handed May to Randall and started toward the front. I made my way up to the lectern and gently pushed the reverend aside.

It was like when Kanye stole the microphone from Taylor Swift at the Grammy's, but judging by Wheeler's gaping mouth, much, much worse.

"I'd like to say a few words," I said.

The many faces staring back at me were a combination of amusement, curiosity, and bewilderment. I overheard one woman near the front whisper, "Is that the same guy who brought the pigs?"

Yes, ma'am, I am.

I hadn't anticipated speaking, but I felt it was my duty to make sure people knew that Mike might have had some degree of mental illness, but he wasn't a liar.

"Most of you don't know me. My name is Thomas Prescott. I recently moved into the Humphries Farm." I paused for a breath, then said, "I only met Mike once. We only chatted for about an hour. Mostly we talked about the Save-More murders."

There was a collective shift in the crowd. Everyone seeming to rock back on their heels simultaneously. Even Randall, as sturdy as humans came, seemed unsteady on his feet.

I had intended on telling everyone that Mike Zernan's mental illness diagnosis was coaxed out of a psychologist by Chief Eccleston because Mike wouldn't let the Save-More investigation go. That Mike had every reason to be paranoid. And that contrary to what the Chief said, it wasn't a robbery gone wrong. That Mike's death was connected to the Save-More murders. That the man who just spoke so lovingly about their fishing trips together was hiding something from all of them.

But as I looked out on the faces, I could see these people didn't care. The Save-More memories were too painful. There was nothing I could say that could possibly justify bringing those memories to the surface.

It wasn't the somber look on Victoria Page's face at my mention of the Save-More murders, or even the nearly audible gulp by the farmer whose pant leg May attacked. It was Sarah Wheeler Lanningham. From even thirty feet away, I could see her bottom lip trembling.

Who was I to come into these people's town and throw around wild unsubstantiated theories and accusations? There might be a time when these people would have to come to terms with the unresolved past, and I might very well be the conduit, but now wasn't the time.

I glanced at the Chief. His eyes were narrowed. I could sense him daring me to continue, almost threatening that if I thought I was an outsider now, I would find myself on the other side of an invisible dome if I uttered the word Save-More one more time.

I broke my gaze with the Chief, then said, "Anyhow, Mike said he'd never seen a town come together like your town did after that horrific crime. He said that although it was the worst time in Tarrin's history, he'd never been prouder to call himself one of you." I forced a smile, then said, "I just thought he'd want everyone to know that."

Then I stepped down.

Chapter 17

It took Randall and me three weeks to cut down the 250 acres of brush. It was late June and the backbreaking labor combined with the warm Missouri afternoons—not to mention a half-hour workout with the dumbbells each night—and I'd shed ten pounds.

As for Harold and May, for every pound I lost, they each gained two. They had both tripled in size—Harold and May were now eating a diet of corn meal plus some fruits and veggies—turning into little porkers and taking up more of the bed's real estate each night.

Randall and I decided to take a couple days off before we started tilling the soil, a task that hopefully would only take us a week. And presently, I was enjoying a long run and listening to a playlist Lacy sent me.

In the time since Mike Zernan's funeral, I had limited interaction with the community of Tarrin. When I did go into town, to grocery shop or buy feed, I could feel the looks, sense the whispers: *that's the guy from Mike Zernan's funeral who was talking about the Save-More murders…and whose pigs desecrated a mound of dirt.*

As for the investigation into Mike's murder, according to the last article I read on the *Tarrin Weekly* website, they were still looking into a number of different leads. If I was one of those leads, they were keeping me in the dark. I kept waiting to be pulled back into the station for another round of questioning, but it never happened.

Which meant the Chief never really thought I had anything to do with Mike's death. Or they were just biding their time and the entire Tarrin gestapo was going to crash through my front door in the middle of night.

Time would tell.

As for my actions the past few weeks, I'd flipped through the copied pages of Will Dennel's notebook a half dozen times, but found no anomalies. Other than that, I'd done little in the way of investigating. After the funeral, Chief Eccleston had taken me aside and threatened to arrest me if I so much as sniffed in the direction of Mike Zernan's murder investigation, and I didn't doubt his sincerity.

With that said, the threat of arrest had never stopped me before. Why was it stopping me now?

I sighed.

Who was I kidding?

I knew exactly why I didn't want to look into the murders.

Wheeler.

The look on her face when I brought up the murders at the funeral.

I didn't want to hurt her, to make her relive any more of that pain.

There was a loud chirp in my ear, and I stopped. It took me a moment to realize it was the sound of an incoming text message. As I pulled the phone from my pocket, I felt myself hoping the message was from Wheeler.

It wasn't.

It was from Will's sister, Bree.

Her text was four words long. Four words that would change the entire course of my investigation.

The notebook isn't Will's.

~

"What do you mean the notebook isn't Will's?"

She didn't answer. She was too busy playing with Harold and May. She'd gone bonkers when she first saw them and leapt from her car.

"Bree!" I shouted.

She stopped petting them and looked up. She was wearing nearly the same outfit as before, yoga pants and a halter top, but today with a tan military jacket.

"The notebook, Bree. The notebook."

"Oh, right." She reached into her car and grabbed the notebook off the passenger seat. She tossed it to me and said, "It's not his."

"How do you know?"

She hefted May up with a grunt, holding her like the gigantic baby she was, then said, "Because, dillhole, I know what my brother's hand-writing looks like, and that's not his."

I flipped the book open.

She added, "It's almost exact, even down to the columns and every-thing. It's just not his handwriting. He didn't write in block lettering. And it's too neat."

"And," Bree said, using May's front hoof to wave at me, "that book isn't four years old."

I closed the book and gave it a long survey. The cover was tattered, the pages starting to yellow, the large coffee stain permeating nearly half the book. It looked aged, beaten.

But Bree was right, the book wasn't old. It was made to *look* old.

I said, "Why are you just telling me now?"

"I didn't really look at it after you gave it to me. I mean, it was a nice thought, you giving me my brother's notebook and all. But, I mean, I have a bunch of his other stuff that means a lot more."

"But you cried when I gave it to you."

She squished her face together, squinted, and sniffed.

"You were faking?"

"You totally thought you were giving me something priceless. I didn't want to take that away from you."

In a weird way, this was really sweet, and I was again reminded of how much she was like Lacy.

I let out a long exhale, then asked, "You want to stay for dinner?"

"Can't. Got a date with Billy the checker." She smiled, then added, "Well, not exactly a date with Billy. He's got a date with his girlfriend—at least according to his girlfriend's Snapchat—and I'm gonna listen in."

"You need therapy."

"Probably."

"How are you gonna listen in?"

"I have my ways."

"Okay, call me when you get arrested."

"Will do."

She kissed both the piglets on the snouts, told them she loved them and that they were both very special, then hopped in her little car and peeled away.

~

I sat down at the dining room table and stared at the notebook, taking a moment to process everything I just learned: 1) the notebook wasn't Will's, and 2) it was made to look like it was older than it actually was.

"Why did you send me this, Mike?" I said out loud.

Then it hit me.

It hadn't taken Mike three days to find what he was looking for, it had taken him three days to *create* it.

Mike must have spent three days creating a replica of Will Dennel's notebook. He filled over one hundred and twenty pages with entries. It must have taken him thirty hours. Then he went through the trouble of making it look as though it was four years old. Beat it up. Put it in the dryer. Spilled coffee on it. Probably dragged it behind his friggin' truck. Then he popped it in the mail with an Arizona return address.

But why? Why not just send the real notebook?

For the entries to look exactly how Will did them, Mike must have had access to the real notebook.

What was he trying to tell me?

I'd spent countless hours poring over each page of the notebook looking for hidden messages in the margins or even within the bets themselves, but I hadn't noticed anything.

I flipped open the book and gazed at the top entry:

JOSH / PACERS / -3 ½ / $50.

Then the next three:

PHIL S. / CELTICS / +4 / $25.

JENNY / BRUINS / +130 / $25.

MORRIS / STANFORD BB / -12 / $100.

I continued going through pages. Two hours later, I'd found nothing.

Zip.

I thought back to the padded mailer the Moleskine had come in. I'd only given it a cursory glance, much more concerned with the contents it held.

I dug the orange-gold mailer out of the trash and surveyed it. The return address was written in block lettering, an address in Phoenix. Then there were ten stamps, all US Flag Forever Stamps, in the top right corner. It was postmarked June 7th from the post office in Mexico.

I considered this for a moment. I'd first gone to visit Mike on Saturday, June 4th. I'm guessing it had taken Mike two days to copy the notebook and make it appear worn and aged, then on Monday night he drove the thirty minutes to Mexico and dropped it off at the post office self-drop. Later that night he was killed. Then the package was picked up on Tuesday, postmarked, then made its way to my doorstep the next day, Wednesday, June 8th.

The timeline fit.

But it didn't tell me much, other than the fact that Mike Zernan was being extremely cautious.

I glanced down at the mailing address: HUMPHRIES FARM, TARRIN, MO 64607.

Like the return address, everything was written in block lettering.

On closer examination, there was something slightly odd about the word TARRIN. The second "R" in the word was only about two-thirds the height of the first "R."

It was only noticeable because the rest of the letters were so uniform.

Almost too uniform.

I thought back to what Bree had said about the handwriting.

It's too neat.

I bit the inside of my cheek and made my way back to the table and the Moleksine. I opened it up and slowly, moving my finger over each number, letter, and symbol, I looked for any discrepancies in height.

It was painfully slow.

One page.

Five pages.

Seven pages.

Twelve pages.

Nothing.

Not a single anomaly.

Ten more pages.

Nothing.

I was on the twenty-seventh page of the notebook and I was dangerously close to throwing in the towel. I traced my finger over the third-to-last entry on the page.

PAUL / ST. LOUIS CARDINALS / -135 / $75.

I smiled.

The last "L" in Cardinals was slightly smaller than all the other letters.

"You sneaky sonofabitch," I muttered with a smile.

I continued flipping through pages. I was starting to think it was a fluke when I found a second height discrepancy.

MORGAN / HOUSTON ROCKETS / +150 / $100.

The "U" in Houston was distinctly smaller than all the other letters around it.

I pushed forward in my chair a few inches.

May and Harold pawed at my legs. They must have sensed my rising adrenaline.

Six pages later, there was another entry, this time the "N" was slightly smaller.

It took me another hour of combing through all the entries. There were seven letters in all that stood out: L-U-N-H-I-L-L.

I pushed back in my chair. My hands were shaking.

Lunhill Corporation.

Big Biotech.

And the most hated company in the world.

Chapter 18

I didn't know a whole lot about Lunhill, but my sister, who became extremely food-conscious after she was diagnosed with MS, and rightfully so, mentioned them a few times.

GMOs are destroying the planet, Thomas!

Lunhill is poisoning people, Thomas!

You have no idea how fucked up this corporation is, Thomas!

They are the most hated company in the world, Thomas!

She'd even gone to a couple anti-Lunhill protest rallies when we were living in Maine.

I searched "Lunhill" on my phone and spent the next hour reading everything I could find.

In a nutshell, Lunhill was an agrichemical and agricultural biotechnology corporation. They had been around for more than a hundred years, starting out as a chemical company in the early 1900s. At some point in the 1980s, they turned their focus to biotechnology, and in the last thirty years had become the leader in genetically modified organisms.

Controversy followed them at every step, from their involvement in the creation of Agent Orange during Vietnam; to being the leading producer of saccharine in the 1930s; to DDT, one of the most dangerous insecticides ever created; to a horrible dioxin spill that destroyed an entire town; to their glyphosate-based herbicide Spectrum-H; to most recently, their Spectrum-H(R)—Spectrum-H *resistant*—line of genetically modified seeds.

According to Lunhill, they were saving the world.

According to most of the world, they were destroying it.

Many people believed genetically modified organisms (GMOs)

were making people sick and Big Biotech firms, specifically Lunhill, were suppressing data that showed GMOs cause harm. Others felt Lunhill was going so far as to deliberately cause food shortages to promote the use of genetically modified food.

There were several other allegations, including Lunhill's incestuous relationships with government agencies like the Food and Drug Administration (FDA) and the Environmental Protection Agency (EPA). An unprecedented number of Lunhill employees either worked at the FDA or EPA before they were hired or went on to work at the FDA or EPA after working for Lunhill.

Then there was the Lunhill Protection Act, signed into law by President Barack Obama, which essentially gave biotech companies like Lunhill immunity in federal court. The bill stated that even if future research showed GMOs caused significant health problems, cancer, infertility, birth defects, kidney or liver damage—anything really—the federal courts no longer had any power to stop their spread, use, or sales.

My favorite of all the accusations against Lunhill was that they had banned GMOs from their own cafeteria while promoting them for sale and consumption by the public.

All science mumbo jumbo aside, most disturbing was the fact that Lunhill spent millions of dollars each year to strike down GMO labeling laws even though the vast majority of the world supported such laws and wanted to know what was in their food.

Why didn't Lunhill want people to know their food contained GMOs?

I made a mental note to keep this in mind the next time I went to the Harvest Food and Market.

Lacy had mentioned they were the most hated company in the world, and I wondered if this was hyperbole or gospel truth. According to a number of different websites, it was closer to the latter. Though Lunhill wasn't always ranked number one, they were usually in the top three, surrounded by the likes of BP, Dow Chemical, Haliburton, Bank of America, and Bayer.

But get this, though Lunhill might be a global company, they were based less than a hundred miles from Tarrin, just outside of St. Louis.

"Shit," I swore under my breath.

Still, their proximity didn't explain their connection to the Save-More murders.

I Googled, "Lunhill and Tarrin, MO."

There were several hits, but only one that caught my eye.

Save-More Victim Worked at Lunhill.

I clicked on the link.

It was from a blog called *GMOs, Guns, and the Uprising.*

It read:

November 17, 2012

Last month, there was a horrific massacre in the small Missouri town of Tarrin, population just over two thousand. A disgruntled ex-employee returned to the grocery store he worked at and took his revenge on the manager who fired him, as well as five other individuals (there was a sixth, one lone survivor). Lowry Barnes, a convicted felon, had legally—yes, legally—acquired a semi-automatic pistol just the week before. Nice work, Show-Me state. Show Me just how fucking easy it is to get a gun. Anyhow, one of the five who were killed had worked for the Lunhill Corporation.

Forty-seven year-old Neil Felding worked for the Lunhill Corporation for nearly twenty-two years. He was one of the lead scientists on a number of their big hitter projects, including possibly their worst Frankenseed creation, Bt-corn, which has been genetically modified to produce its own insecticide. Only it doesn't stop producing that fun insecticide after little Joey eats his taco shell, and two years later he gets colon cancer. Yes, this is happening, people. Here's the link: http://www. medikjournal.com/2349484

Anyhow, three weeks before his death, Neil Felding stepped down from his position at Lunhill after a heated quarrel in the corporate cafeteria with Lunhill CEO, David Ramsey.

Yes, THE David Ramsey.

AKA Vader himself.

One can only wonder what the argument was about. Had Felding had a change of heart? Had he decided to turn his back on the Dark Side? Had he decided to join the Rebellion?

But because of one stupid asshole and a state with possibly the most lax gun laws in the known universe, we'll never know.

I set my phone down on the table.

There was only one word on my mind.

Whistle-blower.

What if Neil Felding uncovered something mind-blowing, something he felt the public had a right to know about? Then he confronted his boss, this David Ramsey, in the cafeteria. There was a heated argument, and Neil stepped down. Now maybe it was just semantics, but usually when you verbally assault your boss—at least from my experience—you don't "step down," you're "fired." But then again, maybe the CEO begged Felding to stay. Maybe Felding knew too much for this Ramsey guy to let him go.

With a company like Lunhill, Felding would have been forced to sign all sorts of non-disclosures with likely heavy repercussions should he break them. If Felding leaked anything, it would have been sure to cripple him financially.

But what would stop Felding from leaking whatever he knew anonymously?

Is this what Mike Zernan thought, that Neil Felding was the real target of the Save-More murders? Is that why he sent me the notebook with "Lunhill" as the clue? Did he think Lunhill was behind it?

I ran my fingers through my hair and thought about the theory that was taking shape.

Neil Felding was about to blow the whistle on Lunhill. Something big, something groundbreaking. And coming from Felding, one of their top-dog scientists for more than twenty years, it would carry unquestionable validity. It would shake Lunhill to the core. It would cost them millions, maybe even billions.

So they (Lunhill) need to get rid of Neil Felding.

But if Felding gets murdered or has an accident so close to his stepping down, it will look suspicious. A good investigator—like Mike Zernan or yours truly—might even trace it back to Lunhill. They would need Felding to go away, but it couldn't look like he was the target—just that he was caught in the line of fire.

But how do they do this?

I smirked.

Where is the only place in a small town everyone is going to go at some point?

"The grocery store," I said out loud.

Somehow Lunhill learned about Lowry Barnes, a felon who was just fired from the grocery store. They get to him. Offer him money, threaten his family, or both.

For the first time, I thought about Lowry Barne's family. He had a wife and two kids. Where were they now?

I made a mental note to find out.

Anyhow, Lowry Barnes agrees to do it, to kill Neil Felding but make it look like it is a revenge murder and Felding was simply in the wrong place at the wrong time.

I thought back to what Victoria Page had said, how Lowry Barnes had come into the Save-More just a few seconds after Neil Felding.

My head unconsciously began to nod up and down. Maybe this was plausible after all. Maybe this wasn't science fiction.

Lowry does the deed. Then he makes his getaway. The police find him in his car on the side of the road where he'd supposedly killed himself. But what if he hadn't?

What if he was there to meet someone? Maybe to get his money. And they overpowered him, shot him in the temple, and made it look like a suicide.

"Holy shit, Mike," I said. "You could have this right."

I wondered what Mike stumbled on to make him think this. And if he thought this, why would the Tarrin Police Department and Chief Eccleston not want this to come out?

Did they have ties to Lunhill?

I would have to find out.

Regardless, there was still one giant piece missing. Lunhill was a multibillion-dollar corporation. They spent millions on lobbyists, they spent millions on lawyers, but if my theory was correct, then they also employed murderers.

I searched "Lunhill and murder" on my phone. There was only one article that contained both words. It was titled "Lunhill tied to Elite Murder Squad, Blackwater."

"No way," I said, staring at my phone.

Blackwater.

Them I knew.

In my decade-long tenure with a number of different law enforcement agencies, I'd heard rumblings about the private military for hire. Founded by a former Navy SEAL in the late nineties, Blackwater provided contractual security services for the federal government, including a $250-million contract with the CIA. They were infamous for a 2007 incident when a faction of Blackwater's employees killed seventeen unarmed civilians in Iraq.

According to the article, Lunhill and the controversial security firm were in bed together, or as they put it, "Lunhill contracted with the shadow army in order to protect the Lunhill brand, to develop an acting intel arm of the company, and to collect intelligence on anti-Lunhill activists, politicians, and competitors."

No wonder Mike Zernan was so paranoid. He must have feared this *shadow army* was listening to his every word and watching his every movement.

I thought back to the ligature marks on Mike Zernan's neck.

The garrote.

A military weapon.

Chapter 19

Lunhill headquarters was located on the outskirts of St. Louis, a little over an hour drive from Tarrin. It resembled a college campus, and not just because of the twenty activists picketing on the sidewalk in front of the Lunhill Corporation sign. They were all ages and races. They held signs and chanted.

I read a few of the placard signs as I drove past.

Protect the Land.

Protect our Farmers.

Stand against Lunhill.

No One Should Own a Patent on Mother Nature.

I am not an Experiment.

Quit Trying to Get in my Genes.

Lunhill = Evil Seed of Corporate Greed.

Geez Louise.

These guys really were hated.

I drove down a long expanse of road until I came to a sprawling building of glass and sharp angles. There were over a hundred cars in the parking lot, but I expected more considering Lunhill employed close to twenty thousand people. But then again, the company had offices all over the world.

A minute later, I pushed through the glass doors and into a wide atrium. I wasn't surprised to see two security guards manning a metal detector. One was older and graying. The other, young with a wispy blond goatee.

They scrutinized me as I approached, my handsome mug not being one of the hundred they saw on a daily basis.

"Hey, fellas," I said.

"You need an ID badge," Wispy Goatee said, "or a visitor's badge."

"How about this badge?" I quipped.

It's funny how people react when they realize you work for the FBI. Or had worked for the FBI. Or had stolen the badge of someone who worked for the FBI.

Both men's backs straightened.

I handed Old Gray the badge, hoping he wouldn't look too hard at the picture—I was a decent looking guy, but Todd Gregory had been pretty to a fault—and notice that although Gregory and I had similar hair and eyes, it wasn't me in the picture.

After a moment, he said, "Go right on through, Agent Gregory."

I walked through the metal detector, the light blinking green, and the guard handed back the badge.

Easy peasy.

Technically, I just committed a federal crime and possibly an even bigger ethical one. I impersonated an FBI agent. A *dead* one. One who would most likely be alive had a severely pissed off serial killer not been exacting his revenge against me three years earlier.

Sorry, *Turd*.

Anyhow, I had no doubt the security guards made a call alerting someone to my presence and I wasn't shocked when a striking woman stepped off the elevator and headed in my direction.

She was clad in a pencil skirt and a flowing white top. An executive. She reached out her hand and said, "Welcome, Mr. Gregory. I'm Allison Daniels, head of PR."

We shook.

"What brings you to Lunhill Corp?" she asked.

That was a good question. I didn't want to play my hand too early so I went with, "I was in the area and just hoping for a tour."

She scoffed, though she attempted to hide it as a cough, and said, "We don't really do tours here."

"Great, then I'll be your first."

She reached out, grabbed my elbow and attempted to turn me back toward the entrance. "I think maybe you are confusing us with the St. Louis Science museum."

As I may have mentioned previously, I don't like having my arm grabbed.

I shook off her hand and said the two words that not only make people's butts pucker, but are the skeleton key to 99.9 percent of the world. "Actually ma'am, this is a matter of *national security*."

If I was already in deep, I was now in the Mariana Trench.

Allison rose two inches in her heels. "Are we in danger?"

"There's no immediate threat, but there have been some rumblings. I was sent out here to get a better lay of the land and see up close what's happening behind these walls."

"Oh, well, I guess I can get someone to show you around."

"That would be great."

She told me to sit tight, then headed back up the elevator.

I twiddled my thumbs for two minutes, then the elevators opened and a young man stepped out. He had glasses, a white shirt that was half untucked, and a half-eaten sandwich in his hand.

"Hi, I'm Brian," Brian the twenty-five-year-old virgin said, his mouth half-full of egg salad.

"Hi, Brian."

"I, um, guess, I'm like supposed to show you around or something."

I was curious if Allison had told Brian that I worked for the FBI, but it appeared he was under the impression I was merely your average Joe.

I forced a smile.

He took another bite of sandwich and said, "So, um, like what do you want to see?"

I was overcome with a fatherly instinct to admonish him for talking with his mouth full, to tell him to tuck his shirt in, and maybe spank him.

"How long have you worked here?" I asked.

"Like, um, three days."

I glanced around until I found one of the many security cameras on the walls and glared into it for whoever was watching.

Then I turned back to Brian and said, "Lead on."

~

I followed Brian into the elevator. He hit the button for the third floor. Then he asked, "So, what exactly do you want to know?" He finished his sandwich, but there was a big piece of yolk on the side of his mouth.

I scratched at the side of my mouth. Once, twice, three times. Brian didn't react.

I said, "You have egg on your face."

He forced a laugh, then wiped it away.

The elevator stopped, and I followed him into a gray-tiled corridor. I still hadn't answered his question and I said, "I really just want to know the basics about what goes on here."

"Do you know much about the company?"

"Just what I've read."

"So you pretty much think Lunhill is the evil face of corporate greed and that we are silently trying to kill everyone on the planet."

"Pretty much."

"Well, we'll see if I can change your mind a little."

"Challenge accepted."

He pointed down the corridor and said, "Down there is where most of the science takes place."

"Is that what you do?"

He shook his head. "I work in sales."

Of course he did.

I said, "For the past three days."

He flashed a toothy grin.

I asked, "What made you want to work here?"

His brow furrowed as he gathered his thoughts. A moment later, he said, "I grew up poor. Like poor, poor. Single mom. Food stamps, food banks, all the stuff you don't want to be associated with when you're a kid. For the first ten years of my life, I went to bed hungry half the time. It was miserable." He paused for a second, then said, "I know in America, I didn't go to bed hungry because of a lack of food. It was more of a money issue. But for a lot of the world, it is a food issue. They can't grow enough. There either isn't enough arable land or enough water or a thousand other agricultural problems. And it's only gonna get worse. In twenty years, the Earth's population will need 55 percent more food than it can produce now."

I tried to put myself in Brian's shoes, which for a kid who grew up as a One Percenter wasn't easy. The only time I could ever remember going to bed hungry was when I was a hostage on a cruise ship. A cruise, I might add, that probably cost as much as Brian's yearly salary. But I could remember the kids at my elementary and middle schools who ate for free and who seemed mortified by this fact. Hunger played an impactful role in Brian's life, and he wanted to alleviate that pain for someone else, someone a generation, or three generations down the road. I respected that.

As for his population statistics, I'm sure they were overstated, but there was no question that with a booming global population more food would need to be produced. Someone had to take the reins and look for an answer to this problem.

I said, "So, that's what made you want to work at Lunhill?"

"No, that's what got me interested in biotech. I wanted to work at Lunhill because they spend the most money on research and development." He paused, then said, "Nearly a billion dollars a year."

"That's a lot of money."

Though, to be fair, Lunhill was a $91 billion company.

Brian started down the corridor and waved for me to follow. We walked for thirty yards before coming to a series of plate glass windows. It was one part greenhouse, one part meth lab. There were two people in the room, one man and one woman. The woman was dressed in jeans and a blouse. The man looked more scientisty, with a white lab coat and clear goggles pulled down over his eyes.

"Is that Walter White?" I asked.

Brian turned to me and smiled, "You know what's funny? His name really is Walter."

I laughed, and Brian and I went on a quick *Breaking Bad* tangent.

"I watched all five seasons in five days," I told him.

"You watched an entire season each day?"

"I'd just been dumped by a girl," I confided, not really sure why.

"Been there," he replied, gazing down between his feet. I guessed he'd been dumped more recently than me. Or, he was still pining over his middle school crush.

I changed the subject back to science. "So if Walter there isn't trying to grow meth, what exactly is he trying to grow?"

Brian snapped back to life. "Golden Rice."

"Golden Rice?"

Brian nodded. "A genetically modified strain of rice that will provide a significant amount of Vitamin A."

I suppose I didn't look as impressed as Brian anticipated, and he explained, "Vitamin A deficiency plagues many parts of the developing world. More than a million deaths a year and half a million cases of irreversible blindness. If widely planted, Golden Rice could help reduce those numbers dramatically."

"Wow," I said, genuinely dazzled. "That's pretty cool."

"Super cool," he echoed.

"So how does it work?" I asked. "What exactly does 'genetically modified' mean?"

"A GMO is any plant or animal that has been genetically modified through the addition of genetic material from another organism." He paused to take a breath, then continued, "My favorite example is Bt-corn."

The term Bt-corn rang familiar, but I couldn't place it.

"Bt-corn," Brian continued, "has been genetically modified to create its own insecticide. The donor organism is a naturally occurring soil bacterium that contains a gene which produces a protein that kills the larvae of the corn borer."

"The corn borer?"

"Yeah, it's an insect. A moth, actually."

"And they destroy the corn?"

"The larvae bore into the stalk of the corn and feed off it. They can really cut into a farmer's yields. Here in the Midwest, they are particularly bad."

"You seem to really like the science behind all this. Why do you work in sales?"

"I failed organic chemistry in college twice."

"Really? You seem like a whiz with all this stuff."

"Biology, botany, all that stuff I get, but for some reason, no matter how hard I studied, I just couldn't get OC to click." He sighed, then said, "I was gonna take it a third time, but I was going to have to wait a full year, and I wanted to start making some money. So I changed majors."

We watched Walter play with a plant for another minute or so, then Brian said, "There isn't really anything else interesting to see. Most of the people who work here either work in marketing, or accounting, or sales—like me."

"I'm pretty hungry," I said. "How about we go grab one of those egg salad sandwiches?"

He smiled and nodded.

Chapter 20

The cafeteria was state-of-the-art. Ready-made sandwiches, salads, pizza, plus a few gourmet food stations. After inhaling Brian's egg salad breath for over an hour, that was the last thing on my mind, and I opted for a salad with grilled chicken breast. Brian grabbed two more egg salad sandwiches, a bowl of cottage cheese, and a Coke.

The thought of sitting opposite him and watching him eat his meal made me shudder, but I still had some questions I wanted answered. There were twenty tables with ten people spread between them. Brian and I took up seats at one of the empty tables.

I glanced down at my salad, then asked, "Is it true the cafeteria here doesn't use any GMOs?"

It was bad timing on my part as Brian had just taken a bite of his egg salad sandwich. He snorted, sending egg salad spittle onto my face and into my open mouth.

I wiped at my face with a napkin and fought back a series of dry heaves.

Brian seemed mortified by what he'd done, and when I said, "Well, that was maybe the grossest thing ever," it didn't help matters.

After we both composed ourselves, Brian said, "I'm so sorry, it's just that your question is so absurd that it caught me off guard."

"So, they do use genetically modified foods in the cafeteria?"

"Of course!" He pointed to my salad and said, "Everything in here is GMOs."

I'd found this hard to believe when I read it, but I was glad to know it wasn't true.

I stabbed at my salad with my fork, took a bite, then asked a follow-up question. "So you don't think genetically modified foods are making people sick?"

"People have been eating GMOs for going on twenty-five years now. If they were making people sick, then there would be concrete evidence by now."

A few minutes after Brian had finished explaining how Bt-corn worked, I recalled why the term sounded familiar. It was the guy's blog, *GMOs, Guns, and the Uprising.*

I said, "I read somewhere that Bt-corn is making people sick. Studies show something about liver and colon cancer."

"Do you have a cell phone?" he asked.

"Yeah. A smartphone." I'm not sure why I felt compelled to add the second part other than my wanting him to know I was hip.

"Well, there are a thousand studies out there that say the cell phone you're using is causing cancer."

My eyebrows rose. "Really?"

"Yeah, but for every study out there that says cell phones are causing cancer, there are ten studies saying that they don't." He paused. "Same thing for Bt-corn. There are tons and tons of studies—done by independent agencies not affiliated with Lunhill—that prove it's completely safe."

He had a good point. There was probably a scientific study out there that said sitting on the couch for six months watching Netflix and gaining forty pounds was actually good for you.

"What else you got?" he said with a grin. He was having fun debunking all the conspiracy theories.

I asked, "Why is Spectrum-H banned in a bunch of countries?"

"Spectrum-H isn't banned in any countries. Glyphosate, the active compound, is banned in a few. All I can say is that glyphosate has been around since 1970 and it is wildly considered the safest herbicide every created."

"Then why did the International Agency for Research on Cancer declare glyphosate a 'probable human carcinogen' in 2015?" I read this from my smartphone. The one that was giving me cancer as we speak.

He smirked slightly, then said, "Every regulatory agency in the world has given Spectrum-H the green light."

I waited for him to add to this, but he let the statement stand for itself.

I put the phone on the table and said, "Regulatory agencies like the FDA? Which Lunhill has hired a disproportionate amount of people from?"

"Makes good business sense. No different than hiring an accountant who used to work at the IRS."

He got me there.

"Okay, what about food labeling guidelines? Don't you think people have a right to know what's in their food?"

He took a long sip of soda and said, "Personally, I'm with you on that one. But, assuming GMOs are safe, *which they are*, it shouldn't matter."

"But you agree that GMO labeling would be a bad thing for Lunhill?"

"Worse than bad. It would be devastating. Studies show your average consumer, if given the choice between buying the same product for the same price, would choose the one not containing GMOs."

"Hence, Lunhill spending millions of dollars each year on lobbyists to prevent this from happening?"

"Like all business enterprises, they have shareholders and a board of directors to answer to. They are in the business of making money."

I appreciated Brian's candor.

"What about farmers?" I asked.

"What about them?"

"I read that many farmers feel like they are being forced to use Lunhill's genetically modified seeds."

"No one is forced to use anything. Farmers *want* to use Lunhill seeds. The fact of the matter is, American farmers average 160 bushels of corn per acre each year, up from 109.5 in 1979. And it's even higher for soybeans, cotton, and many other crops."

I hadn't talked to any actual farmers about this, so I could hardly rebut.

"Tell me about Simon Beach," I said.

I only knew the bare details from what I read on the internet. Simon Beach was a ghost town, but at one point it had been a thriving community of two thousand—not all that different than Tarrin. In 1990, the town was completely evacuated due to dioxin contamination from a Lunhill manufacturing plant. It was the largest civilian exposure to dioxin in the country's history. A year later, the State of Missouri disincorporated the city.

Brian looked over both shoulders. I had a feeling Simon Beach was as taboo here as Save-More was in Tarrin.

He leaned forward and said, "That was awful."

"First, explain to me what dioxin is."

He looked over both shoulders a second time, then deciding the coast was clear, he said, "Dioxin is a chemical by-product of the manufacturing process. Anything manufactured, from soap to toothpaste to household disinfectants, are all going to produce dioxin."

"And these dioxins are toxic?"

"They are when they reach a certain level in the human body."

I took this in, then asked, "So what happened with the Lunhill plant in Simon Beach?"

"Lunhill wasn't entirely at fault. It was their dioxins, but they weren't the ones who spilled them. It's actually a crazy story."

"Let's hear it."

"So this is what happened," he said. "The Lunhill plant wasn't in Simon Beach, it was actually in a town in Southwest Missouri called Verona. Like I said, when you add all the chemicals together to make Spectrum-H, trace amounts of dioxins are created as a by-product. It would accumulate in the bottom of the stills as a thick, oily residue. For many years, Lunhill would send the still bottoms to a waste facility in Louisiana for incineration. This is the best method to destroy dioxins, but it's also the most expensive. So trying to save a couple bucks, Lunhill contracted the services of the Midwest Petrochemical Corporation. But unbeknownst to Lunhill, MPC didn't know shit about waste disposal. So they subcontracted the job to a guy named Russell Canto, who owned a local waste oil business."

He took a sip of Coke, then asked, "You with me so far?"

I nodded.

He continued, "In addition to the waste oil business, Canto owned an oil spraying business."

"Oil spraying? This is a thing?"

"Yeah. They spray oil to keep the dust down on farms and dirt roads."

This made sense, and I waved for him to keep going.

"In 1986, the town of Simon Beach hired Canto to oil its twenty-three miles of dirt roads. Over a two-year stretch, he ended up spraying 160,000 gallons of waste oil, much of which he was getting from the Lunhill plant in Verona.

"Over the course of the next few years, a bunch of animals started dying and a lot of the citizens of Simon Beach were diagnosed with chloracne, horrible lesions on the face and neck, which is consistent with dioxin poisoning." He paused, then said, "That's when the EPA came in and started testing the soil. They found dioxin concentrations as high as 0.3 parts per million along the entire network of roads."

"What concentration is considered safe?"

"0.1 parts per *billion*."

Yikes.

I asked, "So why didn't they just go in and clean up all the roads?"

"A week after the tests came back, there was the worst flood in Simon Beach history. The Meramec River rose to like fifteen feet higher than usual."

"And that contaminated the entire town?"

He nodded and said, "So President Ronald Reagan created the Simon Beach Dioxin Task Force and they came in and bought out the eight hundred residential properties and thirty businesses for like forty million dollars."

"And just like that, it's a ghost town?"

"Yep."

"Did Lunhill get sued?"

"Everyone got sued: Lunhill, MPC, and Canto. But because Canto was subcontracting with the MPC, who had the account with Lunhill, he claimed ignorance—that he had no idea what was contained in the oil. He had to pay out a couple hundred thousand dollars, but he filed for bankruptcy and I'm not sure what ever happened. But Lunhill and MPC both had to pay out two hundred million."

"Do you think Lunhill should have been held responsible?"

"It was their oil," he said, matter-of-fact.

I asked, "So, ethically, you have no problem working for Lunhill?"

Brian puffed out his cheeks. "I fully understand why people don't like the company: Agent Orange, saccharine, DDT, Simon Beach. I totally get it. But over the last couple decades they have done far more good than harm. And now they are leading the fight against the world's imminent food production problem. So no, I have no problem working for them."

"Okay," I said. "You're off the hot seat."

He let out a long exhale, then asked, "How'd I do? I have my first sales call next week."

I told him he did great, then inquired, "Is your sales call over the phone or in person?"

"In person."

"Will you do me a favor?"

He scrunched his nose. "I guess."

"That day," I said, "maybe lay off the egg salad."

~

Brian excused himself to use the bathroom, and I made my way to the dessert bar and grabbed a tapioca pudding. I was disappointed it wasn't the same Snack Pack Harold often snuck from the cafeteria at the nursing home. In actuality, it was rice pudding. I wondered if it was *Golden Rice* pudding. Was I meeting my daily requirement of Vitamin A while ingesting such a delicious snack?

I made a mental note to mention Golden Rice Pudding to Brian. And that I wanted royalties when it saved all of humanity.

As for Brian, he had laid a good deal of information on me over the past hour. Many of my initial judgments about Lunhill had been, if not completely refuted, then at the very least, softened.

But learning more about Lunhill and what they did was only half the reason I made the road trip. The other reason, the *main* reason I came today was to talk to someone who knew Neil Felding. I wasn't sure if it was a calculated decision on the part of Allison the executive, but I wasn't going to get much from the guy who had worked at Lunhill for three days.

I surveyed the tables of the cafeteria. It was closing in on 1:30 p.m. and there were only a few lunch stragglers remaining. Two men at one table. Then a lone woman at another. The men were both in suits and ties. The lone woman, on the other hand, was clad in jeans and a gray blouse, and her hair was in a bird's nest of a bun. Even from twenty feet away, I could see the dark bags under the woman's eyes. She was either a cook, a custodian, or an overworked scientist.

I finished the last of the pudding, stood up, and meandered over to the woman. I asked, "Do you mind if I join you?"

The woman gazed up at me. Up close, the bags under her eyes were a light gray. She moved around her salad with her fork and said, "Uh, okay."

She was maybe in her late forties and had an unmistakable aura of owning three or more cats.

"I'm Thomas," I said, taking the seat next to her.

"Sheila," she said, more to her salad than to me.

I came right out with it. "Did you know Neil Felding?"

Her eyes doubled in size, but she didn't answer.

"You knew him, didn't you? You worked with him?"

She glanced around, then slowly nodded.

"How long did you work with him?"

"Six years."

"Did you guys get along?"

"Yeah."

I waited for her to elaborate, to say how nice a guy he was, that he was brilliant. She didn't.

"Why was he fired?"

She stirred her salad around but said nothing.

"What was he working on?" I prodded, loud enough the two men at the opposite table both glanced over.

"Um—" she began to answer, but was interrupted by a loud clomping.

I turned and gazed over my shoulder.

Striding into the cafeteria were five people: Allison the executive and four gentlemen. Two of them were my friends from the security screening, Old Gray and Young Wispy. The third man was tall, at least 6'5", with a thick frame to match. He had a shaved head and a well-trimmed gray beard. He might be wearing a suit today, but I could tell he'd spent the better part of his life in combat fatigues. He might as well have been wearing a sticker that read "Hi, I'm Dolf. I work for Blackwater."

As for the fourth man, he wore his suit like a second skin. He was my size, but had the build of a distance runner. His white hair was perfectly coifed, and small rectangular glasses were held snug against the best rhinoplasty had to offer. Though he could easily pass for a man in his fifties, he was actually seventy-three years old.

Lunhill CEO, David Ramsey.

According to what I'd read on the internet, David Ramsey had become the majority shareholder of Lunhill in the late eighties after making a small fortune working as a top executive at Exxon for two decades.

I stood as the five approached, but not before Sheila uttered a single word under her breath. The word meant little to me, but I didn't have time to inquire further as Female Executive, Old Gray, Young Wispy, Dolf, and Vader had closed to within mere feet.

"You need to come with us," Old Gray barked.

"Okay," I complied. Well, I complied verbally. Physically, I sat back down in my seat.

Young Wispy stepped behind me and gave me a little push in the back. I turned and shook my head. "Don't."

He slipped a stun gun off his hip and held it at his side.

The stun gun wasn't what stopped me from putting my elbow through his face. It was Dolf. He looked on with a cold stare. If I so much as flinched in Young Wispy's direction, I had no doubt my next memory would be of a hospital bed.

I stood up and walked forward.

"Impersonating an FBI agent," David Ramsey said dryly, "trespassing, corporate espionage. You've had a busy day, Mr. Prescott."

I was tempted to ask him how he found out my real name, but I didn't want to give him the satisfaction of telling me how easy it was.

I did say, "Good thing I ate my Wheaties."

He shook his head ever so slightly, like a father might at seeing his child's B+ on a report card, and said, "The police are on their way."

"Bullshit."

He glared at me.

"The last thing you want is me getting arrested. My name carries weight, and if it leaks that I impersonated a dead FBI agent to infiltrate your headquarters and that it was ridiculously easy, it's going to get a lot of conspiracy theorists talking."

He was silent a beat, then said, "You're right. There will be no record of this."

The way he said it, I think he was hinting at something more sinister. That maybe if I was to go missing or get my head blown off, there would be no record of that either.

He gave a nod to Old Gray and said, "See him out."

The two security guards began ushering me toward the cafeteria entrance. When I was halfway there, Brian walked through the doorway on his return from the bathroom.

He looked on in bewilderment.

I smiled at him and said, "Find me on Facebook."

When I was just steps from the door, I turned around and glared at Ramsey and the mercenary. "I know what you did to Neil Felding!" I shouted.

I watched them both closely, waiting for either of them to react.

But neither of them so much as blinked.

~

Simon Beach was an hour drive south.

I had to see it for myself. I had to see the destruction the evils of Lunhill and its co-conspirators had wreaked.

I followed the directions on my phone until I came to the town limits. Spray painted on the road was a white line. Just beyond the line was the word "DIOXIN" in thick ominous lettering.

The meaning was obvious: once you cross over the white line, you have entered into a new world, one of contamination and destruction.

I slowly rolled the Range Rover over the line. I continued on for several blocks. It was a lost world. Trees, brush, and weeds had overtaken most of the roads. What was left of the houses and businesses were in shambles. The flood waters that had besieged the town had weakened the buildings to the point of failure. No reconstruction efforts were made. They were left alone. Left to die. It reminded me of the opening shot of any post-apocalypse movie.

A few more blocks inland there was a giant water tower. It listed slightly to the left and had "Simon Beach" etched around its circumference in black letters. Underneath this, in red graffiti, was a skull and crossbones.

It was all very eerie.

I crept along the road. After a couple blocks, a river came into view. The water swept by, taking whatever poison still lay in the soil with it downstream.

I drove for another half mile, then slowed to a crawl. On the left side of the road, hidden in a thicket of brush, was an abandoned school bus. I wondered how it had ended up there. Had the floodwater deposited it there? Had it been abandoned by a sick driver? Had it been the bus Ronald Reagan's Simon Beach Task Force arrived in?

Just past the school bus, there was a large sign next to the road. It read "Heavily Contaminated Area. Stay in your car. Keep your windows up as you drive."

Uh, no thanks.

I put the car in park.

Lunhill was not entirely to blame for what happened to Simon Beach, but it had all started because they were trying to save a buck. They had no longer wanted to shell out the money to send the dioxin barrels to Louisiana where they could be properly disposed of.

They had been found responsible. Forced to pay $200 million. They had paid for their sin.

But what other secrets did they have?

How many other Simon Beaches had they gotten away with?

I knew one thing for certain: whatever one of these secrets was, Neil Felding had found out. And that's what killed him.

I thought back to what Sheila said when I asked what Neil had been working on.

She'd only said one word.

Terminator.

Chapter 21

"It's okay," I said, rubbing May's shaking body. "They're just fireworks."

There was a loud explosion and May's pink-and-ink-spotted body jerked. She let out a loud whine. Harold, who was curled up under a pile of hay, lifted his tan head slightly and squealed.

Earlier in the day, I'd driven into town to check out the Fourth of July festivities. Half the town was blocked off as the high school marching band, several fire trucks, and a stream of different floats paraded down Main Street, then wended their way through the many side streets. The sidewalks were cluttered with residents in lawn chairs, drinking beers, not to mention little kids running amok with sparklers in hand.

It was all very celebratory, but I wasn't in the mood. I was too pre-occupied with analyzing everything I'd learned at Lunhill HQ three days prior. There was no doubt in my mind that Neil Felding had stumbled onto something he shouldn't have. It could have been any number of things to do with Lunhill: dioxin, GMOs, fraudulent polit-ical practices, something to do with the EPA or the FDA, or possibly something that Neil had been working on—something that had to do with the movie *Terminator*.

I had stayed in town just long enough to watch the parade, then I'd headed back to the farm. That's when I noticed the front door to the farmhouse was ajar.

At first I thought of Caroline, but unless she'd teleported off the float she was riding on in the parade, then it wasn't her. And it couldn't have been Randall; he and his family were spending the holiday at a lake a few hours north. It possibly could have been Wheeler, but her truck was nowhere to be seen.

After combing the house and half the farm for the two piglets, I finally found them hunkered down in the far corner of the barn.

My best guess was that someone from one of the neighboring farms had been shooting off fireworks, and in their angst, the piglets had pushed up against the front door of the farmhouse and somehow gotten it to open. Then they'd made their way into the barn.

I'd been trying to coax them back into the house for the past several hours without much luck.

A series of fireworks exploded, and after May recovered from another shaking fit, I asked, "You sure you guys don't want to go back in the house?"

I tried lifting Harold out of the hay, but he dug himself even deeper.

"Okay," I said. "We'll stay in here."

I fluffed up some hay until I was comfortable, then I pulled out my phone and hit play.

I'd watched so much television the past six months that the thought of spending two hours staring at a screen disgusted me. But I had to watch it. I had to know what Neil Felding's coworker, Sheila, meant when she uttered the word "Terminator."

Two hours later, I was no closer to understanding.

Was she saying that Neil Felding was the Terminator? Or that Neil Felding was John Connor? Or Sarah Conner? Was Lunhill Skynet? Had Lunhill been working on time travel?

What did it all mean?

But maybe I hadn't heard all of what Sheila said. Maybe she actually said, "*Terminator II.*" Or maybe even "*Terminator Genesis.*"

How many movies were there?

I did a search on my phone.

There were five.

Five fucking movies!

"I'm not watching the one with Christian Bale. I'm just not," I said out loud.

I put the phone down.

The fireworks had fallen silent an hour earlier and both the piglets were asleep.

A few minutes later, I was too.

~

"Welp," I said. "That's a lot of chickens."

There were probably close to fifty running around, squawking, flapping their wings at one another.

It was July 6th and Randall had returned from his little vacation. He chuckled and said, "I told you I had a good chicken guy."

I grinned, then asked, "So will the chickens just go into the coop on their own?"

"Yeah, just watch, they'll play around for a little while out here, but they'll find their way into the coop eventually."

"Where are the roosters?"

"Roosters?"

"Yeah, you know, the birds that knock these chickens up so they start laying eggs."

He slapped me on the shoulder. "You don't know shit, do ya?"

"What?"

"Chickens don't need to get knocked up to lay eggs."

"They don't?"

"No. They do that all on their own. Now if you want those eggs to actually turn into little chicks, then ya got to get a rooster."

"Oh."

He glared at me for a long second then said, "You want a rooster, don't you?"

I did. Mostly because there was a rooster in the picture I colored. I didn't dare tell Randall this.

"Don't worry," he said, giving my back another nice hard slap. "I got a rooster guy too."

~

Unlike the Brush Hog, which was pulled behind the tractor, the tiller was attached up front.

Randall had been behind the wheel for the past thirty minutes, and we'd already tilled close to an acre. This would be a far easier task than the brush removal.

According to Randall, the purpose of tilling was to break up the hard crust of the dirt and to oxygenate the soil.

The tractor did a tight turn, and from the passenger seat of the tractor, I gazed across the several rows of tilled dirt.

I took a deep breath and shouted over the rumble of the tractor engine, "What do you know about Lunhill?"

The tractor slowed, then came to a halt. Randall turned and asked, "Lunhill?"

"Yeah, what do you know about them?"

"Bunch of gutless sonsofbitches." His eyes narrowed and it felt as though he were looking through me, almost as if he were glaring at their headquarters ninety miles due east. "Remember how I told you I lost my farm?" he asked.

I nodded.

"Well, the reason I lost it was because those assholes sued me."

"They sued you?"

He cut the engine.

"Yeah, this guy comes onto my farm, dressed in a suit, carrying a briefcase. Tells me he's there to audit my seeds."

"Audit, like the IRS?"

"Shit, I wish it had been the IRS. I would have stood a chance against them."

I gave a slight scoff. Lunhill was scarier to these people than the IRS. "Did you let him?"

"I told him in so many words to piss off."

Thatta boy.

"So he leaves. I didn't think anything of it, and another month passed. It was now August and I was doing a harvest. Great year. The best year I'd ever had. Little guy comes back. Has some paperwork signed by a local judge, and get this, he's got the police with him."

"Let me guess," I said. "Chief Eccleston?"

"How'd you know?"

"Just a hunch."

"Well, they said they had probable cause. That someone had turned me in."

"Turned you in? For what?"

"For using Lunhill seeds."

"Those Spectrum-H things?"

"Spectrum-H(R)—means they are resistant to Spectrum-H—so when you spray it, all the weeds die, but the corn, or soy, or whatever doesn't."

"And you weren't using these seeds?"

He leaned back an inch, like I visibly slapped him.

"Course not. I'm all organic. I don't spray shit, least of all, those assholes' poison." He lay on the word poison. I was tempted to ask him to elaborate, but I didn't want him to lose focus.

"Sorry."

He shook me off like a pitcher shaking off a pitch. "Don't worry, I just get a little riled up." He took a long breath. "Anyhow, I had to watch while this sonofabitch went through my fields taking samples of all my plants."

"What is Eccleston doing during all this?"

"Just sitting in his car like a dumbass."

"And then they just leave?"

"They said they were gonna run some tests and get back to me."

"Were you worried?"

"Not really. I mean, I wasn't using their seeds."

"So then what happened?"

"Six months later, I got served papers. Lunhill was suing me for patent infringement. Sixty thousand dollars."

"What'd you do?"

"I hired a lawyer, hired a bunch of independent researchers to test my seeds…" He paused, then added, "and thirty thousand dollars later, I got the same results. I was using GMOs."

He said *GMOs* the way a doctor might say *syphilis*.

"How is that possible?" I asked.

"Cross-contamination."

"What?"

"All the farmers around me were using Lunhill seeds. They must have blown over in the wind and cross-pollinated with my seeds." He shook his head. "I should have known when I had such a good year. I was growing those Frankenseeds."

"Did you still go to trial?"

"Had to. I was in too deep. Only way I would be able to recoup my lawyer fees and research costs was if I won."

"But you couldn't prove the cross-contamination?"

"Nope." He sighed. "I lost at trial. The sixty thousand-dollar fine on top of the thirty grand I spent on my own and I couldn't make the mortgage. Bank foreclosed on the property a few months later."

"Shit." I shook my head, then asked, "You ever find out who turned you in?"

"No."

We switched seats, and I took over the tilling.

Randall didn't speak the rest of the afternoon.

~

I could color between the lines like a pro—I had two adult coloring books to prove it—but when it came to freehand drawing, I was a five-year-old with carpal tunnel.

I looked down at the picture I'd drawn on a piece of computer paper: big round head, receding hairline, droopy jowls. I added some peeling skin to his forehead and scribbled "Chief Eccleston." Then I taped the picture to the bedroom wall.

After what Randall had told me about Eccleston accompanying the Lunhill man to his farm, I didn't have a shred of doubt that at some level the Chief was connected to Lunhill.

I'd drawn pictures on several more pieces of paper and taped them to the wall as well. "David Ramsey" looked like the character from *Guess Who* with the glasses. "Neil Felding" was a stick figure with a lab coat. He had a whistle in his mouth and was blowing it. "Lowry Barnes" was a circle face with a single arm coming out of it holding a gun. I was especially proud of that one. Then there was a picture of a big gorilla, or what I intended as a gorilla, but looked more like a huge rabbit. This was "Dolf," the Blackwater goon.

Then there was a picture with five circle faces with X's for eyes. On this, I wrote "Save-More Murders." Then there was a single face with the same X's. On this I wrote "Mike Zernan."

These six pictures encircled a final piece of paper. On the page were two words: "Cover-up."

I knew everything was connected. I just didn't know what they were covering up or how the pieces fit together.

Was it something to do with Neil's research? Had there been a dioxin spill in Tarrin, and Neil Felding uncovered it? Or had Neil uncovered that Lunhill was unfairly suing farmers like Randall? Was it specific to Tarrin or was it something bigger? Something about corruption at the state level? Federal? Presidential?

Obama had signed the Lunhill Protection Act a few years earlier. Had Neil Felding found out something about that?

How high did this go?

I stared at the wall for a long time, until the floral wallpaper pattern began to separate like one of those 3D images.

Out of the corner of my eye, I noticed a flicker and turned. Through the upstairs window, I could see flames.

"Wha—"

The barn was on fire.

I took the stairs three at a time, smashed through the front door, and hightailed it toward the blazing barn. Fifty feet away, I could feel the heat, a pulsing wall pushing outward.

I pulled my shirt up over my mouth and ducked, making it to the paneled door. I pushed the door aside, the wood hot, but still bearable. The fire was louder than I would have expected, a symphony of cracks and pops. Smoke billowed from the open doors, and I dropped to my knees.

"Harold! May!" I screamed.

Since hiding there to get away from the fireworks on July 4th, the piglets had been spending most of their time in the barn, dug into the hay.

Coughing, I crawled to the piglets' new home. Through squinted, watering eyes, I could see two shapes. I crawled to them.

They both whined.

"It's okay."

I picked one of them up in each arm—no easy task as both weighed nearly thirty pounds—took a deep breath, and darted through the approaching flames. The fire nicked at my flesh, but a moment later, I was safely through with the piglets. I continued running with them until I was back in front of the farmhouse. I set them down and took a few satisfying breaths.

"Are you guys okay?" I wheezed.

They were both covered in a fine layer of soot. Harold seemed fine, but May's breathing was labored. She sat down on her butt, taking in small wheezy breaths. I wiped her nose clean of soot, hoping that would help, but it didn't.

Turning to look over my shoulder, I gazed at the barn. The entire thing was ablaze, flames whipping in the soft breeze. If I'd gotten there a minute later, there was no doubt in my mind both Harold and May would be dead.

Who did this?
Lunhill?
Blackwater?
The Chief?
Was this a warning?

May's breathing broke me from my reverie.

"It's gonna be okay," I told her, rubbing her head gently.

Then I ran inside and grabbed my cell phone.

She answered on the third ring.

"Wheeler!" I shouted.

"Yeah, what's wrong?"

"Someone lit my barn on fire."

"Oh my God. Did you call the police?"

I half expected the fire trucks to show up any moment. But then again, if any of the far-off neighbors did see the flames, they probably just assumed I was burning brush. "Not yet," I said.

"Do you kno—"

"The pigs were in the barn," I blurted.

"Shit! Did you get them out?"

"Yeah, just barely, but May isn't doing so hot. She's having trouble breathing."

"I'll be right over."

~

She must have driven twice the speed limit because she showed up ten minutes later.

Her truck screeched to a halt in the drive and she jumped out. She had a black bag in her right hand and sprinted to where Harold, May, and I were sitting on the ground near the front steps.

Thankfully, over the course of the past ten minutes, May's breathing had improved.

"How is she?" Wheeler asked, falling to her knees.

"I think she's doing better."

She turned and looked at the barn, squinting into the flames, and asked, "How long do you think they were in there?"

"I'm not sure. Maybe five minutes, maybe longer."

Wheeler seemed satisfied with this, then spent the next few minutes examining May. She took her blood pressure, listened to her heart, checked her oxygen levels, felt around her throat, looked into her mouth, and swabbed the inside of her nose.

Finally, she said, "Well, the good news is she seems to be doing okay. She definitely inhaled some carbon monoxide, but it doesn't look like it was enough to do any real damage. Oxygen levels are a bit down, but should improve. Biggest concern was burned airways, but those look fine."

"And the bad news?"

"Sometimes symptoms of smoke inhalation don't appear until a few hours after exposure, so she could still—" She stopped. Didn't say it.

"She could still die?"

She reached out and grabbed my hand. "I think she's going to be fine. You just need to keep an eye on her for a little while."

I gave her hand a squeeze and let go.

She switched her focus to Harold, giving him a quick examination, then declared him "Fit as a fiddle."

As if on cue, Harold oinked then pawed at May. Wheeler and I both stared at the little girl, on edge how she would react. She pawed back at her brother, and the two scampered a couple feet away and began wrestling.

I let out a long sigh.

"I told you, she's going to be fine," Wheeler said, taking a seat on the ground next to me.

We were both facing the barn. It was an inferno, the flames at their peak. You could still feel the heat from a hundred yards away. After some debate, I'd decided not to call 911. They would have had too many questions that I would have to circumvent. For example, "*Who would have torched your barn? And why?*"

Oh, I don't know, maybe a little company you may have heard of called Lunhill. And maybe because they wanted to give me a not-so-subtle warning to stop probing into their involvement in the Save-More murders.

That said, there was nothing the fire trucks could do. There was no saving the barn. And having de-brushed the immediate area surrounding the barn, there was little risk the fire would spread.

Wheeler asked, "What were the pigs doing in the barn?"

"They went in there when the fireworks were going off over the weekend and I think they liked it. They've slept there the last couple of nights."

"Did you see anybody when you came out?"

"No," I said, shaking my head.

"Why would someone want to burn down your barn?"

"A warning."

Her eyebrows jumped. "A warning?"

"Yeah, to stop poking my nose where it doesn't belong."

She narrowed her eyes at me. "Does this have something to do with the Save-More murders?"

"Yeah."

"You think there's more to it than just Lowry?"

"I *know* there's more."

It's the way I said the words. With purpose. Each letter granite. Each syllable as strong as the steel frame of her truck.

She looked at me. A look of want. Seductive. In any other situation, I would read the look as pleading for my lips against hers. But it wasn't my lips she wanted. It was information.

"What do you know about Lunhill?" I asked.

"Not a whole lot. Big Biotech." She scrunched her nose. "What have they got to do with anything?"

"I think they were behind your dad's murder."

She cocked her head to the side.

"Come with me," I said, pushing myself up. I held out my hand to her. She glanced at it for a moment, uncertain, as if by taking my hand she was giving credence to the ridiculous statement I just uttered.

She ignored my hand and pushed herself up. "Follow you where?"

"To the bedroom."

She cut her eyes at me.

"Not like that."

Unless.

Wheeler followed me up to the bedroom, and I flipped on the lights. Her eyes found the far wall, where I'd taped all the pictures I'd drawn. "What is that?" she asked.

"That's my investigation."

She took a couple steps forward and said, "Your investigation looks like the wall of a kindergarten classroom."

"Oh, come on, they aren't that bad."

"Uh, they're pretty bad."

I smirked.

Then I tapped the picture of Neil Felding and said, "It starts with him."

~

It took me twenty minutes to run Wheeler through everything I knew so far. At first, she seemed reluctant to believe a word out of my mouth, but inch-by-inch, the way a glacier etches a canyon out of rock, I could tell she was coming around.

She said, "So Lowry getting his revenge against Odell was just a cover?"

"I think so. I think the Lunhill guys got to Lowry. I think they paid him to make it look like a revenge killing when Neil Felding was the target all along."

"Because Neil Felding was going to blow the whistle on something big at Lunhill."

"That's my theory."

"But Lunhill couldn't risk Lowry getting caught and they killed him in his car and made it look like a suicide."

"Right."

I could see her running everything over in her head. This didn't change the fact her father was still in the wrong place at the wrong time, but it did change who was responsible, or at least partly responsible, for his murder.

Wheeler's next words would say a lot about who she was.

She said, "We need to find out what Neil Felding knew."

I tried to fight back a smile.

"What?" she asked.

"Nothing. I just like your spunk."

This made her blush.

There was a loud crack and the two of us darted to the window and peered through.

"The barn," Wheeler said. "It's crumbling."

The two of us ran outside.

We slowly made our way closer to the barn until we reached the point of being singed by the flames.

Maybe it was the fire's destructive power, its absolute disregard for anything but oxygen and fuel, but it made me think about Lunhill. They were just like fire. They didn't care who they hurt—people, animals, the planet—as long as the flames continued to burn.

"We're gonna bring them down," I said.

Wheeler turned.

I could see a crack in her veneer. Her eyes were moist, her breath caught in her throat.

I wondered what she was thinking about. Her father? Lowry? Lunhill?

Our hands were hanging a couple inches apart. Her fingers grazed mine, touched, fled, touched, fled. Then slowly her fingers climbed into mine. Her fingers were soft but strong.

She tilted her head upward just slightly. This time there was no questioning what she wanted.

Me.

I closed the distance between us, my lips brushing lightly against hers.

There was a loud *whoof* as the barn collapsed. Dust and ash swept over us and we covered our heads.

A moment later, we walked back to the farmhouse. I thought about grabbing her hand, pulling her to me, but like the barn, the moment was gone.

Chapter 22

I was exhausted. I spent the entire night awake checking on May every twenty minutes to make sure her breathing was regular. Finally around 5:00 in the morning, I decided she was okay and that I could get some shuteye.

That's when I first heard it.

COCK-A-DOODLE-DOO!

I sat up in bed.

COCK-A-DOODLE-DOO!

What the?

The piglets remained undisturbed by the sound, and I crept to the window. I pulled the curtains apart. The sun was just beginning to wake. I squinted in the direction of the chicken coop, and low and behold, standing on the outside fence just like in the picture hanging on the fridge, was a rooster.

Randall must have dropped him off at some point after we'd finished up for the day.

I shook my head.

If I had access to a time machine and I only had one thing to change about my past thirty-five years, I would travel back to when I asked Randall to acquire a rooster and hit myself in the face with a sledge hammer.

I ambled back to the bed and flopped down between Harold and May.

COCK-A-DOODLE-DOO!
COCK-A-DOODLE-DOO!
COCK-A-DOODLE-DOO!
COCK-A-DOODLE-DOO!

"Shut up!" I screamed. "Shut the fuck up!"

He didn't.

I slept fitfully for a few hours, then finally gave up. I pushed myself out of bed. I threw on some clothes, fed the piglets, ate, then made my way outside.

The sun had risen a couple inches on the horizon, showering the rooster in an aura of yellow.

I was already plotting ways to kill him.

My eyes traveled from the rooster to the still smoldering pile of rubble that had once been the barn.

The previous night, I'd been too worried about May to concentrate on anger. But not now. My fists flexed into knuckled balls of white. My teeth gnashed together, and I wouldn't have been surprised if droplets of venom began to squirt from my canines.

A moment later, I felt a sharp pain in the back of my mouth and cringed.

~

"How did you do this?" Donald Roberts DDS asked.

I debated telling him the truth, how I'd been so angry I bit down and cracked my molar in half or how the tooth had first been loosened by a spinning round kick to the side of my face. But that would lead to a series of other questions or a series of awkward silences, neither of which I was in the mood to deal with.

"Just eating cereal this morning," I lied. I'd actually eaten three waffles, Chocolate Chip Eggos, which were now being carried at the Harvest Food and Market thanks to my bribery.

"What kind of cereal? Must have had some nuts or clusters."

"I think it's called Tons of Clusters."

He eyed me suspiciously, then said, "Well, you need a crown."

I nodded.

"It's gonna take a couple days to make, need to send it to the lab in Kansas City." He smiled, showing brilliant, nearly perfect teeth. "But we can give you a temporary today."

"Will that make the pain go away?"

After my tooth broke, I'd walked back into the house to rinse out my mouth. When the water hit my tooth, or lack thereof, it felt like someone drove a nail into my jaw. I could literally feel my heartbeat pulsating through my gum the entire time I searched my phone for a dentist with an opening.

Dr. Donald nodded. "Right now it hurts because the nerve is exposed. The temporary crown will take care of that."

"Good."

"Now, let's get you numbed up."

After shooting me up with novocaine, a hygienist stopped by to say she needed to do some impressions, though she didn't say who. Hopefully, she did a good De Niro. She said that she'd be back in "a bit."

While waiting for the novocaine to take effect, I took out my phone and loaded the second movie in the *Terminator* franchise: *Terminator II: Judgment Day*.

I watched ten minutes of the movie, then the hygienist returned. I waited for her to break out her Pacino, but apparently, she was taking impressions, not doing them, and she proceeded to stick this metal plate with pink goop in my mouth. Several minutes of gagging later, she removed the hardened material and allowed me to rinse my mouth out.

Once my temporary crown was fitted by Dr. Robert, I made an appointment to come back in a week, then returned to my car, where I decided to watch the rest of the movie.

Two hours later, the credits were rolling and I was ripping out my hair.

I was more confused than ever.

Now Arnold Schwarzenegger was a good guy?

WTF?

I really didn't want to watch six more hours of robots and I searched "Terminator and Lunhill" on my phone.

And wouldn't you know it…

The name of the article was "Lunhill Terminates 'Terminator Seed' Technology." The article was dated March 23, 1999.

I skimmed it, reading aloud bits and pieces.

"Sterile seed technology—dubbed 'terminator technology' in the press—is a gene-use restriction technology whereby second generation seed (seed produced by the crop) will be sterile…After consulting with international experts and many small landholder farmers, Lunhill has made a commitment not to commercialize Sterile Seed Technology in food crops and has no plans or research that would violate this commitment in any way."

I tossed the phone onto the passenger seat.

In 1999, Lunhill did away with their Terminator seed research, but according to Neil Felding's coworker, that's exactly what he was working on.

~

When I made it back to Tarrin, it was close to noon and Randall's truck was parked in front of the farmhouse. I could see the tractor moving off in the distance. Nearly half of the 250 acres had been tilled and it was beginning to resemble something of a farm.

I parked and watched as Randall and the tractor cut across the perfectly manicured lines in my direction. Coming abreast of me in the large red tractor, Randall killed the engine and stood up.

"What happened to the barn?" he belted.

"Id barned dine."

"What?"

"It baruned deen."

He jumped down and squinted at me. Maybe he noticed the slobber on the left side my face.

"What happened to you?"

"Boke may ooth."

"You broke a tooth?"

I nodded.

"Was this before or after you burned down the barn?"

"Agger."

"Right. So what happened?"

"Unill."

"What?'

"Undild!"

"What?"

I took a deep breath, concentrated. "Lundild!"

His brow furrowed. "Lunhill?"

~

It took a few hours to tell Randall everything. Partly because half my mouth was numb, partly because Randall had a thousand questions. But by midafternoon, Randall knew everything I knew.

Of all the things that should have upset him the most—that five members of his community who were murdered, then later a sixth with Mike Zernan; that it appeared Chief Eccleston was more involved with the company than anyone could have imagined; that Lunhill sent some ex-military goons to do their dirty work—he was most rattled by the fact Lunhill and Neil Felding were still working on Terminator seeds.

"I remember when I first heard about that shit," Randall said. "Lunhill was sick of farmers reusing their seeds, not paying them for each year, and they were trying to find a way to make sure that wouldn't happen. So they decided to *design* this seed that kills itself after each harvest."

I was up to speed on this part and motioned for him to continue.

"But what these idiots didn't realize is that most farmers don't reuse seeds to save money—I mean, a lot of them do, especially in third world countries—but the main reason to reuse seed is because those seeds have adapted to certain conditions and environments. You save only the best seeds from the harvest, year after year. Those seeds have adapted to each climate's individual conditions, soil, nutrient level, adapted to each farm's unique farming practices."

"Survival of the fittest?"

"Sort of. But naturally. Not in a lab."

I nodded.

"And because each farmer is saving their own seeds from their own farm, they're all a little different. It's called 'crop genetic diversity.' Those seeds are our global food security. If farmers start using Terminator seeds, centuries of biodiversity will be wiped out."

"But don't farmers have to decide to buy those seeds?"

"They sure do. But look what happened to me—cross-pollination. Say my neighbor buys Terminator seeds and the wind or bees bring a couple of those seeds onto my land. They cross-pollinate with my seeds, and after a couple generations all my seeds are now sterile. But that's not the worst of it. Sure, here in the US we have a choice. But in third world countries that's not how it works."

He locked eyes with me and said, "A defining feature of poverty is a lack of choice."

I wondered if these words stemmed from the topic at hand or growing up in a rough part of Alabama.

He paused for a moment, then said, "These farmers in third world countries are under pressure from their governments to use Lunhill's seeds. Lunhill kicks in a few million bucks to these fat cats at the top, and they start pressuring, sometimes mandating, that these farmers use high-yielding varieties, which is cockamamie bullshit for GMOs. And worse yet, some of these governments force the farmers to buy the seeds on credit or extension programs."

"Shit."

"Yeah, shit. And then you know what happens?"

"What?"

"They get in over their heads, have a bad year, and then they blow their brains out."

"Suicide?"

"Since the late nineties, when GMOs first started gaining popularity, 300,000 farmers in India have killed themselves."

"Did you say 300,000?"

He pursed his lips. "Yeah, and that's just India."

"And if they introduce Terminator seeds, farmer suicide might go even higher?"

"No ifs about it."

We both sat in silence for a long moment, conjuring the implications.

"So if that's what Neil Felding was working on..." I said, more to myself than Randall.

"Then maybe he had a change of heart," Randall said, "or maybe he finally realized what these seeds would mean for the world."

I spit-balled, "And he decided he wouldn't be a part of it."

"And then he confronts Lord Ramsey and threatens to go public."

"And that would have cost them millions."

"Try *billions*," Randall corrected. "Several countries have already banned the use of Terminator seeds, and they haven't even come out yet. It's not a stretch to think that if a country found out the ill effects of Terminator seeds, which are just slightly altered GMOs, they might ban GMOs altogether."

"True."

"And if Felding had solid proof, some hard science proving just how bad they were—shit, coming from one of Lunhill's top scientists—it could have bankrupted them."

I thought about this for a moment, then said, "What if they were already out there? What if the GMOs these farmers think they're planting are actually Terminator seeds?"

"If Neil found that out or was part of it and was gonna blow the whistle on it?" He blew out his cheeks. "I'd say that's motive for murder, my friend."

I was still thinking about Randall's last statement when he asked, "So what are you gonna do?"

I didn't have a lot of options. The murder was four years old. Neil Felding was long dead. Lunhill was locked down. And I was on Blackwater's watch list. I didn't for a minute imagine there was any evidence out there that would prove my theory. And without evidence, there was only one option—confession.

I would need to get the players to talk.

"I'm gonna do what I do best," I said. "I'm gonna ruffle some feathers."

I told him my plan.

His eyes lit up and he ran to his Bronco. He came back a moment later with a copy of the *Tarrin Weekly*.

He slapped the paper into my hand and said, "This would be a good place to start."

I looked at the article on the front page and read aloud, "Mayor Van Dixon Campaign Luncheon."

There were a couple pictures of some of her biggest backers.

One was Chief Eccleston.

Another, Lunhill CEO David Ramsey.

"If you're gonna ruffle some feathers," Randall said, "you might as well get some lunch while you're at it."

Chapter 23

The Mayor's luncheon was supposed to be outside, a white tent affair in the park, but the torrential rains of the past few days sent the organizers scrambling for another venue. I'm guessing there weren't many options capable of holding the one hundred or so guests who would be attending the $500 per plate gala, hence, the Tarrin High School gymnasium.

The bleachers were pushed back into the walls, the basketball hoops were retracted up near the ceiling, and the court below was crowded with round tables, each with a different colored or patterned tablecloth.

It wasn't all that different from my prom, except in place of the banner that read "Puget High Prom '99" there was a big banner that read "Paula Van Dixon, Mayor '16." And instead of green and blue balloons—our school colors—the balloons here were red, white, and blue.

God bless America.

The luncheon began at noon and it was now fifteen after. Most of the seats at the tables were taken, and I approached a woman sitting behind a desk near the entrance.

"Well, hi there," she said. She had an aura of PTO president or the lady who ran the local bake sale. "Is it still raining outside?"

I should note that I was drenched. Head, drenched. T-shirt, drenched. Jeans, yep, drenched.

"Uh, yeah, it stopped raining."

"You look wet," she said with a cock of her head.

"I had a water fight with some pesky kids out in the parking lot."

"Really?"

I wasn't sure why I was harassing this poor lady and I decided I would attempt to act like a functioning member of society for at least a little bit. "I was just joking. It's still raining."

"Oh," she said, blushing. "Of course you were." She gave her head an imaginary smack, then she asked, "Are you here for the luncheon?"

"I'm here for the dodgeball tournament."

Dammit, Thomas.

I took a breath and said, "Yes, I'm here for the luncheon."

She checked a printout to make sure I paid my $500—which I'd done online twenty minutes after Randall showed me the article in the paper—then handed me an adhesive tag with my name and occupation from the online form.

"Here you go, Mr. Prescott," she said, glancing at my occupation with raised eyebrows. "You are assigned to the lavender table right over there." She pointed to a table that had a lavender tablecloth.

I made my way through the many tables, searching out the faces. I saw a few I recognized from around town, but not many I knew by name. There was a long rectangular table up front, and I could see Mayor Van Dixon, Chief Eccleston, David Ramsey, plus a few other official looking people and presumably their spouses.

I came abreast of the lavender table and stopped.

Filling one of the six seats, wearing a dress nearly the same color as the tablecloth—which I'm positive was not a coincidence and took a few phone calls to accommodate—was Caroline.

Our eyes met and she tried to bury a smile in her cheek. The man to her left glanced at her, then up at me. He was ten years my senior, with salt-and-pepper hair and a trim goatee. I didn't recall ever seeing him before.

There were three other gentlemen at the table, and the only seat available was on Caroline's right. After searching for an empty seat at any of the nearby tables and coming up empty, I reluctantly sat down.

"Caroline," I said with a light nod.

"Thomas," she said, her hand gently brushing over my thigh under the table.

Ruh roh.

The man to her left cleared his throat, and Caroline straightened. "Oh, forgive me. Thomas, this is my dear, dear friend, Jerome."

Jerome and I shook hands. I read his nametag: Jerome Bidwell, Law firm of Bidwell & Benson.

I could see him reading my nametag, then sneering in annoyance. Caroline followed his eyes to my nametag, then read aloud,

"Thomas Prescott, Farmer, Detective Extraordinaire, and *Naked and Afraid* Enthusiast."

She stifled a laugh. "What is *Naked and Afraid*?"

"It's a show on the Discovery Channel."

"It's amazing," quipped one of the three gentlemen to my right. "They put a guy and girl in the wilderness naked and they have to survive for twenty-one days."

"They're naked?" Caroline huffed.

"Naked as the day they were born," I said.

"Sounds pretty dumb," said Jerome.

"No, really, it's great," another gentleman said. "We have a viewing party every Sunday."

I gently slid my chair a couple inches to their side of the table.

Battle lines had been drawn.

The three gentlemen introduced themselves as the Fulton brothers: John, Mark, and Luke. They owned a tire business on the south side of town.

"You guys Muslim?" I asked.

All three laughed.

A few moments later, the first course was served. A tomato and corn salad. The waitress gave a long-winded explanation of each and every ingredient and which farm it came from. *Mallory Farm's butter lettuce, Wildwood Farm's tomatoes, Joe Schmo Farm's roasted corn...*

I made small talk with the three brothers, mostly about *N & A*, but a little about tires, and some about my being a famous detective.

Caroline kept sneaking glances my way, but Jerome was clearly threatened by my nearly dry Hanes T-shirt and furrowed his brow at every snippet of conversation he overheard.

At one point during the main course—hazelnut-crusted halibut on a bed of purple cauliflower puree—I counted the number of tables.

Twenty tables.

Six people at each table.

One hundred and twenty guests—nearly five percent of the entire town of Tarrin—and at $500 a plate that was nearly $60,000 for the Mayor's reelection campaign.

I fixed my gaze on David Ramsey up front.

How many people would have paid the $500 if he hadn't been speaking? And more importantly, how much was he being paid to speak?

The servers took coffee orders and since they didn't have Pumpkin Spice Lattes available, I declined. But I was interested in dessert. I'd been eating healthy for nearly a month now and I was eager for some crème brûlée. But first, I had to use the restroom.

I excused myself, then made my way through the hallway and to the restroom. Halfway through my whiz, the door opened and in walked Caroline.

She teetered on high heels, a consequence of the several glasses of wine she'd slugged down over lunch.

"You never called," she said.

I finished, zipped up, and turned around.

I never called, but that didn't mean I hadn't thought about it. That I hadn't thought about what she'd whispered in my ear: *Oh, the things I would do.* I dialed her number twice but stopped short of hitting *Call.* Finally, I ripped up the card she wrote her number on and flushed it down the toilet.

I didn't know what to say, so I didn't say anything. I just washed my hands instead.

"What?" she said, with pursed lips. "You don't want my apple pie?"

"I don't know if your apple pie is exactly what I need in my life right now."

She closed the distance between us. Put her hands around the back of my neck and pulled my head down toward her chest. Caressed her fingers through my hair. My nose was inches from her breasts.

I knew I should stop this.

But I couldn't.

The ship had left the harbor.

SS Dingdong.

Bound for Mistake Island.

She pressed her hips against me.

Against *it.*

Then her lips against mine.

~

The Mayor was speaking when I returned to my seat. Caroline had left a few minutes ahead of me and she was turned in her chair, eyes focused on the woman behind the podium on the dais. I don't know how she explained the five minutes she was gone, the five minutes she had her tongue rammed down my throat in the high school bathroom.

Whatever she said, Jerome knew the truth. I could feel his eyes boring into the side of my head as I sat. Jealousy and anger will do that.

He was probably thinking of something he could sue me for. *Wrongful making out with his luncheon date. Three counts of violating the Bro Code. Acting like a horny sixteen-year-old in public.*

I ignored him and turned my attention to Mayor Van Dixon. She was wearing a green blouse and tan pants. Her gray-streaked hair was tucked behind her ears. She had a massive gold and bejeweled broach on her shoulder that was the size of a small bird's nest.

"Our town is prospering," she spoke. "Small businesses are not only surviving in Tarrin, they are thriving."

Many of the guests applauded. I guessed many in attendance, like the Fulton brothers, were small business owners.

She prattled on about the many great things she'd done over the past eighteen years and the many great things she planned for her next term. I listened halfheartedly, giving the majority of my attention to the crème brûlée in front of me.

Finally, after what seemed like an hour, but was probably closer to twenty minutes, she said, "Now it is my great pleasure to introduce my dear friend: visionary, benefactor, Lunhill president and CEO, David Ramsey."

There was a smattering of applause. Tarrin was decisively a pro-biotech town. But then again, in a time when many farmers were struggling to make ends meet all across the country and the globe, farmers in Tarrin were thriving. And I didn't doubt this was in large part to the higher yields they were getting from using Spectrum-H(R) seeds.

Ramsey gave Mayor Van Dixon a quick hug, then took the podium. Like before, he was impeccably dressed in a suit with a navy blue tie. He adjusted the microphone, then said, "How good was that halibut?"

There was a murmuring of agreement.

"Have you guys ever seen a halibut?" he asked with a smile. "The ugliest damn fish on the planet. Both their eyes are one side of their head. Mutant looking things. But man, do they taste good."

I had intended on waiting a few minutes to make a scene, but patience has never been my virtue.

I cleared my throat and shouted, "Maybe the fish you saw came from the river in Simon Beach. Maybe it just had a bad case of dioxin poisoning."

One hundred and twenty heads snapped in my direction. Most appeared shocked at my outburst. Others, like Jerome and the Fulton brothers, seemed embarrassed at their proximity to me, as if they might be guilty by association. Like when your plus-one gets hammered at the Christmas party and starts getting handsy with your lieutenant.

Up front, I could see Chief Eccleston's gaze narrow as he realized the words had come from his BFF. I half expected him to stand up and attempt to have me forcibly removed, but either he thought it would only make things worse or Ramsey had given him some sort of signal to stand down.

Ramsey glared at me for a long second, then said, "If you aren't aware, what Mr. Prescott is referring to is the tragic dioxin poisoning that occurred in Simon Beach twenty years ago. Though not entirely Lunhill's fault, we did play a role in the tragedy, and we were forced to pay upward of two hundred million dollars in settlements and restitution."

The gymnasium was silent. You could actually hear the rain outside.

Ramsey continued, "We could have stopped there, but we at Lunhill felt obligated to do more. That's why we invested nearly half a billion dollars into the research and development of a new technology that eliminates dioxins more safely and efficiently. Because at Lunhill we want to set an example that we must protect and preserve this planet we call home."

This was met with heavy applause. A handful of people glanced smarmily in my direction as if to say, "Suck on that."

For good measure, Ramsey added, "And just for the record, Mr. Prescott, halibut is a saltwater fish."

Most of the audience jeered. Jerome was smirking so hard his cheeks would probably be sore tomorrow.

"I know about Neil Felding," I said. "I know what he found out."

I watched his face. For the first time, I saw a small twitch in his forehead.

"Terminator seeds," I said. "He was working on a second iteration of them."

There was a soft murmuring. Many of these farmers knew the danger of Terminator seeds, knew that it was an ecological disaster waiting to happen.

"Yes," Ramsey said. "Neil Felding was working on revamping what you refer to as Terminator seeds or what we call Sterile Seed Technology."

"That's bullshit," yelled someone from behind me.

"Please, please," Ramsey said, putting his hand up. "What Neil was trying to accomplish, and I must admit he was doing so in secret, was to add a gene into the seed that would make it impossible for cross-pollination. But four years ago, Neil convinced me Terminator seeds were just too dangerous and we shut down the project. You have my assurances Sterile Seed Technology will never be used."

He locked eyes with me. He'd laid everything out in the open. He had nothing to hide.

But then what accounted for the twitch in his forehead?

I asked, "What was the dust-up in the cafeteria between the two of you about?"

"Oh, that," he said with a smirk. "That was just a little misunderstanding. Neil thought I went back on a raise that I'd promised him a few months prior. He was extremely tightly wound when it came to money. I explained to him that the raise was in company stock, not salary, and that he would see it in his next dividend check."

"Then why did he resign that same day?" I asked.

"He wanted to work on something new. He'd been thinking about leaving for quite some time. And going back to my office and hashing through his raise confusion, we got to talking about his future. And yes, he resigned."

"And then he was killed three weeks later?"

"Yes," Ramsey said. "*Tragically.*"

I'd heard enough.

Thirty seconds later, I was back in the rain.

Chapter 24

The usual puddle in the road leading to the farmhouse blossomed into a small pond as a result of the weekend's rains. I splashed through, the muddy water seeping into my Asics, then continued down toward County Road 52.

I'd been so sure the reason Neil Felding had been killed was his threatening to blow the whistle on the revamping of Terminator seeds, but after listening to Ramsey at the luncheon the previous day, this didn't seem plausible.

Was I way off base? Did Lunhill not have anything to do with Neil Felding's murder? Nothing to do with Mike Zernan's death? Did I want there to be a cover-up so badly that I was creating one in my mind?

Over the course of my career, for the most part, where I smelled smoke there was fire. But every once in a while, it was just a kid lighting off a smoke bomb in the alley.

I'd been wrong before.

Was I wrong now?

As I ran, I thought about everything I knew about Lunhill. Could Neil have stumbled on something else? A dioxin spill? Proof GMOs were causing illness? That Spectrum-H was causing cancer? Some illicit relationship between Lunhill and the FDA? Some governmental fraud? Something to do with Obama?

Three miles later, I was convinced I wasn't crazy.

Barns don't get burned down because of crazy. Police officers don't get strangled because of crazy. You aren't told to leave things alone because of crazy.

No.

Neil Felding found something.

Now I just needed to find out what.

~

Neil Felding's widow lived on a street where the houses were bigger and nicer than any I'd yet seen in Tarrin. Stepping from the car, I walked through a well-manicured front yard and rang the doorbell.

The door opened.

Darcy Felding had a pleasant face, nearly black hair, and brown eyes.

I'm not sure why it hadn't occurred to me earlier to track down Neil Felding's widow. I suppose I was trying to limit the collateral damage that my investigation would cause.

That said, I was done playing nice.

I said, "I was wondering if I could have a couple moments of your time."

"Oh, um, I'm not interested in whatever you're selling."

"Actually, my name is Thomas Prescott. I'm a retired homicide detective. I'd like to speak with you about your husband."

Her breath caught and she said, "Oh, okay. Can you give me a minute?"

I nodded and she closed the door.

Two minutes later, the door opened and she waved me in. "You want to go out back?"

"Sure."

"I can make up a pitcher of lemonade." She motioned me to a small sliding glass door. "It will take me a few minutes, maybe you wouldn't mind finishing up watering my garden."

"Fair trade," I said, then slipped through the sliding glass door and stepped into a small back yard. Unlike most of the neighborhoods in Tarrin, the backyard was fenced.

There was a flower garden abutted by a small vegetable garden. A hose lay on the ground, small droplets of water beading around the head of a nozzle. Lying on the ground just in front of the hose was a white spray bottle.

I picked it up.

Spectrum-H weed killer.

I scrunched my eyebrows together. If Darcy was using Spectrum-H in her garden, Neil must have felt the product was safe.

I set the bottle down and picked up the hose. I sprayed for three or four minutes, stopping when I heard Darcy move through the back door. I clicked off the nozzle, then met her near a table with an umbrella and two cushioned chairs.

"Thank you," she said, handing me a tall glass of lemonade. It had a red purée on top and she said, "Strawberry purée." She nodded at the garden and said, "I grew the strawberries myself."

I hesitated, all of Randall's words rushing into my brain, *I don't spray shit, least of all, those assholes' poison.*

She watched me closely as I picked up the glass and took a long sip.

"So," Darcy said. "You wanted to speak to me about Neil?"

I set the glass down on the small table with an audible clunk and nodded. I considered offering a quick disclaimer, something along the lines of: I need to warn you, the questions I'm about to ask may upset you, may flip your world upside down. But her brown eyes were steeled. I think part of her had been waiting for someone to come asking questions. Maybe even wanting them to.

"Did you ever question your husband's murder beyond him being in the wrong place at the wrong time?"

"I did."

"In what regard?"

"The timing of it all," she said. "Neil resigning from Lunhill just three weeks before he was killed."

"And why exactly did he resign?"

"Creative differences," she said. Then pursing her lips, added, "At least, that's what it said in the non-disclosure."

"But that isn't why he really resigned?"

She shook her head.

I could feel my pulse quicken.

"Did you know what your husband was working on before he resigned?"

She nodded. "Sterile Seed Technology."

"Did you ever have an ethical problem with anything Neil was working on?"

"You mean like the bottle of Spectrum-H I use on my garden."

She must have seen me looking at it. But more than that, she was testing me with the lemonade. Waiting to see how I reacted when she said the strawberry purée was from her garden. That's what she'd been doing the two minutes I waited outside her front door. She was setting up the hose and the bottle.

"Did I pass?" I asked.

"What?"

"Did I pass the strawberry purée test?"

She looked at me for a long second.

I said, "I was a detective for more than a decade."

Finally, she let out a long exhale. "Yes, you passed."

"Were you checking to see if I was one of Lunhill's people?"

She nodded and said, "They never drink."

"Seriously?"

"Never."

"Because they know it might make them sick?"

She shrugged and said, "Who knows?"

I asked, "What's in the bottle?"

"Vinegar."

I grinned, then asked, "If Neil felt Spectrum-H was poisonous, then why work at Lunhill?"

She turned around and waved her hands at the house.

"Money?" I asked.

"Yes, *money*."

"How much did he make?"

"A hundred and fifty thousand, give or take."

"That's pretty good."

"Especially when you live in Tarrin."

"Did Neil commute?"

"About half the time. There are sleeping quarters at the lab. He would stay the night a couple times a week."

"And what about you? What did you do?"

"I stayed home with the kids."

"Where are they now?"

"On summer break from school. They're backpacking through Europe right now."

"Where do they go to school?"

"One is at NYU. One is at the University of Colorado."

"Those are both pretty expensive."

She nodded.

"Do you work?"

"I garden."

Her husband had been dead for four years. If they were smart with their money, he could have left her a sizable nest egg. Maybe a million, maybe more. Plus whatever life insurance he had.

"How much money do you get from Lunhill?" I asked.

"Fifty grand."

I was surprised she answered so candidly. "A year?"

She shook her head. "A month."

I whistled.

She said, "That was part of Neil's *release* package."

"More like hush money."

She raised her eyebrows.

"What was it?" I asked. "Did he threaten to go public with details about Spectrum-H? That it was dangerous?"

"No."

"He must have had something on them. Must have threatened to blow the whistle on something."

She stared at me.

"Come on," I prodded. "What was it? A dioxin spill? GMOs causing cancer? Fraud?"

She took a sip of lemonade.

"I can protect you," I said.

"They will sue me for everything I'm worth. Take the house. Take everything."

I guessed her name was all over the non-disclosures as well. If she broke her silence, they could do exactly what she was talking about.

"These people killed your husband."

"What do you mean?"

"It wasn't just strange timing, your husband resigning and dying three weeks later. Lunhill had him killed."

She looked at me questioningly, but said nothing.

I scooted my seat a couple inches closer to her. "Your husband found something out. Threatened to blow the whistle on Lunhill. They made him sign a bunch of NDAs, but they didn't trust he would keep his mouth shut. They couldn't risk killing him outright, even an accident would have looked suspicious so close to his resigning, so they paid Lowry Barnes to do it."

"That's absurd."

"Is it?" I asked. "Where is the only place in a town everyone is bound to go at some point?"

She glanced upward for a moment, then back down.

"The grocery store," I said for her. "It wouldn't have been hard for them to find out that an ex-felon had recently been fired from the Save-More and was in desperate need of money. They paid Lowry to kill Neil and make it look like he was going after his ex-manager."

"But Lowry committed suicide."

"It could easily have been made to look that way."

I could see her running the logic over in her head, see it slowly going from impossible, to plausible, to probable.

"There is just one question," I said. "Was what Neil knew worth killing over?"

She took a long breath, then said, "It would have ruined them."

~

We moved inside. Darcy joined me at the kitchen table. "They searched the house," she said, "a couple weeks after Neil died."

"Lunhill guys?"

"Yeah, it was actually written into one of the NDAs. If Neil died, they would get to search the house."

"No shit."

"So they put me and the kids up in a hotel for a week and went through everything."

"Did they find anything?"

"They never said. But the money kept coming, so I guess not."

I looked up at the ceiling, the walls. "You ever check the place for bugs? Wiretaps, I mean?"

She shook her head. Then she leaned forward and whispered, "You think they bugged the place?"

"I wouldn't doubt it."

Part of me wondered if someone was listening to our words this very second.

"Why don't we go to my car?" I offered.

She followed me out the front door and into the Range Rover. Once inside, I could see the manila envelope on her lap.

"Is that it?" I asked.

"Yeah."

"Why didn't they find it when they searched the house?"

"It wasn't in the house. I found it in our safety deposit box at the bank six months later."

She stared at the envelope for a beat, then handed it to me.

I slowly unclasped the brass fastener and pulled out the contents. There were several documents and a handful of pictures.

After a couple seconds, I said, "Wow."

I glanced at Darcy.

She shifted in her seat.

I looked back down at the picture in my lap. It was a picture of more than a dozen cows. All on their sides. All dead. Another picture was a close-up of a single cow. It's udders were swollen and red. A man stood over the cow.

The first thing that popped into my head was *dioxin*. Brian had said how a bunch of animals died after they sprayed the waste oil at Simon Beach.

There must have been another dioxin spill.

I moved to the documents. It was a bunch of numbers and graphs. I was sure Darcy had studied the documents at length and I asked, "What am I looking at here?"

"Those are the data sheets Lunhill sent to the FDA from the testing of their recombinant Bovine Growth Hormone."

"Recombinant what?"

"You ever hear of rBGH?"

"Maybe. I think I've heard my sister talk about it. Something in milk."

"It's a hormone that makes dairy cows produce up to twenty percent more milk."

I said, "But according to these photos, it also kills them."

She nodded. "Twenty years ago, Lunhill was testing their recombinant Bovine Growth Hormone, what they were calling Recom 6. They treated seventeen cows with it. Fifteen of them died."

So it wasn't dioxin after all.

I looked down at one of the documents. "But it says right here that the only side effect was one cow getting something called mastitis."

"They fudged the data."

"They can do that?"

"The FDA only looks at the data the company sends them. They don't do any outside testing themselves."

"But that's ridiculous."

"Yes it is. But it would be impossible for the FDA to run experiments and tests on all the new products that come out each year. It would take a hundred thousand employees. It's a government agency, they only have so much in the budget."

"So they rely on these companies to send them accurate data from their experiments?"

"Yes. They set rigorous guidelines that have to be met over the course of months, sometimes years. And most companies send the real data."

"But if Lunhill had sent the real data, it never would have passed."

She smirked. "Exactly."

"It passed?"

"Twenty years ago."

"And is it still being used?"

"Lunhill sold the rights a decade ago for something like four hundred million dollars, but it's still in production."

I thought about the repercussions of this. If this information leaked, sure it would hurt Lunhill, but it wouldn't ruin them. They didn't even produce the hormone anymore.

"If farmers have been using Recom 6 for the past twenty years, then where are all the dead cows? It would be impossible to cover up. They must have tweaked it and made it safe."

"Lunhill did," she said, "before it went to market."

I took a breath, then said, "I'm not so sure if this went public it would ruin them."

"You're looking at it wrong. It isn't about the cows. It's about the fudging of the data. If they sent the FDA falsified testing data for Recom 6, what's to say every product they've ever produced hasn't also been falsified?"

She was right.

Spectrum-H.

Spectrum-H(R) seeds.

All their GMOs.

If this got out, it *would* ruin them.

"Did Neil tell you about this?" I asked.

"No."

"So you have no idea how he found this out?"

She glanced down at her lap, then back up at me. Her eyes softened. "He left a note in the safety deposit box. It said not to take the folder out of the box, to leave it there, to only use it in an emergency."

"Like if they stopped paying?"

"I guess that's what he meant." She took a breath. "He said he stumbled on the pictures and documents when he was going back through the Sterile Seed data from when they first started doing research in the early nineties. Evidently, someone buried a folder in the Sterile Seed files. He opened it and saw the pictures and documents."

"Let me guess, he confronted David Ramsey about it at work and they had a dust-up in the cafeteria?"

"That very day. He was extremely emotional about it."

I'd had a hard time believing David Ramsey's version of the dust-up at the luncheon. A shoving match over a raise?

"I can see why," I said. "He'd been working for the company for twenty years."

"That was part of it, but I think what upset him most was that it happened here."

"What do you mean *here*?"

She grabbed one of the photos and showed it to me. "This dairy farm is in Tarrin."

My breath caught.

I riffled through the pictures. Something in one of them had caught my eye, but I didn't think anything of it until now.

I found the picture I was looking for. It was the picture of the single cow, udders grotesquely red and oozing pus. A man was standing over the cow.

His hair was fuller and his glasses a touch thicker, but there was no mistaking it.

It was Tom Lanningham.

Wheeler's father.

Chapter 25

I hit the small bell on the counter.

"Just a minute," she called from the back.

A couple seconds later, she pushed through the back door.

"Hey," Wheeler said. "What are you doing here?" Her face grew concerned, "Are Harold and May okay?"

"They're fine," I assured her.

I took a breath, then said, "I need to talk to you about something."

Her concern faded and her arms crossed. "If this is about Caroline, I already heard."

I let out a small sigh.

How did she find out? Had Caroline told people? Jerome? Or had it been so obvious everyone at the luncheon had known?

"In the high school bathroom," Wheeler said, shaking her head. "Seriously?"

"That isn't what I came to talk to you about, but since you brought it up. Yeah, it was stupid. She followed me into the bathroom, and we made out like hornball teenagers."

Her arms crossed a couple inches farther. Her shoulders threatened to dislocate.

Against my better judgment, I asked, "What is it with you two, why do you hate her so much?"

I could see her debating whether to disclose her reasoning. Finally, after what seemed like an eternity, she said, "Miller."

"Your ex?"

"Yeah. She slept with him the day after I broke off the engagement."

"Which time?"

She huffed. "Both times."

"Jeez."

"Yeah, she doesn't waste any time."

I almost said, "If you broke up with him, then technically neither of them did anything wrong," but the bell on the counter was within arm's reach and I didn't want it chucked in my direction. I went with, "I'm sorry."

"Now she's doing it again."

I scrunched my eyebrows together.

"Don't act like you don't know I have a thing for you."

I grinned sheepishly and said, "If it's any consolation, I have a thing for you too."

Her arms relaxed slightly, then flexed once more. "Then why did you make out with that floozy in the bathroom?"

"I'm an idiot."

I've learned over the years this is the best answer to a question that has no right answer.

"Yeah, you are."

She took a couple steps forward, her white lab coat swaying, then said, "So what did you want to talk to me about?"

And just when we'd gone and made up.

I thought about turning and leaving, burning the photographs and documents. But I had to tell her. She had a right to know. And, to be honest, I needed to see her reaction. I needed to know she wasn't aware her father was involved in a twenty-year-old cover-up with the Lunhill Corporation.

There was a bench in the small waiting room and I said, "We should probably sit down."

For the first time, her eyes moved to the manila folder in my right hand. She followed me to the bench and sat down next to me. Our legs touched. I handed her the folder and said, "I found out what Neil Felding had on Lunhill."

"Where did you get this?"

"Darcy Felding."

"Neil gave this to her?"

"He left it for her in their safety deposit box."

She swallowed, then pulled the documents from the folder.

I watched as she peered down at the first photo. The one of the fifteen dead cows lying in various positions on their sides.

"Oh my God," she said.

She moved to the next photo. Then the next. I didn't need to see her face to know when she reached the one of her father standing over the sick cow. I would have known by her audible gasp. She whipped her head around. "That's my dad."

One of the hardest emotions to fake is surprise.

Wheeler didn't know.

"I know," I said.

She was silent for the next few minutes, moving through the remaining photos and the documents.

Finally, she looked up at me. "No."

"No?"

"No, my father was not involved in this cover-up. If he was there, he was there to help those animals."

"That's possible."

"*Possible?* No, that's what happened. He was the most loving, gentle man on the planet. He would never have signed on for anything that would hurt an animal."

"Did he ever tell you about this?"

She inhaled sharply, then said, "That doesn't mean he did anything wrong."

"Fifteen of the seventeen cows they treated with their hormone died. You don't think that's a story your dad would have shared with you? If not as his daughter, then as a fellow veterinarian?"

Her eyes started to water. "He wouldn't."

I took her hand.

She pulled it away. She folded the pages up and shoved them back in the large envelope. "Take these," she said, slamming the folder against my chest, "and leave."

"Wheeler?"

"Get out!" she screamed.

I stood and walked toward the door. I turned. Wheeler had her head in her hands, openly sobbing.

I cleared my throat.

She glanced up at me.

"Lunhill gave Neil Felding fifty thousand dollars a month to keep this quiet. They probably gave your dad money too."

Then I left.

~

"This is my wife, Joan," Jerry said, nodding at a fair-skinned blond woman in a blue summer dress. "And this is Tyler. And that little guy is Patrick."

Tyler was seven. He inherited his mother's blond hair, freckles, and blue eyes. Patrick was four. He had darker hair like his father but, like his sibling, he had his mother's light blue eyes.

I gave Joan a hug, then shook hands with both the boys.

"Where should I put this?" I asked, lightly shaking the bottle of red wine I brought.

"I'll take that," Joan said, taking the bottle. Then, giving the label a cursory glance, she quipped, "Oh, goodie. I love Malbec."

She headed off toward the kitchen and instructed Jerry to give me a tour of the house.

Jerry spread his arms wide and said, "So this is the house."

"Nice tour," I said.

Tyler gave a tug on the bottom of his dad's collared golf shirt and said, "Can we finish up our game before dinner?"

Jerry glanced at me and asked, "You play Madden?"

"It's been awhile."

Thirty-five years to be exact.

Jerry gave Tyler a little shove in the shoulder and said, "Me and this punk are tied with five minutes to go."

Tyler smirked and said, "But I've got the ball on his six-yard-line."

The four of us made our way to a door off the hallway and headed down to a finished basement. There were two huge black leather couches, the kind with the reclining chairs built in, surrounding a curved flat screen TV.

Jerry and Tyler plopped down on the couch and picked up their respective controllers.

"Who's who?" I asked, taking a seat next to Tyler. Patrick climbed up on the couch and nestled in next to me.

"I'm the Redskins," Tyler said, "and my dad is the Cowboys."

On-screen it showed the score was tied 31-31.

I nudged Patrick and said, "Who are you rooting for?"

His little face scrunched, then he said, "Tyler."

"Good man," I said, giving him a poke in the belly. "Always stick with your brother."

He giggled.

"You picked the wrong side," Jerry said with a maniacal laugh.

The two boys chuckled.

You could tell the three of them were great buddies.

The game resumed, and I watched the last five minutes, which I have to be honest, was almost as exciting as watching a real game. With just twenty seconds left, Tyler was winning by four points. Jerry marched the Cowboys down the field and they were on the Redskins' fifteen-yard line.

"My dad's gotta score a touchdown to win," Patrick said, bobbing up and down in his seat.

Jerry threw a pass into the end zone, but it was batted away by one of Tyler's Redskins at the last moment.

Jerry yelled, "Shit!"

"Daaaaaddddd!" Patrick screamed, then extended his hand.

The game was paused. Jerry stood up, took out his wallet, and gave both Tyler and Patrick a dollar.

"I wish I would have known about this rule on the golf course," I ribbed him. "You'd have owed me sixty bucks after that shot out of the sand trap."

Jerry laughed.

Three plays later, the game was over. Tyler won. He did a quick victory dance, then his dad took his wallet out a second time and handed him a five-dollar-bill.

I asked Jerry, "Does he have to give you five dollars if he loses?"

"No," Tyler said. "I have to clean his car."

"My turn," said Patrick, grabbing Tyler's controller off the couch.

Jerry said, "Why don't you play, Uncle Thomas?"

Uncle Thomas.

I wasn't technically their uncle, but if Lacy got knocked up, I might someday be an *actual* uncle. I, Thomas Dergen Prescott, would be partially responsible for helping to shape a child's life.

God help us all.

Tyler coached me in my game against Patrick, but it was still a bloodbath, and he beat me 46–14.

When the game was over, Patrick glanced up at me and said, "It's okay, you don't have to give me any money."

"Do you take plastic?" I asked.

He looked confused. I took out my credit card and swiped it behind his ear. He went into hysterics.

Joan called down a minute later that dinner was ready.

~

After dinner, the boys took their dessert—cherry pie and vanilla ice cream—down to the basement.

Jerry topped off both Joan's and my wine glasses, and I asked, "Where did you guys meet?"

Joan, who hadn't spoken much over dinner, save for the occasional reprimand of one of the boys, said, "We met at work."

"At the bank?"

She smiled. "I was working at a branch in Springfield when my first marriage went south. I was looking for a fresh start somewhere and put in for a transfer. Tarrin had an opening."

"How long ago was that?"

She took a sip of wine, set it down, then said, "Ten—no, eleven—years ago."

I turned to Jerry and asked, "How long did it take you to get her to go out with you?"

"Six months," he said. "I asked her out on Halloween."

I turned to Joan and saw her grinning.

Jerry continued, "She was working one of the teller windows and she'd worn these little cat ears and drawn whiskers on her face." He turned to Joan and said, "She just looked so damn cute."

Joan said, "I still have the ears."

"Then what happened?" I asked.

Joan answered, "After we started dating, I had to transfer to the Mexico branch."

"Company policy that you can't date someone at the same branch," Jerry explained.

"I worked in Mexico for a few years," Joan said, "got promoted from teller to loan officer, then I got pregnant with Tyler."

Jerry smiled and said, "Then I chivalrously asked her to marry me."

We all laughed.

Joan said, "Been home with the kids ever since."

We chatted for another hour, then the boys returned. Patrick really wanted to show me his room, and I let him take my hand and lead me up the stairs.

He was big into Teenage Mutant Ninja Turtles and his room was painted dark green with posters of all the turtles on his walls.

There were a couple pictures on his dresser and I picked one up. It was Patrick riding a horse with a big smile on his face. He was a little smaller, and I guessed the picture was taken about a year earlier.

"Do you like horses?" I asked.

He crooked his head to the side, "Yeah." Then he added, "But not as much as Ninja Turtles."

~

It was closing in on 8:00 p.m. when I returned to the farm.

There was a blue sedan parked in front of the house.

Caroline's car.

Bollocks.

I stepped from the car, then pushed through the front door. Harold and May attacked me with kisses.

"Hi guys," I said, craning my neck into the living room. She wasn't there. "Caroline?" I shouted.

There was no answer.

Maybe she was outside somewhere.

"Where is she?" I asked the piglets.

They didn't know. Or they were too hungry to care. While filling their food bowls, I heard a creak. From upstairs.

My stomach dropped.

I made my way upstairs. The door to the master bedroom was closed.

"Caroline?" I shouted. "Um, if you're in there, can you come out so we can chat?"

I waited a long minute.

Maybe she wasn't in there. Maybe I closed the door myself. Or maybe the wind blew it shut.

I closed my hand on the doorknob and pushed the door in.

Caroline was on the bed. She was lying on her side, her head resting on her hand. She was completely naked.

I took a deep breath and said, "Hey."

"Hi," she purred.

She massaged one of her large—and I must admit, perfect—breasts with her left hand.

"So," I said, "I need you to put some clothes on."

"You don't want to finish what you started?"

She swiveled from her side to her back. Then ever so slowly, she began to spread her legs.

A better man may have been able to shield his eyes. To look away. But not me. I stared at her vagina as if there was an endangered fresh water dolphin on my bed.

I mentally splashed cold water on my face and said, "Put some clothes on. This isn't going to happen."

Then I walked out of the room.

She came downstairs a couple minutes later. She was wearing a black robe and sandals. Apparently, that's the only clothing she brought.

"You really know how to make a girl feel unwanted," she said brusquely.

"I'm sorry, Caroline, but this," I moved my hand from her to me, "just isn't going to work."

She took a couple steps forward. She was only a foot from me. She pulled her robe open. "Don't you want to touch them?"

I took a steadying breath. "Caroline."

Finally, accepting defeat, she closed her robe.

"Please leave," I said, nodding toward the door.

She stalked to the door, then slammed it.

Headlights appeared through the window and I walked outside. It was a truck. Wheeler. She parked and stepped out.

Caroline was just getting in her car and rolled down the window. "You can have him," she belted, then gunned the engine and accelerated away.

Wheeler looked at me questioningly. "What was that about?"

I told her.

"She spread her legs?"

"*Basic Instinct* style," I said with a laugh.

"Then you kicked her out?"

"I did."

She fought down a smile, then said, "About earlier, about my dad." She paused. "I know you were just showing me what you found. I shouldn't have screamed at you."

"Don't worry about it. I probably would have reacted the same way."

She handed me a couple sheets of paper.

I looked down at the pages. They were bank records.

Wheeler said, "My dad had been getting ten thousand dollars a month from Lunhill for *twenty years*."

~

"He told me the money was coming from a rich guy whose dog he saved many years ago," she said. "It was when my dad was first starting out. Some bigwig was traveling through town and his dog got hit by a car. My dad saved the dog, and the guy was so appreciative that he set up a trust to give the clinic ten grand a month."

"And you're sure this isn't the truth?"

She shook her head. "I have a friend at the bank. She traced the account number. It's not a trust. It's something called Hillman Enterprises, which I've been researching on the internet for the past few hours and doesn't seem to exist."

"And you think it's Lunhill?"

"Don't you?"

I did and told her so.

"There's more," she said. "The year my dad started taking the money. That's the year my mom left."

"You think she knew?"

"I called her." She took a deep breath. "The clinic was struggling. My dad could barely keep up with the bills. Then Greg Mallory called him to come look at some of his cows. There was a guy there. Offered my dad money to keep what was happening at the dairy quiet. My dad took the money. My mom was disgusted. Left him and me a month later."

"I'm sorry."

"Why didn't your mom ever tell you?"

"She said she didn't want me to hate my dad."

I put my arm around her shoulder.

"He was my hero," she sniffed.

"I remember when I found out my dad wasn't perfect," I said. "I was fifteen. I walked in on him doing a line of coke in his office."

"Really?"

"Yeah."

"What did he do?"

"He told me he didn't do it very often. Only when he had a bunch of work to do. Then he said if he ever caught me doing it, he would cut off my balls."

"Wow."

I said, "I'm sorry about your dad."

She sniffed and said, "And I'm sorry your dad was a cokehead."

We both laughed.

I took her hand and said, "Think about how many animals your dad helped over the past twenty years. If he hadn't taken that money, he might not have been able to do that."

She brushed a tear off her cheek, then she turned her head, her soft eyes gazing into mine. I leaned down and brushed my lips against hers. We are only allowed a few perfect moments in our lifetime.

This was one of mine.

Chapter 26

"I'll be back on Thursday," I said.

She wasn't looking at me. She was too busy blowing raspberries on May's belly.

"Bree!" I shouted. "Did you hear me?"

"Yeah," she said, glancing up. "You're gonna be back on Tuesday."

"*Thursday*. Today is Tuesday." For having a near-genius IQ, Bree was the consummate scatterbrain.

"Right," she said, then bent her head down and blew on May's belly. May squirmed with delight.

"Come over here."

She sighed, then walked over.

I pointed to the piece of paper I taped to the fridge. I went over the piglets feeding schedule with her, plus a few other notes. "If you give them baths, you need to use the Johnson's Baby Shampoo on Harold, he's sensitive to anything else."

"Thomas," Bree said, grabbing my shoulder. "They're gonna be fine. They're pigs. Now say goodbye and go wherever you are going."

"Ohio."

"Yeah, go to *Ohio*. We're gonna be fine." She turned and ran toward the piglets—her blue hair flopping up and down—chasing them into the living room.

I followed the three. Bree was on her back on the floor and Harold was standing on her chest licking her face.

"Piglet kisses!" Bree screeched. "Yay!"

I said goodbye to May first. I gave her a kiss on the head and said, "You be good." Then I softly grabbed Harold's face and said, "You're the man of the house now. You watch over your sister."

He oinked.

"Here," Bree said, handing me my backpack from off the couch. "Leave."

"Okay, I'm going."

Ten minutes later, I pulled up to Wheeler's house. She was standing in the driveway. She was wearing blue jeans, a white T-shirt, and her trusty red St. Louis Cardinals hat.

I rolled down the window and said, "You know, we're only staying two nights." For some reason, I assumed Wheeler was the type of girl who would travel light.

I was wrong.

She had a huge overnight bag and then one of those enormous plastic suitcases.

I grabbed her suitcase, which would *not* have flown for free on Southwest, and said, "What did you pack? Gold bullion?"

"Just the necessities."

I pulled on the zipper of her suitcase and she screamed, "Don't you dare."

I laughed and re-zipped it, then I jumped back in the driver seat and said, "You ready for this?"

"Columbus or bust." She gave my knee a light slap.

She was in a jovial mood and she had packed for a three-week Caribbean cruise, but this wasn't a personal trip. This was all business. There was one more thread we needed to pull. That thread was in Columbus, Ohio.

And it had once been married to Lowry Barnes.

~

Eight hours in a car with someone you don't know all that well is a big gamble. It's Russian roulette. You could easily have your brains splattered all over the inside of the car. Luckily, with Wheeler, each time the trigger was pulled, it was a blank.

The conversation was easy and light. We chatted about past relationships, our families, sports achievements, anything and everything. As we entered Ohio, though still a few hours from Columbus, I steered the conversation toward the reason for the trip.

"Did you know Kim?"

I'd burned a lot of bridges over the years, at the Seattle Police Department, at the FBI, but I still had a few contacts that hadn't deleted my number from their phones. One of these was Kevin Bolger, whom

I'd met while working in Philly. He'd retired from the force a few years back and now did contract investigation for a law firm, but he still had access to a number of different law enforcement databases.

He'd found Kim Barnes, now Kim Harrison, living in Columbus, Ohio. He'd run a background check on her, digging up everything he could find, which proved rather anticlimactic. She worked at a nail salon, had a few grand in credit card debt, rented a small house, and owned a seven-year-old Ford Focus.

But her past was a different story.

Kim grew up in a trailer park on the outskirts of Tarrin. Her parents weren't just poor, they were shit poor, or as Bolger put it, "They didn't have a pot to piss in." This is where she met Lowry Barnes, whose parents also lived in the trailer park. At seventeen, she found herself pregnant with Lowry's child. Two years later, a second child would come. The couple married a few years after that, moving into a trailer of their own. Soon thereafter, Lowry's troubles with the law began and it wasn't long before Kim found herself raising her two children by herself and working two jobs to keep the lights on.

"I knew of her," Wheeler replied. "But I didn't know her personally. She got in a fight with one of my friend's little sisters once."

"Over what?"

"I'm not sure. Probably a guy. What else do girls fight over?" She gave my knee a squeeze.

I grinned, then asked, "What about after the murders?"

"It was such a whirlwind with my dad, getting everything in order for his funeral, that I don't really remember much." She paused then said, "But I do remember when I heard she moved out of town. It was three or four weeks after my dad's funeral and I was going over my dad's appointment book with his receptionist. She told me how she had seen Kim loading up a moving van the day before."

"I'm surprised it took her that long to leave. She probably couldn't go into town without being shunned."

She nodded, though I didn't detect a whole lot of sympathy.

An hour later, we reached Columbus. It was closing in on 8:00 p.m. We grabbed a quick dinner, then made our way to a Holiday Inn across the street from the restaurant. We were both tired from the drive, and after a quick kiss goodnight, we retired to our respective rooms.

~

My phone chimed and I picked it up off the pillow.

It was a little after 9:00 a.m., and I had five missed texts. All from Bree.

I sat up with alarm. Something must have happened to one of the piglets. I scrolled through her texts and gave a sigh of relief. It was just a bunch of pictures. Harold and May in the bathtub. Harold and May rolling around in the mud. Harold and May asleep on one another. Harold and May eating waffles.

The last text, the one that woke me up, read: **I started Harold and May an Instagram account. They already have 500 followers!!!**

I laughed.

I texted back: **How did they like the waffles?**

She instantly replied: **They looooooooooooved them!**

Me: **Chips off the old block!**

I dressed, then knocked on the adjoining door. Wheeler opened it a moment later. She smiled meekly and said, "Good morning." She was wrapped in a towel and her hair was wet.

"I'd say."

I showed her the pictures Bree sent. She snickered, then said, "Oh, what a proud papa you must be."

I beamed.

Wheeler finished getting ready and twenty minutes later, we zipped through the McDonald's drive-through—Sausage and Egg *McMuffin* for me, Sausage and Egg *Biscuit* for Wheeler.

"How could this ever work?" I said, handing over her breakfast sandwich. "We're like the Capulets and the Montagues."

She found this amusing.

It took ten minutes to drive to where Lowry Barnes' widow lived. I pulled onto a side street, continued for two blocks, then Wheeler said, "That's it right there."

It was a small, cookie-cutter, stucco house with a tiny lawn. The house next door was nearly identical, save for the large truck parked in the driveway.

I made a U-turn and parked on the opposite side of the street. I told Wheeler to hang tight and I jogged up to the house and rang the doorbell. It didn't appear anyone was home, and I wasn't surprised when no one came to the door. On my way back to the car, I took a minute to check out the large black truck in the neighbor's driveway. It was facing away from the garage, which struck me as odd.

Back in the car, I asked Wheeler, "What kind of truck is that?"

She raised her eyebrows as if to say, "Really?"

"I'm not a truck guy," I protested.

"A Ford Raptor."

"What does one cost?"

"Fully loaded? Probably high fifties."

"How old do you think that truck is?"

She gazed out the window, then pointed to the truck's front grill and said, "They changed the grill on the newer models. I'd guess it's three or four years old." She glanced at me questioningly, "Why? You thinking about buying a truck?"

"I'm gonna have to if I want to fit in with all you rednecks."

She gave me a quick slap on the leg, which led to some light kissing, then some heavy kissing. I was getting ready to round second when a blue Ford Focus pulled onto the street and Kim Harrison's garage door began to lift.

Wheeler and I waited a long minute, then stepped from the car and started toward the house. It took Kim Harrison half a minute to open the front door. No doubt she was finishing up putting the frozen items in the freezer and she shouted, "I'm coming!" on two separate occasions.

When Kim did come to the door, the first thing I noticed was she was bone thin, which I attributed more to DNA than to anything illicit. She was medium height with her blond hair up in a bun.

I asked, "Are you Kim Barnes, widow of Lowry Barnes?"

I could see her contemplating lying. Her eyes moved to Wheeler, a spark of recognition flashing after a moment, and then she said, "Yes, I am."

I glanced at Wheeler. Her jaw was set and her eyes narrowed. The abstract blame she felt toward Kim was palpable.

I nudged her with my arm.

Perhaps sensing the same tractor beams, Kim said, "I'm sorry about your father."

It was only five simple words, but they could have been five million for the amount of power they held. Whatever hatred, blame, censure, or rebuke Wheeler felt dissipated.

Kim took a step forward and the two women embraced.

I was reminded Kim was also a victim. Not only did she lose her husband, she lost her town. I would need to keep this in my periphery when I interrogated her.

The two women wiped away tears, then Kim invited us inside.

"Just give me a moment while I finish up putting the groceries away," she said, then instructed us to go to the living room.

Wheeler and I sat down on a tan sofa. The room was simple, void of any noticeable extravagances.

"You okay?" I asked Wheeler.

"Yeah," she said, wiping away the last of the moisture from beneath her eyes. "I don't know what came over me. The second I saw her, it was like I saw him. Saw Lowry."

I nodded.

"I keep forgetting that she suffered even worse than me. She had to live with that guilt."

"Yeah, I was thinking the same thing."

"Promise me you'll take it easy on her."

"I promise."

"Why did you just cross your legs before you said that?"

I didn't have a chance to respond. Kim stepped down into the living room. "Would either of you like something to drink?"

Wheeler and I both declined.

Kim took a seat in the recliner opposite the couch. When she was comfortably seated, I asked, "Can I use your restroom?"

I used the restroom, then took a quick detour into the kitchen. Kim's purse was on the kitchen counter, and I rummaged through it quickly, then returned to the small living room. The two women were mid-conversation.

"Where are your kids?" Wheeler asked.

"Summer camp." Kim smiled. "Thank God."

"Is it a day camp?" I asked, resuming my seat on the couch.

"No, three weeks. On one of the lakes about an hour from here. A bunch of the kids from the neighborhood go each year." She took a breath, then said, "But I'm guessing you guys didn't come all this way just to ask about my kids."

I decided to be straight with her. "I'm a retired homicide detective and for the past couple months I've been reinvestigating the murders your husband committed."

"Ex-husband," she said.

"You guys were divorced?"

"No, I mean, he's dead, he's not my husband anymore."

I wasn't sure if I only knew the correct terminology because I'd dealt with widows on a number of occasions while working as a detective, but I felt obligated to correct her. "Lowry isn't your ex-husband, he's your *late* husband."

"Late?"

"Yes, late refers to deceased."

I looked over at Wheeler. She raised her eyebrows. I wasn't sure if this meant she also didn't know the correct terminology or that I was acting like a nincompoop.

"Anyway," I said, "that doesn't really matter. What matters is that over the course of my investigation, I turned up evidence that proves your husband didn't act alone."

"There was another shooter?"

"No. Lowry was the lone gunman. He shot those people. But the reason he killed them isn't what everybody thinks."

"What do you mean?"

"It was made to look like Lowry was waging this vendetta against his manager at the Save-More because he was fired."

Kim must have thought this was a question and said, "Yes."

"But Odell, his manager, wasn't the target. The target was Neil Felding."

"Neil Felding?"

"Yes. He was one of the people killed."

"I know," she scoffed. "You think I don't know the names of the people my husband killed?"

"I'm sorry."

"You should be." Her eyes began to water. "I watched every single one of their funerals you know."

"You were there?" Wheeler asked.

She shook her head. "I made my friend Tally go and record them on her phone. I watched them all. I still have them saved on my computer." She lowered her head and sobbed.

Wheeler grabbed my forearm and I said, "I'm sorry."

I gave Kim a few moments to collect herself, then said, "Then you know that Neil Felding worked for the Lunhill Corporation?"

"Yeah."

"But what you probably didn't know is that Neil was about to blow the whistle on a huge cover-up Lunhill had been hiding for more than twenty years."

I tried to read her reaction. She appeared genuinely surprised. "Really? What was it? The cover-up, I mean?"

"It's complicated, but basically, Lunhill introduced a growth hormone in the early 1990s that when administered to cows would cause them to produce more milk."

I wasn't surprised when she said, "rBGH."

"Correct. Lunhill tested the hormone at a dairy in Tarrin."

"Mallory's?"

I nodded. "They tested the hormone on seventeen cows and fifteen of them died. Then they fudged the data on the reports they sent to the FDA and their product was passed."

Her eyebrows rose. "But if they fudged the data on that, then they could have done it for everything, all their stupid GMOs and pesticides and all their other shit." You could almost watch the anvil fall. "That would have destroyed them."

"Exactly. And Neil Felding was about to blow the whistle on them when, quite conveniently, he was murdered."

I could see her thinking everything over.

I said, "Neil wasn't an innocent bystander. He was the target. Your husband went to Save-More to kill Neil. He made it look like he was there to kill the manager."

"But why would he do that?"

"Money."

The word sat in the air for one second. Then two. It was the Hindenburg, hovering around the small room. And just as bright as the explosion of the floating hydrogen bomb, so too was the look of acknowledgement on Kim's face.

Wheeler and I had driven eight hours to see Kim's face flush.

That was the last thread. Lowry getting paid was the first domino. Without that, the others would never fall.

"You know about the money," I said.

She frowned. "Money? What money?"

I tried to remind myself Kim was also a victim. She had to deal with growing up poor, getting knocked up by Lowry Barnes, supporting their two children while Lowry was locked up, Lowry murdering five people, being ostracized from her town, forced to pack up and leave. What was the big deal if she got a little money? In the grand scheme of things, did it really matter?

Yes, it did. At that moment in time, it mattered a whole fucking lot.

She might not have known where the money came from, but she sure as shit knew it had blood on it.

"How much did they give you?" I asked.

She shook her head.

"How did it come? A big bag of cash? A money transfer? Stock options?"

"I don't know what you're talking about."

"Bullshit!" I belted.

She was stunned into silence and I said, "You think you were so smart. Move to Columbus. Rent a small house. Don't flash the money. And you did so well. Except for one thing." I grinned. "Yeah, you know what I'm talking about."

She glanced up at me.

"You grew up shit poor. Parents didn't have money. Then you had a couple kids. Then your husband gets locked up. You worked two jobs just to put food on the table. And then finally, you get some money. And let's call it what it really is, blood money. And you can't help yourself, you had to have it."

Wheeler grabbed my arm and turned me toward her. "You promised."

"I had my legs crossed," I snorted.

I turned back to Kim. "But you were smart about it, you didn't buy it in your name. You just wanted to prove to yourself you made it."

"What are you talking about?" Wheeler blurted.

"The truck, the one in the neighbor's driveway. It isn't theirs." I tilted my head toward Kim, "It's hers."

"I don't know what you're talking about," Kim said, her teeth gritted.

"You mean to tell me this key doesn't belong to that truck?" I rattled the keys that I found in her purse. There were two Ford keys on the ring. They looked similar, but they were slightly different.

"Give me those!" Kim said, jumping off the couch.

I pushed past her toward the front door. I pulled it open and walked across the lawn to where the truck was parked.

"Thomas."

I turned.

Wheeler was a step behind me.

"What are you doing?" she said, shaking her head. "You're being ridicu—"

I hit the unlock button on the key fob and the truck lights flickered.

Wheeler's mouth hung limp.

I glanced to where Kim stood on her doorstep, her face looking like a wax sculpture under a heat lamp.

"How did you know?" Wheeler said, still shaking her head.

"I haven't seen many trucks since we reached Columbus city limits. This isn't truck territory. Then I checked the odometer. The truck has less than a hundred miles on it, but it's a few years old." And I found it odd the truck was parked away from the garage. It was as if was on display. And it was. It was a trophy. Kim's trophy.

"That's not a whole lot to go on."

"I was just slightly suspicious at the beginning. That's why I wanted to check her keys. When I saw the two Ford keys on her keychain I found it odd. Most people wouldn't keep their spare key with the primary key. When I checked the grooves against each another, I noticed they were different keys altogether."

I locked the truck then made my way back to Kim. I handed her the keys. Her hand shook as she wrapped her fingers around them.

"How did the money come?" I asked.

"Cash," she said. "A big bag of cash."

~

"Did you get the license plate of the truck?" Wheeler asked.

We were a mile from Kim's house, nearing the highway.

I shook my head.

"It might come in handy," she said. "If we need to prove any of this. Prove a money trail."

$250,000.

In a paper bag.

Kim Barnes said she never knew where it came from. She found it three days after the murders. It was under the bathroom sink. She didn't know if the money had come from drugs, guns, or what, but she did know Lowry hadn't come into the money legally. She swore on her life she never once suspected the money had anything to do with the Save-More murders. Tears ran down her cheeks as the words flew from her mouth. It must have felt good in a way. To get it off her chest.

She led us to a safe in her bedroom closet and showed us what was left of the money. There was $20,000 in cash. Then there were two envelopes. Inside were forms detailing the college trusts she'd set up for both her kids. Both for $90,000.

I think she expected me to confiscate the money. But I had no intention of telling anyone about the money Kim received. She'd been through enough. What she did with it was her business.

I only cared that there *was* money. I only cared that Lowry Barnes was paid to kill.

All the same, Wheeler was right. At some point we might have to actually prove a money trail. And Kim Barnes, her truck, and her new life might end up as collateral damage.

I pulled the car over on the shoulder and made a U-turn.

A minute later, I was cranking the wheel to turn onto Kim Barnes' street, when I eased my foot down on the brake.

"What?" Wheeler asked.

There was a car parked in front of Kim Barnes' house. It was a black SUV. Two men stood on Kim Harrison's doorstep. Even with their backs facing the street, I recognized one of them.

Dolf.

"Blackwater," I said.

Wheeler raised her eyebrows. "You think they were following us?"

I thought about it. I was pretty good about spotting a tail. "No, I would have seen them."

"Then how did they know to come here?"

I let out a long breath. "They bugged my car."

"You think?"

"They must have done it when I was at Lunhill headquarters. That's how they knew where I lived." I'd always suspected the Blackwater goon was the one who lit my barn on fire and now I was positive.

I started to drive away.

"What are you doing?" Wheeler asked. "We need to get the truck's license plate."

"I don't want to risk them seeing us. Plus, I don't really want to get

Kim involved. We'll find another way to prove the money trail."

She nodded.

A few minutes later, I pulled into a gas station.

It took me five minutes to locate the GPS beacon. It wasn't under the car, which was the normal location. It was under the hood of the car, stuck to the inner wall near the engine.

"It's so small," Wheeler said.

And it was, maybe half an inch square.

Wheeler cocked her head at a car filling up its tank. "We should put in on that car so they follow it." She grinned. "Like they do in the movies."

"I have a better idea," I told her.

~

There was a good chance it wouldn't work. It all depended on how closely Dolf and friends scrutinized the GPS data. If they were looking at each and every turn we made, they might notice the Range Rover doubled back toward Kim Barnes' street. They might put two and two together and realize we'd seen their car and realize we were onto them. But that's why I drove directly to a gas station. Hopefully, they would think we simply did a U-turn realizing we needed to get gas before we started on the interstate.

Still it would look suspicious.

"Do you really think this is going to work?" Wheeler asked over the phone. "This is pretty remote."

"That's the point."

The houses were half-built. Frames and windows only. A couple had the beginnings of drywall. Probably the funding ran out at some point and the project was abandoned.

An hour earlier, we'd parked the Range Rover in front of one of the houses for thirty minutes, then we drove a few blocks away where we saw a man getting ready to get in his car. Wheeler approached the man and asked for directions before stealthily sticking the GPS beacon on the side of his car.

Wheeler said, "And the goons will see that we were here for half an hour and come to check it out?"

"Hopefully."

"And then they will think we are the car that I stuck the GPS beacon on?"

"Yes, just like the movies."

I could hear her smile on the other end.

I was parked a few streets down from the decoy house. Wheeler was huddled somewhere near there, waiting to give me the go-ahead.

"I hear something," she murmured. "A car."

It was silent for a few seconds.

"It's them!" she yell-whispered. "It worked!"

"Settle down," I said. "Let me know when they both get out."

"Okay...right now they're parking, right in front of the house where we did...one of them got out. Shit, he's huge."

"That's Dolf."

"Who?"

"I'll explain later. Was he driving?"

"No, he was in the passenger seat...Okay, Dolf is going into the house...he's looking under boards and stuff."

That's what I'd hoped. I wanted them to think that I hid something in the house. Maybe something either Kim Barnes or Darcy Felding had given me.

"Okay, now the driver got out. He's a little smaller. But he looks mean. Let's call him Snake."

I laughed. "Okay."

"Now Dolf and *Snake* are both in the house."

That was my cue.

I put the car in drive and slowly idled my way up the two streets, then parked. I grabbed the red canister out of the back and crept my way around the four houses to Dolf and Snake's black SUV.

Wheeler was hiding behind a low wall across the street and I signaled for her to go to the car. I might need a quick getaway.

She darted toward the car and I uncapped the red gas can and began pouring the liquid on the hood of the SUV, then all over the roof, the tires, the back bumper, emptying all three gallons.

"Hey!"

I turned.

Dolf stood in the doorway of the house.

He pulled his gun from his hip and pointed it at me. He barked, "Don't you do it."

I think he was talking about the match in my hand.

Snake came up behind him. He was half a head shorter than Dolf. His head was shaved and he had a scar running down the side of his right cheek. I watched as his eyes took in the situation: Dolf pointing his gun at a handsome man holding a box of matches next to their SUV dripping in gasoline.

I could sense Dolf giving serious thought to pulling the trigger, putting three in my chest, but at the sound of Wheeler screeching up in the Range Rover, he slowly lowered the gun.

I flicked the match against the box and tossed it on the car. It erupted in an inferno of flames.

Both Dolf and Snake stood with their hands at their sides, seemingly dumbfounded. I guessed they hadn't been bested too many times in their lives. Then again, they'd never crossed the likes of me.

I pulled open the door to the Range Rover. I turned and thought about yelling, "Now we're even."

But we weren't.

Not by a long shot.

The gun Dolf was pointing at me.

He was holding it in his left hand.

~

The Blackwater goons knew where we stayed the first night so we switched hotels. And we upgraded from a Holiday Inn to the Crowne Plaza downtown.

At the front desk, I asked for two rooms.

Wheeler glanced up at me, then told the clerk, "Actually, we'll just need the one."

Chapter 27

The investigation was on hold while Randall and I busied ourselves fixing the irrigation and planting seed. Lady Justice would just have to wait. But I wasn't worried, she'd waited four long years; she could wait another couple of weeks.

Just as I had the previous ten mornings, I woke up to the rooster's crow, then made my way out to greet him. "I hate your guts," I told him with a smile.

He replied with a couple clucks.

Besties.

I then made my way into the chicken coop and snagged a half-dozen fresh eggs. I scrambled them up, then divided the eggs equally among myself and the piglets.

Then I went for a quick jog. When I returned, Randall's Ford Bronco was parked in front of the house. He was heaving a large bag from the trunk.

He turned as I approached and said, "This is the last of it."

After fixing the irrigation over the course of the previous week, we'd spent the last few days seeding 150 acres of corn, which with the many eco-fuel companies out there, would fetch the highest price per acre. After much deliberation—at least on Randall's behalf—we decided to seed the remaining 100 acres with sorghum, a grain that had increased in popularity over the past decade as a gluten-free substitute to wheat.

Needless to say, all the seeds were non-GMO.

The tractor and the attached ten-row seeder were parked twenty feet away, and Randall and I spent the next twenty minutes emptying the bags of seed into the ten separate bins.

"How long will this stuff take to grow?" I asked.

"I've never grown it before, but a buddy of mine said he usually does his harvest right around day ninety. It all depends on how hot it gets over the next month."

This was a bit longer than the sixty to eighty days it took for corn to mature. According to Randall, the range accounted for temperature, precipitation, and several other variables.

Today was July 18th, which meant the corn would be ready for harvest sometime in September and the sorghum sometime in October.

Most people planted their crops in early June and we were definitely behind schedule. I asked, "Is it risky to wait until October to harvest?"

"Can be," Randall said, his lips pursed. "We've hit freezing a few times in October, but it's rare. We should be good, and really, if the weather stays the way it has been, we should harvest the last week of September."

Randall and I spent the rest of the day trading off driving the tractor and refilling the seed.

At 7:00 p.m., after seeding half the remaining acreage, we called it quits. Randall and I had somewhere to be.

Wheeler and Randall's wife had set up a date night.

We were going bowling.

~

Tarrin Lanes was fifteen bowling lanes plus an attached bar. The lighting was drab and the place smelled faintly of shoe polish. A baseball game was finishing up on the big screen in the bar, and through the glass partition you could see a healthy crowd slugging back beers and cheering loudly.

All the lanes but one were occupied, and I spotted Alexa and Randall in a lane near the middle.

"Look at you," Alexa said as Wheeler and I approached. I hadn't seen her since their church revival the first week of June. She pulled me into a hug, exclaiming, "How much weight have you lost?"

"Thirty pounds."

I was still another ten pounds from fighting weight, but I was no longer fat. In fact, after six weeks of running, working out with dumbbells, and the long days on the farm, I felt stronger than I had in a long time.

Alexa released me, then said, "Well, don't you go losing any more weight, you gotta give this girl something to hold on to." She winked at Wheeler.

Since returning from our road trip, Wheeler and I had spent countless hours intertwined: at my house, at her house, even once at her clinic, which I'm guessing had to break some sort of oath.

Wheeler grinned and grabbed what was left of my deteriorating love handles. She said, "Oh, there's plenty to hold on to."

Wheeler was wearing a black tank top and a pair of tight blue jeans that accentuated her exquisite backside. Her hands gripping my waist, I was currently struggling with a temptation of the flesh.

Down, Boy.

"Now my guy," Alexa said, tilting her head toward Randall, who was on his haunches examining a purple, sixteen-pound ball. "He could stand to lay off the Thin Mints."

Randall let loose his infectious cackle and said, "You're the one who bought twenty boxes."

The four of us were all giving this a good laugh when the rest of our bowling party arrived: my cousin and his wife. Being a small town, Jerry and Joan had met Wheeler, Alexa, and Randall at various points and I didn't need to make introductions.

After some idle chatter, Jerry clapped me on the shoulder and asked, "So, when was the last time you went bowling?"

"Probably a decade ago, when I worked at the Seattle PD."

"How'd you do?"

"I want to say I bowled a 240...no....a 242."

Wheeler was tying her bowling shoes nearby and glanced up. She said, "Don't listen to him. He rolled a 68."

"I told you that in confidence!" I huffed.

Everyone laughed.

A waitress came over and we ordered one of everything: chicken wings, nachos, pizza, cheese sticks, French fries, chili fries, potato skins, sliders, you know, healthy stuff. Randall, Jerry, and I ordered a pitcher of beer and the women went the martini route.

Alexa, who seemed by far the most eager to do some actual bowling, sat down to the computer and started setting up our game. Randall had mentioned how she was always the one to get things going, whether it was rounding everyone up for a board game or getting people on the dance floor. "Okay," she said, "everyone needs to come up with a nickname."

She typed hers in first: Winky Dink.

"Randall?" she asked, turning around.

He thought for a moment, then said, "How 'bout Pokémon?"

Alexa laughed, then typed it in. "What about you Wheeler?"

She said, "I'll be Sarah."

I cut my eyes at her and said, "Hardy-har-har."

She smirked, then said, "Thomas will be Dergen."

So much for Ice Man.

"Dergen?" Jerry bellowed.

"It's my middle name," I explained.

"You know it means 'shit'?"

I glared at Wheeler. "I have been apprised of this, yes."

Joan said, "I'll be Jo-jo." Then she pointed at Jerry and said, "He'll be Fuzz."

It took a moment for it to register.

Fuzz?

I scoffed, loud enough that Wheeler turned and asked, "What?"

"Nothing," I said, waving her off.

I thought back to Will Dennel's Moleskine—*Fuzz*. I'd thought it was a nickname for someone at the Tarrin Police Department, but was it possible that it was Jerry?

Jerry had proven he was a betting man, first on the golf course, then when he was playing video games with his kids. It wouldn't be a stretch to think he would have had action with the local bookie. Could Jerry have been the one who owed Will Dennel $83,000?

I glanced at him. He was clad in another of his token golf shirts, this time red. If he was in fact Fuzz, did that change anything? Everyone had their vices. Maybe gambling was his. Who was I to judge him?

But $83,000?

Still, I didn't know what had happened in the past. Maybe he won that much previously. Or more. Maybe over a lifetime of betting he was up a million dollars. He drove a nice car, lived in a nice house, had nice things. If he did owe $83,000 it didn't appear to have affected him financially.

Then it struck me.

He never had to pay off this debt.

Will Dennel was murdered.

I asked Jerry, "Where did the nickname Fuzz come from?"

He sighed, then said, "I've had it since high school. When I was a sophomore, I tried to grow a mustache. Didn't turn out very well and all my buddies starting calling me Peach Fuzz. They shortened it to Fuzz, and thirty years later, half the town still calls me that."

The pitcher of beer and the martinis were delivered. Jerry poured three glasses of the amber liquid, and as if reading my mind, he asked, "You guys care to make this interesting?"

"Sure," Randall said. "I'll bet a few bucks."

"Let's just play for fun," I said brusquely, perhaps more brusquely than I intended. Forcing a smile, I added, "I won't sleep tonight knowing I took your guys' money."

They both laughed and we compromised on a small wager of five dollars for whoever bowled the high score over the course of the night.

Alexa overhead our banter and said, "Wait, I want in on this."

"Let's play couples," Wheeler offered.

So we made a second bet. But this one wasn't for money. Losing couple of each game had to buy shots.

A few minutes later, the food came. After eating healthy for over a month, my stomach churned at the bombardment of grease, but everything tasted so delicious that I powered through.

"All right," Alexa said, after ten minutes of chowing down. "Let's do this thing."

~

Four of my first six balls were gutter balls. Things started to come around for me the second half of the game, and I ended up tied for fourth. Alexa rolled the best game, a 157. Jerry second best at 146. Wheeler third with 121. Joan and I tied with 97. And Randall brought up the rear with a measly 84.

As the losing couple, Wheeler and I were on the hook for shots. I hadn't seen our waitress in close to half an hour and I made my way to the bar at back where the crowd had doubled since we first arrived. Fifty people were spread between a handful of tables, three pool tables, a dart board, and three Big Buck Hunter machines.

I wormed my way through the standing crowd, then plopped

down on the only open stool. A moment later, I ordered six shots of tequila from a bartender with a man bun.

"Looky here," a voice shot from behind me.

I turned.

It was Officer Matt Miller.

It was the first time I'd seen him out of his police uniform. He was wearing shorts, a T-shirt, flip-flops, and a trucker hat. His hat was lifted up a few inches, his curly hair flopped sideways across his forehead, and his cheeks had a rosy, alcohol-fueled glow. He looked like a kid on Spring Break in Daytona.

We were nearly eye level with my being seated and I stood up. "Hey, shithead," I said.

It was dark, so I'm not sure he noticed that one of my chins had dissolved since he'd last seen me.

"What are you doing here?" he spat.

"Bowling with your ex-fiancé," I grinned. "Sorry, your *ex-ex*-fiancé."

I probably wouldn't have said this if it weren't for the three beers I drank.

Then again.

He craned his head back and peered through the glass partition of the bar. He squinted, then said, "Ah, and I see you brought your big nigger friend with you."

I'd heard the n-word plenty on the basketball court. I'd even had a number of assholes I was arresting call *me* the n-word. But I'd never heard the n-word directed toward a black person whom I knew personally.

"What the fuck did you just say?" I demanded.

He grinned.

A few bar patrons had taken notice of our exchange and turned around. I pondered cold-clocking Miller in the face, but that's exactly what he wanted. He was a cop. Even off-duty, he couldn't throw the first punch. But he sure as shit could throw the second, fifth, and thirtieth.

Luckily, Man Bun finished pouring my shots, and in the time it took for me to grab cash from my wallet and pay, I talked myself down.

I took the tray of shots, pushed past Miller with a sneer, then made my way back to our bowling lane.

After the six of us toasted and drank our shots, I beckoned Wheeler toward the bathrooms and told her what happened.

"He actually said the word?"

I nodded, then asked, "Did you know he was a racist piece of shit when you dated him?"

She bit the inside of her cheek, then nodded. "It comes out when he's drunk."

"You knew and you still dated him? You still got *engaged* to him?"

"He hid it pretty well. He never said anything around me, but a couple years ago I saw a video his buddy took of him when he was wasted and saying all sorts of terrible things. I broke the engagement off with him the next day." She crossed her arms and silently dared me to criticize her.

I was unfairly judging her and I said, "I'm sorry."

She nearly started to cry and I pulled her into a hug.

"I love Randall," she said.

"I know," I said, wiping a tear from her cheek. "I do too."

"Are you gonna tell him?"

I was guessing it would make Alexa far more upset than it would Randall. "Not tonight," I said.

~

"Here you go," I said, handing Jerry fifty bucks.

Jerry rolled the high score of the night—a 188. I rolled a bit better the second game, a 121. And Randall finally broke a hundred, actually he rolled exactly 100, but by the little dance he did at the end you would have thought he rolled a 250. As for the women, the two martinis and the shots of tequila did both Alexa and Joan in, and both women rolled scores in the fifties. It was almost hard to watch. Wheeler, who apparently had a higher tolerance than the two mothers, beat me by two pins.

"What's this for?" Jerry asked. "We only bet five bucks."

"I owed you forty-five from our golf game."

"Oh, right," he said, pocketing the cash.

Technically, Randall and Alexa were responsible for buying another round of shots, but Alexa was having trouble getting her bowling shoes off, and no one else seemed eager to consume any more alcohol.

Ten minutes later, our group shuffled our way to the front desk to return our shoes.

I plopped mine down on the counter. That's when I saw him out of the corner of my eye. He was returning from the bathroom, flip-flopping his way in our direction.

Wheeler followed my gaze and I could feel her tense up next to me.

"Hey guys," Miller said as he came to within ten feet. "Did you all have a fun night of bowling?"

"We did," Joan replied drunkenly.

Randall was behind me, and I instinctively turned and glanced at him. He was the only other person who knew about Wheeler's history with Miller. He might even know that Officer Miller wasn't the most tolerant of folks. I tried to read his expression, but for the moment, he seemed undeterred by the little guy's presence.

"How'd you bowl, Wheeler?" Miller said, taking a drink of what I guessed to be a gin and tonic. "You bowl good?"

"Sure," she said. "Been awhile."

"Yeah, probably not since the last time we came together. What, like two years ago, was it?"

Jerry, Joan, and Alexa all glanced at one another as they realized this wasn't just a friendly bar patron stopping for conversation. I wondered if they knew Miller was a police officer. With only five officers in town, I was sure they did.

Wheeler didn't answer.

I was about to say something when Jerry took a step forward and said, "Why don't you keep it moving, buddy?"

"First, my name isn't buddy, it's Officer Miller. And second, fuck off."

"Come on, Miller, there's no need for that," Randall said calmly.

I willed him to say it, to call Randall a nigger to his face so I'd have a reason to beat on him. Or attempt to at any rate.

Miller glared at me, then back to Randall. He didn't have the balls to do it.

Coward.

He took a deep breath, squared his shoulders, then started past us. But he kept close, too close, to within a couple feet. When he was parallel with Wheeler and me, he turned on his heel and flung his drink. I'm not sure if he was aiming for me or Wheeler, but Wheeler took the brunt of the drink in the face.

Jerry was the closest one to Miller and he lunged forward to grab him. Miller easily sidestepped him and pushed him to the ground.

Randall went after him next, but with the same result.

I took two steps forward. I didn't know what to say, so I said the first thing that came to my mind.

"I volunteer as Tribute."

Miller grinned.

This was what he wanted the whole time. Everything he did was to provoke me into this showdown. So he could kick the shit out of me in front of Wheeler.

"Don't," Wheeler said, pulling at my arm. Her hair and face were wet, her mascara beginning to run from her eyes. "He's not worth it," she said.

"Of course he's not," I said with a sneer. "But you are."

Someone from the bar must have heard the commotion because half the patrons had spilled out and surrounded us.

"You know what you're doing?" Randall whispered in my direction. "You remember what happened last time?"

Yeah, I sure did.

And so did nine million YouTube viewers.

"Get your phone out," I told Jerry.

He did.

The crowd circled around Miller and myself. No one appeared remotely interested in stopping the fight. In fact, all the bowling alley employees had joined the group of onlookers.

Matt Miller was ten feet away from me. He'd thrown his hat to the ground and kicked off his flip-flops. He didn't do any stretches or any fancy MMA pre-fight bullshit. He just stared me down.

I closed my eyes and tried to teleport. When I opened them, I was still in the bowling alley.

Dang it.

I reminded myself that I wasn't the same guy I was six weeks earlier. That was Fat Thomas. Slow Thomas. Weenie Thomas. Now I was Fit Thomas. Strong Thomas. Hero Thomas.

Miller took a couple steps forward. I matched him. Four feet separated us. He moved his right foot back into a fighting stance. I glanced down at his foot. At the foot that had turned me into the Elephant Man.

I thought back to all the videos of Miller I watched. All his fights. He had two knockout moves. One was a left hook. The other, a spinning back kick, the same one he'd used on me.

I found my fighting stance. I knew he would wait. Wait for me to make the first move.

I took a step forward and threw an overhand right. Miller ducked it and hit me with a left hook to the liver. It knocked the wind out of me and I doubled over.

I forced the pain away and lunged forward with an upper cut. I grazed Miller's cheek. He countered with a straight right into my ribs.

There was a collective gasp from the onlookers as I fell to my knees.

He was toying with me.

A cat with its prey.

I fought back the rising bile in my throat.

Come on, you can do this.

You're Thomas Fucking Prescott.

I pushed myself up.

I glanced back at Wheeler. She looked like she'd just eaten some two-week-old gas station sushi.

There was no way I could compete with Miller in these normal exchanges. He was too quick. Everything I threw was telegraphed. Fighting was a science to him. If I did this, he would counter with that.

I needed him mad. I needed him to go for the knockout.

"What did you do with the rings?" I said.

He eyes flickered.

"Did you get your money back at least?" I prodded. "Or do you sleep with them under your pillow?"

I took a step forward.

I watched his feet.

His toes flexed.

And he spun.

It was lightning quick.

A beat quicker than the last time if that's possible.

Luckily, I started ducking when I took a step toward him. Still, his foot only missed my head by half an inch.

As Miller planted from his failed kick, my arm was already in motion. I pushed down on my back foot, the power coming from my legs and hips, channeled through my shoulder and into my fist.

Miller's head whipped around, his eyes open wide as my right fist smashed into his jaw.

If I had a thousand punches, I couldn't have hit him with a more pure, more powerful punch.

I heard his jaw crack.

He fell to the carpet, his eyes rolling backward. His mouth was open and one of his front teeth was chipped in half.

Everyone was silent as I took the card from my wallet, the one Dr. Roberts D.D.S. had given me, folded it up, and put it in his pocket.

Chapter 28

The receptionist's eyes opened wide at the sight of me. I half expected her to have resigned from her post. But apparently, she decided she wasn't to blame for Mike Zernan's murder. Or she buried the guilt down somewhere where only three glasses of wine could find it.

I didn't tell her why I was there or whom I came to see. I simply strolled past her desk and made my way to the back of the room.

Sitting at a desk, halfway to the back, was none other than Officer Matt Miller. Apparently, he was confined to desk duty for the immediate future.

It had been four days since I clobbered him in the face.

There was a smoothie cup next to his computer with a straw, which made sense as I'd heard through the grapevine that his jaw had been wired shut.

I sidled up to his desk and said, "How ya feeling, Champ?"

He glared at me, but said nothing.

I didn't blame him.

"Did you get a chance to watch the video yet?" *Guy Gets Revenge on Cop* had over fifteen million views on YouTube. I added, "There's a nice remix where you can see part of your tooth fly out in slow motion."

He mumbled something through his caged mouth that sounded like, "Rugg Goo."

I gave him a good Ice Man chomp, which had the added bonus of showing him what teeth are supposed to look like, then I continued to the Chief's office at back.

The door was slightly ajar and I pushed it open. Eccleston was sitting behind his desk. He looked up, spit into a cup, and said, "What do *you* want?"

I tossed the manila envelope on the desk in front of him. Inside were copies of all the pictures and documents Darcy Felding had given me, plus a couple other things I'd stumbled across in the past week.

"What's this?" he asked, the right side of his mouth lifting in a sneer.

"Oh, just a little something I've been working on."

He picked up the folder and pulled out the contents.

As he flipped through the pictures, it was like he was river rafting. At first it was calm waters, then I could see him stiffen as he hit a couple rapids, then he hit the waterfall: a picture of him and David Ramsey from 1992.

He glanced up at me, his sunburned face somehow a pale ivory.

"I know everything," I said.

Eccleston swallowed hard.

I handed him a small piece of paper.

"I'm gonna text you tomorrow at 3:00 p.m. with a meeting spot. And if everyone on that list doesn't show up, I'm sending copies of everything in that folder to my friends at the FBI."

~

"I can't believe this used to be a town," Wheeler said, glancing at the forgotten, near-apocalyptic landscape.

"Yeah," I said, "it's pretty depressing."

"This all from a dioxin spill?"

"Some idiot sprayed nearly 160,000 gallons of Lunhill's waste oil to keep the dust down on the streets. Then there was a horrible flood that ended up contaminating the entire town."

But that wasn't why I chose Simon Beach as the location of the meeting. I chose it because it was secluded and I highly doubted anyone from Lunhill had been there in more than twenty years. And it was located roughly one hour from all parties who were invited to this little soirée.

As for me, I'd been there three times in total, twice in the last twelve hours.

I parked the Range Rover on the side of the road near the ancient water tower that had once been the lifeblood of the small town.

"This is where you told them to meet?" asked Wheeler.

I nodded.

I'd texted Eccleston at 3:00 p.m. It was now closing in on 4:00.

I wondered how much dialogue had passed between the people on the list I'd given Eccleston over the past twenty-four hours. Would everyone show? Or did a couple of them dig up their go-bags and head for South America?

"Look," Wheeler said.

I glanced out the window. There was a line of five cars headed down the small street.

Part of me wondered if they would carpool seeing as most were coming from Tarrin. It appeared they hadn't, which boded well for the cause. They were all looking out for their own hides.

The cars rumbled closer, then four of them stopped. Only the black Escalade in front continued down the hill and parked.

I wasn't surprised when my two friends stepped from the vehicle.

"Hey, guys," I said.

Dolf and Snake both greeted me with a head tilt. Both men were dressed in combat fatigues. It was a power play, one to remind me of the things both men had seen and done. It was the first time I'd seen Snake up close. He had heavy brows angling toward a wide nose and, to Wheeler's credit, there really was something reptilian about him. The scar on his left cheek was thick and raised. Whatever had happened, it was brutal.

I cocked my head toward the SUV and said, "Looks like that fire damage buffed out nicely."

"It's a different car," Snake spat.

Dolf glared at him and said, "He's fucking with you."

Snake's face dropped. "Oh."

I smiled, then said, "What's the holdup? Why are they parked back there?"

Dolf said, "They want to make sure you aren't wired."

I'd expected as much.

"I'm not."

He pulled out a scanner and ran it over my body. Then Wheeler's. Then he ran it all over the Range Rover. After a long couple minutes, he pulled out his phone and said, "They're clean."

One by one, the cars pulled back onto the road. A Porshe SUV was in front and I spotted David Ramsey behind the wheel. His car was soon followed by two trucks and a small sedan. They made their way to where we were standing, then rumbled past.

Dolf headed back to his car and said, "Follow us."

I knew what they were doing. Even if I wasn't wired, I easily could have planted small recording devices in the general vicinity and, depending on the technology, it wasn't certain they would show up on the scanner.

Wheeler and I reluctantly hopped back into the Range Rover and followed the cars for three-quarters of a mile to the sign that read "Contaminated Grounds. Stay in Your Car."

I would have been surprised if they drove past the sign. At least a couple people in the cars ahead would have known how dangerous the area still was, even two decades after the spill.

Directly across from where the cars were parked was the abandoned school bus, lifeless amongst the surprisingly thick foliage.

For the second time, Wheeler and I exited the car and for the second time, Dolf ran the scanner over our bodies. Satisfied that we hadn't added any recording devices during the three-minute excursion, he gave the thumbs-up.

Four doors opened and David Ramsey, Chief Eccleston, Greg Mallory, and Mayor Paula Van Dixon stepped out.

Greg Mallory, the dairy farmer, was the only one who I hadn't seen before. He was sixtyish, with shaggy gray hair and a trim goatee. His skin was leathery, a consequence of so many hours under the sun.

The eight of us arranged ourselves in a loose circle on the cracked asphalt, the faded lines of the road hardly visible. Clockwise, it was Greg Mallory, then Mayor Van Dixon, then Dolf, then David Ramsey, then Snake, then Chief Eccleston, then Wheeler, then myself.

It was a tense atmosphere, everyone exchanging quick glances, but perhaps the most strained of all glances came when Wheeler locked eyes with Greg Mallory. The look on the old farmer's face was pained. It reminded me of when the nerve in my tooth was exposed and I took a drink of cold water.

Wheeler was a raw nerve for Greg Mallory.

"I thought you guys were bringing margaritas," I said, attempting to break the ice.

I failed.

My four friends knew I held their fate in my hands, and there wasn't enough Maalox in the world to quell that type of indigestion.

"A twenty-year cover-up," I said. "I gotta hand it to you, to keep a secret that long in a small town where everybody knows what type of toothpaste you use, well, that's something you ought to be proud of."

For the briefest of moments, I could see a couple of them, most noticeably, Greg Mallory, give a nod in acknowledgement. He must have expected their house of cards to come tumbling down long ago.

I decided he was the most likely candidate to break down in tears and confess on his knees in the middle of the street.

Time would tell.

No one said anything for several tense moments. I had no intention of being the first one to talk. I would let them squirm in silence until morning if need be.

"You called this meeting," Eccleston said, finally. "What exactly do you want?

"I want you guys to tell me how it all went down. I have my theory, but I want to hear it from you guys. From the players."

"And if we do?" asked Mallory.

I shrugged.

For a long minute, no one said anything.

"Fine, you guys don't want to talk. Then I'll talk." I took a breath. "So, this is how I think it all went down. It starts with Lord Vader over there," I pointed at Ramsey, "and his constituents discovering recombinant Bovine Growth Hormone in the early nineties. Several companies were working on their own product, and he knew whoever was first to market stood to cash in. Ramsey wanted to begin testing but he wanted to do it somewhere there wasn't a whole lot of dairy farming. He chose Tarrin because of its proximity; it was near enough to keep a close eye on, but not too close as to be in Lunhill's backyard. Plus, there was only one dairy.

"Ramsey sold Mr. Mallory over there on the idea that by using rBGH, what he was calling Recom 6, Mallory would get twenty percent higher yields from his cows. I don't doubt that he got some under-the-table funds as well."

I glanced in Mallory's direction. His hands were in his pockets and he fidgeted back and forth.

"At first, everything went smoothly," I said. "The Recom 6 was administered, and quicker than anyone would have imagined, the cows started producing vastly higher yields of milk." This was all according to the data that was recorded in the documents. It showed how much of the hormone was administered, then compared the yields of the seventeen cows being treated with Recom 6 to the group of control cows who were not. "But after just a few weeks, several of the cows developed mastitis, their udders growing swollen, red, and infected. Mastitis isn't all that uncommon and Mallory called the local vet, Tom Lanningham, to come take a look."

I unconsciously gave Wheeler a quick glance. I could see the pain in her face at the mention of her father. I desperately wanted to reach out and grab her hand, to pull her into a tight embrace, but now wasn't the time.

I looked directly at Mallory and said, "Did you tell Dr. Lanningham what you'd been giving the cows? About the Recom 6?"

"Not at first," he said.

"Shut up!" Eccleston shouted, glaring at the farmer. "We decided we weren't gonna say anything."

"Piss off, Leonard," Mallory spat. "I'll talk if I want to talk." He looked at the ground, then back at me. "I didn't tell him at first, but it was too suspicious, seven cows getting mastitis all at once. Finally, I came clean, told him about the hormone treatment."

"What did he say?" Wheeler interrupted.

"He was furious. He told me how irresponsible I was. That I was threatening the lives of my cows for a few extra dollars."

Wheeler nodded, appeased for the time being at her dad's response.

"But he didn't understand," Mallory continued. "Only a farmer would understand. The margins are so small. If you don't have a perfect year, if everything doesn't go right as rain, you're lucky to break even. Sure, I love them cows, love 'em to death, but twenty percent higher yields, that keeps the banks away, keeps food on the table, and might even pay for one of my damn kids to go to college." His voice started to break near the end.

"What did my father do?" Wheeler asked.

Everyone present knew Dr. Lanningham was Wheeler's father, but the word somehow seemed underlined as it left her mouth.

Greg Mallory once again had his hands in his pockets.

"Greg!?" Wheeler shouted.

"He treated them with antibiotics and made up a salve. And he talked to them, you know, like how he did." Mallory's eyes were beginning to moisten.

Eccleston barked, "Get ahold of yourself, Greg! For God's sake!" He spit on the ground. "And quit talking. You're only gonna make things worse."

"Worse!?" Mallory bellowed, wiping his eyes. "Things couldn't get no worse."

"When did the first cow die?" Wheeler asked.

Mallory kicked at the dirt and a small plume was whipped away by the light wind. "The day after your daddy came, I woke up to go check on the cows. Three of them were dead." He let out a long exhale. "Then the next day, three more died. Then it seemed like one or two died every day for the next week."

"Fifteen in all?" I asked.

He nodded.

"Out of the seventeen who were being treated with Recom 6?"

Again, he nodded.

"So what did you do? Did you call Ramsey?"

"Sure as shit. I called him the day the first few cows' udders started to swell. He told me to just keep on with it, that it was one of the side effects and it would clear up."

I glanced at Ramsey, waiting for him to react, but he stood resolute—a statue.

"When did you stop giving them the injections?" I asked.

"Oh, I stopped when Dr. Lanningham came to check on the first seven. He didn't even give me a choice. I showed him the vials, and he up and took 'em."

Wheeler fought down a smile in my periphery.

"How did you guys keep it a secret? Fifteen dead cows in a small town. Surely, it would have gotten out."

"I made Tom promise he wouldn't tell. There was a good chance I might end up losing my farm if it got out." He turned to Wheeler and said, "Your daddy was a noble man. One of the best. I'm just sorry I got him mixed up in it."

She said, "Yeah, well, it was his decision to take money from Lunhill for twenty years."

I said, "Just like every single one of you."

The Mayor, Eccleston, and Mallory all traded glances.

"*Money*," I said. "That's how a couple bad decisions became a two-decade-long cover-up."

I watched closely to see how the four would react. Ramsey again did nothing. Mallory gulped. The Mayor glanced at Ramsey. Eccleston snorted and spit on the ground.

"Let me guess," I said. "After Ramsey found out about the fifteen dead cows, he rode in with his piggy bank and started throwing money around. Said that if you could somehow keep a lid on their Recom 6 testing, he would pay you a nice little chunk each and every month for the rest of your lives. That's ten thousand a month for Mallory and ten thousand a month for Tom Lanningham. Meanwhile, Ramsey's scientists have discovered what was wrong with Recom 6—why it was killing the cows—and for the most part, now have a safe product. Ramsey didn't want to have to go back to the drawing board, to do all the rigorous testing the FDA requires, so he instructed the scientists to fudge the testing data."

I pointed at Mayor Van Dixon. It had taken me awhile to realize she was up to her big broach in the cover-up. I hadn't thought much about why David Ramsey would speak at her election luncheon. I just assumed she'd paid him to come speak. She mentioned they were friends, but it wasn't until I had my Philly PD contact, Bolger, dig into her past, that I realized they were once *colleagues*.

I said to her, "You worked at Lunhill for seven years, then you took a job at the FDA. When Ramsey realized the problems with Recom 6, he bribed you to input the falsified data into the FDA records. You did, Recom 6 got the green light, and Lunhill was first to market four months later."

Mayor Van Dixon wrinkled her nose at the mention of her involvement but said nothing.

I glared at her. "A year later, you leave the FDA in St. Louis and coincidentally enough, you end up in Tarrin. Two years later, with the aid of Lunhill's checkbook, you win the Mayoral race. You stay mayor for the next eighteen years keeping a close eye on the town and making sure Lunhill's dirty little secret stays buried. And of course, you get a nice little bonus check each month as well."

I turned toward Ramsey and said, "You knew how much was riding on this all staying a secret, so you didn't stop there. You had the Mayor in your pocket, but you also wanted boots on the ground. So you plucked a police officer from St. Louis that you'd crossed paths with, and with the help of Mayor Van Dixon, you installed him as the Tarrin Chief of Police."

I whipped my head around and stared at Eccleston. The picture I'd found of him and David Ramsey from 1992 came from Bolger. While working for the St. Louis Police Department, Eccleston had padded his income as a part-time security advisor for the Ramsey Foundation, a non-profit started by David Ramsey's wife, Jeanette. Turned out that Eccleston had attended high school with Jeanette Ramsey in the early seventies. The picture came from the *St. Louis Post-Dispatch*. It was a picture of Eccleston standing with Ramsey while Ramsey's wife cut a ribbon at a playground.

Eccleston spit on the ground, not two feet from where I stood, but remained quiet.

"How much were you paying out?" I asked Ramsey. "To these three and Tom Lanningham?"

"Odell too," Mallory said.

"I told you to shut the fuck up!" Eccleston yelled, picking up a rock and throwing it at Mallory. It missed by a foot, but sent Mallory diving to the ground.

Wheeler and I traded glances. She mouthed, "Odell?"

As Mallory pushed himself up, I asked, "Odell? The Save-More owner? He was on the take?"

Mallory nodded. "Before the cows got sick, I convinced Odell to sell the milk at the Save-More. He did, but a bunch of people ended up getting sick. A little boy almost died. Odell blamed it on the refrigerators—that the milk must have gone bad without his knowing—but we all knew it was from the milk I sold him."

My brain was whirring, trying to synthesize the new information. I made a few adjustments to my theory.

I said "If that would have gotten out, that not only did Recom 6 kill nearly every cow treated with it at the dairy, but that the milk illegally made its way into the hands of consumers and made them sick—" I was laughing. "Wow, I can't even contemplate the fallout. It would have been devastating."

I turned to David Ramsey and said, "No wonder you had them all murdered."

"Murder?" Mallory gasped. "What is he talking about, David?"

I raised my eyebrows. "You didn't know?"

"David?" the Mayor barked. "What the hell is he talking about?"

For the first time, Ramsey reacted. His brow furrowed for the briefest moment before quickly snapping back taut.

I said, "The Save-More murders."

The Mayor and Mallory traded glances. Eccleston leaned his head back slightly.

I said, "Lowry Barnes didn't go into the Save-More to kill his manager because he was fired. He went in there to kill Neil Felding."

"Neil Felding?" barked Mallory. "Why?"

"Because three weeks before the Save-More murders, Neil was combing through the computers at Lunhill when he stumbled across the pictures and documents that I'm sure Chief Eccleston has shared with you." I explained further, "You see, Neil was working on a second iteration of Terminator seeds, which were first studied in 1994, just about the time all those cows were dying. Someone involved with the Recom 6 testing buried the pictures of the dead cows and the falsified data in a Terminator seed research folder."

Finally, finding his voice, David Ramsey said, "All those pictures and documents could easily have been faked."

He was right. Alone, the pictures and documents wouldn't be enough to convict anyone in court. The pictures proved nothing except that a bunch of cows died. They didn't prove *how* they died or *when* they died. And the only person in any of the pictures was Tom Lanningham, the town vet, who could have been tending to the cows for any number of reasons. As for the documents, though I was certain they were real, they could *easily* have been faked.

Luckily, the burden of proof in the court of public opinion was significantly lower than a court of law, and Lunhill would have been crucified. Which, of course, was why Lord Vader was here and not sipping scotch with the Emperor.

"You might be right," I said. "But you and I both know the pictures and documents are real and if they ever got out, they would cause a shit storm that would bankrupt Lunhill."

No one said anything for a pause, and I resumed my narrative.

"That very day Felding discovered the Recom 6 folder, he approached Ramsey about the pictures and documents, which upset him greatly as they involved the very town where he lived most of his life. There was a small dust-up in the cafeteria and Neil resigned from Lunhill."

"Like all employees of Lunhill," I continued. "Neil signed his life away on a series of non-disclosures when he was first hired, and if he wanted to avoid litigation, he would stay quiet about what he uncovered. But what you might not know is that Felding was promised an extra fifty thousand dollars a month in perpetuity if he remained silent. And so he did. Or at least planned to."

Out of the corner of my eye, I noticed Eccleston wrinkle his nose at the mention of $50,000. Apparently, he wasn't receiving nearly the same amount.

I glanced toward Ramsey, "But Lord Vader didn't trust that Neil wouldn't blow the whistle on Lunhill's almost two-decades-old secret. And he knew if it got out that Lunhill had falsified data sent to the FDA, there was nothing to stop the public from thinking they'd falsified data for every single one of their products from Spectrum-H to all their Frankenseeds."

"So Ramsey puts his two goons," I nodded at Dolf and Snake, "in charge of making their little problem go away."

Dolf's lips crawled up into a smirk.

"They could just murder Neil on his own, but coming so close to his resignation from Lunhill, it might look suspicious. And making a death look like an accident in this technological age isn't quite as easy as it might look on television. So our friends from Blackwater—that's right, *the* Blackwater—stumble on some timely information: an ex-felon had recently been fired from his job at the local Tarrin grocery store. And if there is one place in a small town where everyone is bound to go at some point, it's the grocery store.

"They approach Lowry Barnes and give him two hundred and fifty thousand dollars to kill Neil Felding and make it look like he was there retaliating against the manager who fired him two weeks earlier."

I glanced at both the Mayor and Mallory. "And if you're curious how I know the exact amount Lowry Barnes was paid, it's because just last week Lowry Barnes' widow showed me the money. I saw it with my own eyes." I didn't find it necessary to explain that the money was actually in the form of a $50,000 truck, $20,000 in cash, and two $90,000 college trust funds.

The Mayor looked as though she might puke.

Mallory did puke, leaning forward, letting loose a small hiccup of whatever he last ate. He wiped his mouth with the bottom of his flannel and I continued, "Lowry waited to get word from one of the Blackwater goons that Neil was headed toward the Save-More, then he followed Neil in, made a couple statements for the surveillance cameras about how he shouldn't have been fired, then shot all six of them." I counted on my fingers, "Odell McBride, Peggy Bertina, Will Dennel, Tom Lanningham, Neil Felding, and Victoria Page."

It happened when I was counting. Seeing each of the victims' faces. It was one thing for two members of the cover-up, Tom Lanningham and Neil Felding, to both be at the Save-More. But minutes earlier, I'd learned Odell was part of the conspiracy as well. For all three of them to be there at the same time...

I smiled.

Wheeler cut her eyes at me.

I always found it odd that Odell was there all by himself. That big store and no checker, no one stocking shelves.

The anvil fell.

They were having a meeting.

I turned to Mallory and asked, "Why didn't you go to the meeting?" Neil might not have been aware that Chief Eccleston and the Mayor where in on the cover-up, but from the pictures, he would have been certain Greg Mallory was involved.

"What meeting?" he asked.

I could feel Wheeler's gaze on my shoulder.

"The night of the Save-More murders." I was guessing that Neil wanted to meet with the parties involved before he did anything rash. That would mean Tom, Odell, and Mallory.

"I was on a cruise," Mallory replied. "My wife's and my fortieth. I don't know anything about a meeting, I swear."

I believed him.

If he'd known, he would have been there, and he would be dead.

I wasn't exactly sure how the meeting changed things. I wasn't sure if the group was the target or if it was just Neil. Maybe Ramsey decided to clean house. Maybe he planned on killing everyone involved. Then again, the Mayor, Eccleston, and Mallory were all still alive. Surely, there were chances in the last four years to get rid of them. Ramsey must have decided it would have looked too suspicious and that someone would eventually put the pieces together.

I looked at Eccleston and asked, "Were you invited to the meeting?"

His face flushed.

He was.

I turned to the Mayor. "What about you? Where you invited to the meeting?"

She shook her head.

I didn't know whether or not she was lying. I would need an hour in a locked room with her to know for sure.

"Anyhow," I said, "Lowry shoots the six of them, killing five. Then he jumps in his car and makes a getaway. He pulls over on the side of the road." I pointed to Team Blackwater and said, "I'm guessing that Lowry was meeting someone. That he was to get another big bag of cash for having completed the job. But Team Blackwater has strict instructions from Ramsey that Lowry needs to be terminated. It's too big a risk to let him walk. So they kill him in his car and make it to look like a suicide."

"You sonofabitch!" the Mayor yelled, running toward Ramsey, banging her manicured hands against his shoulder. "You murdered all those people!"

Dolf peeled Mayor Van Dixon off David Ramsey and stood between them. She screamed, "You've made us all accessories to murder!"

"Calm down, Paula, just calm down." Ramsey put his hands up. "I did no such thing." He turned toward me and said, "You spin a good yarn, Mr. Prescott, but I hate to disappoint you. Neither I nor anyone I employ had any part in any murder."

It was the way he said it.

Wheeler glanced in my direction.

She must have felt it too.

"Neil Felding was getting fifty thousand dollars a month for the rest of his life," Ramsey continued. "There's no way he ever would have risked that by talking. Trust me, I knew the guy for twenty years. Money talked with him. There was no need to murder him."

"Seems like you were paying out a lot of money," Eccleston spat.

Ramsey snorted, then said, "You think you were worth more than twenty thousand a month, just to sit on your fat ass?"

"Twenty thousand a month?" Eccleston huffed. "Try half that. And I did plenty. I protected you."

"Protected me?"

Eccleston glanced at me. I could almost see him straddling an invisible fence. Keep his mouth shut and hope for the best or speak his peace and accept the worst.

He chose the latter. "Mike Zernan."

"Who?" asked Ramsey.

"Don't act like you don't know," Eccleston scoffed. "He was the Save-More investigating officer. He wouldn't leave the murders alone. Kept at it even a couple years after. Said it just didn't feel right. Then he came to me one day and told me that he thought maybe Lunhill was somehow involved in the murders."

I'd never been able to figure out what had tipped Mike off and I asked, "What made him think that?"

"Something about the murders had never set well with him. I think it was the way Lowry yelled at Odell. Mike thought it sounded rehearsed."

I'd never seen the video, so I couldn't speak to this.

Eccleston continued, "So he started looking into all the victims' backgrounds. Will Dennel ran a sports book, even had his little notebook on him when he was killed, and Mike thought maybe there was something to that. But that quickly sputtered out and he started looking into Felding. He thought it was suspicious that he'd had this skirmish with the CEO of Lunhill, then resigned just three weeks before he was killed. Then when he found out that Lunhill had ties to Blackwater, that's when he really started to think that they might be involved."

I'd cracked open many cases following the same formula—a gut feeling substantiated by coincidence and correlation.

I said, "And that's why you made Mike see a psychologist and paid them to diagnose him with PTSD from his time in the military. Not to mention bouts of paranoid schizophrenia. Anything that would mandate he retire."

Eccleston nodded. He was all in now.

I almost said, "*That's when Mike stopped investigating the murders and turned that energy into restoring his hot rod. But then when I came to his house asking questions, he found a way to pass his suspicions along to me. He'd been paranoid that perhaps the unfriendly folks from Blackwater had bugged his house, hence the cloak-and-dagger operation of creating a replica of Will Dennel's Moleskine and its surreptitious message of 'Lunhill.'*" I kept this to myself.

"But I liked Mike," Eccleston said. "We were fishing buddies. I leveled with him. I told him that if he retired and stopped looking into the Save-More murders, I would get him a full pension with benefits."

"And he took it?" I asked.

"He did, but apparently he didn't stop poking his head into the investigation, which is why Ramsey over there had him taken out, just like he took out Tom, Odell, Neil, and Victoria."

Something about this statement pinged something in my brain, but I didn't get a chance to ruminate on it before Ramsey belted, "I told you I had nothing to do with any murders."

Eccleston jerked his chin toward the Blackwater guys, "Just because you pay men to do your dirty work doesn't mean your hands aren't dirty." He took a couple steps toward the two mercenaries. "Which one of you assholes did it? Which one of you strangled my friend?"

I turned to Dolf. "It was you. You broke into his house, came up behind him, and put a garrote around his neck. You had him by fifty pounds, so it wouldn't have been hard for you to strangle him. And you just happen to be left-handed, which is why the ligature marks were so much worse on the right side of Mike's throat."

Dolf moved his tongue around the inside of his bottom lip, took a breath, then asked, "This Mike Zernan, you said he was a military man?"

I nodded.

"If I'd been paid to kill this guy, this would have come up in my research and I never would have taken the job. I would never kill a man who put his life on the line for his country."

The way he said it was so matter-of-fact I found it hard to believe he was lying.

I said, "But you had no problem killing Lowry Barnes."

He shook his head and said, "Sorry to tell you, but the worst thing I've done contracting with Lunhill is taking some embarrassing photos of a couple politicians."

"What about my barn?" I asked. "You burned down my fucking barn. You almost killed my two piglets."

"Again, not us."

Wheeler shouted, "But you bugged his car!"

"That we did. We were hired to follow you and see who you talked to, then report back to Mr. Ramsey."

"I told you," David Ramsey said. "Neither I nor anyone I employ had anything to do with any murders." He turned to Eccleston and said, "If you would have told me about this Mike Zernan guy, I would have paid him to be quiet. Or found a reason to sue him. Payoffs, bribes, lawsuits, this is what I've done for thirty-five years. And guess what? It's worked. Why would I go and change that?"

He was making good points.

Actually, he was making great points.

Why change your MO when it has proved successful for more than three decades?

He looked at the Mayor, Mallory, then Eccleston, then said, "I've paid out twenty-three million dollars to you guys over the past twenty years, why wouldn't I have paid another half a million to keep a guy quiet?"

Eccleston's jaw went slack. "Did you say twenty-three million dollars?"

Ramsey nodded.

The Mayor and Mallory turned and glanced at each another. Then both turned and looked at Eccleston.

"How much were you getting?" Eccleston demanded of Greg Mallory.

"Ten thousand a month," he said.

Eccleston turned to the Mayor and asked, "What about you?"

She glanced at me, then said, "Same. Ten grand a month."

"Okay, okay." He turned to Wheeler and said, "And how much was your old man getting?"

"Same."

Eccleston looked upward, his eyes closed. After a moment he said, "By my math, we were getting collectively seven hundred and twenty thousand dollars a year for twenty years or so, which is roughly fourteen million dollars." He turned to David Ramsey and asked, "How the hell did you come up with *twenty-three million*?"

Wheeler leaned into my side and said, "How did he come up with seven hundred and twenty thousand? I thought there were only five of them on the take."

She was right. Eccleston, Odell, Tom Lanningham, Mayor Van Dixon, and Greg Mallory.

Each getting $10,000 a month was a $120,000 a year, times five, which was $600,000 collectively.

"There was a sixth person," I said.

"Who?" she asked.

And then it hit me.

It was what had pinged my brain when Eccleston mentioned her name and not Will's or Peggy's.

For the first time yet, Ramsey appeared somewhat baffled. He said, "I paid you guys each ten thousand dollars a month for the first couple of years. But then after she came to see me, I upped it to twenty thousand a month."

"After who came to see you?" asked Mayor Van Dixon.

But I already knew.

The sole survivor.

David Ramsey said, "Victoria Page."

~

Thirty minutes later, Wheeler and I watched all the cars drive away.

I'd set up the meeting to prove murder, but all I'd done was prove a twenty-year-old conspiracy, which in all honestly, didn't hold much weight with me. Sure, some cows died, some people got sick, data was manipulated, payoffs were made, and a corporation profited billions, but no one at the meeting was involved in the Save-More murders.

That's why I promised the pictures and documents would never see the light of day. Of course, for a price.

Ramsey came prepared to deal, and after I signed several documents promising to destroy all copies of the pictures and documents Darcy Felding had given me, David Ramsey handed me a briefcase with $2 million in it.

My only stipulation was that I be the one to deal with Victoria Page. All parties begrudgingly agreed.

"What are you going to do with the money?" Wheeler asked me. Though she hadn't voiced it at the time, I could tell she was embittered, even resentful, that I'd taken the money.

I ignored her question.

I took a few steps toward the school bus across the street and yelled, "You can come out now."

I hadn't told Wheeler. I couldn't risk her glancing in the school bus's direction.

Blue hair popped up in one of the broken windows of the school bus and Wheeler asked, "Who is that?"

"My friend Bree. She's Will Dennel's little sister."

"How long has she been in there?"

"I dropped her off earlier this morning."

"How did you know they would stop right here?"

I hadn't known for certain, but I figured David Ramsey would be in the lead car and he wouldn't drive past the signs warning of contamination.

Luckily, I'd been right.

Bree exited the school bus from the back, jumping down into the thick brush, then clambered toward us.

"You get everything?" I asked.

She patted the radar gun looking device in her right hand, which was actually a parabolic microphone she often used to listen in on Walmart Guy and his girlfriend's dates, and said, "Yep. Got it all."

Chapter 29

"They're beautiful," Bree said, her face pushed up against the back window.

"They're called quarter horses," I said. "Race horses. This lady breeds them."

We'd driven directly from Simon Beach to Page Ranch and it was closing in on 6:00 in the evening.

I glanced at Wheeler. She'd been out to the ranch just three days earlier to remove a nail from one of the horse's hooves. She fidgeted in the passenger seat.

"Is that why she stole so much of the money?" Bree asked. "To help pay for her breeding program?"

Wheeler locked eyes with me.

Neither of us had disclosed our theory to Bree, but to her credit she had been listening to the entirety of the meeting at Simon Beach. Still, to put this together was nothing short of astonishing.

"She's like a genius or something," I said.

Bree laughed from the back.

I parked between the house and the stable.

"Stay put," I said to Bree, knowing full well she would be over the fence petting the horses the moment we stepped inside the house.

"Sure thing, boss." She added, "You sure you don't need me to record this?"

"I'm sure," I said.

Both Wheeler and I had our phones in our pockets set to record. And I highly doubted Victoria would pat us down.

I told Bree to keep her cell phone on her just in case.

"I'm just gonna be in the car," she said.

"Your hand is already petting an invisible horse."

She put her hand down, then opened the door, and sprinted in the direction of the horses, blue hair bouncing.

"I like her," Wheeler said.

"Yeah, me too."

A moment later, I knocked on the front door. No one answered, and Wheeler and I headed toward the stable.

Wheeler took the lead, walking through the open door. Victoria Page was inside the second stall. She was brushing the coat of a large brown horse. The horse eyed us, his head swishing lightly back and forth.

"Oh, hi there," Victoria said, pushing her hat up an inch with her free hand.

Wheeler went up to the horse and rubbed her hand on his nose. "What's this guy's name?" she asked.

"Retro," Victoria said with a smile. "He's my old man."

"And how's Macy?"

I guessed Macy was the horse whom Wheeler attended to three days earlier.

"She still won't put all her weight on that back foot, but she's doing a whole lot better."

"No redness or swelling?"

"I checked on it a few hours ago and it looked pretty good." She turned to me and said, "Is that why you guys are here?"

Wheeler and I glanced at one another.

I said, "Actually, it's about something else."

She nodded, gave Retro a few last brushes on his side, then exited the stall.

"Why don't we go inside and have a drink?" she offered.

We followed her from the stable toward the main house. At one point she stopped and asked, "Do you guys see a blue haired girl out on the fence?"

Bree was straddling a black post, petting one of the horses. I said, "Yeah, she's with us."

"Oh good. Just wanted to make sure I wasn't seeing things."

I forced a laugh.

Wheeler didn't.

We made our way into the living room and Victoria excused herself to fix us some drinks. Several minutes later, she entered the room with a tray. She set two martinis on the coffee table near where Wheeler and I were sitting, then gingerly lowered herself onto the couch opposite us with her own glass in hand.

"That hip giving you some trouble?" I asked.

"No more than usual," she said, then took a sip of her drink. She set it down, then said, "You still looking into those murders?"

I nodded.

"I figured that would be the only reason you two would be here together."

"We have a couple more questions."

She looked at Wheeler and said, "I've told you before how brave your dad was those last few minutes of his life. You should be proud."

Wheeler moved her hand to mine and gripped it. At first I thought she was doing it to keep herself from crying, but she wasn't. She was doing it to keep herself from leaping across the room and burying her fist in Victoria's face.

"That night," I said, "you went to the Save-More to get butter for some cookies you were baking."

"That's right, macadamia nut and white chocolate chip." She gave a slight grin at the mention of her famous cookies.

"But that's not really why you were there."

Her grin vanished. "Yes, it was. I ran out of butter."

"No, you were there for the meeting."

"What meeting?"

"The meeting that Neil Felding called."

She set the martini glass down. "Neil Felding? Why would I be meeting with Neil Felding?"

"Because he was about to blow the whistle on a twenty-year cover-up?"

"A cover-up? I don't know what you're talking about."

"We just had a long chat with Chief Eccleston, Greg Mallory, Mayor Van Dixon, and David Ramsey." I glanced toward Wheeler. "We know everything."

Victoria's face fell.

I said, "Mayor Van Dixon told us how, as town comptroller, you stumbled on a secondary account that the Mayor was keeping. You knew it was something illegal, but instead of turning her in, you told her that you would be quiet about it if you got the same payoff.

The Mayor contacted David Ramsey and made it happen. You then convinced the Mayor to let you control the payoffs, that you would launder them through the town budget and into a series of different bank accounts and trusts. Eventually, you convinced Dr. Lanningham, Greg Mallory, Odell, and Chief Eccleston to also let you control their payoffs, and pretty soon all that Lunhill money was coming directly to you."

Victoria Page's chin moved down slightly.

"But after a year, you got greedy. You decided to approach David Ramsey on your own. You got him to double everyone's payout from ten thousand dollars a month to twenty thousand. You decided there was no reason to tell the others and that there was no way they would ever find out while you controlled all the money. So pretty soon you were getting twenty thousand a month, plus an extra forty thousand you were skimming off the other four. Sixty thousand dollars a month. For almost eighteen years. That's nearly thirteen million dollars."

I waited for Victoria to speak.

One minute. Two. Five.

Finally, she said, "After a year of getting an extra ten thousand dollars a month, I bought my first quarter horse. But it was so much more expensive than I thought it would be: the training, the travel, all the expenses. Soon, I was in over my head." Her eyes started to water. "I went to David Ramsey, demanding that he double all our payouts. I couldn't believe how easily he agreed to it. I had no intention of skimming from the others, but then I realized all the money came through me and that the others would never know."

"Then you had nearly three-quarters of a million dollars coming in each year. So you bought yourself some property and a bunch of horses."

She nodded.

"So there was no inheritance from your father?"

"No."

I said, "But with Neil Felding threatening to blow the whistle on Lunhill, you stood to lose it all: the ranch, the horses, everything. Not to mention spending a few years in jail."

"Neil wanted to meet," she said. "I'm not sure how he knew I was involved. I got a text from Odell saying that I needed to meet at the Save-More at 8:30 p.m. that night."

I doubt Neil Felding knew about Victoria's involvement. I'm guessing he only knew about Tom Lanningham, Odell, and Greg Mallory. But Odell either decided that if he had to meet with Neil, then everyone had to, or he thought because Victoria controlled the payoffs, she would be able to reason with him.

I said, "You didn't know exactly what Neil Felding knew. But you assumed that if he wanted you at the meeting, then he could very well know about the money and how you'd been ripping off your partners for almost twenty years."

She shook her head, but I was on a roll.

"That's where Lowry Barnes comes into play. You knew him from when he was a boy. You said it yourself. And you knew he was just recently fired from his job at the Save-More. So you offered him five hundred grand, half up front, half on completion, to kill Neil Felding. And while he's at it, you tell him to clean house and get rid of Tom, Odell, and anybody else who shows up for the meeting. You *masterminded* the whole thing."

"No," she insisted.

"It would have looked suspicious if you didn't get shot yourself, so you told Lowry to shoot you in two places where you knew you wouldn't be mortally wounded."

Tears were streaming down her face.

"Lowry did exactly what you told him to do, killed everyone else there, and put one in your shoulder and hip. Then Lowry leaves. What I don't know is whether or not Lowry really did commit suicide or if you paid someone else to kill him."

"I didn't...I didn't," she muttered.

"After you've recovered from your injuries, all your problems have gone away. They all died that night. Except a couple years later, you hear from Eccleston that one of his officer's, Mike Zernan, is still looking into the murders. Then you get word that I, a retired homicide detective, had been to see him."

Here is where I was on shaky ground. "I'm guessing you used the same guy you used to kill Lowry. Who knows, you have millions of dollars, it wouldn't have been hard to find someone. After all you've gone through, you couldn't risk Mike divulging his suspicions, so you have him killed too."

Victoria glanced up, her eyes red, swollen.

"You had my father killed!" Wheeler shouted. She picked up her martini glass and chucked it across the room at Victoria. It smashed into the window behind her, raining glass down into her scarlet hair.

"No, no…please," Victoria cried. "Please, no…please no…"

Victoria fell to her side, curled into the fetal position, and began whimpering. A moment later, In the crotch of her jeans, a dark stain began to blossom.

I'd joked about having PTSD from falling out of the tree. And Eccleston had paid a psychologist to diagnose Mike Zernan with PTSD. But I was pretty sure what was happening to the woman in front of me was the real thing.

Had the crack of the martini glass reminded Victoria of gunshots and triggered something in her subconscious? Had it sent her back to that day? Or was she faking?

If so, she would be receiving an Oscar nomination come January.

I turned to Wheeler.

She was biting her lip, her eyes heavy and moist.

I grabbed her by the shoulder and said, "She didn't do it."

"What?" Wheeler asked. "What do you mean?"

"She wasn't the mastermind," I said, glancing at the broken woman on the couch. "She was the *target*."

Chapter 30

The license plates were from all over. Texas. Florida. Colorado. Pennsylvania. Illinois. South Carolina. Evidently, people drove thousands of miles to come to Brookfield, Missouri the first weekend in August.

Brookfield was thirty minutes north of Tarrin, a small town of four thousand, which blossomed to around twenty thousand each summer for the Great Pershing Balloon Festival.

It was 2:00 in the afternoon on Sunday. According to the festival website, more than seventy-five hot air balloons would take flight in just under an hour.

Wheeler and I stepped from the car and headed toward the crowd gathered a quarter mile from the overflowing dirt parking lot. A storm threatened in the distance, white thunderheads overlapping above a graying sky, which I'm sure was causing some trepidation among the pilots and crowd.

"You said you came here a few times with your dad?" I asked.

Wheeler nodded. "Yeah, when I was little." She hadn't said much on the drive. She'd simply held my hand and glanced out the window. I think she had a bit of pre-game jitters. Or maybe she was more scared of heights than she let on. "One year, it got rained out, or the wind was too strong, I can't remember. We ended up going to see a movie at the theater in town."

"Do you remember what movie?"

She wrinkled her nose, something I noticed she did when she was thinking, and said, "*The Adam's Family.*"

"Really? I can't believe you remember that."

"I only remember because I started the seventh grade a month later and I wore my hair in pigtails like Wednesday."

We stopped walking and I pulled her hair to both sides, making mock pigtails. "Maybe we can try that again sometime."

"That's your fantasy, huh? Wednesday from *The Adam's Family*?" She punched me in the shoulder. "You sicko."

"You know my fantasy."

"I know, Selene from *Underworld*." She smiled. "I told you I'm working on it."

I punched her in the shoulder. "Thatta girl."

She'd yet to tell me her fantasy and I said, "I know you have one. Just tell me already."

She sighed. Glanced at me. Nearly spoke. Blushed. Sighed again. "I don't even know where it came from," she said.

"Just tell me. I'll take it to the grave with me."

"Like when the balloon crashes with us in it."

"The balloon isn't going to crash. They are very safe."

"How would you know?"

She was right. I'd never been in a hot air balloon. I'd never even been near one. "You ever hear about someone crashing in a hot air balloon?"

"Yes."

"Really?"

"After I found out we were coming here, I searched videos on the internet and watched about twenty videos of hot air balloons crashing."

I laughed, pulled her to my side and gave her a kiss on the side of the head.

"What was that for?"

I shrugged, then said, "Now tell me your fantasy."

She took a deep breath, then said, "You know the actor Val Kilmer?"

"Of course," I said, grinning. "What is it? Ice Man? Please tell me it's him as Ice Man! And why would you be ashamed of that!?"

"I know how happy that would make you, but no, not Ice Man."

"Him as Batman?"

"Strike two."

"Doc Holliday?"

"Nope"

"Him as Jim Morrison? That's got to be it."

She shook her head and said, "Think more recent."

I didn't recall Val Kilmer having any title roles in the last decade, let alone anything that would get a girl's motor running.

I was a detective.

I should be able to figure this out.

Val Kilmer.

And she was ashamed of it.

I stared at her, my eyes doubling in size. "No!"

She dropped her head.

I screeched, "Fat Val Kilmer!?!"

Keeping her head down, she nodded.

I let loose a giant laugh. "You have a thing for Fat Val Kilmer!?"

And then I realized why she was ashamed. Why she didn't want to tell me.

I looked myself up and down. I said, "Please tell me—"

She looked up. She was biting her bottom lip. "When I first saw you—"

I screamed, "I reminded you of Fat Val Kilmer!?"

She nodded.

I burst out laughing.

Pretty soon the both of us were laughing so hard that two groups stopped walking and turned around.

It felt good. It helped assuage some of my fury. And some of my guilt. About what I would have to do next.

~

We wended our way through the barrage of spectators to the sectioned-off portion where the pilots were readying their balloons. The employees working the event all had red T-shirts on with a yellow and blue hot air balloon on the front. On the back it read "33rd Annual Pershing Hot Air Balloon Derby."

Two of these employees were sitting behind a small table, and I gave them my name. They checked a printout then handed over two plastic nametags and lanyards. It'd been awhile since I'd worn one, not since the last FBI task force I was a part of.

"When's the last time you wore one of these?" I asked Wheeler.

She pulled the lanyard over her head and said, "I went to a conference last year in Ohio. Future of Veterinary Technology."

"You're a vet?" asked the woman who'd handed us the badges.

Wheeler nodded and the woman asked a quick question about

which dog food she should be giving her two-year-old labradoodle.

Wheeler told her a couple of her favorite brands, which the woman scribbled on a piece of paper. Then Wheeler asked the woman, "Has anyone ever gotten hurt on one of these?"

"Not here. Only had one balloon crash in thirty-three years and no one got hurt. But I'd be lying if I said there wasn't a small risk."

"What about that storm?" Wheeler pointed toward the approaching clouds.

"We're keeping an eye on things. It's still a hundred miles off according to our resident meteorologist. You should be back down well before then. And if it does come close, your pilot will be notified and he'll get you down."

Wheeler thanked her, then we made our way toward the many tents and balloons.

"What's a labradoodle?" I asked.

"A Labrador and poodle mix." She said it all nearly as one word. She was nervous.

I said, "You don't have to go. We don't have to do this now." It had been a week and a half since the powwow at Simon Beach.

"Yes, we do. And yes, I do."

And we left it at that.

The balloons were staged thirty yards from one another. About half were assembled, filled, their patterned designs and bright colors reaching sixty feet into the air. The other half were on their sides, being attached to baskets or tended to in some way.

We bypassed a balloon that was yellow and blue. Then a purple balloon with white stars. Then one with vertical stripes of several different colors. Another balloon was checkered in every color of the rainbow. Finally, near the center, we came to a balloon that had red, black, and white zigzagging stripes.

There was a loud roar as the man in the basket released a barrage of fire and the balloon pulled against its tethers.

"Jerry!" I shouted.

He turned around. Smiled. Turned down the flame. He said, "I was wondering if you guys were gonna show up."

Wheeler and I approached the basket. It came up to right above my sternum. It was roughly eight feet square and according to Jerry, held four people comfortably or six people uncomfortably. But as Jerry's wife and boys were at a big soccer tournament in St. Louis, it would only be the three's company of Jerry, Wheeler, and myself.

"You guys ready for this?" he asked.

I gave him a thumbs-up.

Wheeler smiled nervously.

Jerry spent the next ten minutes telling us what everything was and how everything worked. He was interrupted by a bullhorn, whereby Jerry told us to climb into the basket, or *gondola*. There was an extra propane tank in one corner. Then in all four corners, there were two large sandbags fastened to the side. Jerry explained the extra weight helped balance the basket when in the air. The balloon itself, he referred to as the *parachute*.

A minute later, a team of red shirts unleashed the first balloon—yellow and green striped—and it slowly rose into the sky. On the opposite end, another balloon was released. Thirty seconds later, two more began their ascent.

We were closer to the middle, so we had to wait a good seven or eight minutes before two red shirts began untethering our ropes from the tie-downs.

"Have fun!" they screamed as Jerry pulled down on the burner throttle and we lifted off the ground.

The basket rocked, and Wheeler reached out and grabbed my arm. She held tight for the next few minutes as we smoothly rose and the spectators below shrunk to figurines.

"How high will we go?" I asked loudly.

He turned down the burner, the thundering roar dissipating some, and you could feel our ascent slow. He nodded toward an altimeter near the burner and said, "A few thousand feet."

I gave Wheeler a reassuring smile, then said, "And how do you steer this thing?"

"Winds change directions at different altitudes. Just need to find the right altitude then stay there for a few minutes. But I'd be lying if I said it's an exact science."

"Roger that."

He grinned, then blasted the burner, and we were yanked toward the heavens.

Wheeler let out a small involuntary whine.

I laughed.

She hooked her arm through mine, her other hand gripping the basket's edge. We inhaled the view. Arguably, it was one of the most beautiful landscapes I'd ever seen. The rolling green hills, the neatly sectioned-off farm plots, a small lake in the distance, the seventy other balloons scattered in every direction, even the thunderheads miles and miles away.

Under different circumstances, I might have enjoyed the moment.

I turned around and shouted, "You killed Mike Zernan!"

~

Over the roar of the burner, it's possible he didn't hear me. He pulled his hand off the throttle, the rumbling quieting.

I repeated, "You killed Mike Zernan."

I watched his eyes. I'd been wrong twice already. I couldn't handle being wrong a third time.

If he were a deer, he would have been inside the windshield of the car that had just blinded him.

I said, "And you did it to cover up the fact you paid Lowry Barnes to kill Victoria Page."

He blinked twice, then shook his head. "What are you talking about?"

"You were Victoria Page's banker."

The picture I'd seen at his house. Of Patrick on the horse. In the foreground, you could see the black fence post. It was the same one Bree had been straddling the day we'd gone to visit Page Ranch.

"It's a small town," he said. "Half the people bank at First Missouri."

"I'm sure they do. But how many of them do you help embezzle money?"

He fought against his urge to swallow, but lost. His Adam's apple disappeared twice, then he said, "Embezzle?"

"Victoria could have opened bank accounts and trusts anywhere— the Cayman's, Switzerland, Canada—but she felt more comfortable using someone she trusted. She felt better with all that money near her. How big was your cut? Five percent? Ten?"

He didn't answer.

"Did you even know where she was getting the money from? Did you even care?"

I doubt he ever knew how Victoria Page came into the money. And I *highly* doubted he knew about the Lunhill cover-up. Most likely, he figured she was just stealing the money from the city budget.

I continued, "Of course you didn't care. You just needed the money. To fuel your habit."

He glared at me.

"Your gambling habit," I said. "You bet a lot with Will Dennel. Or should I say, you lost a lot." I waited a half second then added, "*Fuzz*."

He took a tiny step backward.

I continued, "It's hard to keep a habit like that from your spouse. And I'm guessing that was the reason you and Joan separated for a year. It was your gambling. And you knew if she found out you were up to your old habits—that you were into Will Dennel for eighty large—that she would take the boys and leave. And this time for good. That's the leverage Victoria had on you. And that's why you couldn't just take freely from Victoria's accounts. She couldn't tell the police what you were doing without you guys both ending up in jail. You were the US and Russia in the cold war in that regard. Mutually Assured Destruction. But that didn't mean she couldn't tell your wife about your gambling."

I waited for him to react, but other than a slight dip in his shoulders, he did nothing.

"You attend a weekly Gamblers Anonymous meeting, something that you promised your wife you would do. I checked at the community center. According to the guy who runs it, you've been going for the last six years. I'm sure that's one of the deals you made with Joan when you two got back together. Maybe that's where you ran into Lowry Barnes. His court mandated AA meeting started right after your meeting. It was part of his parole. You guys get to talking and you find out he'd just been fired from the Save-More. That's when you get this brilliant idea.

"Maybe you thought about having Will Dennel killed, but all that would do is erase your eighty-thousand-dollar debt. If you get rid of Victoria Page, then you can access her account and her millions. You'll be able to gamble to your dick's content. But then you think, why not both?"

I watched him closely, then said, "I don't care if you jump, but don't do it until I'm finished."

I waited for him to acknowledge me or jump.

He did neither.

"You offered Lowry Barnes half a million dollars to kill Victoria Page. Half up front, half on completion. Lowry Barnes was a desperate man and half a million dollars is life-changing money. So you stake out Victoria Page, see when she's going to go to the Save-More. Maybe when she's en route, you call Will Dennel and ask him to meet you there. Maybe you tell him you have some money for him."

I debated telling him why Victoria was going to the Save-More. Telling him about the meeting. The one that Neil Felding had called. But it didn't matter. It had nothing to do with why Victoria was targeted.

"When Will and Victoria are both inside the Save-More, that's when you give Lowry the go-ahead. He goes in, makes it look like he's there to settle the score with Odell, then rounds up everyone and shoots them."

I took a breath, then said, "Lowry Barnes used to cut Victoria Page's lawn when he was a kid."

At this, Jerry turned around.

He didn't know.

I said, "She was one of the only people who was ever nice to him. Fed him when he came over to cut her grass, even let him stay the night a few times when his old man was in a bad way. That's why he couldn't go through with it. That's why he only shot her in the hip and the shoulder."

Jerry snorted.

I didn't blame him.

If Lowry Barnes had killed Victoria Page then Jerry would have been in the clear. He would have her money, and I wouldn't be here now.

But he didn't get her money.

And I was here.

I said, "I don't know exactly where you got the two hundred and fifty thousand dollars. I'm guessing you took it from Victoria's account late that afternoon. By the time she noticed it missing, she would be dead."

Jerry looked as though he was about to speak, then decided against it. Maybe he was thinking about the big picture. About lawyers, and due process, what could be proved and what couldn't, not to mention his chances of making it out of this with a wife and without being raped by a cellmate.

"Lowry is supposed to meet you somewhere on the outskirts of town where you were going to give him the second half of his money. But you never had any intention of paying him the second half. You get in the car with him, wrestle his gun away, and shoot him in the temple. He will already have gunshot residue on his fingers from his killing spree, and it will be deemed a suicide."

I let out a long breath, then said, "Damn that felt good."

I glanced at Wheeler.

Twice already, she'd believed she was in the presence of the person who had paid Lowry Barnes to kill her father. First with David Ramsey, then with Victoria Page.

"Say you did it!" she screamed at Jerry. "Say that you paid Lowry to do it!"

He didn't say anything.

I took two steps forward and grabbed him. I yanked him toward the burner then raised his left arm.

It took him a moment to realize my intentions.

I pulled his arm straight and inched it near the flames.

"You heard the lady," I said.

He whipped his head from side to side.

With my opposite hand I pushed down on the burner's throttle. The small flame doubled. I moved his arm toward the flame.

"I did it!" he screamed. "I paid Lowry Barnes to kill Victoria!"

I wrenched his arm from above the burner and pushed him away. He sank to his butt against the basket wall, rubbing his arm with his hand.

Wheeler took two steps across the basket and kicked him. Once, twice, three times, until he was curled in the fetal position moaning.

I pulled her away, the tears running down her cheeks. "You motherfucker!" she screamed.

I held her for a long minute until her breathing calmed. Finally, I stepped back over to where Jerry cowered.

I said, "And you had him kill Will Dennel and everyone else there."

He shook his head. His eyes were moist. "I told him he had to kill everyone in the store. That it had to look like a massacre. But I didn't know Will was there."

"Bullshit."

"Will and I were friends. Hell, other than my wife, I probably talked with him more than anybody. And I had no reason to kill him. With Victoria gone, I would have had millions."

Jerry's face was pained and it wasn't from Wheeler's kicks.

Maybe Will being there had just been a crazy coincidence?

I asked, "Will didn't threaten to tell Joan about your gambling if you didn't pay?"

"No, Will was easy. He told me to pay what I could. But he said I couldn't bet with him anymore."

I said, "So let me guess, you started betting elsewhere. With other bookies. With that Graham guy?"

"Yeah, and Graham, he isn't so easygoing. I got into him for about forty large. He told me I had till the end of the month, then he was gonna rough me up."

Wasn't easy going was an understatement.

He was terrifying.

I mentally kicked myself for missing such an obvious piece of the puzzle.

I said, "And if you came home roughed up, your wife would know right off that you were gambling again."

He nodded.

After a couple seconds, I said, "Tell me about Mike Zernan."

He didn't answer and I kicked him in the ribs.

"Tell."

Kick.

"Me."

Kick.

"About."

Kick.

"Mike Zernan."

He held his ribs. Wheezed. Finally, he said, "I'd known Mike since we were kids. He was a couple years ahead of me, but he used to buy me and my buddies beer once in a while. When he got back from the war, I looked in on him, mostly because I was working my way up at the bank at the time and I wanted him to invest whatever money he made while he was in the military."

He took a long wheezing breath. "He did and he would come in every couple weeks to check on things. Mostly, I think he just knew I would listen to him. We became sort of friends, I guess. After the murders, he started to come in a bit more often. I guess I was like his therapist in a way. He would tell me everything about the investigation."

I said, "The investigation into the murders that you orchestrated."

He nodded.

"And since Victoria survived, you wanted to know everything you could."

"Yeah, that bitch."

I kicked him again.

Victoria made some horrible choices, but she didn't deserve to be shot. And if I was being truthful, I couldn't muster the strength to dislike her.

"Keep going."

Jerry grimaced, then said, "So Mike told me everything about the investigation. One day, I asked him about Victoria, asked if she had any suspicions. But, like everyone else, she just thought she was in the wrong place at the wrong time."

"What about the two hundred and fifty thousand that you stole from her account to give to Lowry?"

"I don't think she ever noticed. Or if she did, she never said anything about it to me."

"How did you get it? Banks don't usually keep that much cash around?"

"I ordered the cash a couple days earlier. No one would have noticed. I'm in charge of all that stuff."

"And what about after the murders, did you and Victoria keep the same arrangement?"

"Yeah."

"And how much were you getting?"

"Fifteen percent."

"Of the sixty grand she got each month?"

He seemed surprised that I knew the exact number. "Yeah."

So he got $9,000 a month. Roughly $110,000 a year. On top of his banker's salary.

"You must be a shitty fucking gambler," I said.

He bristled, but didn't disagree.

"When did she first approach you about assisting her in her embezzlement scheme?"

"Twelve years ago. I was at a horse track in St. Louis. I ran into

Victoria and it turned out that a couple of her horses were racing. After her horses finished up, we met for a couple drinks. I'd gone to the track to try to make some money to cover a couple bad beats that I'd taken with my bookie the day before. But I'd just gone deeper in the hole. I confided this all to Victoria after a few martinis and she proposed we help each other out. I couldn't say no."

"And then you helped her set up accounts and trusts at your bank?"

He nodded.

"Okay, back to Mike."

He sighed, then said, "Mike kept me updated on the investigation. He told me that he was going through one of the victim's belongings—the stuff they had on them when they died—and he found a notebook."

"Will's Moleskine, his sports book?"

"Yeah."

"So what?"

"So, my name is all over that thing."

"Fuzz?"

"Right."

"So what?"

"So I'm thinking that if Mike traces all those bets back to me, that I owe Will eighty large, that he might see a motive and start, you know, digging a little deeper."

"But the case was open and shut."

"Not for Mike. He always thought something was off."

According to Eccleston, it had been Lowry's statements about being fired that had nagged at Mike. Mike thought they had come off as rehearsed—lines from a play.

I said, "Tell me how you killed him. And why?"

"*You.*"

"Me?"

"I heard you'd been to see him. I didn't know who you were at the time. I'd just heard this new guy in town—who used to be a homicide detective—had been to see Mike."

"So you went over there?"

"Yeah."

"To get Will Dennel's notebook?"

"When Mike was forced to retire, he confided in me that he'd taken the book. That he thought there was still something to it."

Of course, Mike never thought there was really a connection to the sports book. That was his cover. What he really thought was that Lunhill was involved. I didn't have the time or the energy to explain this to Jerry.

"So you strangled him with a garrote?"

He nodded. "I ordered one online."

"But Mike was much bigger than you, it couldn't have been easy."

Now that the cat was out of the bag, it appeared Jerry was in the mood to talk. He said, "I went over to his house late Sunday night, the day after you went to visit him. I told him my car had broken down not far from his house and that my cell phone was dead. He offered to take a look at the car. I told him that would be great but asked to use his restroom first. When I came out of the bathroom, he was in the kitchen. I came up from behind him, then I wrapped the garrote around his neck." He paused then added, "But since he was bigger than me, I did it like they show on YouTube and pulled him backward over my back."

That was it.

Everything about my theory had fit, except that Jerry was right-handed. I knew this from golfing with him. And this didn't fit with the bruising on Mike's throat. But as Jerry described it, it did make sense. Since he was smaller than Mike, he'd pulled Mike onto his back, using Mike's own weight to help strangle him. And putting the garrote around Mike's neck, then crossing his arms and pulling Mike onto his back, things would have been reversed. Like looking in a mirror. So Jerry pulling harder with his dominant right hand would have resulted in deeper bruising on the right side of Mike's throat.

I asked, "Then you searched for the notebook?"

"Yeah."

"Where did you find it?"

"It wasn't hard to find. It was in the drawer of his desk."

That's because Mike had just spent a day and a half copying the notebook to make a near replica that he'd sent to me.

"Then you made it look like a robbery?"

"Yeah."

There were three loud chimes. It came from a small speaker nestled near the extra tank of propane.

"What was that?" Wheeler asked.

Jerry pushed himself up and gazed over the top of the basket. "Weather advisory. They want us to go back."

According to the altimeter, we'd been floating along for the past ten minutes at right around three thousand feet. What I hadn't noticed was that we were moving laterally toward the approaching storm.

"Take us back," Wheeler barked. "Now!"

I guessed we were a few miles from the Pershing grounds.

Jerry pushed himself to his feet. "What are you gonna do to me when we get down there?"

"I'm gonna drive you to the Tarrin Police Department and you're gonna tell them everything you told me." I gazed down toward the ground. "Or you can jump."

He gazed down.

He appeared to genuinely be considering his options.

"No!" yelled Wheeler. "He isn't jumping. If he jumps, we have no way of getting down."

I felt pretty confident I could get us down safely, I mean, it was pretty self-explanatory.

Fire, up.

No fire, down.

Jerry eased down on the throttle and we began to descend.

I joined Wheeler against the far wall, keeping my back to the basket so I could keep an eye on Jerry.

A few minutes passed in silence.

"Can you hurry up?" Wheeler said. "That storm is getting a lot closer."

She was right. It would be on us in the next few minutes. I gazed down at the ground and saw we had moved farther from the Pershing grounds. Jerry was heading us toward the storm.

"Hey," I yelled. "You're taking us in the wrong—"

Jerry picked up the extra propane tank. I shielded Wheeler, thinking he was going to throw it at us. He didn't. He tipped it over the edge and let it fall.

"What are you doing?" I screeched.

He ignored me, then began fiddling with the burner. It roared to life, sending the balloon soaring.

We caught a gust of wind, the balloon leaning hard to the right, and headed directly toward the thick gray clouds.

I pushed him out of the way and attempted to turn the burner off, only the throttle was gone.

"Where is it?" I said, grabbing him by the shirt.

He opened his hand. The large throttle was held tightly in his palm. I reached for it, but before I could grab it, he tossed it over the side.

I punched him in the gut.

There was a loud *oof* and he sank to his knees.

"What's going on?" cried Wheeler, holding tightly to the corner of the basket.

"He just threw the throttle overboard."

"Oh my God."

I turned my attention back to the burner. I tried to get the flames to stop, but I couldn't. We continued to rise. Continued directly into the storm.

~

There was a lightning strike, then a boom unlike I'd ever heard. It was like an M-80 exploded inside my ear canal.

"If we survive this," I screamed over the pelting rain, "I'm going to potato peel your entire body before I hand you over to the police."

Over the last ten minutes we'd risen to nearly six thousand feet. The storm had overtaken us and the wind and rain turned us into its own giant washing machine.

"Thomas!" Wheeler screamed. "I'm scared."

Yeah, me too!

I yelled, "It's gonna be okay."

A moment after I said these words there was a soft choking, the flames dying out. At first I thought maybe the rain put out the flame, but it hadn't.

We were out of propane.

The flame flickered one last time, then went out completely.

The balloon halted its ascent, hung limply for a long moment, then slowly began to descend.

"We're going down," Wheeler yelled, a big smile on her face.

I glanced down at Jerry.

Going down was a good thing, right?

But then, why would he have dumped the extra propane tank?

A minute later, I realized why.

Our rate of descent was increasing. Without the hot air to slow us

down near the ground, we were going to impact hard. And the parachute whipping in the wind certainly wasn't helping.

I checked the altimeter. "Four thousand feet," I said.

I began counting in my head.

When we hit three thousand feet, I stopped.

"You any good at math?" I asked Wheeler.

She nodded through the rain.

"How fast is a thousand feet in forty-six seconds?"

Ten seconds later, she said, "Right around fifteen miles per hour."

"Shit."

"Is that how fast we're going?"

I nodded.

"We need to slow this thing down."

"I don't know how."

"We need to get rid of all the dead weight."

"The sandbags!" I shouted.

There were eight in total, each weighing thirty pounds. Wheeler
and I started picking them up and heaving them over the side.

The wind whipped us violently, and I rammed my side into the top
edge of the basket. Blinding pain shot through my torso.

"You okay?" Wheeler asked.

"My ribs."

I gritted my teeth but forced myself to my feet. I checked the altimeter. Seventeen hundred feet.

I counted until we hit twelve hundred.

"Five hundred feet in sixteen seconds."

"That's over twenty miles per hour!" Wheeler shouted. "Why are
we going faster?"

I didn't know. Maybe the wind.

I looked down at Jerry. He probably weighed 150 pounds.

"Stand up," I said.

He gazed up at me. Shook his head.

"Stand the fuck up!"

He wouldn't so I heaved him up myself.

I turned and looked at Wheeler.

She fixed me with a panicked stare.

I turned Jerry around and pushed him up against the basket wall.

"No!" he screamed, whipping his arms back and forth. "Think
about Patrick and Tyler! They need their father!"

His words gave me a half second's pause, but that was long enough for a gust of wind to send the balloon nearly sideways. I was tossed to the other side of the basket and I smashed into Wheeler, who went down in a heap.

I wasn't sure how many seconds passed since I last checked the altimeter. I pushed myself up and glanced over the side. Trees and houses were much bigger than the last time I gazed down. I guessed we had fifteen seconds at best. Ten at worst.

I started to count.

One.

Directly below us was a field. Better than a rock quarry, but we were still gonna hit hard.

Two.

I hauled Wheeler to her feet.

Plenty of people survived impacts going faster than twenty miles per hour. Most of those people were in cars and had seatbelts on and airbags, but yeah, most of them survived. At the same time, a lot of people died in impacts going much slower.

Three.

If we could keep ourselves in the basket, we had a much better chance of surviving.

My instinct was to hug Wheeler as tightly as possible, but logic told me to keep my distance. At twenty miles per hour we were each other's biggest threat.

Four.

I pushed her toward the corner nearest me and screamed, "Try to hold onto that rope! Use your legs as shock absorbers!"

She nodded.

Five.

I grabbed the parachute rope with my hand, dug my feet into the bottom of the basket and bent my knees.

Six.

I locked eyes with Wheeler.

She was crying.

Seven.

"It's gonna be okay."

Eight.

"Bend your knees!" I yelled.

Nine.
"We're gonna be just—"
I never made it to ten.

~

"Were you really gonna do it?" Wheeler asked, holding her arm to her stomach. "Were you really gonna throw him over?"

We were sitting on the ground, leaning against the hot air balloon basket, which was on its side, the parachute billowing in the light wind that remained from the storm. I had a huge gash on the side of my head and my left knee was hurting, but I'd escaped serious injury.

"I'm not sure," I said, answering Wheeler's question.

When Jerry had mentioned his children it had given me serious pause. I had to weigh that burden with the prospect of Wheeler's and my own survival.

But as fate would have it, I never had a chance to make a decision one way or another.

"Let me see your arm," I said.

She held her left arm up with her right. There was a giant lump halfway up her forearm.

"It's broken," she said.

"How would you know?" I said. "You're a veterinarian."

She smiled weakly, then asked, "Are you gonna go check on him?"

I let out a long exhale and pushed myself to my feet. I couldn't put much pressure on my left leg—I was guessing my knee was badly sprained—and I began limping toward Jerry's body.

With Wheeler's and my combined weight on one side, the basket had hit the ground at an angle. This turned out to be a blessing as Wheeler and I had both somehow stayed in the basket. Jerry, on the other hand, who had been clutching the high side of the basket on first impact, had been flung into the air.

As I limped toward his body, I could hear a soft moaning.

He was alive.

At least for the time being.

When I finally reached him, I cringed.

He was a mess.

A bone splintered through one of his shins, his hips seemed out of line with the rest of his body, and his head was caked in red.

A siren slowly began to intensify, and I turned and glanced back over my shoulder. Two ambulances were driving through the field, kicking up dust. Someone must have seen our balloon plummet to the ground.

I knelt down next to Jerry.

His body started to shake.

I reached out and gently touched his arm.

I don't know if he knew I was there. And I don't know if he deserved to have someone by his side when he took his last few breaths.

But he was family.

Chapter 31

September 19th, 2016
Tarrin, Missouri

"That is some good looking corn," Randall said, twirling a golden cob in his hands. "Man oh man, is that some good looking corn."

According to Randall, it was his best harvest to date. Nearly 160 bushels per acre, which was right on par with the yields of GMO corn.

Randall had already sold our entire harvest, save for a few bushels, which we would eat, give away, feed to the pigs, and use as seed next summer. As for the sorghum, Randall wanted to wait another couple weeks before harvesting, but he had high hopes for that as well.

Presently, we were celebrating. Both the harvest and that, as of two days ago, the Humphries Farm finished probate and was now officially mine.

Randall and I were manning a large grill, roasting about fifty ears of corn. Alexa was on another grill, cooking up enough hotdogs and hamburgers to feed the seven adults, four children, and two pigs.

Wheeler's arm was in a cast, but she was doing her best to help Joan set the two picnic tables delivered the previous day. So far, Joan had put on a brave face, even cracking a smile here and there. It must have felt good to get out of the house for a few hours, to take a break from waiting on her husband hand and foot.

Turned out that Jerry didn't die. Though he probably wished he had.

He broke his spine in two places. He was a quadriplegic, confined to a wheelchair for the rest of his days. He would need a full-time nurse to feed him, to bathe him, to empty his colostomy bag. He couldn't talk, but according to Joan and the straw Jerry blew in to communicate, he had all his wits about him. I couldn't think of a worse suffering. He was locked in a biological prison. A skeletal Alcatraz.

Which was why, after the events of the balloon crash, Wheeler and I had decided that Joan didn't need to know what Jerry had done, didn't need to know that her husband was responsible for the deaths of six people. It would only make her life that much harder. And I didn't want Patrick and Tyler to know their father was a murderer. I didn't want them to carry that burden the rest of their lives.

Like Jerry's wife and children, the town of Tarrin would also continue on without knowing the truth. For most of the town, the wounds had healed. Nothing could be gained by divulging the real motive behind the Save-More murders.

As for Mike Zernan's murder, it would remain an open investigation, though without any family to champion his case, it had already faded from most of the town's consciousness.

I glanced over my shoulder to where Patrick and Tyler were running around with Randall's twin girls in the dirt. The four of them were chasing Harold and May—now each weighing close to sixty pounds—who were squealing in delight.

The remaining adults were Bree and her boyfriend, Billy.

After stalking him for nearly nine months, true to Bree's plan, Billy and his girlfriend had broken up, and she had slid right in.

But that wasn't all that Bree had been up to over the course of the past month. She'd also been busy uploading the recording she'd taken at Simon Beach and posting it to a website called Reddit. She'd cut and spliced the recording so that it was only Chief Eccleston, Mayor Van Dixon, Greg Mallory, and David Ramsey talking about the cover-up. She eliminated anything said by Wheeler or me, as well as anything related to the Save-More murders. Then she anonymously uploaded the file with pictures of the four and titled it "Lunhill rBGH Cover-up."

The post quickly gained traction and within a few days, the mainstream media jumped on the story. By week's end, downtown Tarrin was teeming with news vans from all over the country. It wasn't long after that when the FBI took notice.

The story dominated the news cycle for the next few weeks and so began the fallout:

Both Chief Eccleston and Mayor Van Dixon resigned from their posts and were under investigation for a slew of different charges, including government fraud, kickbacks, and of course, public corruption.

Greg Mallory was also under investigation, but having not held a position in government, he would probably receive the most leniency of the bunch.

As for David Ramsey, after Lunhill stock plummeted 45 percent, the board of directors voted him out as president and CEO. His stock options were worth $670 million, which would come in handy when hiring a team of lawyers to fight the onslaught of lawsuits that awaited him.

As for Lunhill, there were rumors swirling that pharma giant Bayer would buy them out by year's end.

But the person facing the most serious charges was Victoria Page. An FBI forensic accountant had sifted through twenty years of her work as Tarrin comptroller. He uncovered that she had not only laundered nearly $20 million in payoffs from Lunhill, but she'd also siphoned off another $13 million from Tarrin taxpayers.

She'd been indicted on seven different charges and, if convicted, would most likely spend the next twenty years behind bars.

Jerry's involvement in the embezzlement scheme, setting up bank accounts and trusts, and moving money all over the globe, had yet to surface. But it was only a matter of time. At some point in Victoria's trial, or should she plea, the story would come out.

But hopefully, in the wake of Jerry's tragic hot air balloon accident and that he would need help wiping his ass for the remainder of his life, they would let him slide.

~

After we ate, I grabbed two beers from the fridge and made my way toward Randall. He was sitting between his wife and Wheeler.

I handed him one of the beers and said, "Take a walk with me."

He glanced at me suspiciously, shrugged, then took the beer.

Wheeler tried to fight back a smile.

Randall stood up and the two of us started toward the charred remains of the barn. I never did find out who burned it down. It could have been Chief Eccleston. Or it could have been Matt Miller. There's even a chance it could have been started by a wayward firework from one of the neighbors.

I would never know.

"What's going on?" Randall asked.

I ignored him and just kept walking.

A few feet later, there was a soft pitter-pattering and I turned around.

It was Harold and May.

I crouched down on my haunches and let the two attack me with kisses. "Hi, guys," I said. I gave them each a long rub, then a kiss on the snout.

"The looney bin, I tell you," Randall said with a laugh.

I stood and wiped away a bit of moisture on my cheek with the back of my hand.

"Are you crying?" Randall asked.

Again, I ignored him.

I continued walking, Randall following next to me in silence. We pushed through the now earless stalks of corn, walked for a good ten minutes, until we came to the fence that signaled the far edge of the Humphries Farm.

I took a sip of beer, then pointed with the bottle at the farm next door.

"What do you see?" I asked.

Randall cocked his head at me and said, "I guess I see a four-hun-dred-acre farm."

I reached into my back pocket and pulled out a folded piece of paper. I handed it to him.

He set his beer on the fence post and unfolded the paper.

I said, "No, that's *your* four-hundred-acre farm."

He blinked, his head shaking from side to side, then exclaimed, "What? How?"

"Let's just call it reparations," I said, then added, "from our friends at Lunhill."

The $2 million that David Ramsey had given me in exchange for my silence—and true to my word, I had destroyed everything that Darcy Felding had given me—had covered the cost of the farm, a re-model of the farmhouse, and two brand new tractors.

Randall leaned forward and pulled me into a giant hug, then he lifted me off the ground.

"Be careful," I wheezed, "I'm not as big as I used to be."

After nearly four months, I was finally back to my original weight. Randall set me down, wiped his eyes, and said, "I can't believe this." I smiled, then said, "And you're gonna have to rip down this fence." He looked confused.

"I'm leaving," I said.

"What?"

"This isn't me. I'm not a farmer."

I'd come to Missouri a broken man. But the Humphries Farm, Randall, Wheeler, Bree, Harold, and May...

They'd healed me.

"What about Wheeler?" Randall asked.

"She knows."

I'd told her a couple weeks earlier. She made no plea to come with me and I made no plea for her to join. I think we both understood what the relationship had been. A treasured summer. Never to be forgotten.

"What about these guys?" He looked down at Harold and May.

They were both sitting down on their rumps staring up at me with their big brown eyes. I think they sensed something was happening.

I shook out my arms, took a halting breath and said, "I was hoping you would look after them." My voice carried a slight quiver.

"Of course I will. And the girls already love them."

Then he asked, "When are you leaving?"

"Tomorrow."

"Where are you gonna go?"

"France."

Lacy was all the family I had left. But she was also all the family I needed.

I said, "My sister is pregnant."

Randall smiled. "Uncle Thomas?"

"Yep." I grinned. "Uncle Thomas."

Author's Note

The idea for this book came to me in the last days of December 2015. I live in South Lake Tahoe, but I'd spent Christmas (and my birthday, which is on Christmas) with my family in Colorado. I have two dogs, so instead of flying, I'd driven the grueling sixteen hours. I left Colorado to return home on Dec. 28th, but I didn't want to do the drive all in one fell swoop, so I stopped at a hotel in Primm, a town near the Nevada/California state line, about thirty minutes from Las Vegas.

A couple hours after arriving at the hotel—a grimy, less than desirable room in a dingy casino—my stomach started to gurgle. You know that feeling, the "Dear God, please don't let this be what I think it is" feeling.

But it was.

Food poisoning.

I spent the rest of the night "sick" and slept on the floor in the bathroom.

It was, in a word, awful.

The next day, still seven hours from Tahoe, I pondered trying to drive home. But I couldn't go fifteen minutes without getting "sick" and I still had to drive through Death Valley, which is more than a hundred miles without services. There was no way I was going to make it.

So I got on the internet, and started searching for a room at another hotel. The thought of being "sick" in the room I was currently staying in for another night was terrifying. I was able to get a room at a four-star hotel in Las Vegas for $150, which wasn't all that bad. At least I would be sick in a nice room and I could take a bath. (I like baths.)

But first I would have to drive thirty minutes to Vegas without getting sick. It was a close call, that's all I can say. Seconds separated me from getting "sick" in my car and getting "sick" in the hotel lobby bathroom.

Long story short, I ended up getting the sickest I've ever been in my life. I'm not sure if it was food poisoning or the flu, but I spent the next FIVE days confined to my room at the hotel. I was so weak and my stomach cramps so severe that I could barely lift myself off the bed. And I was far too sick to try to drive to a cheaper hotel, so I continued to pay $150 day after day.

But, here is the worst part: I had my two dogs with me!!

So I had to force myself to take them outside to go to the bathroom four or five times a day. I can just imagine what some of the people who saw me thought. Me walking my dogs, doubled over, Lamaze breathing because my stomach was cramping so badly, yelling, "Just poop already!"

So from Dec. 28th until January 3rd, I was confined to a bed in a Las Vegas hotel.

It was a nightmare. (A nightmare that cost me almost $1000.)

But two good things did come out of the experience. While sitting in my hotel bed, I came up with two great book ideas. One was for *Speed of Souls*, the book I will be writing next about a dog that dies and comes back as a cat. And the other one was *Show Me*.

For the longest time, I had my heart set on the fourth Thomas Prescott book being titled *Walking in Memphis*, in which Thomas would reinvestigate the assassination of Martin Luther King Jr. If you know anything about the event, James Earl Ray was the killer, but there are so many different conspiracy theories out there about who really killed him that there was room for a good story. (Even Martin Luther King Jr.'s son said that he didn't think JER was the killer.)

Anyhow, I ordered a half dozen books about the assassination, about Memphis, and about all the conspiracy theories. I had the entire story outlined but...I couldn't get it to work. Thomas' personality wasn't going to mesh with the subject matter.

So I scrapped it.

Fast forward to my Las Vegas hotel room, and between getting sick, taking my dogs out, and convincing myself I wasn't going to die (I'm kind of a hypochondriac), I had this epiphany: Thomas needs to inherit the farm that Harold grew up on in Missouri.

It was perfect.

But that's all I had. Sure, throwing Thomas into this small town would be great, making him learn how to farm would be great, but I needed a story.

I still liked the idea of Thomas reinvestigating an actual crime as he would have done in *Walking in Memphis*, and I started searching up "small town murder in Missouri" on the internet.

There were a few things that came up in Missouri, but the crime that really interested me was "The Be-Lo murders." It happened in North Carolina in 1993. The Be-Lo was a small grocery store. After closing one night, the store was robbed and three people were killed. The murders were never solved.

Initially, I had planned to base the crime that Thomas reinvestigates directly on the Be-Lo murders, but in the end, the only part I used was that the crime occurred at a grocery store.

So I had the setting, a small farming town in Missouri. And I had the basis for the cold case that Thomas would need to investigate. But I still needed IT. That big thing that brought it all together.

I had recently watched the movie *Spotlight* and I was enthralled by the slow burn of bringing down this corrupt institution of the archdiocese. I wanted to write something similar. At first, I planned on just having the "grocery-store murders" tied to small-town corruption. But this seemed boring. Overdone.

(Though, while searching "small town corruption" on the internet, I did stumble across an article about Rita Crundwell who, as appointed comptroller of the town of Dixon, Illinois, embezzled $53 million from the town budget to help finance her quarter horse breeding program. She would become the basis for Victoria Page.)

For a couple days, I kept waiting for that "magic" moment that happens when you are coming up with a great book idea. For *Gray Matter*, it was when I read about all the anti-wolf legislation that was out there. For *The Afrikaans*, it was the AIDS epidemic still plaguing the small villages of South Africa.

Then it happened.

And it was so obvious.

It needed to have something to do with farming!

From there, the logical next step was GMOs.

And when you think GMOs, the first word that comes to mind is…Monsanto.

And here is where the magic comes in. I had already figured out where the farm that Thomas inherits would be located. From *Gray Matter*, I'd established that it was somewhere in Missouri. And while sitting sick in my hotel room, I'd narrowed it down to an exact county. Audrain County, located in north-central Missouri.

On a whim, I searched, "Monsanto headquarters."

And wouldn't you know it?

Monsanto headquarters was located just on the outskirts of St. Louis, about a hundred miles from where I'd decided my fictitious town would be.

Even on my deathbed, I remember letting out a little "whoop, whoop!"

A few days later, I finally made it back to South Lake Tahoe. (I'd lost close to ten pounds.)

But there was one last thing: the book needed a title.

I'm not sure where I first saw it, but the moment I read that Missouri was the Show-Me state, I knew I had it. (I mean, the golden rule in writing is to *show* not tell.)

And *Show Me* was born.

~

Show Me is a work of fiction.

I took MANY MANY creative liberties in regards to small towns, farming, piglets, weight gain, weight loss, Missouri as a whole, embezzlement, horse breeding, hot air balloons, not to mention a hundred other things, as well as everything that has to do with Big Biotech.

But if I had just read this book, I would want to know what was actually true. So here we go. (Some of this stuff I've taken from Wikipedia.)

Tarrin

Tarrin is a fictitious farming town located in Audrain County, Missouri. Tarrin is loosely based on a number of different small towns all over Missouri as well as my experiences visiting small towns throughout my life. The county seat of Audrain is, in fact, named Mexico, which has a population of right around 16,000.

Lunhill

Lunhill is a fictitious corporation based on a number of different Big Biotech firms. Though the location of its headquarters and some of its history are based loosely on Monsanto, Lunhill is equally based on DuPont (US), Bayer Crop Science (Germany), Syngenta (Switzerland), Groupe Limagrain (France), and the Delta and Pine Land Company (US), among several others.

rBGH

Recombinant Bovine Growth Hormone (rBGH), also known as Bovine somatotropin, is a peptide hormone produced by cows' pituitary glands. Four large pharmaceutical companies, Monsanto, American Cyanamid, Eli Lilly, and Upjohn, developed commercial rBGH products and submitted them to the US Food and Drug Administration (FDA) for approval. Monsanto was the first firm to receive approval in 1993.

The FDA, World Health Organization, and National Institutes of Health have each independently stated that dairy products and meat from rBGH-treated cows are safe for human consumption.

In the United States, public opinion led some manufacturers and retailers to market only milk that is rBGH-free.

A European Union report on the animal welfare effects of rBGH states that its use often results in "severe and unnecessary pain, suffering and distress" for cows," including "serious mastitis, foot disorders and some reproductive problems."

Glyphosate (Spectrum-H)

Glyphosate is a broad-spectrum systemic herbicide. It is used to kill weeds, especially annual broadleaf weeds and grasses that compete with crops. It was discovered to be an herbicide by Monsanto chemist John E. Franz in 1970. Monsanto brought it to market in 1974 under the trade name Roundup.

Farmers quickly adopted glyphosate, especially after Monsanto introduced glyphosate-resistant Roundup Ready crops, enabling farmers to kill weeds without killing their crops. In 2007, glyphosate was the most used herbicide in the United States' agricultural sector and the second-most used in home and garden, government and industry, and commerce.

An increasing number of crops have been genetically engineered to be tolerant of glyphosate (e.g. Roundup Ready soybean, the first Roundup Ready crop, also created by Monsanto) which allows farmers to use glyphosate as an herbicide against weeds. The development of glyphosate resistance in weed species is emerging as a costly problem. While glyphosate and formulations such as Roundup have been approved by regulatory bodies worldwide, concerns about their effects on humans and the environment persist.

Many regulatory agencies and scholarly reviews have evaluated the relative toxicity of glyphosate as an herbicide. The German Federal Institute for Risk Assessment toxicology review in 2013 found that "the available data is contradictory and far from being convincing" with regard to correlations between exposure to glyphosate formulations and risk of various cancers, including non-Hodgkin lymphoma.

In March 2015, the World Health Organization's International Agency for Research on Cancer classified glyphosate as "probably carcinogenic in humans" based on epidemiological studies, animal studies, and in-vitro studies.

In November 2015, the European Food Safety Authority published an updated assessment report on glyphosate, concluding that "the substance is unlikely to be genotoxic (i.e. damaging to DNA) or to pose a carcinogenic threat to humans."

Terminator Seeds

Genetic use restriction technology, colloquially known as Terminator technology or suicide seeds, is the name given to proposed methods for restricting the use of genetically modified plants by causing second-generation seeds to be sterile. The technology was developed under a cooperative research and development agreement between the Agricultural Research Service of the United States Department of Agriculture and Delta and Pine Land Company in the 1990s, but it is not yet commercially available.

From Monsanto's website: *Monsanto has never commercialized a biotech trait that resulted in sterile – or "Terminator" – seeds. Sharing the concerns of small landholder farmers, Monsanto made a commitment in 1999 not to commercialize sterile seed technology in food crops. We stand firmly by this commitment, with no plans or research that would violate this commitment.*

Golden Rice

Golden rice is produced through genetic engineering to biosynthesize beta-carotene, a precursor of vitamin A. It is intended to produce a fortified food to be grown and consumed in areas with a shortage of dietary vitamin A, a deficiency which is estimated to kill 670,000 children under the age of five each year.

Golden rice has met significant opposition from environmental and anti-globalization activists who claim there are sustainable, long-lasting, and more efficient ways to solve vitamin A deficiency that do not compromise food, nutrition, and financial security.

Golden Rice was one of seven winners of the 2015 Patents for Humanity Awards by the United States Patent and Trademark Office.

As of 2016, it was still in development.

Times Beach (Simon Beach)

Times Beach is a ghost town in St. Louis County, Missouri. Once home to more than two thousand people, the town was completely evacuated early in 1983 due to a dioxin contamination that made national headlines. It was the largest civilian exposure to dioxin in the country's history. In 1985, the State of Missouri officially disincorporated the city of Times Beach.

I stole bits and pieces from what actually happened. You can read the entire saga here: https://en.wikipedia.org/wiki/Times_Beach,_Missouri.

Farmer Assurance Provision (Lunhill Protection Act)

The Farmer Assurance Provision refers to a bill that was passed by the Senate on March 20, 2013 and then signed into law by President Barack Obama on March 26, 2013. The bill is commonly referred to as the "Monsanto Protection Act" by its critics.

Legal effect - if a biotech crop had already been approved by the USDA and a court reversed that approval, the provision directed the Secretary of Agriculture to grant temporary deregulation status at the request of a grower or seed producer, to allow growers to continue the cultivation of the crop while legal challenges to the safety of those crops would still be underway.

Support – the provision was a response to frivolous procedural lawsuits against the USDA which were attempting to "disrupt the regulatory process and undermine the science-based regulation of [agricultural biotechnology].

Criticism - those who opposed the provision referred to it as the "Monsanto Protection Act," on the premise that it "effectively bars federal courts from being able to halt the sale or planting of controversial genetically modified (GMO) or genetically engineered (GE) seeds, no matter what health issues may arise concerning GMOs in the future."

Monsanto and Blackwater

From Newstarget.com:

Millions of Americans remember the private mercenary force known as Blackwater for its involvement in an unprovoked attack that left scores of Iraqi civilians dead in 2007, but most have no idea that the firm had a business relationship as well with Monsanto.

As we reported in May 2013, the relationship between the world's largest bio-ag company and producer of genetically modified foods and seeds and Blackwater was described by blogger Randy Ananda as "a death-tech firm weds a hit squad."

As further reported by The Nation magazine, it appears that Monsanto hired Blackwater shortly after the Iraq incident to "protect the Monsanto brand," which meant essential [sic] conducting intelligence operations against anti-Monsanto activists and their allies.

Read the full article here: http://www.newstarget.com/2016-04-28-monsanto-hired-the-infamous-mercenary-firm-blackwater-to-track-food-activists-around-the-world.html.

Monsanto/FDA/EPA

This is from a post on Rense.com:

The "revolving door" - the interplay of personnel that assists the industrial alignment of public service and regulatory authorities - has led to key figures at both the US's FDA and EPA having held important positions at Monsanto, or else doing so shortly after their biotech-related regulatory work for the government agency.

An article in The Ecologist's famous 'Monsanto Files' by Jennifer Ferrara, 'Revolving Doors: Monsanto and the Regulators,' looked in detail at this issue. As an instance, Ferrara noted the FDA's approval of Monsanto's genetically engineered cattle drug rBGH which failed to gain approval in either Europe or Canada despite intense lobbying and accusations of malpractice.

You can read the rest of the post here: http://rense.com/general33/fd.htm.

FDA and testing of new drugs

From the FDA website:

Drug companies seeking to sell a drug in the United States must first test it. The company then sends CDER (FDA's Center for Drug Evaluation and Research) the evidence from these tests to prove the drug is safe and effective for its intended use. A team of CDER physicians, statisticians, chemists, pharmacologists, and other scientists reviews the company's data and proposed labeling. If this independent and unbiased review establishes that a drug's health benefits outweigh its known risks, the drug is approved for sale. The center <u>doesn't actually test drugs itself</u>, although it does conduct limited research in the areas of drug quality, safety, and effectiveness standards.

Suing farmers

Since 1997, Monsanto has filed 147 lawsuits against farmers who have "improperly reused their patented seeds." This includes when farmers tried to sue Monsanto over cross-pollination of their organic crops with GMO seed. For example, a federal court dismissed one of those cases, saying that it couldn't protect Monsanto against unfair lawsuits should they side in the farmers' favor.

According to Monsanto's website, they have only proceeded through trial with nine farmers.

They have won all nine cases.

~

You are probably curious about where I stand when it comes to this whole GMO controversy.

It may come as a shock, but I don't have a firm stance one way or another. And that's how I wanted Thomas to come across in the book. It is definitely a hot-button issue for some people, on both sides of the equation, but I wanted Thomas to have more of a problem with the institution (Lunhill) than the science (biotechnology).

Which is how I feel.

Sure, Monsanto and friends have done some really shady things, but to blame biotechnology and GMOs as a whole just doesn't seem fair.

I, personally, do not think GMOs are harming people. We have been eating them for going on twenty-five years, and I think if they were making people sick, we would know by now. So basically, yes, I believe genetically engineered foods are safe.

But even if I feel GMOs are safe, it doesn't mean that I want to eat them. I do try to eat organic whenever possible. (But I'm not going to spend $3 on a fucking apple. I'm just not.) I prefer to eat organic, mostly because I try to avoid pesticides and herbicides. But I'm celiac so I already have to eat gluten-free, and I avoid dairy, so trying to eat organic as well seems like a full-time job.

Although I don't consume dairy very often, sometimes it is unavoidable. And I'm going to eat ice cream every once in a while because I don't want to live in a world where I can't eat ice cream. Anyhow, I haven't drank a glass of milk in over a decade. But, if I were a dairy consumer, I would only drink milk that was rBGH-free. From my research, Bovine Growth Hormone sounds pretty awful. It harms the cows, most notably giving them mastitis (infected udders), whereby they are put on antibiotics. And it has been proven that those antibiotics can sometimes make their way into the milk on the shelf.

No thank you.

All in all, I'm kind of a health nut and I want to eat food that is natural.

Which brings us to GMO labeling laws, which like Thomas, I do have a stance on.

Even if I believe that GMOs are safe, and I do, I still want to know if I'm consuming them. I realize this is hypocritical. I mean, if I think they're safe, then why should I care? Because I want to have the choice. I want to be able to avoid them or gravitate towards them if I choose.

But I can also see this from a business perspective and I fully understand why Monsanto and friends spend millions of dollars on lobbyists trying to fight down these labeling laws. It would cost them dearly. If I were in their shoes, I would be doing the exact same thing. It's business. And lobbying, though it could be perceived as unethical, is perfectly legal.

~

While doing research for this book, I was inundated with books, studies, blog posts, news articles, left-wing rhetoric, right-wing rhetoric, a shit storm really of the good, the bad, and the ugly when it came to Big Biotech.

After sorting through it all, I could only chose a limited amount of this material to bring into the book. I didn't want to overwhelm the reader with science and I could only have so many plot points. In an attempt not to alienate anyone, one way or another, I wanted to showcase the bad, but also the good. That being said, I did cast Lunhill as the villain, so I did have to lean more toward the bad.

~

This was a tough book to write. I hadn't written a full-length novel in close to five years and I forgot how big the scope of the project was. Now, at the finish line, it seems almost impossible that this seed of an idea I had a year earlier (between visits to the bathroom) has come full circle and is now a book.

Thank you so much for reading. And if you enjoyed the book, please tell a couple people and/or write a review for the book on Amazon.

If you would like to see some ridiculous pictures of me and my pups, go to www.nickpirog.com.

God is love.

Nick

Acknowledgements

As always, thank you to my mom for being the first to read the book. She is not afraid to tell me when I have failed to be funny, or that something just has to go, or that something doesn't make sense and needs more development.

I would like to thank my editor, Kari Biermann, who did a magnificent job. It is amazing what a little tweak of a word here and there can do. I look forward to working with you for many years to come. You can check her out at www.karibiermann.com.

Thank you to my good friend and beta reader, Nelda Hirsh. Your corrections, comments, suggestions, and insights are always spot on.

Thank you to Nadine Villalobos, another friend and beta reader, for your last-minute corrections. (Still haven't gotten them! Hurry up!)

Can't wait to do it all over again.

(Actually, yes, I can.)

Printed in Great Britain
by Amazon

51084708R00180